ROADS, WHERE THERE
ARE NO ROADS

Roads, Where There Are No Roads

A Novel

ANGELA JACKSON

TRIQUARTERLY BOOKS

NORTHWESTERN UNIVERSITY PRESS

EVANSTON, ILLINOIS

TriQuarterly Books
Northwestern University Press
www.nupress.northwestern.edu

The anonymous Yoruba love poem that appears on pages 39–40 was translated by Robert Cameron Mitchell and is used with his permission.

Printed in the United States of America

10 9 8 7 6 5 4 3 2 1

This is a work of fiction. Characters, places, and events are the product of the author's imagination or are used fictitiously and do not represent actual people, places, or events.

Library of Congress Cataloging-in-Publication Data

Names : Jackson, Angela, 1951– author.
Title: Roads, where there are no roads : a novel / Angela Jackson.
Description: Evanston, Illinois : TriQuarterly Books/Northwestern University Press, 2017.
Identifiers: LCCN 2016036600 | ISBN 9780810134720 (pbk. : alk. paper) | ISBN 9780810134737 (e-book)
Classification: LCC PS3560.A179 R63 2017 | DDC 813.54—dc23
LC record available at https://lccn.loc.gov/2016036600

For My Brothers

George Jackson Jr.
and
Prentiss James Jackson

For Memory and Dream

CONTENTS

ROADS, WHERE THERE
ARE NO ROADS

Sunflower

The sun was roasting him. And the Southern road was swallowing him up. The land seemed ravenous. And there was a hunger in his head that had been there for a long time. Since he had been born. Blind as a potato. Now he could see. Maybe the hunger had been there before he was born. Maybe he had been born into it. Blind. Without a hope of seeing until his mother had done what she had done, and what had happened to her had happened to her.

He could see. Earth was visible everywhere, stark in the sunlight. Trees and grass and fields in a static, lush, violent aliveness. They all welcomed him. As they never had before. He inbreathed them deeply, thinking he could pull it all inside himself and manage it someway. If he breathed deeply enough he could hold the brown-gray shanties, the brown spindly-legged children tumbling in the dirt, rolling in worn-out weeds, like out of an old family photograph that stood forever on the edge of the heart's first ventricle. If he could pull it all in, then he could manage his heart.

"What am I missing?" He was looking.

He shaded his eyes from the sun. He slowed the coughing car and watched the children kick the soft shadows in clouds of dust that whipped and dressed their ankles in ash. Right now he could feel the earth itself. The centrifugal force of a century spinning to a close. Sooner than they thought. He could feel it. So why couldn't Mississippi?

He pulled his car to the side of the road. Lit a cigarette, dragged, and blew the heat through his nostrils. The sun was eating everything in sight. He moved into the passenger seat. Crouching into shadow, searching out the window like he was missing something, or somebody, he thought he shouldn't miss.

After a while in which he pulled in deep drags of cigarette smoke and heat, he focused on one of the children. In the center of the boy's forehead the mark where he had probably stood too close within the zone of a mule's hind kick. The hoof had only scraped him. But it had force enough to etch a half-moon in the center of his forehead. A kick like that should have killed him. If it had been a kick. God knows what it had been. He should have been dead. The man thought.

Instead he was alive, his head thrown back and laughing out a song.

> Peckerwood, peckerwood, don't peck me.
> Peck that nigger behind the tree.

Then the boy ran and hid behind a tree. The man watching him from the car was thinking of woodpeckers, how they knocked on wood, listening for food. Wasn't that the way it was? Woodpeckers and peckerwoods. Why peckerwood? He knew why. "Get that through your wooden head, boy."

With his eyes the man who had been born blind had seen some things. He'd been to war and back. He'd worked in a factory in a textile town. He'd picked cotton that bit his hands like an ungrateful dog. He'd loaned his body out for day labor that only a mule should have done. Once he'd outworked a machine, drilling a hole in the side of a mountain. Or had it been a hill? It was a mountain. He'd beat that machine. Doing the work no man was born to do, but which he especially had not been expected to do. He was a minister's son. He'd been born behind enough prayers to line the streets of his life with gold. But he hadn't chosen those.

His father, Reverend Doctor Jeremiah Stone, was an African Methodist Episcopal minister and a scholar who knew ancient secrets. His historic old church had been a way station on the Underground Railroad. For some, it had been the last stop. Others went right on to Canada, afraid to stop running, determined to be freely free somewhere. When he was a boy, Reverend Stone's son would go down into the caverns beneath the church and play down in the dark. Once he'd fallen asleep, and awakened to the sound of whispered voices, one plaintive, one harsh. "Goooooo," the harsh voice pounded the walls and woke him up. A low plaintive cry answered this harsh command. He looked around and there was no one else there. Frightened by the failure of his sight to see, he'd run to his father and told him what he'd heard, what he'd dreamt he'd heard. His father just kept writing his letters to the editors of newspapers and magazines. His favorite pastime: correcting White people. A hobby that gave him much pleasure. Finally, Jeremiah Stone put his pen aside, and looked into his son's eyes.

"You heard voices? In trouble?" he asked the boy. "And what did you do to help them?"

Thinking of that time, the man rubbed his eyes and watched the boy with the mark on his forehead and wondered what his father would want of him now.

He thought of all the lives he'd led. It seemed to him that some years were centuries long and some months, decades. He thought, "Didn't it take four hundred years for the Israelites to come out of captivity and cross the Red Sea?" Once he had lived a lifetime in a moment. The moment his father had died. That was it. He felt himself fill up and empty out tears from a river of memory he had not known he'd known of. The moment was of such torment and such bliss, he'd thought he'd died then too. Except for his mother, he would have vanished. Peeled away skin, then bones, then cartilage, then muscle, then arteries, then veins, then organs. The last to disappear would have been his eyes. They weren't totally his anyway. The seeing parts.

But he hadn't died. Or maybe he had, because since that moment he'd been searching for a life to lead that would balance out into that 1:09 A.M. moment. Where hadn't he searched? Searched to find a life out of which would flow that rich flight of love, so exhilarating that the loss of it was a plummet into a lake of tears, but never a death. No. Not a death.

His early life had been a strange one. He'd come out of his mother like a comet, trailing afterbirth like a bloody, messy comet's tail. After one live birth and six miscarriages he'd been born to Reverend Jeremiah Stone and Mrs. Mercy Stone. Born blind. Yet his mother was not one to submit to circumstance. For years she searched a way out of the dark for him. It was she who had done what God didn't do. She who gave him sight. Thinking about the gift made the man put out his cigarette half-smoked. His throat half closing with the ache of his love. But he didn't want to think about it. He'd thought about it enough. It was the reason he'd run so fast through so many lives.

In one life he'd been a college student, tall and younger than usual, graduating early and with distinction from a Black university in the Northeast. And on to law school. Then more distinction as a graduate student at an Ivy League university. That life had pleased his parents. He'd lived it for them.

His brief time in the service he didn't like to think about. His father brought his only son home and probably saved his life. In another life, three months long, he'd been a gambler. But he'd given that up because living solely by chance and wit seemed presumptuous, begged too much favor from God. He'd awakened one morning in a rented room in a boardinghouse, and the first words out of his mouth were, "You're always waiting to get something." He had nine thousand dollars in the bank. Nine hundred dollars on his person, in his pockets and shoes.

Having lived solely for money, like a spoiled child might live for jawbreakers and bubble gum, he needed something for his soul, which lumbered and squalled inside of him. Too big for his body.

He went looking for a life that fit his soul, the way a man shops for a suit or a pair of shoes. The biggest thing he could find was music. It was everywhere, coming out of storefronts, record shops, churches, or on street corners, in parks, in barbershops, in his mother's kitchen.

He'd hung around musicians for months. He fit inside the musicians' schedules, staying up until the sun crawled out of bed. Sleeping two or three hours, then going to work as a janitor. He'd taken up the instrument he'd studied as a boy. His mother had given him the horn too. He'd struggled with it until he was certain he had no gift for making music beyond the memorization of notes, their studied execution. His music had no metaphor; not because he'd gone so far into one sense the vocabulary for the other didn't work, but because his music was not rich, original enough to provoke creation. He'd have to just live it. Walk it and talk it. Act it.

So he decided to love music, but to leave it behind, taking only what would stay in his head, or whatever leaked into his consciousness from his soul. He accepted being a religious listener, and translated the freedom and intelligence of music into moody fragments of a life.

One morning he stacked all his records (from Coltrane to Ellington, from Muddy Waters to Mockingbird July, from Louis Armstrong to Charlie Parker, from Smokey Robinson and the Miracles to James Brown, from Aretha Franklin to Nina Simone, from Sarah Vaughan and Ella Fitzgerald to Billie Holiday, from Delta blues to African percussion) in his blue Ford, squeezed himself in, under the boxes tied to the roof, the boxes crammed on the seats and floor, and pulled the music-filled trailer hooked up to his back bumper to the front door of his mother's house.

She wasn't home, so he used his key and began to unload and put the records on the shelves in the room of his boyhood and on the shelves in the basement next to his father's books. After every seventy-eight, every thirty-three, every forty-five had been carefully placed, so that no harm would come to them, no warp disturb their exquisite and delightful and soul-feeding sound, he went to his father's study and began to read every book he had never read and had been meaning to, then he would reread every book that had told him something he needed for his life.

His mother came home from church. She stood in the doorway of his father's old study and listened to the son turning pages for a long time. She could smell the change in him. Was his aftershave more subtle? Later she would tell him he smelled like a man who had just taken a bath and has just begun to sweat. A little salty. And something else. She couldn't put her finger on it. If she could have put her finger on it, she would have been able to see it.

✦

There is always a Sunflower. That is what my daddy says. One place or another is a Sunflower Café. It's not one place. But places that keep replacing another place. There is always, he says, a place called the Sunflower Café somewhere between Mimosa and Letha. One time there were two places called the Sunflower, but people kept getting their addresses mixed up, so people kept complaining to the people who came up with the name after the first one had been in operation for a few months. And, eventually, grumbling all the while that his freedom to think up what come to him had been taken from him against his will, the owner began to call his place the White Lily. He resented it all the while because he remembered the day he'd come up with the name Sunflower, riding one day down Cadoree. It flashed in his mind like a sign. He could see the image, born in his mind, intimate and special, and it was his. Someone might have told him that there was a sign there on Cadoree for the first Sunflower Café, but he would have said the sign didn't matter. And maybe it didn't. Maybe the idea of the Sunflower was just brooding along the road waiting for someone to stumble upon it and pick it. Even if it was already picked.

When he drove into town some people were walking around looking bored with the heat. He drove through the center, which was a gas station, a general store, and a furniture store, a lumberyard, and three other dusty establishments. Then he waited for somebody Black to amble by. When they came, he followed. They stood back from the road and waited for him to pass.

"Can a hungry man get something to eat?" His head and arm out the car window.

"Mmm-hmmm, sugah. You sho can." She looked like she wanted something, but he hadn't been missing her.

"Keep going right down Flood Street. There's a nice little restaurant called the Sunflower Café. Woman named Miss Saphronia cooks there. She do all right with the skillets." She paused. Smiled. "I do a little better."

"Girl, come own." The flirt was snatched, glance and drawl and all ample hips down another road that wasn't so much a road as a way. The man parked his car and began to walk alone and hungry.

Saphronia's was easy to find, once someone who lived in Letha had pointed him in the right direction. He saw the homemade sign, in black scrawl on a gray background. It was a small, once-white dwelling place with a screened-in porch that bridged the heat of the day and the heat that poured from the kitchen. He passed through the screened-in area, where flies swirled crazily on the outside looking in with a multitude of eyes at the foods of the day; he opened the door to the restaurant proper and stepped inside.

At the counter, he dropped his duffel bag and slid into a seat next to a big man who was hunched over a plate that was piled high up to his wrists almost. The man glanced up as the stranger took the seat.

"How ya doin?" Reverend Stone's son offered. They eyed each other—a whole face to last forever in half a second's memory.

"That sun is doin it today!" He wiped his face. In winter his skin was tan. In summer, as in this moment, it was glorious in a well-done pinto-bean sheen, seasoned to perfection. "This is definitely not our sun. In Africa the sun slides on you behind a layer of clouds. They know how to give it to you over there. Nice and moist."

The big man grunted.

Reverend Stone's son couldn't take his eyes off the man's plate.

"Oh, man," he said. "I got to get me some of those greens. Woo!" He clapped and dry-washed his rough hands together. The big man next to him, shirt open and with a red scarf wrapped around his neck, glowed into his plate. He had his corn bread poised in his left hand and in his right hand the fork was so quick it was invisible. It made a tick-tick as it touched the plate.

Saphronia stood in front of him. Evil. Hot. Impatient.

"Good afternoon, ma'am," he said respectfully.

But anything he offered her was inconsequential. She was short. "Whatchu gone have today? We outta croquettes. Willie, we got any biscuits ready?" She shouted the second question over her shoulder. Her blouse popped open in the turn and she buttoned it without blinking or looking down.

He smiled agreeably. "I don't want any biscuits no way, miss." He pointed to his neighbor's plate. "I want some of those greens, some fried chicken, dark meat, fried okra, and tomatoes—"

"No mo' tomatoes."

He looked disappointed. Hunger hollowing out his eyes.

"I gi'ya some corn relish we put up ourself."

"Thank you, miss. That sounds good to me."

Because she found him pleasing, she slid some ice water down the counter toward him. He was nice, even if he did wear the bushy hair on his head and a beard had started on his handsome face.

The men who ate supper at the Sunflower Café would not talk when their mouths were full. Their mouths were filled with pork bits, salty and fatty, muddy-spicy rice, collards, and corn bread. There was rich silence around them. They breathed, sweat, and ate. A few couples talked low over the thin, handwritten menus. He sighed and sank into the silence. When he'd ordered, his voice had been soft, and almost like a boy's instead of a grown man traveling.

Briskly the overhead fan whipped round and round. The heat laughed a little, let up in a thin patch of coolness that ripped through his bushy head. The man on his right, shirt open to his waist, sat back on his stool and chewed with his eyes closed.

The Reverend Stone's son was happy and relaxed. He was certain that the food would be delicious and filling. What his hunger roared for.

He turned on his seat and stretched his legs into the cool flight of air.

He was looking over his life, or lives, thinking that he could travel and collect things for his soul for years and years more. Steam warmed his face and woke him from his thoughts. The woman's voice had come to him shortly. He gave himself to the nourishment at hand.

✦

He had left the Sunflower Café feeling fat and ready to live. At the end of the counter he had passed his coins and dollars to the woman. He was always surprised by the cost of things. So little or too much. They had conversed in that lazy, full-mouthed language that is more like reciprocal humming.

Saphronia had taken all of him into her eyes: blue work shirt and jeans, the hair full and neat, a new beard and mustache outlining the heavy-lipped mouth. She remembered his eyes that etched her body and searched his surroundings so curiously. She thought his ways were "nice and pleasant." He was a kind man. He left a generous gratuity and a boy's grin.

He slow-walked toward the center of town. Absently, he kicked dust into the ditch. He was picking sweet pieces of chicken from between his teeth. The earth took all of his moments' sounds and played with them. He could hear his own steps and the wind moving through his teeth when the dark meat was free of his white teeth.

He looked for a mailbox to drop in a crumpled letter that he'd carried in the pocket over his heart for the last thirty miles. His mother would laugh to hear about the postcard that said, "Letha, Mississippi." He smiled at the thought of her. Laughing.

With that same smile and his inquisitive eyes, he raised his head to see more of this territory of his mother's birth, and of exodus when the great highways had parted the soil. Her father had had to run because he had killed a White man who tried to steal his land. They had lost the land anyway.

He wondered how far he was from Money, where Emmett Till had been murdered for talking to a White woman. Had he whistled? The fourteen-year-old boy from Chicago had been taken from his uncle's house and killed by White men. His beat-up body dropped into the river. He'd never forget the mother of Emmett Till, who'd chosen an open casket for the swollen, ruined body. "Look what they did to my son!" she said. He could never forget. "How far am I from Money?" He spent a long hour walking in circles.

He could smell the wild onions in a nearby yard. He took his breath carefully. When he found his car it would not start. The engine whined under his fingers. No energy sparked and his wheels would not rotate. He sat in the dead car. The window was down and night was floating through on cricket sounds, the rattle of the wind moving as subtly as snakes through the green onion lot and through the bushes. The moon came through his windshield between the cleavage of trees like a candle fed on white fire.

A man with a red flag around his neck was walking under the round white moon. Even in soft moonlight his deep-black skin was blue toned. His shirt was wide open, flapping in the small breeze that his walk created. His chest bare.

It was his stool neighbor from the Sunflower Café. They had shared food together, so they knew each other. The blue-black man grinned at Reverend Stone's son as if they were brothers; he searched under the hood of Stone's car. He performed impromptu surgery. At last he straightened and said, "This thang dead, man. Done seen its last go round for a while."

The minister's son said, "Shit." But without too much conviction, because death was no surprise. He turned around and around in a circle like he was gathering direction. He shuffled one foot in mild disgust.

"My name's Ricochet," the blue-toned man said after a while.

"They call me Stone."

"Stone." Ricochet, who was marked with grease, shook Stone's hand and marked him too. They fell to talking. Stone leaned against the car and took out cigarettes. They traded smoke signals.

"Must be a sign," Stone said.

"What?"

"I came here looking and this afternoon I found somebody and I can't go nowhere I can't walk, so I guess I must be about my business right in these parts. There must be something I gotta do or see."

"What business you in?" Ricochet asked. "Land changing around here. I can hear it. But the White man be steady kickin against it. Steady kickin."

"Yeah," Stone grunted.

Ricochet had to go. Ricochet tossed his cigarette butt away. He prepared to leave.

"Wait a minute," Stone said hurriedly.

"Yeah?" Ricochet asked.

Then Stone didn't know what else to say.

"You must be lookin for the Voter Registration people. None in this town. They over in Mimosa."

"Can I walk it?" Stone asked.

"I'll drive you."

Somehow he decided to go to Mimosa with Ricochet to the Voter Registration workers. That sounded good. He could learn something. He was free, with flexible directions. His bones grew loose in the atmosphere as the tension evaporated. He walked along the highway with Ricochet, moving away from the angry chorus of crickets, the farmhouse dogs relearning the wails of their ancestors, the rattle of leaves when wind spilled on them.

Listening. He was always listening. Straining to learn all the vagrant noises that struggled on the edge of his mind's music, he placed them in a universe rounded and respectable with tone and voices. In the center. Only to his ear, like an echo, came his own voice. He treasured this gift of listening.

He was listening to Ricochet tell him how he'd gotten his name. "When I was a baby boy learning to walk, I'd bounce off one wall and up against another. Plus, I'm wild like a bullet. Don't nobody mess with me, including these crazy-ass peckerwoods." They were driving then in an old beige Ford, dented and scratched.

Stone smiled and listened to the night that rolled past the rolled-down window. Dull and sharp night cries were scattered around him, the trees, the crickets, the distant dogs.

Ricochet was making him laugh. His crazy stories tumbling out one behind the other: the one-legged dog who peed upside down, the woman who washed her hair in dishwater. Stone hoped he'd remember everything later to write in his journal where he kept his life.

Behind them sudden light crushed the studded silence and the dark. Stone turned around, trying to see. A car eased behind them in a quick pass. Ricochet's eyes darted. Inside the passing car, faces hung like angry moons incongruous under sheriffs' hats. The shotgun in the window had a voice that came out of a double-barreled nose. The voice commanded them to stop. They did. Ricochet said, "Don't say nothing to these crackers." Then the double-barreled voice said, "Get out the car." They did that too.

Reverend Stone's son spread-eagled against the car, his hands touching the roof, but not touching Ricochet. Then in a whirl his jaw was on the hood of the car. Blood was at his mouth. Flashlights were spreading his thighs, and fingers following his body.

"Shit," he thought. "Crazy crackers."

From the other side of the car, he could hear Ricochet talking. "Sheriff, I ain't done nothing. I was just taking my cousin over to meet me—" A rough, heavy, puddingy-crushing sound of a rifle butt against flesh. Then again. Then again. The sound came. And Stone heard himself shouting all the while with each thrust. "Leave him alone. Leave him alone, motherfuckers."

Somebody hit him on the back of his head, punched him on his sides, aimed for his groin, but he shifted and the blow glanced across his thigh, stunning him. His knees buckled after someone else beat the caps with a stick. He fell.

✦

When he awoke he thought that he thought he had dreamt he had fallen inside another life that he'd dreamt in a bad dream. It was pitch-dark. The air was thick. He raised his hand to wave it before his face. He could barely see it.

In the corner there was a frame of sky. A full white moon in blackness with lesser flecks of brightness. All of the world that was for him was bound in a frame, steel striped and obstructed. The rest of everything was a stench that had volume and solvency. It rose from a hole in the corner over which insects danced and flashed toward skin. Odors hovered and swelled in the sheetless mattress. Ricochet was thrown across a cot in the next cell. He was halfway on the concrete floor. His blood had congealed and his hair matted with it.

Stone wondered where the sheets were. Then he laughed at the idea. His laugh ripped out of him. Crippled him. He laughed at himself. Why hadn't he known that it was a brutal cliché? A Black man now. He was a rerun of a life that had already been lived. His was ending now.

Then he swore that he was dreaming. He fumbled through the darkness opposite the toilet hole; found bars. He cursed at them and shook them. A deputy came and switched on a light. Brightness stabbed his eyes.

The deputy stood in the doorway, cradling a rifle like a newborn child. Face red under the light. His hair lying red and thin upon his scalp like a baby's. He stood there with his lips moving, saying nothing. His jaws working, grinding, grinding his teeth. A slight man. Medium height. A common face.

Stone knew that there were lines he was supposed to say. Words to spout out of him like blood from the neck of a sacrificial fowl.

"There's been a mistake. This is crazy!" The words flew back at him, crazy and hollow in the emptiness.

"Mistake, huh?" the man said. "You made it. You been traveling with the wrong kind of niggers."

14

Stone was standing in the ancient darkness. His knuckles bent tight around the bars. He was panting and mouthing familiar obscenities. But his eyes were wide and he was startled. "This man is gonna kill me." Came to him. It made him weave on his feet.

He knew that even before the deputy turned. And the door stood empty and open. And he could see into the cluttered, filthy office where piles and piles of paper lay with nigger names and nigger numbers identifying them. His own duffel bag with notes and miscellaneous clothes—shirts, crumpled jeans, a red scarf, clean and ragged with wear.

Nothing moving, but the sound of the deputy's boots gone now beyond the outer door. Now muffled in the old, dry dust. The door to the jailhouse left wide open.

Stone just stood there. His arms raised and his hands still tight on the bars. He was leaning his head against the steel. Listening to the ordinary sounds of night, sharply perceptible through the wide-open door.

What made him so ragingly sad was the meaninglessness of his own end. That he should go down this way in this time. In this time before he had lived the life he was preparing to live. He was going to die with his life unfinished and he was dying because he was randomly Black and unlucky. He should have known so many things.

He had come looking for some magic, but the land held no malevolent magic. People hold to their traditions. Custom was what they knew, the blind behaviors of alleys in the heart. Systems survived.

He listened to his story tightening to a close: cars, the wheels, treads chewing the gray dirt—cars, ordinary, passing and stopping before the open door under the full white moon.

When they came for him, he fought. He fought like his father. He fought like his mother had fought for him. Like his army of uncles. Like Nat. Like Gabriel. But they beat him down with rifle butts and sticks. Six of them. They dragged him to the car, through the night, toward the slow and ripe smell of water. Another car followed. They were rolling on a road with many turns, moving toward water. They were beside him and in front of him, beating him.

"You trouble-making sons of bitches—"

"Ought to leave things alone."

"You trouble-making niggers."

"Who you think you are, boy?"

Who he was came to him then. Exactly who he was. He played limp, sick. The rider beside him reached down. Treemont Stone shoved him hard, down. He reached over and opened the door, shoved the rider out and jumped out after him. Then he ran, his handcuffed hands leading him on. He darted into the bushes and they had stopped the cars and were after him. The bushes were wild; he'd knock down a clump and rush through and the clump would grow up behind him. He'd twist through branches and the branches twisted back, grabbing him. He was panting and his panting was a raggedy chant. The ground grew moist and he ran from his own footprints.

Soon he was back near the road, darting low across it, hunkering down to get to the other side. But they spotted him and came running. He dashed into the darkness.

Then he heard them. Amazing sounds. Screaming and crying children being whipped. It was them. Awe and terror and wonder in their shouts.

"Oooooh," echoes and echoes behind him.

He turned. He could hear them scrambling, scrambling to get away from him. Rushing and stumbling. Some of their guns in the dust. One shot rang out. Then another. And one last one that hung in the darkness.

He felt himself, afraid one of the shots had hit him without his knowing. But he was whole, bloody and heaving. He made his way back a little, and their cars were screeching away, and they were wild-eyed inside.

Then, there in the road, he saw what they had seen.

He smiled.

And fainted dead away.

✦

Three days had passed. He'd slept in a tunnel; one end beginning in darkness, the other opening into light, light like a host of suns. In sleep he'd wandered fitfully from one end to the other. Attracted to the warmth of the light, the obliterating sweetness of all those suns, and pulled back by the comfort and intriguing terror of the darkness. He dreamt of his mother in the darkness. She was weeping. He dreamt of music, a melody he could never have played. But he heard it. Fleshy blues was in it, and soaring like field hollers, grunts like work chants, and jazz like the rise of birds on a high hill. Finally, he dreamt of his father. He was standing in brightness, smiling at him and shaking his head.

Then Stone woke up.

The first thing his eyes focused on was a silver-white spray of hair. Then he saw the kindest face he had ever seen leaning over him, looking into his eyes. She smiled. And he was happy to be alive.

"What time is it?" he asked, like a boy who has overslept.

"Time for you to get up." The white-haired woman walked out of the room.

He didn't get up. He lay there in that high, deep bed and took account of his body. He was sore all over. He felt his face and it was swollen like a cushaw. His legs were still as railroad tracks.

Sunshine came running through the window, so bright the cotton curtains were translucent. He looked into the sunlight and blinked. The light disturbed him.

He remembered something. Men had been chasing him. White men with evil on their minds. Sweat broke out on his forehead. Little bumps of it, like an allergic reaction to dying.

Then he remembered what he'd seen on that road.

He remembered what had saved him.

Who had saved him?

Who would believe him?

From the smell and feel of himself he knew that he was clean. Someone had bathed him. The white-haired lady. He wasn't embarrassed at the idea.

After a while he climbed into his freshly laundered clothes. He was moving like an old man. Railroad tracks don't bend, so he sat on the high perch of the bed and pulled his stiff jeans over his stiffer legs. He crawled upwards into his shirt. Each button was tedious. His fingers had drawn up. Someone had given him a haircut and shaved off his beard.

He combed his tough hair with a big-toothed comb he found on the dresser. The dresser mirror was cloudy like someone had breathed on it to be sure he or she was alive. And the breath lingered, living on the glass. He did the best he could with the comb. By now, the little bedroom with its big bed was suffused with the good smell of food.

There was a plate for him. Grits smooth as satin and white as cotton. Eggs like scrambled-up suns. Light-brown biscuits and pieces of golden fried chicken.

"You better eat that before it turn cold."

So he did as he was told.

And swallowed the hot, black coffee she poured into the white china cup with the gold trim.

He wiped his greasy mouth with a paper towel. And he felt good. She was pouring him another cup of coffee.

"Can I call your family?" she asked. Or did she hum it?

He blinked in amazement and opened his mouth. Dumbfounded.

"Hurry up, Treemont Stone. I got to drive you to the gas station so you can use the phone there. They listen in on this one here."

He called his sister collect. He only said one word, "Viv."

Vivian grilled him. "What have they done to you, Montie? What have they done?"

"I'm okay, Viv."

"You don't sound okay."

"That's just the connection. I'm really okay. I'm staying with Miss—" He drew a blank. She'd said her name, hadn't she?

His sister knew. "Miss Grace told me they brought you to her house and I say praise God for that! You tell her I am thanking her for what she's done. If the doctor would permit Mama would go down to get you. But you know. After a day and no word from you, she cried awhile. Then she brightened up and said you were fine. You know she has her ways of knowing. I'll come and get you."

"No. Don't come. I'm coming home soon. I'll call back when Mama's up."

"Tomorrow. You'll come home tomorrow?"

"No. I'll call tomorrow." He was looking around the gas station. Looking at Miss Grace sitting behind the wheel of her car. Looking past her to the highway. He wouldn't be leaving here for a while, not even to see his mother's smiling face. He knew then he would find the last things.

The last things he needed to know for his life he'd find here in Mimosa, Mississippi. That's where Miss Grace told him he was.

✦

She told everybody who asked who did not know that he was her nephew. Timothy Grace. One of her brothers who'd gone to Detroit and never set foot in the South again. Everyone accepted him because Miss Leah-Bethel Grace said so. They called him T-Baby. He went with her to Mt. Tabor Church. She picked up some flyers and they didn't tarry. She dropped him back at the house.

"We'll talk tonight," she promised him, and gave him the back-door key.

He spent the day cleaning up; gratitude making him even more industrious than usual. He washed the breakfast dishes, made up his bed, swept the house and dusted. When he finished these tasks, he sat and thought for an hour or more. He grew agitated and took all the dainty china cups out of the cabinet and washed them along with the souvenir plates.

He walked around the house and looked hungrily at every picture on the wall. The Graces must be legion. He smiled over a lineup of school photos. Boys and girls in white shirts or blouses and blue uniforms. A brown, apple-faced girl smiled through small, almond-shaped eyes. She looked hopefully into a distance. Like she could barely contain herself. A real dreamer. He read the inscription and signature in the blue ink at the bottom of the photo: "For Aunt Silence, who is golden. Love, from Maggie."

Hanging beside the picture of the girl was the picture of a boy who looked like her. His face masculine and somber, but smiling too in the smile Stone was beginning to recognize as a Grace trademark. The boy's picture scrawl read, "To my dear Aunt Silence, from Lazarus."

And more photographs signed Honeybabe, Pearl, Sam Jr., Ernestine, Shirley, and two grammar-school miniatures from Anne and Frances. That same smile.

"It's a million of them." Mercy Stone's only son chuckled to himself.

His favorite photograph was one of Miss Leah-Bethel (who must be Aunt Silence) when she was young. It was a club shot with everybody dressed flamboyantly and looking celebratory and happy to be together. There she was, Miss Leah-Bethel with a man who looked like her, and a woman who looked even more like her, and a man who looked alone. The photographer had even captured the smoke as it drifted by. He sensed too that she or he had captured the state of each soul. The portraits of four lives moved him. He was drawn to it. He stood in front of it and searched out every detail. Trying to glean the lives inside the photograph. Something here touched him so deeply he felt full of a goodness.

Worn-out, he left the house in a hurry and went into the yard, where he roamed and inspected trees (fig, pecan, pear, crepe myrtle, mimosa), shrubs, fallen nuts, and insects and birds until the falling sun dimmed the air. He thought, "Maybe the land is magic. Black people survived."

He went back into the kitchen this time and looked for something to cook. She would be hungry when she got home.

He put some music on the record player in the living room. Mockingbird July radiated through the rooms as he peeled the potatoes into long, unbroken spirals of skin and bald white balls, sliced tomatoes and cucumbers for a salad, peeled onions without weeping, and opened a can of mackerel and made croquettes. He liked to cook. In one of his lives he'd worked in a restaurant. But he washed more dishes than the ones he filled when he filled in when the cook was too sick or too drunk to do his duties. When everything was ready, he went back into the living room and waited for Miss Leah-Bethel who the kids in the photographs called Silence.

When she came, she wasn't alone. He had fallen asleep in the rocking chair under the wall of pictures. The hubbub woke him up. Hours ago, there'd been a huge boom that had jostled him from his nap, but he'd drifted back into the restorative darkness. Now the house was full of people and they were talking excitedly and angrily. He searched for Miss Leah-Bethel in the throng.

She was in the dining room talking on the telephone. "Nothing left? I suppose they came like the wind and didn't a soul see nothing." She paused and looked around her, not seeing anyone. Not seeing him. Her sight had disappeared; he could tell it was in her ears, coming out of her mouth. She sounded big and stormy. "I suppose we should just thank the God who made us only two people were hurt and we taken them to the hospital. Concussion. Broken ribs."

Then she was talking even more forcefully. "Lord, I am fed up with these people trying to stop us from being free. We doing God's work. I hope the next bomb they call themselves making blow up in their hands. That would be fair. Lord knows it would." She listened again. Nodded. "We working from right here. If they coming for somebody again they better bring an atomic bomb." She hung up. She saw them and everybody was one. Even Stone.

The crowd of people was boisterous, waffling between salvation and relief and outrage. God had not blinked his eyes on them after all. They were still alive. And they were hungry like the living.

They raided the refrigerator. Heated up the food he'd cooked: croquettes, potatoes and onions. Somebody brought in tamales and french fries. A woman was frying fish and a man brought in a kettle of greens from the Sunflower Café and a block of corn bread compliments of Saphronia. Treemont got down every dish he'd washed that day. And they used up a pile of paper plates. Eating like starving children or grown men and women who'd worked hard for a long time with nothing on their stomachs.

He was right with them, answering to the names Timothy or T-Baby, or once or twice Gracie.

When the phone wasn't ringing, somebody was talking on it.

Miss Leah-Bethel wouldn't sit still long enough to eat, and Treemont was right behind her. He and another man carried the big mimeograph machine into the bedroom from someone's car.

In the living room they pushed back the couch and put in a banquet-size folding table. There was a chair in every corner. Some people stood. Others sat on the floor with plates on their laps.

The workers got down to the work and he listened. He listened to the sound of his life.

In the middle of the night Stone was in the kitchen, clarified with joy, and washing dishes. A few workers sprawled on the couch fast asleep. And a man sat straight up in a corner chair dead to the world. There were sentries at windows wide awake and watching. Across the street Mr. Marshall watched all night and slept throughout the day for Miss Leah-Bethel. He was old then, and proud to be needed. And Treemont Stone was proud to be needed, so he broke suds and broke into a soft whistling. Little arabesques and twirls of sound haunting the area over the sink, falling into the dishwater, silent against the stainless steel, the china, and the plastic glasses that could be used again.

It hit him in that moment, a jabbing finger in the solar plexus. He had been grieving all those years. Guilty because his father, who'd been a giant, had died while he had lived. He'd been rudderless. Lost. And spinning aimlessly in a sea of grief-glinting months. He'd told himself he was getting ready all that time to start his life. But he hadn't been fixing to do anything. "Fixing to do nothing," he said to the pane above the sink.

"Digging yo potatoes." That's what the girls on his block growing up used to call it. That hesitation dance, bobbing and weaving outside the double Dutch rope, feigning, but not jumping in and dancing on hot, light feet.

Right then and there he decided to live. And keep learning as he went. The music and the books—he needed them, to keep his head on straight.

He chuckled gruesomely, thinking about what it was like to lose a head, lose it completely, then put it back on.

Miss Leah-Bethel said, "What you in here being happy about?"

He looked at her full in the face, willing her to read his heart. "I got to tell you something," he whispered back urgently. He went and shut the kitchen door.

They sat at the tiny table in the corner. It was piled high with voter registration leaflets, but neither of them moved them. He leaned on them and looked at her close-up again. Outside the window, the wind bobbed inside the fig tree. The tree was beautiful. Profuse and delicate. They looked at each other, and she just burst out laughing. Laughing from way inside. From her feet. Down to the floor. And through the floor. To the earth. And down through the earth.

"You're not supposed to laugh yet," he told her. Laughing too because he couldn't help himself. After a while she quit and started up again in little deep giggles.

"Old Mr. Death thought he had us tonight," she said. Then she sighed. And was quiet, looking at him, and waiting for him to tell her.

And after a while he did.

"Those people who brought me to you, where'd they find me?" he asked.

"Up in the bushes along Old Letha Road. Up around there."

"You know what happened?" he asked her.

"I know somebody was after you. And then something got after them." This cracked her up again. She laughed through the floor and to the earth again. Outside the window he could see that fig tree laughing. But he couldn't see the wind.

"Miss Grace, do you know what got after them?" he asked her curiously.

"Mmmmmmmm hmmmmmmmm," she answered, sweet as a little biddy girl.

But neither of them would say it.

"I've been thinking about my father. He died a while ago and I've been running away from that. Tonight, this morning, I would say, I decided not to run anymore." He'd been afraid the words wouldn't come, but they did.

"So I'd like to stay here a little bit, and work with you before I go home. Is that all right with you?"

"That's fine with me."

After they'd finished talking about room and board and working, he felt better. Content even. He felt like he'd just made a contract with an angel. He told her that.

She said, "You just sold your soul to God, not me." And then she went to bed.

He finished the dishes, and stayed up the rest of the night writing in his new spiral notebook Miss Grace had given him. Writing everything that had happened to him. He wrote like a man in a trance about Letha and Ricochet and the sheriff and the riders and dying and not dying; Reverend Jeremiah Stone; Mercy Stone, his mother, who had given him so much; Vivian; Miss Grace, who some children with the same smile called Silence; the civil rights workers; himself in all his lives; and the shimmering woman who'd saved him on Old Letha Road. Her only weapon her head in her hand.

Watercolors

I've seen the beautiful trees of Eden and been betrayed by them. Those trees I tried to capture in watercolors—I should have used my tears and the fire in my mouth, the smoke from my Afro like soft charcoal smoldering in the air like I do. It is summer and I lie in my bed and in my mind prime a new canvas for my life.

Happy birthday, dear Maggie. Happy birthday to me. I'm eighteen years old. What are my rights? Do I have the right to bear arms? I have the right to marry and make love and war. If I choose. Mama commissioned me to do a portrait of her and Madaddy. I work on it this summer. She pays me. A pretty penny. (Mama—patron of my art, my good angel, my mother most beneficent.) I have the right to call myself an artist. When I tell her I don't want to go back to Eden, she tells me I don't have the right to waste my life. She sits on the side of my bed and she says, "I don't want this society to leave you behind." I don't have the right to be a person of the past, to be cast aside.

When I was a little girl walking down Arbor, I saw a man walking from another direction. A tormented man, youngish, with fuzzy hair. His coat blew open with the wind he made himself as he fast-walked. "Who got the rights?" he shouted. It was fall then, although I couldn't remember the year, what year of Grace when Silence spoke down south and my daddy had to go bring the bail money because there were too many people in jail and not enough money to get them out. "Who got the rights?" a year long before Lazarus went to jail for running to work, or my Uncle Blackstrap got put away for getting his gun when the car dealer sold him a lemon truck and would not undo the trade, and Uncle Blackstrap's savings were gone and he had to start his junk business from scratch again, carrying the world's leftovers in a cart, a pushcart. Nothing happened to the car dealer, or the policemen who beat up Lazarus, or the Mississippi sheriffs who jailed Aunt Silence. That day I stopped in the middle of the pavement, transfixed by that tortured brown-skinned man with the mussed-up hair, and watched him as he went along his way, repeating, "Who got the rights? I got the rights." That was it. The question and another. "Who got the rights?" and "Who withheld the rights?" These questions would form in my subconscious and be underneath, afterimage for the portrait of my becoming. One of my becomings. All my reachings, and strivings, and wonderings and desires and necessities pounded into me by life itself. "Who got the rights?" That was easy enough to answer then. And I was still in elementary school.

This post-freshman-year summer and the splendiferous green beauty of that landscape no longer calls to me. I am tired as the battle weary. I go to a party of my high school class. We call ourselves the Debutantes because we know we were not, although we had a sweet cotillion in the gym of a Catholic boys' high school. I waltzed with my father and watched him and my mother waltz. Then I waltzed with a boyfriend I'd borrowed from another, more popular girl. She had an extra boy who longed for her then liked me better that night when I wore my princess dress and perfect pressed and curled hair. The richest and lightest girl in our class had a mama who glared at me and loud-whispered, "What's she doing here?" Because my dress was sewn by a seamstress and not purchased at the store her daughter's was. I'll tell the truth now: I was prettier.

At the mini high school reunion of Lourdes Academy at Theodora Clarke's house, someone puts on "Theme from Valley of the Dolls" and Yolanda Taylor begins to sing in her voice that haunts like a child's ghost. One by one we begin to cry. Because life is scary. I thought at first it was just Martin Luther King we were crying for and all the others murdered on our Weeping Road, and ourselves, on the brink of nothingness or Revolution. There is a War ahead. And we have to file our way through granite.

26

"I never paid that much attention to Robert Kennedy," Theodora says even while someone else says she did and worked for him. "I heard someone crying and I found out it was me." She goes to the same all-girls college my sister Katherine Pearl graduated from in June. "I didn't think I cared that much."

We'd each brought a forty-five. I put on "This Bitter Earth," by Dinah Washington, then I put on the same song sung by Mockingbird July. It is rare and kills you to listen to. It hurts with painful beauty.

They don't like my music. They don't really like me. They like that I went to Eden, where there was a student Takeover. A Black revolt.

In elementary school we sat under desks with our heads between our knees praying through dreams of mushroom clouds that came out of our heads like question marks, waiting for the air raid siren to stop. That siren lured the fears of an Atomic Age to squat under desks beside us. White kids hid under their desks too. I heard some Whitegirls talking about it at Eden once. In Eden we rolled bandages, egged on by the EARTH, a collective aimed to educate the people about the coming apocalypse, and the sirens of riots across the country that summoned us there. We were certain that we weren't White and never would be, though we suffered what they suffered and suffered because of them. Was the Revolution only a siren luring us to crash our lives against the rocks of the world as we leapt out to the drowning sea?

The Debutantes of Lourdes Academy ask me about the Takeover at Eden University. I tell them about the Takeover with a few details. Their eyes get big at the sound of the guns. About the building burning I say, "It was an old building. And a group of White SDS burned down the ROTC building. We're not the only ones who burn buildings."

But Theodora won't hear it. "He burned that building and burned up his life at the same time. Things are changing for the Negro people and he messed up. You have to keep believing."

Do I believe in miracles? Yes, I have heard the story of my grandmother Sarah Mahalia Lincoln Dancer who walked against her own death. And I believed. But right now a flower bursting out of this troubled soil seems miraculous. America is a mural of fire and barrenness.

How do I put these together—images of For Bloods Only women rolling bandages during the siege at Eden and my high school classmates smoking cigarettes, some of them, and reminding me of our (what we called) Etiquette Class in which we learned about the uses of different forks and spoons and knives at the well-set table. The nuns in their way prepared us for a grand entrance into a desegregated world; at Eden, we prepared ourselves for another. They weren't the same worlds. Did I know something, so many months ago, a life ago, as I stood unblemished in my white graduation dress and smiled my extravagantly bright smile of joy, fear, accomplishment, and anxiety?

It was a convent, only we'd gone home in the afternoons. The nuns who lived their secret lives on the second floor of the vast stone building taught us well. There are teachers who are important as I. B. K. Turner, the only Black teacher at Eden, is important to me. I. B. K. Turner must have taught one of my art teachers who broke the flow in the syllabus after everything went down—the Takeover, the fire, the assassination, the City and other cities burning. One day the art teacher talked about the Wall of Honor in the "ghetto" and how it had recharged so much interest in murals around the country. I liked the inspiration part, but the "ghetto" made me grind my teeth. I'd heard on Blood Island that the Wall of Honor was sublime, awe-inspiring. It had a magical effect on the community in which it stood. Bent backs straightened, and pro-cessed heads turned naturally complex. The people started talking back to the artists as they worked. I wanted to see the Wall, but by the time I was ready to venture forth, it had been torn apart and scattered. Another Wall was going up. I wish I'd been old enough to work on the Wall of Honor. I was still at Lourdes.

Theodora passes around a yearbook. I look at my graduation picture. My smile was one thousand watts as I married tomorrow. At Lourdes Academy we learned about miracles manifold. The lame walked, the blind saw, the terminally ill were healed. The waters of Our Lady were healing waters. Miraculous waters out of which sprang undiluted hope and a faith replenished, verified. She must have been the Black Madonna. But at Eden I'd put Lourdes away. How gawky I'd been, how insecure, how early adolescent! How Negro! How nothing but accommodation and anticipation. That's what some of the girls of Eden whispered. The girls from Lourdes remind me I'd been the "Angel with a Flaming Sword."

"Remember, Maggie? You talked like thunder. I was scared. You were usually quiet and giggly. But you remember when Medgar Evers was killed in Mississippi in June before we came to Lourdes and that next year we were talking about it and you told us what your aunt Leah-Bethel Grace said, 'Hold the line. Don't fall back.' Remember, Maggie?" Distance has made them like me better.

I remember. That is what Aunt Silence said.

At the beginning of every school year we watched *The Song of Bernadette*, starring Jennifer Jones as the ordinary peasant girl who was visited by the Blessed Virgin Mary. I know about seeing ghosts! But the Blessed Mother left miracles in her wake—stories of wonder. Not just tales of quick flight and scared getaways. Actual miracles that lingered. And she used a simple poor girl, Bernadette, to do God's will. I would think, "I want to do God's will." But today I act like who I tried to be. "If I see *Song of Bernadette* one more time . . ." I say.

"Maggie, you aren't foolin anybody. We thought you'd quit Eden and go into the convent."

"We wouldn't have been surprised. You liked that movie, Maggie."

"The Angel with a Flaming Sword spoketh and she sayeth, 'God can work miracles in so common a thing as waters. We must drink and be healed.' Those were your words, Maggie."

I feel my face catch heat.

I've taken Existential Philosophy. I know "the benign indifference of the universe" and a hell that is a room populated by flies. The flies are the myriad little memories of things I once said, once believed. Dresses of bright white and too-light-pink lipstick I once wore on my lips.

Everyone is wearing a natural except for our hostess, Theodora Clarke, who still calls us Negroes. We look so good in our Afros! Bushy and beautiful and together.

So remembering with the Debutantes impels me back to Eden University. That and Mama and Madaddy have an invisible gun at my head—bullets of guilt and expectations. The September day I come back to Eden I sleep the whole day. My roommates, Essie and Leona, wake me for dinner.

✦

My little sisters, Ernestine and Shirley, have come to visit Eden on an October day—eyes sore from burned-out buildings and boarded stores slowly being repaired.

At the Sweet Flats (or Eden Suites, the sophomore and up dorm) they head straight for my side of the room in the new apartment. They are covetous creatures with huge hair and simmering hormones.

The door is open. Trixia sticks her head in.

"What's this? Day camp?"

Her eyes are friendly, inquiring and insolent. But her mouth is just condescending and insolent.

Nobody answers. My sisters look her up and down. Down and up.

"That was Patrixia from Carolina." She's gone.

The sides of their mouths are turned up. The inquiry is etched in the stone of their hearts that keep everything.

"She ought to go back."

"Who want that?"

"She was ugly too. But she believe she cute."

"She ain't got no mirror."

"The mirror broke when it saw her."

And on and on about Trixia, who is a criminal because she has called them young. They are caged young lionesses, haughty and predatory. I gotta get them out of my room before things start breaking.

The Cave has a steady cast of characters, consequently it's cool. Ernee and Shir say it's so, so I feel like a good hostess. We take a booth in the middle of the room, directly facing the door. Ernee checks out the counter—salads, tuna, chicken, and egg; roast beef with a pink heart, corned beef with crusty insides, turkey, lettuce, tomato, cheeses, and pickles and breads—black to white. Mayonnaise, mustard, horseradish, ketchup, butter, and relish. Potato chips hang on a rack, puffed up with air left from packaging. This satisfies her. She comes back to the booth smiling, walking with such assurance she assumes a runway air like my roommate Leona. Ernee acts like she's been places. Like our big sister, Honeybabe. She's been to the end of the El line here to Eden, a college dorm, and now a deli. She's seen more cheeses than she knew existed.

She names them for Shir so she won't have to see. "Monterey Jack, Swiss, Colby, Provolone, American, Cheddah, and Peppah Cheese."

She sips some water. "Some of that cheese is white. I don't think we oughta eat it."

"You prejudice against cheese?" Shirley.

"It look funny. Cheese spoze to be yellow like Miz Wilson's teeth."

"Those are false." Me.

"Well, cheese suppose to be yellow."

"You think it is because that's the only kind you've ever seen." The soft ring of authority in my voice. Slightly elevated.

"I still ain't gone eat no white cheese."

We don't see Steve Rainey much since spring. He's more studious, if more is possible. Even though he was suspended (expulsion pending) from school and is out on bail from one continuance to another, he's around. A brother at the desk of the back entrance lets him in and out the library, so he's holed up in Dark Shadows, deep in the dusty stacks like a nocturnal animal with more hair on his face and a cap pulled down. Only a few people recognize him walking tight across campus like something has him by the arm. Seeing one of us, he sticks his head up out of thought. Sudden. As my brother Littleson named Lazarus used to do. Out of Encyclopedia *S*. Almost through the *World Book* set. Almost knowing everything there is to know. But Steve, I would surmise, is only somewhere around *J*. The J curve we learned in Poli-Sci. A curious swerve in human expectancy. When people expect Justice and Equality, they ask for them. Maybe Steve was at *Z*. And he took everything to *Z*.

A long time ago Mama was cooking tea biscuits, and Anne, the baby, asked to see into the bowl. Mama tipped the bowl for her to look inside. Having seen the batter, Anne's anticipation turned to demand. She cried until she had a sweet biscuit in her mouth. I can see her. Eyes still wet and hot and mouth full with the flour, sugar, eggs, milk, and shortening. When Mama touched her forehead to lay down her bangs, she found out Anne had a fever, and fever made her irritable. Her eyes like little looking glasses polished too high. Mama learned because Anne had to know.

Steve pops his head up over the back of the booth. Arriving so quietly we didn't see him coming. He's banned from campus, but he's hiding in plain sight. We all look alike.

"Uhura," he calls me. That's my name now, as it was during the Take-over. I was the communications officer because I worked the switchboard at Wyndam-Allyn and called Black students to leave their dorms and head to the Finance Building. There I typed inside the building, doing what needed to be done. All of us in it together.

He remembers the names of my sisters; this puts them at ease. Talking, he slides into the booth beside me.

"Did you see the brothers? Bad. Bad. Wasn't it bad?" He's talking about John Carlos and Tommie Smith. "They said that air in Mexico would be too thin, but the bloods were like black light faster than the speed of light. Bad. Bad."

"They sure can run," I say, in awe at the memory.

The Olympics were on TV. The sound took over the house. When I passed through the living room, the bright scene caught me. If you've seen the bodies of Black men who run, you know a body can be a tree. Honed and spectacular. A length of leg and head thrown back. A man can be an antelope and be at no loss of dignity. The beauty of them makes your mouth go dry.

So I would wander through the room, then sit awhile to wait for victory. Because any of their victory is ours. Preeminently ours. Yet sometimes, when the other Americans win, we don't win. The Africans—their pride is ours too.

John Carlos and Tommie Smith raised their fists. Raised their black fists. (We know the officials wanted to kill.) Their feet planted on the victors' platform. Gold medals hanging from ribbons around their necks. They didn't smile. Their running suits shone like the dark on a new road.

Steve says, "Then the fist. The Power and Pride salute on the winners' pedestal of the 1968 Olympics. 1968. It is a very interesting year. I wonder what the wine will taste like from this year." For the benefit of my guests, he flips a napkin across his forearm. "1968. The crop was unusually varied, resulting in wines of a multiplicity of bouquets and tastes. Bitter and tenderly saccharine and robust, indubitably robust." He passes a water glass under his nose. Sniffs and sips. Then, like he's finishing brushing his teeth, he works the front of his mouth. Swallows. Grimaces. And smiles. "Mmmmm. *Magnifique.*"

"Come see. Come saw." Shirley giggles.

He's quiet when he leans back in the seat, acting like he's not here, but I know he's listening. Even with his head turned, the 'fro cut down and lined with a razor at the nape of his neck. Hair shielding his cheeks. I know he observes.

"How'd you remember our names?" Ernestine is happiest because people mix up her and Leah Shirley's names so much.

"How could I forget?" Steve answers.

"Do you have a sister?" Shirley.

"No. I'm an only child."

"You spoiled." Shirley.

"That happens to the best wine. Stored in too much heat. Or the seal is broken too soon. The cork contaminated."

"You must be a wino." Ernestine.

"You're a woman who likes a good joke."

Then he tells one I heard him tell on Blood Island last year when we were young. But it's funnier now because he's so nice to my little sisters. He's called Ernestine a woman and implied the same for each of us. Here he goes.

"This mother was in the hospital. She'd had a baby, days ago. But she hadn't seen her baby. She kept asking for her baby. Nurses came in. Where's my baby? Husband came in. I want to see my baby. Doctor. No baby. Finally, one day the doctor comes in looking solemn, superserious. Mrs. Mother, we are bringing your baby today. We've done all that we can. Is my baby dead? No. No. Just be patient. Doctor goes out. Whispering in the hallway. Doctor comes back in. Bundle of swaddled joy in his arm. Completely covered. Carefully, hands the baby over to the mother. Mother ecstatic. She got her baby. Starts unwrapping, unwrapping pink blanket, till she gets down to—and it's a Eye. Nothing but a big ole Eye. Baby-size. Before the mother can scream or get used to this big ole open baby-size eye, the doctor says, Mother, I'm sorry. The bad news is, it's blind."

My sisters don't even laugh. They start right in on speculation.

"How'd you like yo mama to bring home a eye?"

"I wonder what it eat."

"Feed it with a eyedropper like a baby kitten."

"They cain't see either."

"What color were her eyes?"

"Her eye."

"I guess it don't matter. It's color-blind."

"Frances is legally blind without her glasses."

"How'd you like a eye for a sister?"

"Pearl is a eye."

"Naw. Anne Perpetua is the Eye with her nosy self. You left yo old diary, Maggie, where you be writing to yourself, and Anne read it. She was laughing. Pearl took it from her."

"She read it all."

"I know," I say grimly, still ready for vengeance.

"Now she know."

Shirley rests her hair-heavy head on her two hands on the table. Like she's posing for a baby picture. Her mouth starts to bubble, but she can't get it out. Ernee moves to the side. Starts hitting Shirley to make her talk.

"That's what it means. The Eyes have it."

Steve thinks that's so funny. People in other booths turn around to look at him laugh.

They look fresh, my sisters, when the sun tears its way through foliage, painting leaf shapes on the sidewalk. Ernestine and Leah Shirley, in their minidresses and opaque stockings and buckled-on Mary Janes, look like flowers that have chosen human life. For a day. They are rose and lilac, respectively. Eternally, momentarily, bright and decorous. Their hair brushed up into neat-shaped shrubs, white ribbons binding their bushes.

Steve won't leave. It's like he's been lonely for them all of his life. They are not yet books. They have few leaves. And the ink is thin traces on the side leaves of flowers. How deep the natural dye is I don't know. Mention Aint Kit and they flare up. Their edges crimp. Mouths tight and eyes starting fires.

"Ooooooh, oooooh. I wanna rub her out," Shirley says, still mad about a rumor that began with Aint Kit: they'd been kissing boys in the alley.

"Yeah." Ernestine agrees to rubbing out that lying Aint Kit. She's like a provocateur at a bonfire.

Steve appreciates the purity of their desire for the immolation of our aunt. The immolation of dastardly elder relatives appeals to him. Or maybe it's my sisters who do. They are pretty girls, wicked, and anxious to be women with a say-so. Somebody listen.

Now the street is narrow as a tightrope and we play Follow the Leader. These fearless girls dance on wire thin as fishnet stockings.

It's awkward after a time when Steve doesn't know whether to stay or go. Whether we want him or not. His body is loose and longing, gawky on the corner where one side of campus meets another. He looks at the tops of things. Trees. Buildings. Streetlights.

"Steve, you gonna show Ernestine and Shirley the landfill and stuff? I have to go back to work."

"Sure. I'll do that." Relief. He tries not to look at them. But he does. The excitement the prospect of being alone with him generates in them frees him for excitement too. Jovial now, he is an educator. "Let's start with the library."

"Lie-berry. I don't wanna go to no lie-berry. We wanna see your room." That's fast mama Shirley. No wonder Aint Kit making up tales on her.

I can feel him look at me with the eyes in the back of my head. Steady walking the other way, I say, "Don't take my sisters to no all-male prisons." He's illegally in an all-male dorm. Off campus.

I can feel them forget me. Then I'm free. I wish there were time for me to go to the studio to see what happens.

I've seen a naked man. An artist's model. Wouldn't you know, a brother from the Cave. With clothes he was grungy and dumb. He tended to wear, the times I've seen him with different Whitegirls in granny dresses, a vest with fringes like parlor lamps, cowboy boots that make Leona refer to him as Deadhead Dick.

He sits on a stool. His back very straight. And the invisible gauze I've imagined him swaddled in falls to his loins. His privates are private, but the thin cloth between revelation and discretion make our untutored hands unsteady. Palms sweat.

After half an hour, he shifts position and this is like watching mountains move. So this is what the Masai mean when they say Ol Doinyo Lengai, "the mountain of God." I still haunt Africana. That is how I know. He sits like *The Thinker* on *Dobie Gillis*, that doofus show, torso bent, abdomen drawn in, half fist propped under his chin. What he thinks intrigues me. We were instructed to draw; therefore, I do. It is not good. What he thinks will not appear. What he feels inside the security and insecurity of his leather skin is not what I know.

"I can't do him justice." Inadequate, I sit and watch my classmates forge ahead like the children of conquerors. Apologies for their mistakes not required.

My teacher sees me resting. She will not allow it. She gives me a pencil.

"Three-quarters naked," she says. "And not bad. Think of a man, any man, as an iceberg. It's better that way. Just what you see, Magdalena."

I sketch like an old woman who knows what is not present. Much time is spent on hair; true to our time. (It can take a good half hour to shape an Afro. Brush, then lift, then pull out the dented places. Spray, till you make a sweet, smothering mist in which to envelop yourself.)

The switchboard is quiet and I have time to wonder why I wondered whatever was under that brother's skin. Everybody knows an Oreo has white sugar crème in the middle. I scrape that out and eat the chocolate parts. Always have. One day I'll paint Mama and Madaddy better or Aunt Silence or Aint Kit or Uncle Blackstrap or the Uncles and the Aunts.

When I am good enough there will be Mahalia, Sarah Mahalia Lincoln Dancer.

In a doorway.

In a cotton field circumscribed by a broken fence.

In a kitchen.

In a bedroom. A bed bordered by four posters to turn back the wind and hold her world in place.

In a yard, scattering fowl.

Sam Jr. had a BB gun he liked to use on chickens. Just to watch them jump he'd shoot around them; they'd fly up, startled enough to think flight possible. Then fall down to be startled again. They flapped and scrambled around, hysterically. I would capture them in furious semi-flight. Sarah Mahalia among them. She is gathering eggs in a sun hat.

I see her bathed in light, carrying something under her arm.

"What you thinking about?" Ernestine wants to know. This is her right. They've been places. And they are back.

"Grandmama collecting eggs."

"She carrying a whole lot of eyes."

"I get off in a little while. Where's Shirley?"

"Outside with Steve. She say he cu-uuuuuuuuuuu-uuute."

"Where'd y'all go?"

"To a house with a old man. He was nice. Then to Gorey." That's Blood Island, where bloods go. I told them about it.

"You like it?"

"It was okay. Steve told me to tell you they finished that game of chess they started last year."

"I know."

"Oh, Steve told me to tell you he's takin us home. He got William's car."

I open the front door. I ask Ernestine, "Do you know what size car William has?" For Steve's benefit I say, "Well, wonders never cease, Steve got wheels."

"You ready to raise, M.G.?"

"Me?"

"I gotta make a run for I. B. K. Turner. You want to come, don't you? We'll take Ernestine and Shirley first."

That's how I know I. B. K. Turner has stayed on, even though no one has mentioned him. He must be hiding in plain sight like Steve.

The girls feign protest, but I can tell they're tired. It is time to recreate their expedition in talk. To savor it in the kitchen. They've been to Eden and back. Now they know the geography of my discontent. Sophomoritis.

✦

A little car. Built low like a bug. There's no safety in it. How easy it would be for the front to meet something big and come in all the way to the back and take our bones and guts with it. Like a chicken salad sandwich pressed down hard. When the girls are gone I can think this. Even though Steve says the car is safe, with them in back, I am the mother who had to use her body, if need be, to come between them and catastrophe. On my own, with Steve Rainey, I have no one to protect. Blunt bravery sweeps out of my body. I feel everything. Look through the low windshield. We are down to earth.

Once or twice we see a pigeon in the alley, picking weeds from between bricks like spinach from between great brown teeth.

Soon the only real light comes from the car. It splashes back on us, like water from a fall. First it hits bottom, then some rises back.

"What do you have to pick up?" I ask Rainey.

"I have to take something."

"You not carrying anything."

"It's in the back of my pants. A flat package. I think it's some papers."

"Did you look?"

"It's not mine."

"For all you know you could be delivering a baby."

"An eye that ran into a rolling pin? Girl, you imagine. Your life's gonna be troubles and heartache. Like mine."

Now I know Steve wants to play "memba the time." He's my friend and he remembers for me. Only it's his life. I ask because I sense he wants me to.

"Not much to tell. I had a mother. Everyone has a mother. I had no father to speak of. I said to speak of. Don't be so persistent. What's this? Steve Rainey tells all. Father a work phantom. Mother a wage slave. Until the end. Maggie, you make me crazy.

"I was born in Denver. Yes, there are Negroes in Denver. None in Boulder. But Denver is crawling with Negroes. My mother said they went west before the Civil War. California on their minds. Pike's Peak caught someone's eye. Have you seen that? That's a mountain. Sister, that ain't no hill. I'm used to mountains. Man is a dwarf in the universe. You better know it. The grandeur is in the ascent. That sounds like you. You have a nice mind, Maggie. I always knew. Pretty too, honey chile.

"The details of my birth are scant. My mother didn't want to tell me. I was born in the Great Mother of Blizzards, knocked out power in six or seven states. Some kinda way Moms and Dad got caught miles from a hospital. Out in the middle of nowhere. I was coming through. Like a child in a myth. Feet first. They had to spin me around in the womb. But it doesn't make any difference. I was coming out feet first like a natural man, ready to stand on my own two feet."

"Looking up between yo mama's legs all the while. Real mannish."

"Look out, Maggie! You tryin to play the dozens with me. Actually tryin to signify on somebody's sexual inclinations, when I know you like that wolfsbane keep a man from turnin into a werewolf and devouring you. You ain't never been touched."

"How you know?"

"I know."

"You don't know nothin' I don't tell you."

"I know that."

"No, you don't."

"Yes, I do."

"No, you don't."

"I do too."

"Ya don't."

"Well, let's find out." He looks at me, laughing uproariously at his own wickedness.

"I'm gone write the name of my true love on the wings of a dove and you gonna have to fly to see it."

"Girl, you don't know nothing about love."

"How you know what I know?"

"You read any Yoruba love poetry?"

"No."

"The ritual dancers of the dead, the Egungun, got a love poem for you."

"What they know?"

"This is how it goes. Somethin' like this:

> We only know the one we love
> Not the one who loves us.
> Love is of many kinds.
> One love says, If you die, let me die with you.
> Another love says, If you buy the stew, I will buy the rice.
> There is love of the eye.
> There is love of the mouth . . .
> The love of the wife is different
> The love of the husband is different,
> The love of the father is different,
> The love of the mother is greatest.
> It is love that makes the goat share her husband's beard.

'I see the one I want to marry.'
The father says, 'Don't you know that his father is deaf?'
If the whip howls on my back, and thunder shouts in heaven,
If you tie me to the pillar and feed me with grass like a horse,
I will still know whom I love!"

"What's that about a goat?" I say, ignoring the rest of the poem, but not.

"That's okay, Maggie, you not ready for that poem. It's too deep for you to know it."

"Yes," I say, burrowing into the seat. "What you don't know can't hurt you."

From the El you can see the back of life. A fence is the same from front and back. You know there can't be anything inside. I. B. K. Turner, who has commissioned this ride, says there are scientists now who dig up garbage to know people. That's easy. Ten thousand years from now refuse is artifact, and garbage has birthed a renovated species of bug. A souped-up cockroach. Down here on the ground, the view from the alley is simple: squalor ready to climb out of barrels, in some cans burned back to antiseptic black ash. Useless newspapers, leftover celery stalks, onion peels, the centers of tomatoes, apple cores, dull razor blades, and toothbrushes, the middle bristles flattened to the sides. Decapitated dolls and the entrails of chickens fallen out of old newspapers, the spotted skins of picked-out beans, and ring bones and chewed grizzle, and stiff oatmeal and grits in rigor mortis of breakfast food after morning. Plastic dry cleaning bags and boxes that clock radios came in. Soapless S.O.S pads and empty bottles of Mr. Clean, he of the wrapped muscular arms and bald head like a wrestling genie, or a grinning sailor in charge of galley slaves.

Mostly I use peripheral vision. Ahead the lane is neat, except for the cobblestones sprinkled with buds of glass, divided by weeds and infant trees that birth themselves out of lines of dirt, their roots working under the bricks. Aimless, other than the desire to thrive. Senseless to the imminence of car wheels.

"Is this the place?"

"I'm not sure."

"Don't you recognize it?"

I peek out the window. The alley light is at a distance. The back-porch light further away than that.

"Uh uhn."

"Looks like . . . Have you ever seen the back of a blue rose?" I saw the Blue Rose once.

"It don't smell like a rose."

Halfway out of the car, he turns to invite my company. I decline.

"You wanna rib tip?" he asks me.

I haven't been near Roscoe's Barbeque next to the Blue Rose since the night of that fight and the gang members jumped that boy and my roommates and I got caught up in the chaos. I shake my head no.

"Suit yourself. Lock it."

I lean over and slam the button down. Then, curious, I crack the window on my side, so I can hear the night. Television on. The Olympics. The news. John Carlos and Tommie Smith. Heads down, pious and lethal. Fists. Fists in the air. Replays.

Aint Kit says it was not the Fastest Man Alive who came home. After his victory, an outraged Hitler stole the Black man and made his scientists make a Whiteman black. Then they cut the Fastest Man Alive into little pieces and scraped his scrotum like a pomegranate and froze the seeds they found there. They used these seeds to impregnate Fräuleins and create a master race of athletes who were neither Black nor White, neither male nor female. The Whiteman who was the Fastest liked being the Fastest so much he renounced his purpose and his country. He liked what Fastest liked. He loved what Fastest loved. He wanted what Fastest wanted. He had what Fastest had. That's the story Aint Kit invented about the 1936 Olympics. Madaddy said Aint Kit was more a Whiteman than the one she invented.

"Why's that, Sam?" Mama asked him just so he'd stop his sister's foolishness.

"Tellin lies and casting aspersions on a Blackman's capabilities."

"She didn't say nothing 'bout what Fastest didn't do. She was talking about what the White folks probably did to him." Mama was smiling.

"Probably? That's tellin lies, because you ain't accumulated no evidence for this switching up on some bodies."

Mama imitated Aint Kit: stuck her head forward and pointed a finger at Madaddy. This next low and confidential and conclusive. "You never saw him run as fast as he did in Berlin afterward, did you?"

"That's just ridiculous!" my father spat out, hating his sister's stories that didn't "make any durn sense."

Sometimes Steve Rainey doesn't have good sense. This is one. Leaving me in this alley. Now I know when a rat big as Hitler ambles up and sits up like the Führer at a mouth-foaming rally on the low car hood. Sitting up on his hind legs like he's officiating over garbage, which he is. I can't even scream.

My mouth is open. Steve says, "What's wrong?" He's standing near the car. Yet still in the yard. He's doubled back for me.

"Did you see that rat?"

"Where?"

When I can talk again, I tell.

"You sure?"

"It was like a squirrel."

"You been down here with Rocky the Squirrel. Somethin' told me to take you upstairs with me."

Although I've never set foot here before, never laid eyes on these men before, I know what they may say (a glimpse of it), what they have said at one time or another here (a piece of it), how they might initiate a melody of reflection and analysis (a spirit of it). One will push his top dentures tight into the gum, delicately, almost surreptitiously, looking nowhere, his fingers in his mouth, then startle upon a half-forgotten past. "What com ma—?" "What got with—?" That's the way he will begin. "What got with—?" "What com ma—?"

The times I've heard my father in casual discourse with another man on Arbor, some Saturday he'd look down the alley, the two of them in Saturday work clothes, momentarily idle, he'd count the cobblestones that stretched past his vision and his memory. Then the inquiry. An idle transverse.

"What com ma—?"

"I wonder what ever got with—?"

"They tell me—"

"I seen that ole rascal—"

"You wasn't one of them that was involved in it, were you?" Whatever it was.

So these men must begin something like this. Each of them old enough to be my father's father.

Every one of them old enough to have rubbed shoulders and elbows with men they have lived to outlive, thenceforth to ponder the roads, the back alleys, the boulevards of prosperity, common trickery, and ameliorated contrivance. They know a con when they see one. They know one when they're in one. When they're the mark. When they're the shell. When they're the pea.

It's the way Steve Rainey explained—a shell game at the rear of the bus. Move the pea from shell to shell faster than honest eyes can see. Talk fast and bright so attention is broken. Palm the pea. Move the shells empty and fast. Lift a shell and dark is light and people say, "Ahhh!" or "Shoot!" Some of them say, "Gimme my money back!" Some look injured in the eyes and move away, empty-handed. Faith in benevolent chance lost, having cost too much. That's the con game Steve Rainey describes when I know he means we are the pea, moved around by a lot of con men. Centuries worth of con men. Giving us false promises. Dazzling us with the rhetoric of democracy. Then taking our money. Taking faith.

We are secreted in the folds between sly fingers.

There is another way to see this. I am seeing it now. When the quick trickery is on the other hand. This is a game of peas. Okay. Black-eyed peas. That's good luck and New Year's to me. And these men are hopping John sitting in a pot. I have the feeling some trickery is about to begin. Legerdemain.

Steve is holding a large envelope in both his hands; he is an errand boy, suppliant and earnest. In this room, he is younger than I ever thought possible. On Blood Island it always seems like he and Elder and Yvonne Christmas are old. Old beyond their years.

Between us, Steve and me, we have more hair on our heads than these grandfathers put together over their whole bodies. Little thistles of beard on one of the old men, and his head covered in a gray-white like the softest pigeon feathers, the ones that must cover the tenderest part. The other is clean-shaven; his face like an expensive purse. His mouth clasped. They're sweeping up after what looks like a party.

43

Leftover food, saucers, napkins, and silverware on the table.

"Good evenin'," they say, one behind the other.

"Good evenin'," I say to them. Very proper as I've been taught. I have on a skirt, albeit short, at my thighs. My T-shirt says, FOR BLOODS ONLY. They know me.

Steve Rainey quit saying "What's happenin, what's happenin" a while ago. Now he says, "Excuse us. Sorry to barge in on you, but I have a package for the man who lives here."

"Have a seat." This comes inside the sweep of the broom.

We sit and every now and then the walls of the room go blue. One wall, one corner where no one sits, blinking, an almost imperceptible blue. Someone tells us to rest our feet. When we should be telling them that. We rest our feet. In the corner where the wall goes occasionally blue, I take the stern-backed wooden chair and Steve Rainey sits near my feet, leaning a little on my legs. Soon his elbow is on my knee. I look out the window and see the front of the Blue Nile/Blue Rose, although I cannot see the entrance. Only the luminescence of the sign, and I see now how little blue really comes in. Maybe I never saw, only knew it would be in this corner.

The old men have an audience now. Their talk is fulsome. Like great actors who rise to the occasion of audience.

"I'm DeadandBuried," one sweeping man says. He turns his head toward the corner in which we sit. His voice hits the corner, so deep it is hollow. A voice.

"Yeah. He sho is DeadandBuried now."

I think I'm supposed to say, "I'm sorry about that." Like my mother does when she hears someone has just died.

They sweep some more. Measuring their voices in teaspoons like the gentlemen they are, and shake with the tip of the index finger exaggeration back into the bottle of memory. Whatever misses the mouth they divide. This cannot be true. I lean forward to look at them closely. Steve Rainey leans hard on my legs to keep me from inclining too close, too invitingly.

"DeadandBuried," the men keep saying, chuckling all the while. As if the idea has proven a source of great delight.

"We must be seeing ghosts then," Steve Rainey says.

They throw their heads back, then crunch their torsos in, at that.

"Seeing ghosts."

"Seeing ghosts. Oh, yeah. You seeing ghosts. I see yo hair standing all over yo head."

"Do you know yo older heads?" one man looks dead at me.

"No, sir, I don't."

"You hear that. That girl got pretty manners. 'No, sir, I don't.'" He mimics me appreciatively.

"They ain't answer yo question," the other one says. "Cause they don't know what you talkin 'bout."

"Do you know yo grandparents and such?" He clears it up.

"I know my grandmama Patsy."

"What about you?" The man rests on his broom, and points with his free hand to Steve Rainey.

"No. They're all dead and buried." Steve chances a smile.

"There you go."

"That's why we DeadandBuried. So you know us and tell about us."

"Young man live here putting us all on record. So when we dead and buried you'll still know us."

"They don't know what you talkin 'bout. Look at 'em. They don't know."

"Just let me finish getting these crumbs up off this boy's flo. Then I'm gone have some ghost stories for 'em."

"You gone put on the sheet?"

He leans on the broom, considering costumery. "Naw, they think we the Ku Klux Klan. Light outta here."

He sweeps. "Lift yo feets, Lil Lady. Low I sweep over 'em and you go to travelin."

Steve Rainey lifts his elbow from my knee and gets off the floor. My legs in the air like a magician's assistant, I lean to the side and stare at the contents of a bookcase jammed with books, journals, magazines, and newspapers from Africa and Europe. On top of the case is a stack of *Negro Digest*, and a stack of file folders bulging with newspaper clippings. Steve takes down the clippings and shows them to me while the old men nod and watch. "Massacre at Sharpeville," "King Assassinated," "W. E. B. Du Bois Dies in Ghana," "Malcolm X Meets with OAS." Soon

I just see names: Cabral, Touré, Nkrumah, Nyerere, Mandela, Tambo, ANC, SWAPO, FRELIMO. I look at the books on the shelves: the Holy Bible, the Holy Quran, the Egyptian Book of the Dead, the *I-Ching*, *The Book of Negro Folklore*, and *Mules and Men*. *The Wretched of the Earth*, *Pan-Africanism or Communism*, *Here I Stand*, *The Crisis of the Negro Intellectual*, *The Negro*, *The Rise and Fall of the Third Reich*, *Marx and Lenin*. *Elementary Physics*, *Civilization and Its Discontents*, *Walden II*, *Integral Calculus*, *Advanced Carpentry*, *Negro Art*. A stack of *Black Panther* newspapers and *Muhammad Speaks*. A bookcase of law books.

I look down at a pair of thick white cotton socks in soft brown leather slippers. The smooth, thin, brown cane leaning, wedged between the wall and a chair. The man atop of the slippers, juiceless and wiry. The cuffs of his khakis rolled up to his calves. I think he's looking at me too. But he isn't. He's turned my way, leaning on his broom again, thinking.

Whoever lives here doesn't have dessert dishes. Persimmon preserves brim out of quasi-crystal ashtrays, and toasted wheat bread (with the crust carved off) covers the trays waitresses carry in places like the one downstairs, circular trays for beer bottles, ice cubes rattling in stout glasses, and neat piles of triangular napkins. The two sweepers decide to enjoy the last of the light repast. They invite us to join them. Politely, we nibble at sandwiches.

"Go head now. You got to finish tellin 'bout that time," one old man says to the man in socks, the broom now gripped tight in his tough, shrunken hands.

Nobody says anything. Steve Rainey lifts his arm and puts his wristwatch to his ear. He rewinds it before time stops and the gentlemen know it. I try not to look at the burn places on his hands. I have been avoiding them all day.

"We just gone sit here?" I wonder, but don't give voice to this impatience for some occurrence, any.

They eat daintily like poor men at a high-tea party, alien, cautious of manner, extreme in courtesy. Not even breathing too hard lest that be offensive. They chew each morsel like a praying mantis chews a blade of grass.

Now from the back room comes a third man. He walks like a stick, straight up and down. He has a hat on his head, so his hair is invisible.

He is black as a raisin. And his eyes are heavy lidded. "Got to be going," he says.

But the other two say, "Peddler, come sit."

He sits.

And the broom man starts talking. "I used to like to make them long runs, between the Big Apple and the City of Angels. We used real china on them tables. And we set the table. Used napkins and everything."

"We got that, Lemuel. We got that."

Lemuel!

"Did I tell you 'bout the girl call me 'sailor' of them rails? Chinamen lay them lines. Prison gangs. Steal a hawg and you have to make your own way. I mean make it. Huh! We hit it! Huh!"

"I thought you was a porter, Lemuel. Not no chain-gang prisoner."

"Evvybody got two or three times."

"That's true. You tellin the truth."

"I'm a wanted man."

"Don't nobody want you, Lemuel," cracks the man under the hat.

"Don't?"

"Statue of limitations done run out," the second broom man explains.

"Nope. Nobody wanna old nigger with no teef," the mean man under the hat.

Lemuel sets his jaw stubborn. "One time I robbed the train."

"You didn't. You didn't rob no train," hat man.

"What they call it, then?" Lemuel.

"You run off with the train."

The second broom man shrieks like a girl. "Lemuel, you elope with the train." They all laugh at this. A mixed box of Chuckles, chewy candy with different colors.

The hat man sings, "If the train should jump the track, do you want your money back?"

"How far did it take you?" I have the nerve to interrupt, when laughter is so sweet.

"Far enough."

Then he begins at the beginning.

"We pull into a little town name Blossom. Air not workin, soz everybody gets off. The engineer say I wanna take me a smoke. However, everybody know he got a woman in this town. Got a house the size a gas pump. And two little baby children all the time be necked as lizards. He got off and I get back on board. And 'fore I know anything—we gone. I took her out easy but I rode her hard for two hunnerd fifty miles. I see the station coming up. I set the brakes and 'fore hit stop, I jump down from there and hit the ground runnin. I took off.

"Made it to a highway and wait for some colored peoples in a car. They come and I got on the running board and we ride thataway. That's the way a man spoze to get outta town—standin up in the open."

Steve Rainey and I look at each other. Simply delighted. This dude's a real desperado.

"What it feel like commandeering that railroad train?" Steve asks.

"It feel fine."

His friend, our second host, has to add, "I'da rode that baby on into Union Station in Chicago. Everybody-get-on-board!"

"I seed one child that whole two hunnerd fifty miles. A little Innian boy wave at me. He had eyes like jelly beans."

"How you tell?"

"He was right up on the tracks. He look up. I look down. There his jelly bean eyes is. Then I blew the whistle. Sound like Miss Mockin'bird Joo-lie. I met her one time. She used to sing something called 'Seven Veils Blues.' Couldn't nobody see her face. She sing behind seven scarves she call veils. They say somebody cut her face. Then I heard she was showin her face and there wasn't no scar. She ain' have to dance. I can memba the words, though. They wadna special. It was the way she sing 'em make yo skin come off yo body and wanna dance. It was kinda funny the way she sing and them veils don't move. Like she had a mouth somewhere's elsen her mouth."

"Respect the children. Respect the children," Mr. Hat says. "Yo imagination done run off with yo memory. 'Magination do that."

"Mebbe it is. Mebbe it ain'. One time after she sang, I saw a man put another man head on a platter. They was both of 'em smiling."

"Uhhhh oh! Look out, John the Baptizer!"

"Look at that girl. Eyes big as tablespoons. Don't worry, guh. We missed her again."

"She be right in fronta you in the store you miss her."

"Negro, you blind in one eye and cain't see out t'other one."

This jest stops Lemuel cold, undermines his testimony and hurts his feelings, so he remembers the pain of the present.

"I got to take my medicine," he says, and gets up and pours from the plastic pitcher a half glass of water. He unwraps from his breast pocket a handkerchief and removes a green capsule. Pops it in his mouth, washes it into his body. Then goes and sits back down.

"What that you takin?"

"Same thing I been takin."

"You feel any better?"

"Naw."

"Now why you takin it, then?"

"Feel worse if I don't."

The inquirer piles persimmons on a cube of toast. Sticks his tongue out and lays the whole thing on it. His mouth is full now; he rares back in his seat as if to convey he will seek no more sense from medicine or people who take it.

He chews until the toast and persimmons are out of his mouth, consumed, then he says, "Benjamin drank whiskey just like milk. I seed him turn up a milk bottle one time, oouh, it was fulla whiskey. I say, boy that whiskey gone ride you home. And it sho did. Them doctors wrote it down. The nurses too. They can write."

This drinking talk makes everybody thirsty. It is Lemuel who fills our glasses with water, pouring with a steady hand. Years as a waiter aboard a land-bound luxury liner with an easy sway taught him to hold steady his hand. Taught his body the tasks it takes to do a job. How long does it take a body to forget its work even after it's been laid off or fired, discharged or dismissed? How many jobs, incorporating how many menial tasks can one body master and remember?

My father would say, my mother would say, work is one thing you should be happy to have. Aint Kit would say work is the only thing, and she'd go grinning into the crack of dawn to greet White patients and dirty floors with the same smile. Uncle Blackstrap would say work is the only thing left.

And now I know he is right.

There is only one Body of work. People raise food for it. People prepare the food. People scoop up the leavings. People move and rule and pamper it and whip it to make it do. Wash it and soothe it and perfume it. People make clothes for it. People make potions for its beauty—face, eyelids, lips, skin, hair, and nails. Trinkets for ears and wrists and necks and ankles. People make new parts for it when parts wear out. When its head is bad, people shrink it or lock it up. When its heart is troubled, people pray for it. When it dies, people pray over it, and empty it out, and fill it up again with formaldehyde. They make boxes to drop it in, then drop the boxes in the earth they hollowed out. Or they burn the Body and spread the ashes in the wind or water.

The worst works are the essential ones. And these are the ones these men have done. Kept the vast Body alive. They have always served the Body. Funny, isn't it, now that each of them is old and rusty and quaint? The Body does not serve them.

The horror of this kicks like a mule inside my head.

I observe them and feel inadequate, not in the restless, laconic way in which I was too disarmed to sketch the dimwit of the Cave in figure-drawing studio class. Here I am disabled by the inabilities of my own hands, never raw, scraped, knotted, and calloused with unlovely labors, heavy deliveries. Bolt, or reins, or hammer, or gun, or gutting knife. Or burned like Steve Rainey's.

I am hopelessly young. Hopelessly.

The years they talk about, the years they gaze at when their eyes are cast down, these years are roads underneath other roads. Paths I never see. Roads where there are no roads, only clear ways between trees. And the trees are shiny and wrapped in a sheath of ice, glistening in that astonishing treachery.

Once (is it possible?) they were dumb as I am dumb, fidgety, shy behind a lot of mouth and too-eager eyes? Staunch to hold on to one thing. Big about it. Big behind it like these letters on my chest. FBO. It's funny. That dream I'd forgotten. When I first came to Eden, I dreamed the dorm mother, Mrs. Sorenson, was passing out Biggifying Pills to Whitegirls and Belittling Pills to us Blackgirls.

How many Biggifying Pills have they taken, these old Blackmen? But really, how many Belittling?

What pill offered compensatory dominion? Dominion over hog, possum, water moccasin, castrated bull, mule, bobcat cub, bear, rabbit, rind, boll of cotton, tobacco leaf, feather. The best they could do was supervise death, bring bloody alms to the living god. Take some pride, but not too much in each assignment. Crow over an accomplishment and someone will cut it out of your throat. Call attention to profit and thieves follow. Look up too high and heaven crashed like the stock market. So they took their Belittling Antidote Pills, small ones, on the lam, grew too big for their modified britches, and ran. They swallowed the Antidote during a dance, on a wedding day, at a birth, a harvest, and took a half one every Sunday. At night in bed beside a wife, everything in its place, the chifforobe, the dresser, spoons and forks and butter knives on the sink shining back at the moon that slipped through curtains, no Antidote was needed. Only sweet breath in wisps and currents, only air itself, compensatory and munificent. And ordinary, ordinary. And how many nights like this in a life? Two or two thousand?

As many nights as Belittling Pills? Too many of them. The bee-shaped pills that found whatever honey there was, and hid it.

Sometimes it seemed that every star there ever was was one too many. It made the eyes water. Longing.

Insult lay everywhere.

Disrespect mocked effort.

What was good you forgot. And as good as it got was never enough. Could you see Hercules in a wine jug? Or Buddha on a diet of worms? The Blessed Virgin in the lockup?

Honest labor—the Body exalts. Restless, too tired, the Body punishes. Dishonest pay, a slap in the face.

You. You there. Boy.

There is no glamour in disparagement. That sounds like something Yvonne Christmas would say. She would sit here and understand what I can't. I think of my brother Lazarus the Panther. "Each one teach one," he would say. Each of these old men is teaching me through osmosis.

We've been sitting here a long time. I'm starting to get tired. They act like they just wound the wristwatch on Steve Rainey's arm.

Suddenly the man under the hat gets up from his seat. In a corner of the room where my eyes have not stopped yet is a tape recorder.

"I wonder 'bout this boy wanna put everything on tape," the hat man says, with an island I don't know accent. "A bunch of old men gummin each other brains. Like the hobgoblin. Talkin 'bout de Mind Bank. Look at de girl. She beauty, right?"

Then he is Nigerian, a city dweller with an aggressive undertone. "I have seen her. I know this. She is like a young queen. Ah! She is my bride. We must marry."

"Your mind's playing tricks on you, old man."

"Is not de mind playin de tricks." Island again, insinuating.

My cheeks catch fire.

"It ain't that low, either. My heart be longing for you, Lady." He smiles and I can't make out the accent or why he keeps dipping in and out of them. I can't see his face whole; it's hidden by the hat. Now the hat floats over his head, like his face is a swamp. I lean forward, till the press of Steve's hand on my knee keeps me back.

The man of a thousand accents says, "Beauty speak. Tell this old man wid his heart afire where you been hidin all my long soldier years? I been rippin and runnin across the sea back and forth looking for you, Pretty."

How long we've been here I do not know. Grandmama Patsy told me once when I was a little girl her mother came cross Atlantic River in 1821. A river or an ocean. I don't know. Aint Kit said her grandmother came from Georgia. I don't know how she knows, so I don't know which water. Which water.

All I manage to get out to my admirer is, "I was born in Mimosa, Mississippi." And say Mimosa right, with the silent *a*.

"At last when I encounter you, I am an empty-handed man. Once I dove the blue-bluest waters of High Tea and clasped coral in my hands. The rocks of the reef tore my knees and I bandaged them with my ragged shirt. Now I encounter you, scarred and wasted, and I have no coral to give you. I must go to High Tea tomorrow and ask the priestess to kill a white hen for this desperate love. No, I will offer a snow-white dove."

"I brought some papers from Professor Turner." Steve interrupts the serenade of the man with a thousand accents.

Lemuel reaches for them. And the love-struck man proceeds.

"You think I'm too old." He turns to his cronies. "This girl wants to know how ole I am." Then he does something incredible. Shifts diction and is young and fly. "I'll put it to you this way, mama. If a century be a fish, I eat all but de head and fin. Make stew with the rest. Feed it to the boy who lives here. Girl, you a danger to any man. Make a grown man cry and suck his thumb just to hold yo hand."

This is funny. He sounds like a brother in a lean, walking me home from the grocery store.

"Oh, you a pretty brown-skinned thing. Make me choose what I ain' chosen."

"Is the Occupant home?" That's Steve. Who wants this romantic foolishness to quit.

"He sittin with the cackling women and crowin men like the Little Red Rooster in that song."

Lemuel cuts Hat's accents now and goes into reminiscence. "Zekie try his hand at song some years ago. When this fool here talkin in tongues was workin the boat that run from the island to the Gulf. Everybody hear Zekie sing say 'Uhhh, naw you a bookman. You cain sing.' He marry that pretty girl. Settle down with a thousand books. Then he come here and be a professor. I forget where I met him. Seem like I always knew em. We all like that."

Hat says, "Negro, I don't know you." Sounding like my cousin Bay when she playing with somebody she likes.

"Yeh, you do."

It's awkward to have to ask a room full of men where the washroom is, but I manage to make delicate little signs with my hands and mouth. Say "bath" and gesture a question.

Mr. Hat leads me to the bedroom door. I enter, pass through it, straight to the bathroom. It is a small cell papered in news. I put the toilet seat down, more certain than ever that a man lives here alone. I sit and read the newspapers on the wall. First, whoever lives here has laminated the paper then sealed it to the wall. The news is permanent this way. I think how handsome Malcolm X is, and Paul Robeson and King. After the faces you'd expect, I notice other people. Rent strikers in New York, Panthers in Oakland, H. Rap Brown looking like he's in the middle of saying, "Burn, Baby, Burn." Stokely Carmichael and "Black Power,"

John Coltrane squinting at the distant notes of "A Love Supreme," Nina Simone serenading us "Young, Gifted, and Black," Odetta, Miriam Makeba, Fannie Lou Hamer "Sick and tired of being sick and tired," Rosa Parks, Thurgood Marshall, Muhammad Ali, a group of jazz musicians leaning on bass, holding horns, at piano, a blues singer I don't know (which is a sin because that's my daddy's blood), Mahalia Jackson singing at King's funeral, Aretha Franklin, the Miracles, the Temptations, the Supremes, Otis Redding, the Howard Takeover, the Cornell Takeover, the Eden Takeover, Takeovers, cities on fire, the smoke cresting in the sky, children looking into the camera for something better than what they're standing in. Children playing and laughing. Old people smiling.

I go back to the Eden Takeover. We're coming out of the building. I look for me, but I'm hidden mostly. Behind someone else. At least in this picture.

Wipe. Flush. Wash my hands. In this mirror I am glassy-eyed. Tired and excited. Older. Because age is something that rubs off. The towels are perfect, brown and tan and folded on a rack. I don't want to leave any trace of myself. I wipe my hands on my jeans. Turn off the light, so the faces can keep each other company.

This time I take the bedroom slowly. Lingering long enough to observe the neat arrangement of the dresser. The Afro pick and big-toothed comb, the brush and small hand mirror for checking the back of the head, the eyecup (I never knew anyone who had one before), the nail clippers, the emery board, and floss. Photos in black frames I glance down at, startled to catch my aunt smiling. Her hair like cotton. Silence.

"Find what you lookin for?"

It's Mr. Hat. And my cheeks are really scalding now.

"I didn't know . . ."

"One never know, do one?" He laughs. "Oh, this man, he know a lot a peoples. Know a lotta peoples."

"I think he knows some people I know."

"Is that right? Well, just cause you know don't mean he cain't."

"Who is he?"

"Yo friend 'bout ready to leave. When old buried men quit tellin stories."

"Big shoulders," Lemuel is saying when we come back into the room. "Wide. I still cryin but laughin 'bout that trick he did me. Cry and laugh, sittin on his shoulders, goin up and down. Plum forgot them goobers. And his pretty hands, hands pretty like a woman's hands, hold me steady case I fall."

"How long yo baby brother been dead?"

"Oh, he been done been dead. Oh, 1952, he died."

"You remember," one says, and they start over to remembering childish things, like peanuts, watermelon, and the smell of burning leaves, sweet kisses, and the click of the bedroom door, rain and the melting of snow, the flight of moths at the window, the single lightbulb on the porch, the oven door down on a cold morning, and the radiator hissing heat. They tease less, and their voices are soft, the diphthongs reduced, melted together. Every *th* is *d*. Softened and strengthened in the unity of sounds. A sentence is a song. Our good-byes are mumbles and their gazes hold us. Their good-byes are ghost good-byes, that soft, that longing. Suddenly Lemuel says something that I think would stop Steve's watch if he hadn't already gone out the door.

"I know there is another life," Mr. Lemuel says, "but it's not this one." There is so much in this. Marveling regret, dejection, and an old, firm composure that assumes serenity. In back of these, peeking out, is a whisper in a well-schooled consolation against the abyss. A regretful hope.

Steve Rainey on the landing beneath me, ahead of me, is turned. I look into his eyes. Steve tilts his head to one side. That means, come on down into what waits at the bottom of the stairs. Beer bottles, slim-necked bottles of whiskey and brandy like little princesses, soggy cigarette butts, and ashes leaking out of wet brown paper bags. A placard with a past date on it. "Highway 61" is the name of the show, featuring—this one jumps at me like a cat—"Mockingbird July." I look at the date and it's like the ghost talkers say. You always just miss her.

Sleepers

Leona does not go with us to the men's rooms. Her father is reopening the remodeled barbecue place. Preteen looters, carrying slabs of ribs, scurried from the BoneYard ("Where the Mambo Is Murder") after the murder in Memphis. After the smoke cleared, Mr. Pryor built over the destruction of the dining room, knocked out the vacated neighbor's wall, and expanded his establishment into that space. Now the opulent hickory smell rises again from the three chimneys in which pig, chicken, and cow are cooked separately; all three lavished with the notorious mambo sauce guaranteed to make you want to holler out the spirit dancing on your tongue. Murder!

Instead of tearing down the LakeSide Arms, a deteriorating, once genteel hotel, the owners leased it to Eden University, and the university houses male students here on the isolated upper floors. On the lower floors blue-haired matrons and balding men with tremors in their aging, liver-spotted limbs live off cottage cheese and unspiced vegetables. On the upper floors most of the students are Black. The brothers who stay here call the seventh floor the Ghetto. Sometimes they set speakers in the hallway and blast music up and down the hall. Then they shout, "The ghetto is real! Can ya dig it?"

When the groaning elevator's door opens on the floor, William and some Kappas are right in the doorway. Black Greeks only visited our campus last year. Now they're here.

"Welcome to the ghetto," the men say. They smile lazily like lions. I smile nervously. Steve Rainey, who's come out of nowhere, is looking over William's shoulder, searching for Leona. Before he can ask, Essie says, "Leona had to go to her daddy's ceremony. She's up to her elbows in dried mambo sauce." And Leona has long arms.

Steve's eyes go blank with disappointment that he tries to hide by raising the volume of his small talk. Obligatory flirtation I know his heart ain't in. This doesn't become him. Just like this bright-red shirt he's got on doesn't suit him. But William is in his right mood and color and he pulls me along the hall with Essie bringing up the rear.

When it's Essie William has eyes for, he focuses on me (her friend), so the world won't know. But everybody knows I am the decoy. Essie trails behind picking up the pieces of William's running monologue, which is meant for her anyway. It's been like this for a long time, ever since that night last year when she came home in the wee hours with a smile on her face. Every now and then William will come around and dally with her. Like now. Now she looks sublimely content like movies I've seen of animals who've just given birth to exultant and hungry litters who nuzzle at their tits. The mother's eyes shiny and soft as hot fudge.

William is easy to figure: he wants two women, like that man on the Rekinkification Trip who has two wives. Steve Rainey is the enigma. This is strange because I know him better. I don't know him or exactly what that little kiss meant. It just made me feel guilty for a long time. Why he alone took credit for burning that building when I dreamed William was with him, saw them together, I don't know. The administration accepted Steve's version. The reason was Rhonda's father. When Rhonda's father's friend, the judge, came up to meet with the university administration, we gathered on Blood Island and somebody started singing, "Here come da judge. Here come da judge. Everybody knows that he is the judge." Like they do on *Laugh-In*. It's Judge Simpkins who saw that Steve was suspended pending the results of his court trial, which is being continued. Of course, Steve's lawyer says the case is circumstantial and Steve is crazy and claiming credit for something he didn't do. Hero complex. In the meantime Steve is hiding in plain sight.

The door to every room is open and the men call out to us as we go by. Like prisoners yelling to the prison board of review as they file down the tiers. Everybody here likes company. We break the monotony of card games, war talk, sexual hyperbole, and speculation about what's going to go down when the shit hit the fan.

Sometimes I wonder what else the brothers talk about besides rating women in beauty on a scale of one to ten. If the private talk is anything like the Sweet Flats where we women stay in suites of two bedrooms and a stoveless kitchen. Three or four women per unit. Except for Hamla, who rooms alone because of a fluke. Her roommate got married suddenly (out of necessity) and did not return to school. So I spend a lot of time in Hamla's empty room, where she let me set up an easel. She asked me to move in with her, but I couldn't leave Leona and Essie. I had pulled the lowest number in the lottery, so our room was mine. So I go to Hamla's to work sometimes, but mostly to listen because Hamla has stories she has to tell. When she's not writing poems and I'm not painting, she tells stories.

The sad story was the story of John Olorun, the poet. She invited herself over to his house, appeared one day on his doorstep. She listened to his poems, then she went to bed with him. I should say, she went to floor with him. She said it was like lying down with God; he told her what to do and she did it, only he didn't do much. I've had better, she said. Yet she didn't care. She felt blessed just lying on his floor with him. Sheets of his poems scattered all around them.

Hamla and I were doing a puzzle when she told me the worst story. The puzzle was this: two blue-black Blackgirls peeking through a knothole in a fence into the amazing delights of the reptile-boy, a bearded alabaster virgin, and a two-headed cat. Hamla, her eyes burned red with tears, guided one head of the twin-headed cat into place, and I put down a piece of another.

"I tried to make something out of nothing. John Olorun is a good brother. I threw myself at him. Men don't turn it down too often, I guess. But this other brother came after me. His rap was so strong. He'd been listening to my poems. He told me he was everything I needed. I was lonely after I messed up with John Olorun. So I believed the Slick Black Rapper. I fell for him." She looked down at the mystery of our puzzle. The landscape came alive as Hamla lay down its shapes. She intuited the lock on the edge of the sky blues, the cloud whites, the sun saffron. I searched for the scaly tail of reptile-boy.

When Hamla, holding herself like a glass, went to the bathroom, I was alone with the puzzle table. She promised that I would be good at puzzles, but I'm not. Coherence is a slow process for me, putting the big picture together. I'd rather be creating alone in an empty room, but Hamla had not stopped bleeding extempore and messily from between her legs for four days. It was not her period. She was friendless except for me, weak, and afraid.

The bleeding was mysterious, but Hamla wouldn't follow my urgings to go to the Student Health Center. That day I saw "Viet Murderers" scrawled across the side of the center, because the company that under-wrote its construction makes napalm and other chemical agents. But anti-War graffiti didn't keep Hamla away from the dispensary. I don't know what one or many things did. She became angry when I suggested a doctor. She said she's already been to one. I decided to wait it out a few hours. Maybe then she'd listen to me.

It was Rhonda who cornered me in the cafeteria when I went to get Hamla something to eat. Rhonda asked me about Hamla, but I wouldn't tell her what I thought. Then she asked me if I wanted her to get Christ-mas. I managed to say yes to that.

And Christmas came to the door ten minutes later. Her hair was in braids, a scarf loosely tied around them. She was a subdued Medusa. And my mother came out of her mouth—fear and tenderness tangled in the comb of her voice that raked through Hamla's sleep-wild head.

"Hamla, you got a temperature, baby. Let me see." Her cool hands covered Hamla's forehead. And Hamla, who was uncertain as Camille Loomis, her slave name, didn't argue when Christmas threw back the covers and eased her out of the bed, inspecting the stains on the sheet.

"Hand me her coat, Magdalena," Christmas commanded, and I snapped to. I flattened myself against the wall to let them by in the small foyer. Hamla, walking like an old woman, was leaning on Christmas. For the first time I noticed Rhonda hovering in the hall, outside the door, peeking over Hamla's shoulder even as she took Hamla's other arm.

"Hamla, girl, you've been bleeding bad," she exclaimed. Then she glared at me as if to say all my ministrations were childish and obsolete, idiot work. So Rhonda's part in the rescue I remember as obnoxious instruction, even though she was the one who brought Yvonne Christmas.

I went back to my room and kept my mouth closed. I didn't even tell Essie or Leona.

Everybody found out anyway.

✦

"Was your mother like Leona?" I ask Steve Rainey.

Of course it's happened the way I knew it would. Essie and William are in his room doing what I can only imagine now. The rest of the seventh floor has congregated in one room down the hall, as many girl visitors as boy residents all crowded in playing Wisconsin Sleepers. There's quiet from that end and Steve and I sit in the hall with our backs to the wall. That's the way I feel safe. Steve smiles behind my question and resuscitates one cigarette after another with his skin-grafted hands that are hidden in gloves.

"Nothing like her," he finally says. He drags on the short Kool like it's a roach, or oxygen in a tube saving his life. "My mother was tired," he says. "All the time. She couldn't sit down without letting out a sigh."

"My mother's like that sometime." I wrap my arms around my knees. Out of the corner of my eye I watch Steve Rainey stub out the ember on the roof of an empty beer can. His index finger makes circles in the ashes. Circles in the ashes. Neither one of us wants to be the first to say something significant, something we won't be able to conceal later.

Suddenly he sighs, and I confess, "I'm tired too sometimes. Tired of waiting on—"

"The Revolution?" Steve interrupts. Takes his gaze from the circles in the ash on the wet top of the beer can. The ashes are muddy now.

"Yeah. That and my life. Sometimes I know IT'S arrived. Like when we took over the building. It was scary, but it was exciting. Like we all had one heartbeat and we were beating History. Mosta time, though, it's . . ." Revelation ends in a shrug.

Steve wipes his gloved index finger on his shirt. The red shirt. He dirties his clothes and doesn't care. He's not really into fashion. But the rest of him is fastidiously clean. The just-washed smell comes out of his pores. I breathe him in and forget the dank berry smell of the hotel hallway.

Down the hall Marvin Gaye and Tammi Terrell push voices against each other. I think of what I've been told, how Marvin and Tammi could sing parts to the love song in separate rooms, eyes closed, listening to the other's Voice over a headphone—"Stand by you like a tree / Dare anybody to try and move me." The voices search around each other, soar, and gasp and fall back.

When the record ends, we sit with dreams in the musty old hallway.

After a while Steve begins again, "I wish my mother had been sick and tired like Fannie Lou Hamer. Sick and tired of being sick and tired." He is wistful, a motherless child. "Fannie Lou Hamer is one beautiful sister," he says with all the longing in the world.

Is he for real? I eye him keenly, thinking he must be making fun of the sharecropping woman with half-nappy, unstyled hair, blunt features coated in a deluge of sweat. The furthest a woman can get from Twiggy.

One evening at Blood Island I'd marveled at Fannie Lou Hamer on TV, stumpish like a baobab, steady as a stone. Two brothers parked in front of that old TV set full of ghosts said she looked like BBB: a big black bear. Scorn and glee fused in the naming. My stomach lurched and I wanted to throw them up.

Right now Steve Rainey isn't putting me on. He appreciates the capable muscle of a farm woman; he adores the stubborn mouth of the activist, the profuse sweat of the worker. Her broad facial features I adore; he adores. The spirit that shone out of my Aunt Silence shines in Fannie Lou Hamer. And I suspect that Steve Rainey could love Silence too. And if he can love Silence, he can love my ghost as well.

Right now I can see Steve Rainey burying his whole face in the ample bosom of a ghost, and coming up for air like a boy who has wholeheartedly and whole-facedly devoured the ripest, juiciest watermelon and come up with his face drenched luminously in the satisfying juice. All this comes to mind.

"Yo mama loved you, boy," is all that comes out of my mouth. He lets me call him boy. Like I'm old or younger than most of us now.

"She left me in a world of strangers."

"How could she help dying?"

"She was too tired to love me."

"My mama says love never stops."

"Your mama is alive." He thinks that Death is the last word.

I am going to tell Steve Rainey about my mother's mother, whose love surpassed a severed head and disintegrated flesh. I am going to tell Steve Rainey what I've told no one else. A story that may make me an object of ridicule and derision.

My legacy emboldens me. I touch his chin and turn him toward me. I put my palm on his cheek, positioning his face for the importance of my story. He thinks he's about to receive a kiss. And from Leona's best friend. His lips part in fear and anticipation.

"You have to promise you won't ever tell anybody what I'm about to tell you." I look sternly at him, until anticipation dies in his eyes and a more fearful look is born.

"I promise, Magdalena," he solemnly swears.

I open my mouth and a scream comes out. That's where I think it's coming from at first. The confusion I see on Steve's face must be on mine.

It's coming from down the hall. We scramble from the floor and run to the scream, which hasn't ended.

There's a crowd at the fire escape entrance and Hamla's at the front of it. The scream is dead now, but its shape hasn't left her mouth; her eyes like everyone else's are riveted on a figure dancing on the black metal grate of the fire escape porch.

"What's he on?" somebody asks.

"Probably acid."

"LSD."

"Blackpeople don't take no acid."

"Where he get that from?"

"I don't know."

"He could fall and kill himself."

"I'm so hip."

"Who is it?" Steve asks.

"Russell."

"Russell Garner. Young Galileo."

"Tweedie Pie?"

"Damn. I thought he lived at that White fraternity. What's he think he's doing?"

"Talking to the stars."

"Great."

"He says he's a star. He understands the language."

"Don't he look like a star?" That's Roberto. The voice of irony.

"Oh, please," I say.

"He could kill himself," Hamla says like that's a new observation.

"I told him that already. He says there is no such thing as death in the universe. $E = mc^2$. Energy can be neither created nor destroyed." Roberto repeats this like he's reporting a lazy baseball game.

The figure scrambles up on the grate to the railing, then falls back. A sigh sweeps through his audience. He's just missed death. Seven floors below. Russell is chanting one word now. "Energy. Energy. Energy. Energy. Energy. Energy." As if he were an automaton, memorizing a recipe while making a dish.

"What's he doing now?" I ask.

"Excuse me," Roberto yells to Russell, whose eyes look like two raisins in separate toilet bowls when he turns toward us. "What are you doing now?" Roberto asks.

Russell just looks. And keeps chanting. "Energy. Energy."

"Can't get a thing out of him," Roberto says jovially.

"This is not funny, Roberto," Hamla reminds him.

"I'm not laughing. I'm not crying either. If he wants to die in this stupid-assed way, what am I supposed to do?" Roberto is angry at Hamla, who is close to tears of distress for Russell, who thinks he's a star—an actual star.

"Man, why don't you come down from there?" Steve Rainey asks.

"The cow jumped over the moon," Russell says.

"I'm supposed to take this shit seriously?" Roberto glares at Hamla and tries to make eye contact with me, but I only see him peripherally. It's Russell I can't take my eyes off of. He's still reciting that piece of nursery rhyme, riding the rail now, and looking up at the sky. His head turned away from the moon, which is full. In the distance a siren sounds and Russell starts to howl.

"Do stars howl?" Roberto asks.

Russell throws his head way back and bays.

The siren is louder and thicker now. Russell is more agitated. He's scrambling to his feet on the thin railing. "Energy. Energy. Energy," he repeats hypnotically like one of my baby sisters used to repeat the catch-phrases of a television commercial.

Steve Rainey breaks out of the entranced audience and artfully makes his way across the wobbly grate toward Russell, who by now is taking his nickname Tweedie Pie seriously and standing on the bar while hooking the air under his elbow as he tries to fly. But Steve wraps his arms around Russell's legs and holds him hard against the pull of gravity and hallucination. Russell Garner wavers in midair. The black night all around him like a dry, empty womb. His body wobbling loose, disconnected from life except for Steve's arms. And the fire escape, almost a building-code violation, shivers and rattles, knocking against our hushed warnings and stifled screams.

Russell starts fighting for his right to fly. His torso strains toward stars; he kicks his legs feebly in Steve's powerful, restraining embrace. Steve won't turn him loose. When Russell pitches over the side out of our sight and Steve begins to fall too, we groan like children at the circus when the trapeze artist tumbles or the lion almost chomps off the lion tamer's head.

Then we're all on the wildly swaying fire escape porch, and the white- or blue-haired residents of the other floors stick their heads out of their windows. They gape. Their heads sticking out on those skinny necks like hens at the chopping block. A row of them. They point to the fire truck coming up the street.

It's Steve Rainey and Russell Garner and Roberto and Hamla and me and Trixia with no blouse on (I don't ask her why she's out in public with only a bra and skirt on), all of us rocking back and forth in the dark sky. Steve still won't let go and Russell is vertical, slapping against the grating of the metal staircase.

Now Roberto has Steve's legs and Hamla and I have Roberto's legs (one apiece), holding his feet to the perforated floor. Trixia (wouldn't you know it) has her arms around Roberto's waist.

"Oooooh, baby," Roberto groans. "Just keep on pushing your titties into my back."

"Just hold on, fool," Trixia snarls.

"Everybody hold on to your brother or your sister," Hamla exhorts, because she's a poet and has a religious bent.

Russell Garner, who isn't a star anymore, is hollering for his mama like any other colored child. Just like I used to when I was a little girl riding a roller coaster. Mothers, we believe, have power over gravity. Tonight, Russell's life is in the hands of a man who doesn't even like him.

Nobody is turning anybody aloose, not even when the fire truck stops and the firemen stretch out nets. We ignore them.

There are voices in the hall behind us. More people from the corridor, Essie among them, come to help, and hands reach out for us and haul us back from the edge and the inevitable collapse of the porch. Inch by inch, those hands pull us back, until Russell's legs, then pelvis, then abdomen begin to snake over the side of the little porch. Lastly, his head appears, and Steve, in a burst of power, heaves Russell from the heavy pull of a definite and gut-splattering death. Then they crawl back against the fire escape landing and climb up into the hall.

Russell is babbling about energy again when the ambulance attendants arrive, strap him onto a stretcher, and carry him away.

We're just hanging around the hall congratulating ourselves on the rescue, replaying Russell's bad trip, waiting for our heartbeats to slow down. Essie asks Trixia why she's running around this men's dorm with no blouse on.

Trixia looks surprised.

She says she's just been initiated into Wisconsin Sleepers. A goofy game they play up here. It's a fake wedding night with a dozen people watching on the sidelines of the room as a boy and girl lie down in a bed. They ask the blindfolded bride to take off whatever she needs to take off in order to make sweet love to her new husband.

Essie swears that two years ago Rhonda took off her panties. That's how she got William.

We retreat into a room to continue the game now even as Whitepeople still walk around the corridor. Steve needs to disappear, so he and I get into the bed to play Wisconsin Sleepers. I don't want to, but Essie and William convince me to do it.

I'm nervous as a bride, even though the room is full of people. White-people poke their heads in on us. Retreat. This makes me more nervous. William begins to croon instructions, "It's your wedding night, young marrieds. Now what must you take off to make sweet love?" I start to tremble and shiver.

There is a long pause in which the whole room is breathing. I am not breathing. Then Steve Rainey, lying next to me in bed, leans down and whispers in my ear, "Maggie, take off the blindfold." I snatch it off to see the lights come on and all the laughing bodies up against the wall.

Steve saved me from what? A nasty taste is in my mouth.

In the hallway I pass a girl crying because she took off too much.

In the early morning, safe in my own bed, I have a dream. I am hanging like a spider over an abyss. The only thing I can hold on to is my own breath, my own spit. In the dream I see a spiderweb, pale and shimmering, that I know has been spun by many people. When I think the web will catch me, it disappears. I keep spinning spit, because in the dream I am an artist. A better one than I am now.

✦

Sometimes I feel left behind, as if I'd missed the train to Mississippi and found myself running between rails, chasing behind it. Lazarus in front of me, both of us reaching for the caboose. As if I'd missed the plane and not gone with Aint Kit to my own homecoming. As if my grandmother were motionless and decayed in the Mimosa cemetery and my Aunt Silence had never made herself well. And even if I did make it to Mimosa, one or two memorable times, and have heard of Sarah Mahalia the revenant, her head restored to its rightful place, and have called Aunt Leah-Bethel Silence because silence healed her, none of this has happened to me.

These days I find a thought hanging behind my eyelids, like a piece of my spider dream, whispering out of my mouth when I'm not even aware of it. "I don't want to miss anything."

The book I've been reaching for high in the stacks in the Dark Shadows library slips from my grasp. In the dark caverns of the stacks I look around me nervously, fearful that I can be taken for crazy—talking to myself without knowing what I'm talking about. In the library I hunt for men, for heroes in the pages of obscure volumes. I look at old newspaper clippings of Marcus Garvey, W. E. B. Du Bois, Paul Robeson (who isn't dead yet, just buried), Joseph Cinqué, Malcolm X, Medgar Evers, and now Martin Luther King Jr. I missed them all. That's why I miss them.

One night less than a year ago I waited for a headless woman ghost to tuck me in at night. Now I miss some other tucking in I have never known. One time Aunt Silence said if two people sleep with their heads on the same pillow they'll dream the same dream. Who in Eden would believe that? Besides me. And what would we dream?

I don't want to miss anything, I tell myself in the morning when I take the A-train to the City. Determined at least to witness everything. I sit with a sketch pad open on my lap. The only one on the train except for a brother sipping beer for breakfast. The can innocuously swaddled in a brown paper bag. He places it between his knees. Looks at me as he takes out thin little papers, no bigger than bubblegum wrappers, and a sandwich-size plastic bag with weed inside. He promises me, while rolling his joint with his trigger finger, he won't smoke it until he's sure he's the only one on the train.

"Excuse me, miss," he says, by way of explanation, "I have to go to work and trip out on these hunkies before they trip out on me." He puts the rolled reefer into his coat pocket, and goes back to his beer. I watch him sedately sip his ammunition. I draw that.

That's what I do all day long. Go places and sketch. Filling up the sketch pad with lines and shadows, curves and spirals. I go to Arbor Avenue. I hang around the neighborhood, sitting on our stoop without going inside the house, knowing no one is home, and sketching. Because I don't want to miss anything. When my fingers are nearly numb, and my eyes burn from stringent seeing, I head back to the El. I get off downtown and walk around for a while, looking at all the Whitepeople, then I go back to the subway.

The platform is lonely and clean swept like a Hughie Lee-Smith painting. The gray is heavy, and the cement tunnel narrowing to hold me in it. Strolling from the edge of the platform, where I haven't seen a train coming, I walk to the newsstand and ask the man behind the counter for *Negro Digest*.

The paper-stand man shakes his head and mumbles something.

"I beg your pardon," I say, drawing nearer to catch his reply.

"I could use a little nooky right now. Like to make some money?"

That's what he said.

Now he has two sweating bald heads, two pairs of glasses, two fish slits for mouths. I can't stand to look at him to get it straight. I look for something to kill him with. My numb hands agitated, empty. I could use a gun.

Something rises up through my extremities, through my stomach, lungs. I can hardly breathe. I want a gun.

The subway platform is long, emptily empty, soundless except for my own steps and the sounds of the Roach's hands slithering across pages of the papers he still has to sell. At the invisible end of nowhere a thunder is far away. Not yet close enough for me to see the lightning jumping off the side of the wheels of the black train.

"Who you want to kill?" a friendly voice says. Someone else has come. It's a young brother, acting like a breeze that has blown my way before.

"It might be you." My voice is thick, watery.

"Just cause I'm here, right?" He sizes me up.

"You see that man?" I point to the newsstand. "He is a roach."

"You want me to squash him?" he offers. He scrutinizes the bald Whiteman behind the counter. The paperman acts like he doesn't see us looking at him.

I think about it. The rage is still rumbling in me, so I say, "Yes. Yes. I do."

"Watch this," my friend says. He walks over to the newsstand.

"Hey!" he yells at the paperman.

The lascivious man looks up.

At the black, invisible end of the train track thunder is coming.

"I'm the exterminator," the young man introduces himself. He's very civil, as if he were paying a visit to the man's house. "Come to get rid of roaches and termites and big old ugly water bugs." Then the Civil Exterminator changes. He goes on a cussing spree. Suddenly, newspapers start flying all over. White bats of paper swooping in the air.

"I'll get a cop! I'll get a cop!" the bald man is crying out of his fish mouth.

69

Thin lightning flicks out from under the train. The noise takes over. My eyes go from train to flying papers and two men. The papers fall down.

My savior turns to me.

"Didn't this pervert expose hisself to you?" he asks.

"Yes," I respond just as simply. "He sure did expose himself to me."

The lascivious vendor is livid now. His face red as mainland China. His fish mouth is atremble. His whole fish body shivering and jerking like a fish on sand.

"She can testify to how small you are," my hero says. "You still want to call the pigs, pig?"

"Get away from my stand," the pig-fish man shouts. His voice above the noise of the approaching train. His piggy hand sliding under the counter. The train door opening, at the same time his two hands come up into view, now with a shotgun.

"Robber!" the lascivious pig-fish yells. The shotgun in two hands. His voice carrying so people on the train can hear his version.

"Run!" my rescuer yells. We leap onto the train in perfect sync, like two wild deer. Then we duck down under the seats so the madman with the gun screaming "Police!" won't shoot us through the window.

We scramble up the aisle and jump onto the next car, in case he's after us. He's not. He's running up and down the platform screaming, outraged and guiltless, about vandals destroying his property. People on the train look at us in disgust and apprehension.

The doors close and the train begins to slide forward, so we raise our heads and watch the mad pig-fish man carrying on. Waving that gun like a roach waving an antenna, shrieking and foaming at the mouth, making a lot of noise as he thrashes his feet through his fallen newspapers.

When my hero and I are sure we're safe, we slam down into seats.

"Some knight you are!" I gasp, still pulling my breath out of panic.

He cuts his eyes at me. "If I hadn't come along, you'd still be pacing and trying not to cry." He licks his lips. "Do I get a kiss?"

"You no better than he was."

"I don't have to buy anything. I just wanted a kiss." Now he's got to theorize. His mouth curled under and his eyes gauging me. "Next time I'll let a Black woman defend her own virtue. White women know how to treat gallant men who save them from orangutans."

Behind this, part of me's guilty. A bigger part pissed off. I jerk my head around and won't look at him.

Now his voice is soft, conciliatory. "Can I at least have your phone number so I can talk to you?"

I tell it to him. The exchange isn't City. So I tell him about Eden. He's impressed. That makes me mad. I hate Eden University.

My rescuer is chatty and quick to tell his story. His story is· His name is Moses Outlaw. He's an accounting student at a city university. He's twenty-two and been going to college off and on for three years. Night school. He's trying to stay out of the draft. "That's why I don't sleep under fans or near open windows," he says. It takes me a while. "The draft. Get it?"

We lapse into silence.

"Why'd that man make that nasty overture to me?" I don't know why that question comes out of my mouth. I didn't know it was bothering me.

"You don't look like no hooker, sister. If that's what you're worrying about." He narrows his eyes and considers me. "You look like Edie Eden of Eden. You go there on scholarship or you one of the Black bourgeoisie?"

"I grew up on Arbor Avenue," I tell him. "We still live there."

"You on scholarship." He looks at me. The beat-up sketchbook in my hand. A question in his eyes I won't answer.

My hands resting on the book, I lean back in the seat. He's still looking at me. I don't mind the quiet between us.

I don't mind that I've gotten on the wrong train with him. Going back into the City instead of away from it.

Coming out of Downtown at some invisible line in space the crowded train is pregnant with a Black presence. At some point in time, during the bat of an eye, Whitepeople have left the earth. They leave an edge of weariness on Blackpeople's faces. And some relief, a lessening of pressure. It's rush hour.

Beside me I look at the man who isn't looking at me now. I don't miss anything. His hands are purple palmed with newspaper ink. The ink all under his nails. Just that fast the ink rubbed off.

I lean away from him to get a good look. I can feel the glass against my head. I turn to look at him in the glass. I can see him good. How young he is. Older than me but young. He's wearing an army surplus jacket like the brothers in FBO. He'd fit right in. Hair and costume. I know him. Past him in the glass are the gray backs of buildings, bannistered and fragile. The skeletons of cars and the remains of couches where great ideas were conceived to howl into a tiny space of more buildings with gray backs or impressive bricks emblazoned with words. Words like Cobra, Devil's Disciple, Maniac Apostles. Sounding impressive and flashy like angels carrying swords or the names of all-male singing groups. Belligerent melodies on the otherwise speechless stone.

And beside them on storefront placards and tall corner signs are other words of definitive quiet like dreamlike labors in night: Infinite Mercy Church of God, Mount Calvary M. B. Church, and Richard Allen A. M. E. Temple. There is the silent steeple of St. Augustine Roman Catholic Church.

The sun falling in its perfect place in the west sets fire to the scene. I catch my breath as a bottomless and boundless glow joins earth and sky. The train snakes in a half circle and we turn a corner of the world.

Now I see me in the window with the man and everything. He could be one of my brothers; we look that much alike. High cheekbones and heavy mouths. Broad noses and small ears fine-tuned to hear hidden music. He stirs a little when I sigh. He looks at me. We are in the glass together.

The train rocks and we move with the sway. Keeping the portrait alive in front of our eyes. This is the portrait my life is working on: woman and man moving away from something, moving into something, banished and becoming in a noisome and perfect solitude.

I open my worn book and begin.

3

Sacred Heart

Bay's already married, but Aint Kit insists she get married again. Because running down to the courthouse in a pair of slip-slides with your African pickaninny braids rolled up on pink foam rollers, mumbling "I do," and holding hands all the way back to the lounge on the bus is not the way to get married. So says Aint Kit. That's not how it happened anyway. Mama told me.

Bay wore a pretty African print dashiki dress; her hair was fluffed out real pretty so that it looked like a cloud of cinnamon spice. She dyed her Afro that color. Baby's breath were pinned in her hair and she carried five yellow roses with white ribbon binding them and trailing off and down to brush her scarred knees as she walked beside her darling. That's what she calls that steelworker with his shoulders as big as an elephant's knees. A grin wide as the wide river that runs near Mimosa spreading across his face when he looks down at Bay.

He doesn't call her Bay. He calls her Winnie. "That's right," Lazarus remembers what we Graces sometimes forget. "Been calling her Bay so long I forgot her name was Winona. That's pretty." And Bay acts pretty all the time. All dainty and obliging.

Aint Kit was livid to discover Bay a happily married woman housekeeping for a husband who makes good money. They call it that. Good money. Bad money is welfare checks or unemployment, social security or daywork. Bay's making throw pillows and planters to decorate their love nest (a four-room flat on a street not far from Arbor Avenue) while they save the money for a down payment on a house.

Winnie's husband was married before and has small twin daughters named Alice and Rachel. We laughed when Bay told us that. Alice and Rachel, soap opera rivals on *Another World*. Winnie's husband keeps his twin girls in crinoline dresses and hair ribbons. Bay doesn't mind it taking some months to put the cash for the house aside. Madaddy said Bay used to be "a evil gal." Now she's sweet as peach cobbler Mama makes just right. Just right.

Pearl says Bay's euphoric marital state wasn't theatrical enough for Aint Kit. It lacked drama. Which is based upon conflict. Pearl took a course in World Theater, which didn't include Africa or Asia. Drama comes from conflict, the book says. And Aint Kit must have read it because she believes in drama. Consequently, Aint Kit initiated conflict by insisting that Bay get married to Henry Freeman all over again. The right way. The Aint Kit way. The dramatic way. Henry loves Winnie-Bay, so he went along with it, because he thought his Winnie would be pleased to please her mother.

Now Bay's lips are made only for saying Henry's name. At every opportunity. Sometimes she uses it in random exclamation like Mama says, "Goodness gracious," or Madaddy says, "Go'amighty," or Aint Kit says, "shit." When Bay drops a saucer of straight pins all over the plastic-covered carpet and the pins scatter all over Aint Kit's cluttered living room like thieves caught in the middle of the act, Bay exclaims, "Oh, Hank!" Pearl and I look at each other over Bay's bent back as she retrieves what is lost.

Bay is making a slipcover for an old couch, saving money, while Honeybabe, Pearl, Mama, and me wait for Aint Kit to come home so Aint Kit can take over plans for the rehashed wedding that she insisted on having. Aint Kit had to make a quick run to the store. Pearl said she left us sitting there so we'd all have to wait on her. So she can keep thinking she's the sun. Kit's prestige was badly shaken by Bay's sudden marriage that's turning out to be so happy without her. So Aint Kit is keeping us waiting, and I wait with anticipation because I don't intend to miss a thing.

Mama waits quietly because she understands that Kit's going through a hard time. Letting go of the only person she's tied to herself. That's what Mama said. Trying to evoke empathy for her sister-in-law. It doesn't work. But I feel a twinge.

Aint Kit comes through the door, carrying a lot of bags and making a lot of noise. I'm glad I've already told my mother, sisters, and Bay about Moses Outlaw, my hero, and Eden. And Pearl has told us about St. Ursula College's Black Student Organization voting her president of the Alumni Association—all fifteen women. Honeybabe has told us that C.C. is safe in the jungles of Southeast Asia, and Mama has told us how Madaddy has taken to calling his harmonica Sweet Love, and Bay has told us about Hank and then some more Hank, his grueling but lucrative job at the steel mill, his bowling team, his nice singing voice, his children, his ex-wife with her low-down self, his report cards from grammar school and high school, his last physical, a perfect specimen of a man. More than we wanted to know. Now that Aint Kit is back, she'll be doing the talking. Unless you want your life wedged in between Aint Kit's whoppers. Or even worse, wedged inside one of her lies.

She, balanced by overflowing shopping bags, comes in her door now. She's talking. "You know right after they killed Martin Luther King? You know that play lot they threw up like instant potatoes on that vacant lot next to the viaduct over round your house?" Aint Kit asks us as preamble. As expected, we all nod yes.

"What about it?" Honeybabe asks, not tagging the question with a respectful "Aint Kit" the way I do.

Aint Kit pauses and takes a full breath like she's had it with life. "Shoot. It's tore up now. The seesaw twirling like a whirlybird, and them swings ain't got no seats, just chains swinging in the air. They ought to string up some of them roguish devils on them very same exact chains."

The verdict is too harsh for consensus.

Mama says with restraint, "Kit, you just called those playgrounds instant. We all know King was assassinated April 4 and those facilities were built by April 14. The equipment was pretty enough. The colors were. But the materials like the solutions were flimsy and not constructed to endure."

"I don't care what you say, Ca'line. I know ain't nobody got to be tearing up like that in their own neighborhood. They no-count. White folks never will do nothing else for them." Her voice sounds crisp like new dollar bills.

"Children do have to learn to take care of things," Mama agrees. "But they have to have something decent first." Mama's not budging. Though her mouth is sweet, her eyes have thin lights in them.

Bay puts her couch covers aside. Straight pins tinkle in the little container. "When we going to discuss my wedding, so I can get home and give Hank his foot rub?"

"You so stupid." Aint Kit sounds appalled. "I bet you be rubbing that clown's feet every night when he get home."

"As a matter of fact, I do. Is it all right with you?"

Aint Kit cackles. "His name is Henry, not Jesus Christ. Need to be putting them stanky feet in the tub. Know he got altheletic feet."

"My husband's feet don't stink."

"Next you gone say his pee don't either."

"As a matter of fact that smells like peach wine."

Aint Kit really cackles now, because Bay's toppled her in the duel of tongues. She's happy to be fighting with her daughter. Usually now Bay's just smiling. Aint Kit's happy so long as Bay is talking to her and seeing her; she doesn't care what's said or seen.

"Maggie has to get back to school and Pearl has to study. You know Maggie's in college. And Pearl is studying for her master's." Honeybabe sits on the edge of the chair. Very businesslike.

"I know they're in college. Hadna been for me, Magdalena never woulda made it up to that school." That's not true, but we never mind.

"Honey wants to get started so she can run home and write another fifteen-page love letter to send to Vietnam." Bay is the pot calling the kettle black as magic. She understands the pleasure of wifely devotion. "Girl, I'd be too sick if Hank had to go to the service." She shudders at the thought of the draft.

Aint Kit is an authority on the War. "They ain't fighting nobody over there but women, babies, and old men need false teeth to chew that rice. At least I think they old men. The women and the men look just alike with them little church-top hats and pajamas on in the daylight. They need somebody to wake them up."

"Aint Kit, you ought to be shame," I have to protest even though the word pictures are funny.

Aint Kit cuts to the wedding plans. She's sitting in a wingback ornate chair with sky-blue cushions. She's stuck a cigarette into a six-inch gold cigarette holder, and puffs on it demurely. She taps the ashes into a sterling-silver ashtray with flowers cut into the edges.

The end table squats like a sumo wrestler beside her chair. The legs like two fat baby legs with rickets. The lamp, also on the end table, is monstrous: a golden bowl bottom with fake diamonds dust-brushed into the metal, wearing a baby pink shade in the shape of a hoop skirt.

Behind her, the blue-gray drapes hang heavily over the bay window, preventing the entry of sunlight, which Aint Kit says fades her plastic-covered hot-pink carpet, and preventing the inquiry of neighborhood boys who might covet her treasure-chest disguise for her combination TV–record player–radio. I look at it in amazement. When I walk by it, the TV jumps on. And Aint Kit swears I'm a witch. The only other person it ever did that for is my Aunt Silence when she visited one time. Stayed one day. I didn't see her. She was supposed to stay a week, but an emergency called her back to the Movement in Mississippi. This truncated visit further evidence to Aint Kit that Silence put "Strangers before family. Family. Her own flesh and blood." Aint Kit is into familiarity.

The plates of every persuasion all stand up together in the china cabinet in the dining room. The names of the places Aint Kit's honeymooned are scripted on the plates: Niagara Falls, Hollywood, Las Vegas, Palm Springs. The little Black jockey boy Whitepeople like in their yards waits for a pony in a corner of the living room where we are.

Whatnots crowded with bottles and overdressed knickknacks. A gang of porcelain dogs, long ears and puzzled expression and their heads cocked to the side, line one shelf of a glass étagère. Valentine hearts, white, blue, and red, encase nothing: it's the little containers that delight Aint Kit. The polished artifacts in which only emptiness is saved.

Honeybabe says Aint Kit ain't got no taste. But Pearl says she got too much taste. A taste for everything all together at once. As if anything beautiful not directly under her eyes becomes worthless by virtue of being invisible. Her eyes are bigger than her stomach and her heart.

Aint Kit has talked about it, but I know she's never gone up and down the road searching for a ghost. The search would not be worth the effort. And the answer right before her would elude her. So the mismanaged beauty of Aint Kit's possessions beats me upside the head, and my head hammers as the wedding plans jump out of her mouth like tap-dancing midgets in sequined tuxedos.

✦

"Can't you wear a wig for the wedding?" one night at rehearsal Aint Kit asks with a little pang in her voice, like it hurts to look at my nappy hair. And hurts even more to have to ask me to hide it. I should know better.

She asks Mama to ask me to get my hair fixed. (Like it's broken or something.) My mama calls me at school and, in the middle of a sentence about Lazarus and the Panthers, pines nostalgically, "I'll be glad when you get your hair curled again."

I snap, "We'll all be happy in heaven, sister."

She snaps back, "Don't be so smart, miss."

On the day of the replayed wedding, Pearl and Honeybabe, my sister bridesmaids, are in the hair resistance too.

"Thank God," Aint Kit sighs, "I talked some sense into Bay."

You should see Bay's head with the sense talked into it. She looks like somebody out of Marie Antoinette's court. Marie Antoinette. On her way to the guillotine. Hair piled up on her head in tiers like her wedding cake. With those little decorated-on ropes of ribbon that swing pressed into the sides of the coiffure. Loops of hair twirled and extended, then pressed into a tier of curls. A Korean hair entrepreneur must have had a thousand weeping Asian Rapunzels locked in a tower someplace growing hair. On hair-harvest day he herds them out to be shorn like sheep; their wool to go for American wigs. Dyes and braids are added to wigs like the one on Bay's head. Sold to somebody's bald-headed mama.

Today Honeybabe is thinking about her wedding day. I can tell by the faraway look on her face when I start talking about Korean hair businessmen. Now she's in Vietnam.

Once I swear I saw Honeybabe's husband on TV. He was opening a can of C rations. He was almost anonymous in his dark skin, sweat, khakis, and firearms. I told Honey I saw her man squatting and eating out of a can on TV. She burst into tears. Crying about the army was feeding her husband like a cat out of a can. Like that's the worst that's happened to him.

I wonder how many Yellowpeople he's killed. I just wonder. Because weddings make me think of funerals. They always have. I don't know why.

Bay has submitted so discreetly to Aint Kit's management of her wedding details. Details down to hair and dress and pedicurist. I figure Bay must have something up her sleeve or in her opulent hair. At least slipped a hatpin into one of the tiers of her pre–French Revolution hair. Just in case somebody messes with her on this, her wedding day.

Everything shines. The sunlight does the Skate across the hood of the rented limousine in which Bay, Honeybabe, Pearl, and I must ride. Hank and his groomsmen will ride in another rented limo. Aint Kit will cruise alone in a Lincoln Continental Town Car. Pearl's hair shines like she's sprinkled jewels all through her foliage, but it's Afro Sheen glittering on each strand of her hair.

A light layer of snow has fallen and snow crystals wink at us as we mince along in high heels, lifting our long, fat skirts up at the knees, so that our pilgrim-style shoes show. The satin skirts are baby-girl pink, and the laced-up corset tops are even lighter pinks, and the dainty fur stoles each of us wraps around our shoulders have a whisper of pink in them. Like a rabbit's nose. We are pretty maids all in a row. Everyone tells us.

Bay is smiling sweetly. As she leans back on the plush cushions of her limo, she says she doesn't mind looking like Marie Antoinette.

"Didn't she lose her head?" Bay murmurs through lip gloss and a contented smile. "I've sure lost mine over my Hankie."

I don't tell her the people chopped hard-hearted Marie Antoinette's head off like Grandmama chopped the head off of one of her chickens. The chicken danced awhile and Grandmama caught it, plucked it, and fried it for breakfast. We ate it with biscuits and grits and eggs. Then Silence came and got Lazarus who was Littleson and me after her meeting. Aunt Silence took us to Mt. Tabor Church and the people worked in the fellowship hall while Littleson and I played tic-tac-toe then name the states and capitals then name the countries and capitals glad that Pearl wasn't there to name more than either of us. Mt. Tabor was the epicenter of the Movement in Mimosa, Mississippi. Once it was firebombed.

Aint Kit is a member in good standing at Sacred Heart of Jesus Roman Catholic Church. In good standing because no one there knows she's been married a million times. Or only twenty-eleven. She chose this parish because the church is so thrillingly big and beautiful. God is grand and opulent here. Who can blame her? It is beautiful.

The church is hugely hollowed out like a ribbed cave, with chandeliers hanging down from the ribs. The chains for the elaborate lights are of proportionately increasing lengths as the roof curves up, so that the lights hang down at just the same height all over. Blossoming out of the ceiling like a garden of chandeliers, groomed in brilliance.

Bold, panoramic murals of the Stations of the Cross cover the sides of the church. Jesus is eight feet high—pale and grotesquely anguished—stumbling on the road to Calvary. Floor lights spray each scene with luminescence. The figures glow like giants, noisy while we prayed or rehearsed these evenings. A confessional on each side of the church, ornate as the coach of a Chinese emperor, made of dense, cinematically carved wood, keeps in sin. The walls so thick no words of repentance or absolution slip out of the compartments into the vestibule where the groomsmen are gathered when we open the door and let in snow flurries before us.

Once Sacred Heart of Jesus was the parish of exceedingly wealthy people. So rich they lobbied the archdiocese to change the name of the parish from the pitiable Sacred Heart of Jesus (which makes us think of pierced sides and spent blood) to something glorious like Assumption (which they assumed they'd be into heaven) or Ascension (which they loved even more, a magician Christ pulled into heaven on his own steam around his ankles).

The parishioners threatened to sue the artist commissioned to do the murals of the Stations when at last the cloths were dropped and his work stood huge before them. The agony dwarfing them.

They refused to pay him. "Who wants to look at that?" they said.

And no priest could entreat the sponsoring committee to give the artist his due—the priest slipped the man his commission out of his own money. This priest is known for doing the right thing. He marched with

SCLC. My heart is with the artist, even though his paintings are too damned big. The mastery of technique is there. Check out the perfection of the fingers on Jesus's sweating hands. I respect the meticulousness. And the passion flexing in the figures on the wall. I like best Veronica Wipes the Face of Jesus. Women matter. What I do matters. That's how I take it. Even when I feel I don't fit in.

The bridal party fits right in. Everything is too much in the already too much decorated church. Too many floral wreaths at the entrances of too many pews. Too many ribbons to cut. As each pew is opened to guests, the ushers must cut the ribbon crisscrossed on the row. Bouquets of red roses scattered at the foot of the murals like roses on the garish carnage of a bullfighting arena. And a forest of candles ablaze on the three altars at the front of the church, while in the back every devotional candle is glowing with the fake blessings Aint Kit has prayed on the couple. The donation box beside the bank of red-encased candles my extravagant aunt has filled with silver.

From the chilly vestibule I peek, through the clear edge of the glass that's frosted in the middle, to the church beyond the vestibule. The scene is too crowded, so I give up looking through the glass and look at Bay shivering and smiling like well-schooled royalty who don't mind the inconvenience of cold, a cumbersome skirt, or the weight of an obese wig. She just smiles and her smile shames all the eye-stabbing beauty around her. I smile at her and swear to myself that I'll give up my grouchy, critical ways and just love, love, love Bay's Whitepeople wedding. Even though my feet are killing me in the shoes Aint Kit forced on me, I smile through pain.

Lazarus, my brother the usher, sticks his head out into the foyer, where it's hard to see the floor for all the skirts jammed against each other.

"It's not too late," he winks at Bay.

"It's way too late. I got to go with my heart." Bay sounds all breathy and breathless at the same time.

"Hey, look what I got they going to throw at you." He opens a half-pound pink satin pouch filled with white rice grains.

"I hope people know they're supposed to shower you with this. And don't anyone throw this at you. It'll knock you out." He chuckles devilishly like our father. The joke is on Aint Kit, who issued those bean bags full of rice. And the joke is on Aint Kit because she sent Bay's birth mother a gold-trimmed invitation to show off. Gussie, Bay's real mother, came.

Gussie is short and fat with breasts that have answered the pull of gravity. They hang to her waist naturally, but are held in midair now in front of her by a ribbed push-up bra. The wires of the bra push out through her pastel-blue polyester dress. Her hair is short, half the length of my baby finger, and did not take to the straightening comb or curlers with which some cosmetologist has worked on it. So she's wearing a short Afro and looks really cute.

She is standing shyly in the vestibule, gazing mistily through the frosted glass at the statuesque outline of her daughter the bride. And my heroine, Aunt Silence, in a black wool coat, stands beside her, cupping Gussie's elbow in the palm of her hand. I spy them through the clear part of the window, just as Bay turns too because someone's called her name.

Honeybabe pushes open the vestibule door a little and Aunt Silence slips in and leads Gussie by her hand to her daughter.

"You sho do look pretty. Guhl, you look so pretty!" Miss Gussie exclaims, clapping her hands together in delight, keeping her hands busy when we can tell she wants to lay her hands, if only for a moment, on her daughter's professionally made-up face.

"Hug me, Mama," Bay implores like a little girl. So Gussie does. Gathering up Bay's finery and crushing it within the embrace. To see this, all of us in the foyer swallow at the sweetness. In the middle of the hug and the whispers of "My sweet baby" when I'm looking at Aunt Silence and telling her I know she was the one who brought Miss Gussie and Silence is swearing it wasn't her idea, Aint Kit slams open the door.

"Don't you hear the music playing 'Here Comes the Bride'? You have missed your cue!" She is talking to Bay, but she glares at all of us, especially Miss Gussie and Aunt Silence.

She holds open the door to stare at us as we line up in the vestibule. First Pearl. Then me. Then Honeybabe. Then Bay, with Miss Gussie and Aunt Silence on either side of her. Miss Gussie moves to leave, but Bay says, "Stay with me, Mama. This is my wedding day. See there. You wouldn't come to my first one."

"I was feelin poorly, Baby. You know that."

"Well, I want you right here beside me now." Bay is stubborn as a five-year-old, which is what she is acting like now. That spontaneous. That open.

"Who's giving you away?" Miss Gussie changes the subject, fidgeting with her dress that hikes up in the back, nervous about being in the center of things, in the spotlight, when people turn around in the beribboned pews to look at Day and wait.

"Here come Uncle Sam," Bay says. This is still funny. Our old Grace joke. The very idea of Madaddy being Uncle Sam, when we know Uncle Sam looks like Lucifer with a pointed white beard, a tall striped hat and stars around the hatband, and a tuxedo on his long, snaky body. Our Madaddy does have a tuxedo on, and his hair is turning gray, but there the resemblance ends. He's not the one who sent Honeybabe's husband across the water.

Sam Grace hums to himself merrily and takes Bay's arm. The procession is complete. And Pearl begins the walk toward the shortest groomsman, who waits at the front of the church with Henry, who's staring lovingly past the crowd, his eyes hankering only for her, his Winnie. I follow Pearl's lead, avoiding the critical eyes that light on my Afroed head with much the same disfavor as they fall on Pearl's and Honeybabe's. Our hair isn't dressed up enough. Not quite fit for God. My feet that have died by now are worthy. If I go to Whitepeople heaven, it'll be breach. Feet first.

Miss Gussie and Aunt Silence are sitting beside Mama, and my other brother and sisters fill the row behind them. I pick their faces out of the crowd. They beam at me. Essie and Leona, light and dark, are sitting way off on the groom's side of the church, trying to even up the guests. They hunch each other and wink at me in my ridiculous European getup, daintily keeping time to the march on dead feet.

I can hear them now, what they'll say later at Eden.

"Where were your buckets, Maggie? You looked like a French milk-maid. Maybe Swiss," Leona will say. And about the bride Essie will comment, "Bay has such a beautiful face." Then Leona will finish what Essie didn't say. "Who could concentrate on her face for all that pumped-up hair? Every time I turned around I got twisted up in some ribbon and had to look over the shoulder of a bouquet."

I know they're going to ridicule this wedding so bad I'll get annoyed so as not to get embarrassed over this Aint Kit extravaganza. I think about killing Aint Kit. All through the whispering of vows and fumbling for rings, I think about Aint Kit in the front row wiping her eyes and looking radiantly bereaved.

Maybe I think about Aint Kit because I don't want to think about myself. I am not a bride and may never be one if I look at my batting average at Eden. I try to think of the female artists I've heard and read about: Augusta Savage, Georgia O'Keefe, Loïs Mailou Jones, Grandma Moses, Elizabeth Catlett, Margaret Burroughs, and Betye Saar. Were they or are they married? If not, were they ever in love? Were they each one of them in a star-crossed love affair? Will I ever find my one and only love?

If I do marry, I will dance barefoot to an African drumbeat, wrapped in kente cloth.

As the couple leaves the church and we follow relieved behind, I can hear Aint Kit stage-whisper to no one and everyone, "I'm not losing a daughter—"

"She's gaining a Gussie," Pearl breathes maliciously behind me.

When I turn around, she's smiling devilishly.

"Lucky Bay," I say, because Miss Gussie is here and she is gentle and shy and poor and we like her for loving Bay even to the point of having given her up to a better life she thought.

And Aint Kit, who has caused us such inconvenience, won't get to be mother-of-the-bride on this wedding day Kit has waited for most of Bay's wild life.

I can't wait to introduce my Aunt Silence to my friends. She balances out the impression my family has made. Crazy. At the reception in the church hall, Aunt Silence sits with Leona, Essie, and me for a while. She asks them about Eden. They answer respectfully, in awe like Edie Eden, as Moses Outlaw named us. Then Silence and I speak softly, only to each other.

"Do you know some men called DeadandBuried?" I ask her without preamble.

"They friends of mine." She pulls back to see me better. "Mighty funny you know 'em." She smiles.

"Do you know a man who lives above the Blue Rose or Blue Nile?"

"The what?"

"A blues lounge. A nightclub," I answer, flustered.

"I ain't been jukin in years." She uses the old name for clubbing. "I know a lot of people and a whole lotta people know me."

"He had your picture in his apartment."

"What were you doing in his apartment if you don't know who he is?" She acts surprised.

"I was helpin somebody deliver something."

"It wasn't nothing illegal, was it?"

"I don't think so."

"Well, then." She smiles again. "DeadandBuried be all right. And their friend all right too. Yes. Yes."

Then Silence moves away to sit with her best friend, my mother. Waiters bring out salads. Then they set platters of ham and fried chicken, plates of twice-baked potatoes, and bowls of French-style string beans on each table. Aint Kit got the food right. All but the ham.

Aint Kit surprises us when she yields her place at the bridal table to Gussie. Aint Kit does not sit throughout the reception. She races in chiffon to and fro checking on the fountain, which spouts pink champagne, haggling with the caterer over the color of the deviled eggs and the thickness of the slices of ham. "After all, I know how these things are done. I had a catering business myself once," sniffs Kit, adjusting the streamers on the table decorations, waving to one of the doctors or nurses from her job. They love her. When Lazarus asks, "Who those White people?" I answer, "Aint Kit's Fan Club."

Usually Aint Kit is puffed up like a bantam rooster so that her stature seems greater than it is. Her breasts are pushed out into the air before her like pathfinders. Her hips knock from side to side so forcibly she's been known to knock down a 260-pound, six-foot man, just by bumping into him by accident. Today as she asks Miss Gussie's permission to set her dress shoes down by the bride's mother's place, her entire body sags—shoulders droop, breasts lose their bounce, hips cave in. Even her hair wilts, the curls dropping out of it like petals on an old rose. Aint Kit's eyes, big and heavy and dark and hurt like Miss Gussie's. Our hearts go out to Aint Kit, who has lost her place. Lost.

Soon guests begin to grumble against Miss Gussie. Essie among them. "If she couldn't be a mother for all this time, why she show up at this late date?" She purses her lips on the rim of a champagne glass. She wipes a bubble off the tip of her nose. Then she giggles, "Poor Miss Kitty. Miss Gussie hoggin the spotlight."

I don't like Essie much right now. So I don't say anything for a little while, and just sit unmoving in the quiet of my momentarily hushed-up dress at the table with her and Leona. Watching the drama of the reception. "Miss Gussie doesn't mean any harm," I say from somewhere inside my warring heart.

Leona is locked in conversation with one of Aint Kit's cronies, who's also seated at our table. I was supposed to be at the bridal table. I'd offered my seat to Aint Kit, but she wouldn't take it. She was enjoying the scenario of Miss Gussie the usurper too much. Or maybe, and this is strange, Aint Kit has shrunk so from misery she seems like she just doesn't want to take up any more space. Essie's eyes are bright like a bird's, and she stares attentively like a pigeon at different scenes. Then she pecks at some food on her plate.

She's looking at Bay's new husband and so am I. He looks so uneasy in the rented tuxedo, like a great bear in a collar and bowtie, dancing in a circus. (Have you noticed how subdued bears in captivity are? How awkward they seem in bowties and hats? I mean the last time you saw one. Not like their massive, lumbering, terrible, and beautiful selves covering ground like black or brown mountains on the move.) Hank and Bay dance the first dance now. The musicians are playing Aint Kit's favorite song, the one her jewelry box tinkles out when you open it, "Them There Eyes." Hank has requested Little Milton belting out "We're Gonna Make It," but Aint Kit said that was too bluesy and low-classed. What would the people from her job think?

I think they wouldn't think anything worse than they think so far. I also think they better not think anything.

The hulking man and the top-heavy bride skate clumsily through the tune, bumping into each other, stepping on each other's toes. Bay and Hank smile at each other, and the whole thing doesn't seem so stupid and grotesque. They look like the original Adam and Eve at Lucifer's costume party. Before sin and banishment, I. B. K. Turner says the original Eden was doubtlessly in Africa. Bay-Winnie and Henry could be there now, thinking up words for a kiss.

Leona wants to know why I didn't invite Moses Outlaw to the wedding. I tell her I don't know why I didn't but I didn't.

At the mention of a man's name an eavesdropping cousin asks me, "When you going to get married, Maggie Lena?"

"She got to get her edjumacashun," another cousin answers.

"You girls better try to get you some husbands instead of sitting over here at a table full of women," the first cousin persists.

"I despise weddings," Leona whispers under her breath.

Bay and Hank are feeding each other gobs of wedding cake, like two toddlers playing communion.

Then Hank throws Bay's garter and a ten-year-old second cousin catches it.

"Now what he gone do with that?"

"Mannish thing."

"Use it for a slingshot, I hope."

It takes Aint Kit to clear the floor of men and boys who act real disappointed they didn't catch a garter and a wife. Then the ten-year-old victor twirls the garter on his finger. Kit gives a forced smile. All her smiles, at this point, are forced. Her eyes reek disappointment, but she won't give in to embarrassment. "All you girls, come on up here. We got to get ourselves some husbands. Gussie, Lee-Bet, come on down here. They got marriageable men in Mimosa. I'm gone get me one." How can a voice be so loud and so caught in the throat at the same time?

A flock of women wait to fly after the bridal bouquet.

"Come on, Maggie Lena, you all. College women got to have a husband too," Aint Kit consoles us.

"Yeah, they call that polygamy. One man, many wives." Leona gets all technical when she's griping.

We grumble, but we get up anyway. Essie tries to feign as much reluctance as Leona and me. But she's excited. She has someone in mind.

"Move, Maggie," my older sister, Pearl, shoves me. "You're not getting married before me." She could be joking.

When Pearl grabs the bouquet like a quarterback in satin skirts, Leona gets real political. She doesn't know why we participate in these European customs anyway. Lending credence to the ways of our oppressors.

"Yeah," I agree. Mad at myself for hoping. "This is not very revolutionary at all."

We're in the washroom.

"I wish we could just have fun sometimes." Essie is the wistful one now. "Just enjoy ourselves without judging everything all the time."

I take this as a personal rebuke. "You were judging not too long ago."

"I know. I just wish we could be happy too." The wish comes clearer to her and she talks about it faster and louder. "I wish we didn't have to be Black all the time."

"That's one of two wishes you can't have. The other is immortality."

Leona lifts her hair fiercely. Until her hair looks like it's standing up on its own muscle.

I don't answer. I just stare at myself in my getup. Leona doesn't answer either. We look at each other in the one long mirror that hangs above their face bowls in a row.

Mama, Silence, and Miss Gussie come into the washroom, talking among themselves.

"Maggie, let me use your lipstick," my mother says when she sees me. It's crowded in the little room, so Leona and Essie promise to meet me back at the table. We have to get going soon. Or they'll leave me.

It's just Grace women and Miss Gussie, the mother of a Grace woman, in here.

Aunt Silence, inside a stall, lets out a long whoosh of pee. "Drinking wine always make me make water." She punctuates the noise with her words.

"You sound like Victoria Falls in there, Leah," my mama signifies a little taste. Miss Gussie just giggles self-consciously, not sure if she knows my mama well enough to laugh at the jokes between her and Silence.

"There you go now. Where is the Victoria Falls, Ca'line?"

"Over there in Africa somewhere. Ain't it, Maggie?"

"Uh-huh." I know it's time to show off my expensive education for Aunt Silence and Miss Gussie. "The Nile begins there."

"Is that a fact." My Aunt Silence likes to know anything I tell her.

"Oooooh," Miss Gussie says, like this bit of knowledge is a miracle.

"You know that place the Blue Nile?" Aunt Silence reminds me.

"I've passed by there."

"Next time I come up here, you and me gone go there." Aunt Silence is rinsing her hands and looking dreamy. She smiles as the water runs over her wrist. "Ain't it good to love somebody and be loved back. The Blue Nile."

"I'm going too,' Mama says.

"Ca'line, you don't know nothing 'bout them low-down dirty blues," Aunt Silence challenges Mama.

"Who don't?" Mama takes the bait.

"You don't. You a married woman with a house fulla children."

"I'm a Negro woman just like you." Mama is all defiant. "I'm a Black woman." She's really tough.

"This sure is nice," Miss Gussie says. She is not in the game. She's looking up in the corners of the room. Acting pleased about even the seams of this place.

"Kit sure put together a beautiful wedding. It was nice of her to let me stay and sit in and everything." Miss Gussie appreciates everything.

Mama has my lipstick now, and is keeping her mouth still as she reddens her lips.

"I thought I saw Kit give Hank a bill for all this reception." Silence's voice is noncommittal. She's still cooling her wrists. The hall is very hot and stuffy. Too many flowers. Too many people. Too much to drink. Like that imaginary milk that bubbled up out of Grandmama Patsy's nipple in Aint Kit's lie that Grandmama Patsy breast-fed Bay after giving her up to Aint Kit. A doozy.

"She gave him a big bill to help him pay for everything. That was so bighearted," Miss Gussie says. She doesn't know wedding etiquette and is pleased with the face bowls now. And the paper towels that have flowers on them.

Aunt Silence is real emphatic. "Naw, Gussie, Kit give that man a bill for him to foot the bill."

"Girl, I know you kidding me." Mama stands with my lipstick poised in midair, too stunned to finish her mouth.

✦

My father drops me at the Sweet Flats. I get out of the car clumsily in my bridesmaid regalia. My hat perched precariously atop my sculpted Afro. In the wedding line I was matched with one of the groom's cousins. Here at Eden University I'm not matched with anyone. Is this loneliness I walk into? I have my shoes in hand, tiptoeing into my dorm.

"Hey, Maggie, Halloween been over!" It's Trixia, being smart.

I have to admit I do look like Halloween. And, except for Silence, I didn't even get a treat.

Sleeping Cats Station

Moses is waiting for me just beyond the turnstile in one of the worst El stations in the City. Once a lion escaped from the city park zoo not far from here. The entire city was on the alert—dogcatchers and police crouched side by side, going down the street, peering into alleys, bushes, and crannies. A commuter coming home late from work came upon the lion napping on the El platform, having leapt over the turnstile like a delinquent teenager. The lion awakened to his hysterical scream, yawned, and watched in a one-eyed squint the fleeting footsteps of the man. Of course, when the dogcatcher and the cop came for the beast sleeping amid pigeon doo, he looked as lively as one of his stone brothers who stalk the platform guarding the Institute of Art.

We call this station Sleeping Cats Station. When you come through and go through it, you take your life in your hands. It's one of the coldest stations in the City. In winter the City's wind we call the Hawk nests here hatching out new, impatient baby hawks that scream through the cracks. In summer the Hawk sleeps here; you'd think the coolness of his folded wings would be soothing, but it is not. It is a dank chill that passes over you as you step in from the summer sun. In Sleeping Cats Station you could catch a chill or one could catch you.

Moses looks at me sleepily when I catch sight of him. I think it's supposed to be a sexy look. It works because I turn over inside, like an

El-train just rumbled through my stomach. We are related to trains, I've figured that out. I met him on the platform near the newspaper stand of the despicable man. I wonder where Moses and I are going.

"Check out the vacant space where the Lecherous Merchant used to hawk his wares? You see it going by?" Moses lays his arm heavily across my shoulders.

"It's not there anymore."

"I'm so hip. I took care of that for you, my African Queen."

"I read in the paper where he was arrested for setting fire to it himself."

Moses cackles and his teeth are white and uneven. "Don't believe everything you read in the newspapers, Miss Lady."

Sooner or later I'm going to have to tell Moses how much I hate being called every name but my own. "There were witnesses to the arson."

"There you go again." He sucks his front teeth. "You up at the rich Whitefolk's college believing everything you read in them books. I believe that which I have experienced. I know from my five senses." His free hand he holds before us, the fingers all splayed out. It looks big. The arm around my shoulder he leans on me with, pulling me to him, grabbing my shoulder that's not pressed into his chest. I can hear him inhale and hold his breath.

"You smell good," he whispers into my ear. "You smell real good, Miss Ivory Tower. Like Ivory Soap." He cracks up.

We burst out of the cold dark staircase right into a blast of sunlight. The street is sunny and cold, but our spot is warm. Moses's wool coat scrapes my cheek. I pull away from him a little.

"What time is the movie?" I ask.

"We got plenty of time." He's casual, dismissing my question. "Come go with me, while I run down this niggah owe me fifteen dollars."

He asked me to see a movie about Malcolm X with him. At a liberation school not far from where he lives.

The street is wide, and snow sits in dirty lumps on the curb. The street just shaved by sunlight and snowplow. The streets downtown and in Eden have been plowed. This is a neighborhood of last resources. A peculiar area of poverty situated a block or so away from a high-rent, fashionable area. The one place in the city where the certified rich and the confined poor enjoy the same unobstructed view of the lake. My brother Lazarus says he bet those rich people get out of bed some days and scratch their heads over the unfairness of the lay of the land and the view of the lake. How could God or city planners be so cruelly capricious?

We walk past a boarded-up corner store where a steady flow of customers goes in and out. A young man saunters out, munching a bag of pork rinds.

"Looka here, my man. Looka here," Moses says to the dude in a red black-and-green crocheted cap that's pulled up around his head because his hair is so big.

"I'm trying to catch up with Skin. You seen him?"

They don't look at each other. The conversation is so cool they look over each other's shoulder in opposite directions. I stare at both of them and remind them who they're talking to. They're talking about money. That's why they never say the word. Skin owes Moses some money. Not this munching dude with big hair. So Moses just implies money and urgency to him.

"I'll check you later on, man." Moses is saying good-bye now. "Oh, hey, this my lady. She go to school at Eden University!"

Big Hair salutes me with a pork rind, then he pops it into his mouth.

Moses says, "Tell Skin I'm looking for him."

We go in different directions.

"Niggah lying." Moses spits on the sidewalk. "He know where that joker is. He better tell that rhino skin gimme what he owe me. I don't want his ass, I want my money." Meaning he'll take Skin's ass if that's what he can get.

"What time is the movie?" I ask.

Moses looks at me like I'm disturbing him. He doesn't answer. I'm beginning to think this movie isn't in his immediate plan. He just likes dragging me around his neighborhood.

He touches my elbow, then makes a sharp turn onto a walkway and up some raggedy steps to a frame house. From a landing he calls to me, "You coming? So we can catch that flick." I follow him reluctantly.

I can hear Leona now in my head. "You shoulda gone to the post office so you could be sure his picture wasn't in the gallery down there."

Moses isn't a crook. I've figured that out from hour-long phone calls he's made to me. He keeps a lot of what my mother calls "bad company."

93

Inside the apartment his friends, a man and a woman, offer me a seat on a couch. Moses heads for the back. He starts talking to a guy back there, then he takes a seat, and the guy beckons with a little green tube and Moses begins to sniff something off the top of a kitchen counter like a hound dog.

I'd rather be watching the movie of Malcolm X that we'd set out for, instead of Moses blowing up his nose.

Finally, Moses squeezes his nose with index finger and thumb, real quick. He says, and this time I can hear, "You seen Skin? Tell that chump I'm looking for him."

I can see clean through the gloomy little apartment. Past the dining room that is a bedroom, into the kitchen where a movie projector is sitting on the table.

"You want to catch this flick with us?" The guy, who is named Ronnell, invites me.

"No, thank you," I say. Wily instinct pushing the words out of my mouth. I look at Moses so hard I want to make him levitate out of his seat on the low-down couch.

He looks back at me, brushing his nose. After a while he tells Ronnell he'll see him later on. I say good-bye easily enough.

On the street I don't speak to him first.

"I'm glad you wanted to raise. Him and his ole lady ain't nothing but freaks. They watch dirty movies so they can get it on." He sniffs with disdain. And because he has to sniff. His nose is red. It's not that cold.

"I don't need movies." He takes my hand in his.

"The movie on Malcolm's over, isn't it?" I ask resentfully and rhetorically.

"Yeah. We missed it."

"Where are we going now?"

"To my crib."

Everything is a box. The building, like a cereal box with window holes cut into the sides. Or like a tray of ice with the very tiny orifices for miniature cubes. Everything is a box inside a box, like a disappointing present, with no redeeming surprise in the ultimate tiniest cube.

Moses lives in a box on the fourteenth floor. Outside the door I turn my back to the door and look at the lake. It is shapeless, blue and lovely.

It has no head, no legs; it just is here and what it is. Wandering and situated. Empowered in languor and fury. A sight for sore eyes.

"Oh, look at the lake!" I sigh in awe, releasing my disappointment at missing Malcolm X. Seeing him instead.

"Pretty, ain't it?" Moses fits his key in the lock and does not turn around. He's seen it before.

The apartment is the same as Essie's, only bigger. There are more people in his family. Past the square, predictable living room, Mrs. Outlaw is busy in the kitchen. Moses doesn't call to her the way we call to Caroline Grace the moment we hit the door.

She doesn't look up. But I know she sees us and I nod and smile politely at her blind, busy gestures. I linger in the living room, hoping Moses will introduce me to his mother and tell her I am his girlfriend. But he shuts the door and tells me to come on. I do. I look back at his mother, but she makes like she doesn't see me.

His room reminds me of a cigar box. I hesitate at the door. Behind us, I can hear the rumble of many children. The kind of noise that we used to make in the Grace house on Arbor Avenue. Like distant thunder, earthquake, and stockyard truck rolling by. A stampede of wild African elephants or American buffalo. In the house the box is full of noise.

The walls so thin, I feel like I've stepped inside a transistor radio. Inside the room Moses has turned on his radio, and I watch him close the door and prop a chair under the knob, but not before a little boy announces that Moses has a girl in his room. I try to imagine Sam Jr. (when he was younger and living at home) or Lazarus with a girl in his room and Mama not knocking on the door demanding to know who. I can't.

"Does your mother mind you having company?" I ask him.

"I been twenty-one. I pay rent." He flops down on his bed. "Sit here." He pats the space beside him.

I go to the window instead. I look out. Happy the lake is there.

"There's the lake," I say.

"And the sun is somewhere over it," he yawns. "Come here."

I look at him, stretched out on his bed. Shoeless and sleepy-eyed. He crooks his fingers like he's playing an imaginary bass in the air as he beckons me to sit beside him. I must hear the music because I look back at my view of the water only once. Then I sit beside him on the bed; my buttocks touching him at the hip. The touching is strange and familiar— like we were connected there once and now we're reconnected.

My old self is here and watching me and watching him at the same time. Like I'm wise to what the touching means. But my young self is dumb. Fear and shyness make me not look at him. But I do when he sits up and leans toward me.

His kiss is not like Steve Rainey's—like the play of water on dry lips. Moses's mouth is hot and its pressure on mine is hard. His tongue is hot and shaped like a giant jalapeño pepper, heat all in it; it's slippery and rough like a hot plum. He fills my mouth with it. I give him my tongue. And they tangle in our mouths. But that is not enough and he begins to move himself and me impatiently, swiftly. He dances me down on my back, and himself above me like a viaduct over a dark, small street. The thought of aqueducts from ancient Rome—columned arches over waterways—comes to mind, from some Western Civ text, but I can't hold on to the thought. Moses is still kissing me. And I'm kissing him back because I like him, because I like this kiss, because I'm curious. And I don't want to miss anything, so my eyes are wide open sometimes. Watching him.

He is quick. I've missed the opening of my blouse. But he is languid as he plies my breasts from their cups and takes one into the palm of his hand and the tip of the other into his mouth. He twirls the favored nipple with his magic, jalapeño tongue until it is hard like the pit of a tiny plum.

I have to think about this—the flow of heavy water through me— how it rises to be closer to the viaduct, the aqueduct. I have to think, but I can't. Sounds come in from outside the door to his room. Children rustle and giggle, but I'm not one of them.

He pulls at the zipper of my pants, and clear, panicked resistance shoots through me. I think of Essie, I think of Leona. I think of Eden. I think of babies. I push him off me hard. I sit up and try to collect in my head what I know about forbidden acts. He hasn't given up. He's looking at me in a one-eyed squint.

I think of his mother in her kitchen. I look at him. Around the spare box room. I think of ice.

"Maggie, it was just getting good." He looks disheveled, disgruntled, and incomplete. His shirt half off. His hair an untidy mess. He starts to knead me. But I am stiff and will not give in to his caresses.

"Were you raped or something?" He is perplexed, trying to be compassionate, instead of impatient. But where'd he get that from? Essie was raped and she's been with William. I don't tell him the question's dumb.

"No," I answer. "Not me."

Then he's hurt because I wasn't raped and won't do it either. He falls back on the bed. His voice humble and angry with disappointment.

"How come I can't have nothing I want?" he says.

I am sorry for him and his whole life in this box.

I lay my wet face on his bare chest. When did I start crying? "I like you. I do like you," I whisper. But there's torn surrender in the way I put this. There's only the plea for peace.

The children are louder now. And someone's knocking on the door like a human hammer. I jump up and fix my clothes, go and sit by the window.

"Who is it?" Moses yells. Angry now I know because he thinks he could have talked me into it. Touched me into it.

Moses yanks the chair from under the knob and the door falls open to a young man in knit pants and a knit top. Outside the door is shadowy and the man's face fits into it. Even if I looked hard I couldn't make him out distinctly. I am embarrassed and ashamed to be found in Moses's room when the signs (the tumbled bed and the torn zipper on my pants, the thickened air and Moses's annoyance) tell the story of sex in the afternoon while Moses's mama is in the kitchen. So I don't look hard at the visitor.

"Man, what's wrong with you?" the visitor exclaims. "You look like you been in a fight." He looks from Moses to me and back again.

"What you want?" Moses is sullen, sitting on the side of the bed, putting on his shoes.

"I brought the thang you been looking for."

Moses doesn't look up. The visitor drops a wad of money on top of the record player.

"I was looking for it earlier." Moses looks up at his buddy.

"Hey, I brought it to you." The visitor jumps back and throws up his hands in a gesture of innocence and disavowal.

"Yeah," Moses says, like "I'm so hip."

"I'm gone pull yo chain later and let you finish what you and yo lady was about."

"Yeah," Moses says.

The man waves and is gone.

I put on my coat. Not surprised Moses doesn't help with it.

✦

It is late afternoon. It feels like years have passed and I've made a long, aimless journey with Moses and gotten nowhere. For a moment, sense of place tilts and I could be walking through this dusk street with my head in my hands. My head is so heavy and yet so hollow it feels like a gourd. I think of that and concentrate on balancing the gourd on my neck. I walk self-consciously, imitating what I've seen of African women in photos who carry household appliances, foodstuffs, industrial supplies, and bright patterned bolts of cloth on their heads. But Moses bumps against me and jolts my grace. So I stop being a poised African woman, and I'm just Maggie who had almost made love for the very first time.

Moses is feeling good now. He's walking next to me talking about and against the Whiteman. He says the Whiteman thinks he's God, but he's not.

"I am God," Moses shouts to the street. People ignore him. He's buoyant and proud again as he marches me toward Sleeping Cats Station, where I will catch the subway back to Eden.

I think he's so happy now because he knows one day he'll have me. He's sure of it. Or maybe he's happy because he took some deep drags off a joint before we left his room. He's feeling omnipotent. His friend brought the cash by. He's got a little bit of money.

In the station I pay my fare at the window, while Moses leaps like a big cat over the turnstile. The attendant keeps quiet to see him swing over the revolving bar. To say anything would be like chastising a lion escaped from a cage. Besides, Moses is yelling, "I am God," as he swings across the turnstile. At the top of the stairs to the platform, we stop.

"I'm going to call you to see about us going to a flick or one of them shows up on your campus," he promises.

I don't tell him FBO members don't really attend many frivolous campus events, like the musical comedies the theater department specializes in.

He's acting mighty arrogant now. He stares at my mouth. Suddenly, I'm in a tight hug and we're wrapped in a kiss as deep and hungering as before. In Sleeping Cats Station, public and impractical, I am free, so I open my mouth wide and swallow all of him. Tongues chasing each other around in our mouths.

People come off the trains and up the stairs to the surprise of 3-D passion. Feverish and unconsummated. The kiss substituting for the rest of it. Old women suck their teeth. And grown men giggle. We kiss again and I tear myself away from him, then haul to catch the train, just before the doors clamp shut.

✦

One day in my Negro-girl memory, Mrs. Wilson was jiggling the hot curlers inside a roll of newly straightened and glistening hair on the head of the wife of Reverend Person, pastor of Star of Bethlehem. The pastor's wife had closed eyes and a smile on her face. At their request, Jeannie and me were bringing them ice-cold pops from the corner store. Mrs. Wilson had put out her cigarette in honor of Mrs. Reverend Person's visit that came twice a month. Mrs. Wilson just breathed hot breath through the two nostrils pinched into one by her glasses. No smoke today like an imperial dragon.

"I tell you them Catholic kids don't do nothing but go up in that woman's store after school and steal her blind."

The word *Catholic* stops me cold as I meticulously count out Mrs. Wilson's change and wait for her to bless me with a tip. Mrs. Reverend Person keeps her eyes closed and kind of hums assent behind Mrs. Wilson's sentences.

"She caught one of them boys just stuffin his old pockets full of them butter cookies she keep in the jar on her counter. Now you know that's a shame. All of them uniforms confusing her when they come up in her place in a gang. Hovering around, robbing her barefoot."

Next I suppose they'll be robbing the store lady pregnant. ("Barefoot and pregnant," I've heard Mama and Miss Rose say they go together.) Those roguish Catholic kids. Like me. I guess Mrs. Wilson forgot that.

"I don't steal." Self-defense jumps out of me before I knew it was there. "I never steal."

"What you say?" Mrs. Wilson asked, astonished by my emphatic tone. Mrs. Reverend Person opened her eyes.

"And my mama say everybody good's going to heaven!" I ignored Jeannie and the anticipation of candy money and headed for the door haughtily.

"Come back here, Maggie. Wasn't anybody talking about you," Mrs. Reverend Person hollered after me. But I disobeyed and left the three of them astonished and openmouthed. The two grown women embarrassed and edgy about what my mama or her best friend, Miss Rose, the Missionary Baptist, member of Star of Bethlehem, will say to them.

So I was then. Persecuted for my faith. A martyr. I imagined. An outcast.

"When the brothers let loose in the streets after King was offed I saw a brother on the news running with a whole ham in his hands. I started singing 'Hambone, Hambone, where you been? Round the world and back again.' The call is global. It's global. Four hundred years is over. We want liberation and reparations now. We want what they took." That is what Elder Levergate said one evening when he and Yvonne Christmas were sitting in the communal room on Blood Island. Everybody was in a bad mood whenever we thought about Steve and what would happen to him and how we had to let it.

I was convinced after listening to Elder that the center of things was screwed up. Everything was wrong. And we had been wronged. So when Leona and Essie and I went to the store that evening after leaving the Island, I stood away from the counter and looked cool while Leona bought cigarettes, which she is practicing smoking. Out of the corner of my eye I surveyed the array of candy bars on the wall facing the counter. Swift as a pickpocket who rides the bus that runs down Arbor Avenue during the Christmas season I plucked a PayDay from the rack and slid it into my jacket pocket. I caught myself as if I were painting me as I acted, a slow flow of colors collecting, then rushing out impulsively. When Leona had gotten her cigarettes, we fell out of the delicatessen, bumping into one of the brothers who hung out there as he fell in behind two Whitegirls who were giggling at his attentions. When the air hit me I was animated, angry strokes come alive. "What you got?" Essie asked me.

"A liberated PayDay," I replied.

"You mean you st—took it?" she fumbled.

"Yes, I did." The way they took us and the world.

Leona lit one of her cigarettes and coughed. "These menthols. I ought to take them back." Essie was looking worried. We walked for a while with nobody saying anything. We were walking in the middle of the street. Everything seemed wider that way. Our path. We could travel without being attracted to store windows or bumping into curbs or garbage cans. I thought it was like walking down Old Letha Road in Mimosa, Mississippi. Like I was walking down that road. Then the PayDay was heavy in my pocket. I unpeeled it and began to eat it. But it tasted like dust. And Leona would accept none because she was smoking, and Essie was thinking. Once they had stuffed their pockets with Snickers and Mr. Goodbars while I had stood by. I took another nibble from the candy bar, but it was old and dry and stale. So I heaved it over the street and way over into some bushes that encircle the base of the glass-domed administration building. I didn't even hear it land.

Above us the night sky was loaded with stars, more plentiful than the Graces and the Dancers and the Pryors and the Witherspoons. I couldn't count the stars without losing track.

Then I said, "I'll bet my grandmama could count every last one of these stars and give you its history. Time of birth and death." Essie really looked at me like I was a weird stranger then. A new thief and a crazy woman in one night. Leona just blew some cigarette smoke over her head. And I knew I'd never liberate another petty thing in my life. I am after the big music.

That happened this spring of 1969.

But there was more. Everything got more intense. Nina Simone, our High Priestess, sang this song. (I don't know when she started singing it.) "What's gonna happen now that the King of Peace is dead?" The song tears my heart. Like a door to a house full of monsters has been opened and the monsters have come out. Then, too, it's like we are all travelers and the final emissary has been sent out and murdered, his head propped on a post, and the savagery of the act tells us what we've always known. Malcolm warned us before. And Malcolm was right before the bullets ripped through him in the Audubon Ballroom in New York. And Malcolm was right after the bullets hit King on the balcony in Memphis.

The brothers from the EARTH come up to our campus this spring of '69. They bring their women with them. Everybody is mean. "Every last one of them is mean. Girl, do you hear me? Too tough," Leona says. We go down to the basement of Blood Island. This is the way the EARTH-men explain the role of the Black student to us. Alhamisi talking.

"The role of the Black student is to step aside and let the grassroots grow on through. The role of the Black student is to join with the people in our struggle for liberation and not merely sit back on your collegiate asses and enjoy the fruit of our struggle. The role of the Black student is to be a Black man or a Black woman. That means we must recognize our common goal and refuse to go against the interest of our community. The Black student must be held accountable to his community, by himself and his community. Nothing must come before his commitment to Black Liberation. Not even your God. Not astrology. Not straightening combs. Not birth control pills. Not the chance to sit next to White kids and marry White boys, all you sisters."

We're all squashed into the basement of Blood Island. Backed up against the walls and tucked into crannies. Alhamisi is so sure about everything. The searching thing inside me is quiet. And I can tell Leona is appeased and Essie is sure too. All around the room the bloods of FBO listen. Last year my friends and I made fun of him. But that was before the pain of Eden, and the death of King and the death of Robert Kennedy too. I think about what Mama and Aint Kit and Aunt Silence used to whisper about in their kitchens in the City and in Mimosa. How after the deaths of my grandmother Sarah Mahalia Lincoln Dancer and the others the calendar of days was drawn up around the event. As if calendars were more than markers of time, but markers of memory as well. The days of pain and loss marked in red. The days my mother's mother came to my mother after death, those days marked in blue, with yellow in them like white Easter lilies with yellow pistils. Those days surrounded in black like sky and signifying the mystery of those visitations.

Those days are marked in red, the color of the eyes of pigeons, which is also the color of Alhamisi's eyes. The color deepens into a notation of dried blood; it is loud and definite and we can see it from a long way off. No matter where the other days throw us, we are pulled back into that color. These days are marked in black too, but this is a different Blackness that we talk about all the time. It is strong and unbreakable as certain barks; it is real and reliable as a small gun that fits in some secret place under your skin; it is deadly and profane. But it is glorious and defiant and talks back to all the ugly, annihilating meanings for it. It is Black Is Beautiful, Black Pride, Black Love, Black History, Black Power, Black Man, Black Woman. As a study in contrast to blackheart, black magic, black devil, black mood, black soul, black filth, black terror, black cloud, black fate. They pass out a poem by Margaret Burroughs (I know her work!). It is about black. We here on the Island want to be Black as we can be. Grassroots. The real thing. As removed from big White lies as we can get.

We don't want to lose now what we've paid everything to gain. We are all that we have. Alhamisi says, "We can't be lifting up any more heroes so they can be shot down. We have to place our faith in the grass-roots. The masses. We cannot base our commitment in allegiance to one person. We have to commit ourselves to our community."

When he is finished, the sister with him brings him a glass of water, then she brings him another. Back and forth six times without saying a word. He never thanks her or nods even. Leona lifts her eyebrow at such servitude.

Alhamisi still looks like and talks like an ice baby to me; his style is the ice baby's cool. But what he says is true. I know this.

The human baby's body is 75 percent water. What about the soul? You take some bodies born in cold and a bitter climate and they'll come out ice babies, souls hard to touch, slow to warm. Just old and cold adults who never grow warm with wisdom and age.

Moses Outlaw is grassroots if he is nothing else. But he is something else. He is the one who saved my soul from humiliation. A hero of sorts. A Black knight. Who tore up newspapers and fixed the lecherous-eyed merchant. I lie on my bed and think about him, a psychology book open in front of me. I feign study. My grades vary. But how could I care too much about that now since the calendar of days has been painted in so many colors?

The day of our missed Malcolm movie has become more interesting in retrospect. From safe, virginal distance. And Moses in the midst of dirty movies we wouldn't watch, and what I know was cocaine, and Moses in the midst of unfinished desire is couched in the galaxy of forbidden things.

He called me and said he will come to see me here in Eden. I am thinking of the writing on the wall. A long-ago summer day and Littleson telling me to wash the dirty word I had written off the side of the garage. I try to study my book, but I cannot wash Moses off me. I think of aqueducts and the dark waters beneath them.

There is one exhilarating memory of the summer of '68. 1968. John Carlos and Tommie Smith, two Black runners in the Summer Olympics. Their gold medals glistening at the closing ceremony, they lifted their fists in the Black Power salute. The whole world fell down around them, and that is how I am painting them now in the spring of '69. My easel set up by the window in Hamla's extra room. The two figures larger than anything else. Black and muscular and victorious. In the background I discover surprises. Shadows of sharecroppers and slaves, railroad men and laundresses, wet nurses and soldiers. Each and every shadow lifting a fist. And behind these, Africans with fists. Afterimages of a tender and terrible spiritual triumph.

Painting. That's all I want to do. I get only As in art classes. The professors, all but one, a severe gentleman with an accent, seem to know my name. No one has to coax me. My teachers stand over my shoulder and look onto my canvas approvingly.

They discussed me once. I overheard a conversation about me one day as I was sitting in the Art Library. "The Grace girl is an extraordinary talent," the man says. "Maggie is so good. I hope she can go to France for Senior Honors," the woman says, with great longing in her voice. She wants things for me. This is Miss Julienne. Whose work I love. In whose classes I am happy. The man is a crazy sculptor who gnaws on chunks of bread all through class. He carries around a long loaf of bread still smelling fresh and alive. One time in late afternoon when I'd just finished a tiny piece of abstraction as required, he offered me a hunk. And I took it. Leona, who has heard about him, says he rarely offers his bread. Only to the most gifted does he turn over a piece. "I hope he's not planning to hit on you," she warns. I take him at face value. Yet I am wary and shy around Mr. Charles-Smythe who has a hyphenated name.

That day they were talking about me. They were standing outside the door of the Art Library, worrying about my future like they worried about the future of any student who had the gift. Then Miss Julienne growled, "It's difficult enough for a woman to gain respect in this man's art world. She's got the other problem." The other problem. I am Black. I don't like my Blackness called a problem. I can feel myself get tight all over. "In Paris she'd be okay." Mr. Charles-Smythe tries to sound real sure.

Paris. I think about the Louvre. The paintings by the Masters that hang there. I don't like to call them the Masters, though. That reminds me of slavery. The difference is one set has mastered a craft; another believed in mastering people. I just don't like that word, I told Miss Julienne once.

"Why?" she asked me with that gentle, unknowing smile of hers. Her brow wrinkling more because the barrette on her head has pulled her hair back so tightly.

"I just don't like that word." I was so stubborn and reticent.

"Well," she blew out cigarette smoke to signal we were finished with it. "We won't call them that. Let's call them the Old Ones." Even that doesn't set well with me. Since they are not that old. Western Civilization is a spoiled babe. That is what I. B. K. Turner says. "Western Civilization is a spoiled babe who takes others' treasures, then swears they belong to him. Squeezing the life out of things with his tiny, Western hands." When I don't agree to the Old Ones, Miss Julienne just smiles.

"The Old Boys," she says. "That's what we'll call them."

"The Old Boys instead of the Masters," I agree, but on Blood Island I call them the Old Babies when I call them anything. They are spoiled and prone to imperialist tantrums.

They want me to study in Paris. Mr. Charles-Smythe thinks I will have Paris at my feet. Like Josephine Baker. I should paint in banana leaves. They might give me the Medal of Honor. Yeah. Sure.

I am almost at home in the art classes. Someone stands over my shoulder. Miss Julienne or Mr. Charles-Smythe tells me things and they mean that I should grow.

I paint, favoring watercolors. I paint like the spirit of painting is in me. So I have a vast family of canvases now and no place to put them. Mr. Charles-Smythe tells me he has a loft with a lot of space and I can store my work there. But I tell him no thank you. My family has space.

"Maggie, your daddy says you can't put nothing else on that back porch. It's a fire hazard," my mama says over the phone when I call her to ask.

"Let me see if Rose got some room in her closets." Since Eddie's death Miss Rose and her daughter have lived alone. At least until Jeannie started having babies. But Jeannie got married and left her mama's house. Later Mama calls me back. "Jeannie and her children are back with Rose. Jeannie's expecting again."

"Expecting what?" I ask, just to sound grown-up and annoyed with the world.

"Some more of what she doesn't need and got too much of already, Rose say." Caroline, my mama, mother of nine, says, "A woman can't have that many children unless she got a husband."

"She got a husband," I say.

"Please," my mama says. Finished with Jeannie's husband who is not a husband. "I asked your Aint Kit and she says you can put your paintings in her spare room. You know Kit has too much room."

"I don't want to keep my work in Aint Kit's house," I protest.

"She's not going to hurt your paintings, girl."

"Every time I want to get something, I have to go through Aint Kit." That's like going through a forest of smiling, growling bears. Bears with growling lies.

"Well, I told her you are bringing them now. So you just take them over there."

I am between a bear and a crowded place. So I say okay I'll take them. Knowing that means I'll have to visit with Aint Kit for an interminable time. She's more demanding of time than ever now that Bay has married and moved out. That big house has opened around Aint Kit like a yawn of immeasurable boredom and emptiness.

When Moses calls me again, I ask him to help me take my paintings to Aint Kit. Leona is going too since she has the car. A present from her daddy the barbecue king. When Essie finds out Leona is going, she has to go. I don't know if there will be enough room for all my paintings, so Leona borrows her daddy's station wagon. It's a party. And they get to meet Moses. And Aint Kit again.

Essie looks like she's been struck by lightning. Her just-washed hair unbraided and electrified from the water and the stretch of the braids. Color too is drained from her face and her eyes are glassy from unshed tears of shock. William and Rhonda, we've just found out, got married on the spur of the moment. Or maybe it wasn't the spur of the moment, since everybody understood that they would marry sooner or later. Everybody but Essie. And William. Leona and me and Hamla too because she wanted what Essie wanted. I saw that once and told Hamla so and she denied it. But Essie wanted William. Now Essie is standing in the lobby with Leona and me waiting for Moses to show up so he can help carry my paintings to Aint Kit. We have another stop to make. Leona has impressed on me that what I have to give belongs to the community. The community has the right to the people that dance out of my hands onto canvas.

"It's natural, Maggie," Leona philosophizes. "Even spiders make their art public sooner or later. Everybody's got to cross under a spider's web at some point." This sounds real good to her and to me. To me because I am proud of *Gold* (the painting of the Black Olympic runners); proud of the portrait of a bowl of figs and the Grace women (Mama, Aunt Silence, Aunt Charity, Grandmama Patsy, and Aint Kit), dresses flowing into each other, each studying a task, eating figs or holding them in their laps, in a sunlight-washed scene from the dining room of what used to be Grandmama's house and is now Aunt Silence's; I am proud of a landscape of a long, winding road that rises at dusk. A twilight vision of the dark way of Old Letha Road, heavy with shadows out of which I know haints will walk. Haints whose names I could call. One in particular. This painting I have named *Remember*. Leona wants us to drop by Great Zimbabwe to see or give away one of my paintings, because they are indeed beautiful and deserve to be looked at. And because Leona says they are remarkable and restorative to the heart. Because hearts must be healed.

"Ain't that what your art's about?" Leona asks rhetorically, not waiting for my answer, because she knows she need not. We've talked about this enough. Leona says, "Great Zimbabwe is about restoring us to our traditional greatness as a people. I know they're going to want to use your work. It's great." This is what I like to hear.

Leona is standing around looking pleased with herself. Like she is the successful matchmaker of two of her favorite ideas. Essie is standing with us with a smile on her face standing someplace else. That smile right there on a body, but the soul of her sitting in a chair in a white-walled room, catatonic. "Leona just thinks everything is like she says just cause she says it's so," Essie interjects.

"I beg your pardon, Miss Witherspoon. What's that supposed to mean?" Leona is looking at Essie like Essie is off-the-wall and way in left field, lost in her own private high grass.

"Maybe Maggie ain't as good as you making out."

I'm looking for Essie in the high grass now.

"I mean, I know she's good. But maybe she's not so good that everybody wants her stuff." Essie's having a hard time making herself clear, and stomping on my ego and coming up with clean shoes.

"Well, if our friend Maggie's stuff ain't so good, what you coming to carry it for? We don't want your hands on it!" Leona is putting on her gloves in the lobby, shoving her fists into the leather gloves like they're boxing gloves.

"Maggie wants me to help her," Essie says. "Don't you, Maggie?"

"Sure, Essie," I say, trying not to hurt her like she's hurt me or let Leona or Essie know how bad Essie has hurt me. "I want you to go with us."

We stand around for a minute or two that go like millennia. Then Essie says, sounding all misunderstood and rejected, "I think friends should be honest with each other."

Leona opens her mouth, thinks better of it, and closes her mouth again. We're standing around with too much and too little to say when Moses saunters up the walk. The Hawk battering him, and billowing inside his jacket that cuts him at the waist.

Moses bangs through the lobby door with, "Hey, are you ready to do that thang?" Not shy at all about meeting my two friends for the first time.

"Do what thang?" Leona says archly, so that I blush to my roots.

"Hey, Moses. This is Leona Pryor." I point to my tall friend. Moses nods. "This is Essie Witherspoon." I point to my wild-headed friend. He nods to her. Then Moses and Leona start talking about her father's barbecue and our mission today to find a home or two for my work. Essie and he don't hit it off so well. Each acts like the other isn't there. We button our coats and head out into the Hawk.

Leona and Essie have already helped me load those paintings that were kept in our dorm suite and Hamla's room. Now we're at the Art Department, where my work is stacked in a cubbyhole.

Miss Julienne is the only one there when we get there. She's sitting in a studio staring at a canvas. For once her hair is out of the restrictive barrette and flows and splashes all over her shoulders. Cutting across one side of her face in a blonde descent like Veronica Lake, an actress from the forties known for that hairstyle and a smoky voice. Once Silence called my mother Veronica Lake because in those days Caroline wore her pressed hair cascading down over one eye. Miss Julienne's eyes are smoky and thoughtful as she turns to greet me when I go in. She's still hugging herself and doesn't quit when my friends come in behind me.

"Magdalena," she says. "I was just thinking of you."

I don't ask her what she was thinking. "These are my friends, Miss Julienne. They came to help me take my stuff." "This is Miss Julienne, my teacher," I tell Leona, Essie, and Moses. The three of them look at her like she's Miss Ann and why am I calling her "Miss."

"I've told Magdalena repeatedly to just call me Ana. But she insists on this 'Miss' business," Miss Julienne grins almost apologetically to them. "Ana. A-n-a. One lonely *n* between two *a*'s. That's my name. One *n* quite alone." Now I'm wondering why Miss Julienne keeps hammering in this alone business. She's looking at Moses. And he's looking at her.

And Leona, Essie, and I are looking at the two of them looking at each other.

Miss Julienne's lashes sweep up and down and she is finished with the survey. "Maggie, I don't understand why you've never asked your friend Moses to model for us. I think he'd be excellent. Would you, Mr.——?"

"Outlaw. Moses Outlaw. I didn't bring any business cards with me, but I can give you——"

"Maggie's got your number, Moses. She'll give it to the department. We have to get going." Leona is so smooth when she's obstructing something.

I guess Leona broke the trance because Miss Julienne is Miss Julienne again. All encouragement. "Maggie, please don't take your work too far away, and be sure it's stored securely. You mustn't damage your canvases. I want you to submit to the Paris program." All to me as she walks with us to the room where student work is stored. And to my friends, "Magdalena is one of our most talented students. If not the most talented this old fuddy-duddy department's seen in many years. I take great prideful pleasure in her work." She is walking a little ahead of us.

Leona cuts her eyes at Essie-the-doubtful. I-told-you-so is all in the glance. Essie acts like she doesn't see.

Moses is looking sleepily at Miss Julienne's big, sausage legs. Until he looks at me looking at him. Then he slides into a sheepish grin.

"You got an ID, mister?" the security guard asks Moses when we come out of the building for the last time, having left Miss Julienne gazing smokily at her easel. His hand is poised on his gun like a cowboy marshal entering a saloon. "This is private property."

"I beg your pardon." Leona is always the first to beg pardons. She does it really haughtily.

"Mr. Outlaw is my guest," I tell Mr. Security.

"Yeah. I was invited. Glad you asked instead of shooting to kill." Moses keeps moving to the station wagon and negotiates putting in my paintings. Carefully wrapped.

"Let's see what you people are taking out of here," Mr. Security says.

"You wouldn't happen to have any relatives in Mississippi, would you?" He looks just like Sheriff Columbine of Mimosa and I wish my dead grandmama would take a morning stroll down the tree-lined path. Give him a show, so he'll quit bugging us.

"This is for your own protection, young ladies," the security man says. Then he talks into his walkie-talkie. Telling somebody where he is and how he's about to inspect some materials that "four Black people" are taking out of Pilgrim Centennial Hall. "Let's see some ID here, girls," he says once he's finished his call home.

"Girls," Essie says, like her ears are failing her. Or her eyes.

"These sisters are Black women, mister." Moses is leaning on the car, pissed off.

"I got daughters their age," Mr. Security snaps. "ID, please."

I snatch up one of my paintings in a big gesture so he'll know how annoyed I am. The cloth hanging over it whips in the wind when I unveil the painting called *Gold*. "In the right-hand corner is my name, Magdalena Grace. That's the same name on this ID," I say. "That's the same face on this ID."

He scrutinizes everything carefully, making as big a show as I have. I know he can't really read my signature on the painting, because I'm still experimenting with the way I sign my artworks. He acts like he can read it, though, bending down and squinting hard into the canvas. "Okay, then," he says finally.

And we think the inquisition is over and start loading up again. "Let's see the rest," he interrupts us.

"All these paintings!" Leona exclaims.

"That's right," Mr. Security says.

We are standing there looking at each other when Miss Julienne steps out the door.

"Is there a problem, Mr. Reynolds?"

"Just doing my job, Miss Julienne. You know these—students?"

"I do," she answers simply like a marriage vow.

"I need to know what they're taking out of university buildings."

"They're taking Miss Grace's work out, Mr. Reynolds. I just gave it to them."

"Oh, you gave it to them? All of it?"

"It's all hers."

"Okay, then. Just checking." Then he tips his brim to Miss Julienne. And ignores the rest of us. Never laying an apology—"Sorry for the inconvenience." Or, "You understand it was only a formality"—or any of that on the dark four of us.

Miss Julienne just looks sorrowfully at us. Then she goes on her way. Takes a few steps and turns around. "You really ought to consider that year in Paris, Magdalena."

When she's gone, Leona just says, "Whitepeople, Whitepeople." We get in the station wagon, my work in the back, Leona at the wheel and Essie beside her, Moses and me in the backseat. Then Leona floors the accelerator and we shoot off down the tree-lined drive like out-laws, renegade Blacks too quick and too furious to get hung up again in Whiteman's law. Daring Mr. Reynolds to give chase.

✦

I am a vision in white going up a flight of stairs to a temple. The temple is like the glass-domed administration building here at Eden. Its glass roof shines so the sun must have made its home in it. I am wearing a long white dress and I am smiling. There are presences behind me, accompanying me. Yet I cannot name them, even though I know I know who they are. When I am almost at the head of the stairs and stepping onto the landing, I realize my teeth have fallen out in front and I am holding teeth in my hands. I am horrified. And more horrified when one of my companions tells me I have stained my lovely dress. I have sat in something or my own menstrual blood has soiled me. I am ashamed. A deep well of shame is inside me. I can feel it heavy and bottomless. I am beyond tears, toothless, and spoiled. Everyone can see me.

When we leave Eden behind, the dream comes back to me from the early morning.

Nixon is on the car radio when Leona switches it on. So she switches it off. Moses says, "Naw, naw. We got to hear what he talking about. He might be talking about my life or my death." So she turns it back on. He's talking about the War-that's-not-a-war-only-people-die-anyway.

When Nixon's over, Moses starts entertaining us by signifying on how ugly and ambitious the man is. "You know that Whiteboy's going

112

to want to be president forever. They're going to have to drop a bomb on the White House to get him out."

"Why is that?" I ask, just so he'll keep talking, making us feel cheerful. "It took him so long to get in! He cried for the position in 1960 before the whole nation. Now you know that man has absolutely no cool when it comes to power and losing it. So he is going to be there forever. You mark my words."

Essie is not listening to this. She's looking out the window in a world of her own. Wherever she looks she sees Rhonda as William's bride. Rhonda in a very traditional European wedding dress. William subdued in a tuxedo. And Rhonda in white lace with a train at her back, a trail of white following her. The daddy walking her up the aisle. William waiting at the altar. I know that's who's walking alongside us on the sidewalk. Couples. Duplications of Rhonda and William. The question I asked when I heard is out there walking with the couples hand in hand. Was William the judge's fee for working for free to save Steve Rainey's life, to keep him out of prison?

Leona is right with Moses in the signifying game. Moses is still on Nixon.

"Now that's a face that belongs on a Halloween mask. I swear to God," Moses says.

"Anybody that uugly." (The u is long in *ugly*.) "Anybody that ugly has got to be ambitious." I think Moses and Aint Kit will appreciate each other. She's got a thing about ugliness too. "Anybody that hard to look at got to have power so he can make people have to look at him as punishment. You know ugly people into revenge!"

The car is swerving Leona is laughing so hard.

"Stop, Moses," I say. "She can't drive with you talking crazy." But I don't want him to stop, because the good humor of his talking has loosened the tension of our encounter with the security man, and the tension that reeks off Essie. Even she must laugh now, turned a little in the seat to look at Moses. "You know they even got some Nixon jockey shorts. Yeah, they do." We know he's lying and now I tell him so.

"I have seen them, woman, with my own eyes. His face is on the crotch, his mouth is on the fly. And on the backside is printed PRESIDENTIAL ASS. I'm going to get me some. I'm going to get me some as soon as I get paid. Maggie, why don't you pick me up a pair?"

I just look at him like he's gotten too personal now. The Mouth moves on to something else. And he's like that all the way out of Eden and through the City, heading toward Great Zimbabwe. "I'll be glad to be at this Great Zimbabwe crib where the real kings and queens are. Niggahs at Eden can't even burn up a building without burning their own selves up."

I leap to Steve Rainey's defense. "He said he was into self-immolation like one of those Buddhist monks in Vietnam."

"Self-who? Burning hisself up."

"Never mind." I miss Steve Rainey's sarcasm now.

"Niggahs couldn't pour piss out of a boot if it had the directions written on the heel. That's what I heard this grandpa say about Nixon."

Moses has never been to Great Zimbabwe. The rest of the ride we tell him about it. Our eyes shining again at the prideful activity of the bustling women in the lobby marketplace, the musicians who could make oodles of money on records for Motown but who refuse the Whiteman's marketplace.

He asks about the name, "Great Zimbabwe. I ain't never heard that sound before." He's from a project on another side of the City.

"It's named after the ruins of a great civilization. From around the eleventh century. They're in Rhodesia." I educate the brother.

"Rhodesia, huh? Ain't that named after a hunky?" None of us answers that one. He knows anyway. "How they go in and name something that obviously already been named?"

"Don't act surprised. They named you," Essie says, unnecessarily nasty.

"How you know his forefather ain't take the name of Outlaw after Emancipation?" Leona says, because she doesn't like Essie's attitude, even if she is hurting.

"Lincoln and Washington were already filled up. Yeah." Essie's in a dreadful mood. A misery she's taking out on everybody. "We applied for those names just like we applied to live in projects. We're just stupid," she snaps.

Then it occurs to me that Essie is anxious because the second and last time FBO went to Great Zimbabwe for rekinkification, she got to sit with William because Rhonda had other things to do. So the Great House of

Stone is Essie's house of false hope. And our trip to it now is too much looking back for her. She is salty and wounded. Not Essie at all. And Moses is meeting her for the first time.

He can't stand her.

*

Great Zimbabwe before noon is quiet as a ruin. The lobby stripped of the tables and wares and loud bartering and haggling over the price of things. Moses is not impressed. He just stands in the center of the room with *Gold* in his arms. He's looking around sizing things up and finding it less grand than we had promised. Standing in the bare lobby, I know the magic of Great Zimbabwe is in the people and the music and dance that come with them. The huge mural on the wall is overwhelming, but I know now it is not nearly beautiful enough. I look at the fingers on the figures and can tell the artist had a problem with the delicate, disciplined strokes. The hands are like mittens with lines drawn through them. The fingers on my painting are fingers, each hand individual and well defined. I feel happy now. Maybe they'll ask me to teach an art class here. Of course, they'll be so happy to welcome my work home. And honor me as a new genius of the race. I smile as I keep looking at the hands that look like mittens and boxing gloves on the heroes on the wall.

"Who does this go to?" Moses asks me, lifting *Gold* a little to indicate what he's talking about. He sets it on the floor.

A side door opens and a group of long-dressed sisters comes out. Their hair braided in intricate styles. They sail past us saying, "Habari gani," sailing like a fleet of yachts. Impervious to our blue jeans.

Moses starts to grin real stupidly. Looking like a dope.

"Oh, close your mouth before the last fly flies in," I snarl at him. A sweet expression on my face. The sisters can braid hair, so can I. And I can paint. I can paint like nobody's business but my own.

I ask one of the sisters if she can help us. She pauses for a moment.

"I have a painting. I'd like to know if Great Zimbabwe would want to hang it here." I'm a little shy.

The sister is too. "Let me see if I can get one of the brothers to speak with you. I'll be right back." She bustles away in search of a brother.

"Maggie, you don't want to know if they want to hang it. Of course they want it. You should have just told her you brought a gift of your art for the community." Leona is exasperated by my shy ways. But we don't want to be aggressive with each other. On Blood Island we say Whitepeople are aggressive. So aggression is anathema. Bad form. And so Whitefolkish. We say so much on Blood Island.

We stand there fidgeting for a while. Moses keeps asking the names of different heroes on the wall. Leona tells him who people are. Essie is looking sad. Like an angel locked out of Paradise. That damned wedding.

The sister who cannot speak to us brings a brother who can. It is the priest who wears purple at the performances here. He is tiny and smiling. His smile takes us in.

"You've come to our Manhood Class, my brother?" He addresses Moses. The rest of us are suddenly invisible.

"Naw, I'm accompanying my lady. She's an artist."

"Oh, which—"

Moses introduces himself and me, then Essie and Leona. Moses who's the newcomer.

The tiny priest is still addressing Moses. "Now, my brother, if you were attending our Manhood Classes, you'd understand your lady is not a lady—" He holds up his little hand before Moses can get him good. "This beautiful sister is not a lady. She's a queen. An African Queen. Ladyship is some European nonsense we snatched up in our pathetic Negro days."

"I can dig where you coming from, brother." Moses smiles amiably. "My queen has some business with you. I'm with her." Moses is trying to direct the priest's attention toward me. It's not working.

The priest keeps at it. "Now you've introduced an important aspect of our Manhood Class. Brothers have to learn to TCB—take care of business. And quit forcing our queens into unnatural roles."

"I can dig that!" Moses says very seriously. "I'm accompanying her in order to educate her as to how to conduct business in the community." Moses is talking as verbosely as the priest now. "In case I am unavailable. She's an artist, ya understand. She's brought her painting for you to consider hanging it. Maggie, help me unveil this," he says like he's my lord and I'm not his lady but of a lower class.

"You can take the cover off, Moses," I say, because I'm not going to help him take charge over my work like I ain't here.

"Maybe you'd like Maggie to talk about it," Leona suggests.

The little priest must not have heard Leona, because he doesn't act like he has. But he had the same idea as she. At last he asks me, "Let us see the offering you've brought to the temple, young sister."

Moses has unveiled it by now. He hoists it up so the priest can take a look at it eye level. "Hmmm." Priest considers like he's tasting something.

"What is this called?"

"*Gold*," I tell him.

"Who are these people in the background behind the two gold-medal runners?"

"Drylongso. Just ordinary people," I answer, a shade puzzled because he couldn't figure it out.

"You mean Negroes. Those Negroes in the background indicating that these two perfect specimens of African manhood derived from Negroes shuffling and scuffling down south instead of the magnificent and noble Africans of our ancestry."

"But these are Africans in the background. See? They're in the distance. But you can see them." I just want to amend his oversight. Sure he'll see now. My puzzlement breaks into clarity. He reminds me of my brother who was Littleson in those years who is Lazarus now, standing over my shoulder, his arms crossed like an insolvent genie. Glaring at me authoritatively, then pointing at the letters I'd chalked on the side of the garage. That nasty word. That offended him. My handiwork.

The priest is milder in his reproof—his criticism subtler, in a benevolent guise. His arms are not barricaded across his chest. But there's nothing he need defend. Or so it seems. Other than this omitted gesture, the situation is the same. The supercilious demeanor. The rebuke. Only this time I'm not sure what I'm guilty of.

"Poor ignorant slaves. The Negro zero. And put our African kings and warriors right behind the two victorious runners. Then the young sister would really be making a statement."

"But don't you think it's special?" Leona almost yelps.

I want to cry, but I smile instead.

"Oh, yes, she'll be able to paint for our people one day. You see, all the art forms are the same. I am a musician and I've been practicing for many years. Many hours every day. Now I have perfected my art form and I'm fulfilling the Creator's plan for me. The sister's just got to keep on studying and learning and listening. The Creator's got something in mind for her."

All through this Moses hasn't said a word till he covers the painting back up.

"Nice rapping with you," he tells the little priest. He shakes his hand.

"Can I look for you to be at Manhood Class and you sisters at Womanhood Class?" the priest asks.

"Yeah, you keep an eye out for me, brother man," Moses says jovially. "Great Zimbabwe is really a gas. A natural gas. You doing something here." Moses is walking toward the door all the while. We're following. There's nothing much to say. Leona looks like she's about to explode. Essie looks sorrowful and a trifle smug. And I can feel myself looking like a truck ran over me, but I keep walking.

Moses slams the door to the car trunk. I don't look at anybody. Just sit staring at the front of Great Zimbabwe. The marquee spells out the letters in red. The dream begins to make sense now that I'm feeling so bad. Leona dare not say a word, since it was her bright idea to come here in the first place. Essie is torn between being right about me not being so special and reacting to my pain. If she says a word to me, I'm ready for her. The dream wasn't about her after all. It wasn't about her dressing her dreams in bridal white, then being disappointed by William. It's about me. Silly me. The way I'm feeling now. I can feel Moses climb in beside me. I don't look at him, but I can tell he's not joking now. I can feel his eyes on me, full of sympathy. Leona is at the wheel, paying more attention to driving than I've ever seen her do before.

It's cold outside, but I let my window down a little bit. Nobody complains. I suck in the chilly air, taking big gulps. Swallowing my own hurt. Moses starts talking now. "That little half-size runt got a face like my genitalia." He is trying hard to make me laugh. "That smooshed-in face with that little hole for a mouth. Them ears hanging down on either side of his mug, if that ain't look like my privates, I ain't never seen them."

Moses has the cure for everything. He looses his wild tongue on the perpetrator of my humiliation. I really have to stick my head out the window now. Grateful tears cover my eyes, ready to fall. If I started crying now my eyes would float down with the tears. Two empty sockets be left to accuse the world of my misery.

Because I'm not looking at him Moses keeps on, "I was scared for y'all and myself. Any minute that private-faced fool was going to pee on us . . ."

"He didn't," Leona says, her voice all thick with what she's feeling. "I am sorry I ever told you to go over there. Stupid people are a big disappointment." Essie doesn't put anything warm in this pot of comforting words. She says, "You should go back there when you're real good and famous and make them eat crow." This is so mixed up and mixed hearted I'm mad enough to snatch the imminent tears back. I do. Next I bore holes in the back of Essie's head with my eyes that can turn back rivers. She's got one more time on this day to mess with me.

✦

From Aint Kit's porch you can smell the lake. If her brown brick house doesn't get its immediate breath, it gets its second wind. Winds tend to run cool from the lake around Aint Kit's place.

From the fenced-in yard aback the house her hungry dogs howl like someone's nearly dead. Maybe it's them. Starved as they are for food and gentle affection. Sternly, she goes out back once or twice a week with a tin of bones and spare morsels of meat. On special occasions she hauls out whole cooked hams and throws them down. Racks of roasted lamb and grilled steaks thick as the heads of all her ex-husbands. These occasions are few and yet enough for her dogs to wait for. Aint Kit's acts of love are capricious, difficult to predict. They keep the dogs alive.

"Don't they know they're supposed to howl at the moon?" Leona says. It's afternoon. The day is bright and chilly. And we're bumping against each other on the porch. I've pressed the bell. It has four names on it: Grace, Jenkins, DuValier, and Jones. All of the names are Aint Kit. But she likes Grace and DuValier best. Grace slips off her tongue. DuValier fits her like a pair of white kid gloves. We're waiting for her to answer the door, listening to the dogs yapping and howling. Tearing up the thick, crisp air with their teeth.

"They sound like I feel," Essie says. And I feel sorry for her and move a little bit closer so that our shoulders touch. She gives me a smile, frail and rueful.

Then the door opens slowly, and then the wrought iron gate in front of it. We step back a little so that the iron gate clears us and gives us a good view of Aint Kit in her blue nightgown and negligee. She looks like a movie star. Glamorous and disheveled.

"I was just getting ready to call your mama to see what happened to y'all," she grumbles, her voice sick and atremble.

"Hi, Aint Kit. I'm sorry we're late." I stumble forward, banging my canvases against the doorjamb. Her cheek is cool and silky when I kiss her. You have to kiss Aint Kit. She doesn't leave you any choice. She turns the side of her face to the sound of your face and she waits. As if we owed her kisses. I suppose I do today, since my mother has asked her for storage space for my paintings in her home.

I've stepped over the threshold, and now I face it with her.

"These are my friends who helped me bring my paintings," I introduce them as a group. Then I introduce them one by one.

"This is Essie Witherspoon."

"Oooh, look at all that pretty hair," Aint Kit shouts, marveling at Essie's mane. Aint Kit loves hair, almost as much as she loves money. It, too, is a commodity of a kind.

"This is Leona Pryor."

"Your daddy is a real businessman. He got that good-tasting rib restaurant. That launderette. And that grocery and liquor store all up on Seventy-Fifth Street. His establishments cover an entire block. They call it Pryor Providence."

None of us tells Aint Kit it's Pryor Province and he has a funeral home too. She's too happy sounding, like a reporter for a financial newspaper. I guess Mama told her about Leona.

Essie and Leona step over the threshold into Aint Kit's domain.

"And this is Moses Outlaw."

"Oh, you go to the university too?"

"No, ma'am, I don't." Moses actually acts shy before my would-be movie-star aunt.

"He's my friend," I tell Aint Kit.

"Oh." Aint Kit's voice goes flat. "Well, step on in and leave that cold air out there."

Moses does as he's told.

"Hang yo coats in that chifforobe there," Aint Kit commands us. Pointing to an oaken wardrobe, delicately carved and thin legged, situated in the hall.

"Maggie, take their coats for me. My back been worrying me. I can't lift nothing too heavy." Aint Kit bends her tiny self over a little, and puts her hand on her side. The fabric of her negligee swishes. "I almost couldn't struggle out of bed this morning. But I say let me get on up because my Maggie Lena coming over and bringing her friends."

I blame Mama for this and I'm going to get her. This storage-space ploy was to get me to come see my aunt, who always has an ailment and a story. Or both in one.

"Y'all come on into this big, empty house. Bay done gone and left me here all by myself." This is pity talk that Aint Kit is good at. Her shoulders slump, her head falls into her neck, her hand is on her hip holding that now, and her eyes are full of the pain of neglect. The body of a mother abandoned. Then those pained eyes fall on Moses, and apprehension sets in. He doesn't go to Eden University. He must be a burglar. I can read her mind. Everyone wants what Aint Kit has. Aint Kit starts talking real loud.

"I got me a great big gun, though. I'm in this house all by myself and I got guns and knives planted all over it where only I can get them when I need them. So no burglar better not come up in here looking for nothing or he gone find a double barrel looking in his eye." Aint Kit shouts all this. So loud she must want the dogs to hear. "And them dogs back there all I got to say is 'kill' and a roguish niggah is dead and tore to pieces."

We can't help but laugh at the incredible pictures Aint Kit makes. These extemporaneous threats barely masking her panicky fear of loss.

"Mama said my paintings would be safe here," I comment.

"And anything else you got," Aint Kit assures me.

She's quiet for a little while as she pushes apart the French doors that lead into the living room. When she speaks again her voice is sugary and coy, "Y'all want to see my house?"

So far everyone but me has been struck dumb by Aint Kit's house, in which delicacies jostle each other to delight the eyes. Now Essie breathes out, "Oh, wow." Like she cannot believe her overcrowded eyes.

Aint Kit is not disappointed by their responses as each one creeps close to some individual wonder of craftsmanship—a chair, a sofa, a lamp, a knickknack—in the blind accumulation of good taste and bad. I'm used to Aint Kit's property. She introduced it to me more than once.

After my friends have feasted their eyes on the living room, Aint Kit directs us to pick up my paintings and follow her up the stairs. It is like climbing a mountain of moss. The carpet is so thick we lose our feet in it, and leave depressed footprints.

The second floor of Aint Kit's house is four bedrooms and one and a half baths. Aint Kit likes to say half bath like she's got something historic like a bathtub sawed in two by a magician and the half a tub that belongs to her can still hold water. That's half a bath.

"Maggie Lena knows she always has a place to stay."

Aint Kit had more lives than a cat, and almost as many husbands. Arrogant and silky as a feline she slinks through the rest of the house that's filled with mementos from husbands. "My husband won the Golden Gloves that year. My husband was a heavy hitter in the Negro Leagues. And that year they went to Los Angeles and he brought me back a plate from Hollywood. My husband was a chef. My husband played in Nat King Cole's band. My husband was a railroad man on the Atchison, Topeka and the Santa Fe. My husband was an older gentleman; he served in the Spanish-American War. My husband was a gambler. He gave me his lucky dice. He call 'em Kit Kats." Everything glamorous and dangerous a Blackman could do, one of Aint Kit's husbands has done it. Right now it doesn't make Aint Kit any never mind if she'd actually married all those men or not. They were her husbands; they lived with her, slept beside her, held her, gave her some or all of their paychecks, showered in her half bath, bathed in her full bath, soaked their calloused feet in her silver bucket, and listened to her vast collection of blues and jazz records while misery and delight somersaulted inside of them.

We are in the attic, having circled the second floor and seen the inheritances from husbands and all the niceties Aint Kit's squeezed out of dollar bills, out of the days she bathed the naked behinds of old Whitepeople, sloshed their too-hard or too-soft stools out of bedpans and into blue-water toilet bowls, stripped beds and folded on new, crisp sheets with North Lake Line Hospital stamped on each one.

"I would love a house like yours, Miss Kit," says Essie, who's lived in a project apartment since she was ten. Essie, kneeling, is looking out the tiny diamond window that overlooks the backyard. Leona's looking over Essie's shoulder. Moses is just looking.

"Those are the dogs!" Leona exclaims. "They are big!"

"They not really dogs," Kit says authoritatively, like she's letting us in on the world's best-kept secret. "They really a cross between a panther and a sheepdog."

"How'd those two ever get together?" Moses asks. I don't say a word, just get really busy arranging my paintings in a corner, protecting them from the air that slips like a burglar through the window and the sun that makes its entrance through glass. Trying not to laugh when Aint Kit doesn't miss a beat.

"Opposites attract," she says. Aint Kit eyes Moses to be sure he believes her dogs' lineage. "It was a rainy night and somebody fell asleep on the job. The panther escaped from the Barnum and Bailey Circus and broke in my yard to get at my sheep bitch—"

Leona and Essie look away when Aint Kit says "bitch." Just like they don't say it.

Aint Kit doesn't miss anything. "A bitch is a female dog," she announces with superb superiority. Great respectability.

Moses is caught up in the story. "That panther got away, huh? Like that lion that ran away from the zoo years ago and took a catnap in the subway station around where I live."

Kit's quick. "You live around Sleepy Cats Station?" she asks Moses. She's poised to accuse. Both eyes half close in close scrutiny. "The only Black people around Sleepy Cats Station live in high-rise projects."

"Yeah," Moses answers, surly. Then he starts walking around the attic, blowing dust off boxes. Dust falls thickly to the floor.

Aint Kit circles in for the kill. "Where you say you live?" she sniffs.

"He didn't," I answer for Moses. I'm stern and Aint Kit looks at me to see if my face matches the finality in my voice. She backs off and tries to come another way.

"I used to work at the private hospital over around there. I know that area of the City very well." That's all she says for now. She doesn't want to offend me. I'm one of few nieces who put up with her. So she starts acting like she's only got my paintings on her mind.

"Let me see some of your work you got, Miss Maggie Lena. Show me."

I unveil *Gold*.

"That's very nice," she says.

I unveil *Remember*.

"That's just beautiful."

I unveil *Figs*. Aunt Silence is on it. Aunt Silence is different from Aint Kit and the same. When I wrote her about this guy I was going out with she asked me what kind of dreams he dreams. Not his street address like Aint Kit, but what kind of dreams he dreams. She's worse than Aint Kit. As hard to please as I am.

Aint Kit sighs when she lays eyes on *Figs*. "Oooh, I want it. How much you gone let me have that one for?"

I'm flustered by Aint Kit's enthusiasm and don't have any idea what to tell her. "You don't want this, Aint Kit." What makes me say that? Self-protection? Leona frowns up her mouth at my ineptitude at selling. She's got market women in her lineage. Aint Kit just gets mad.

"Don't tell me what I want," her voice cracks like a starched sheet. "I know what I want. Ain't that me and my mama on there?"

"Yes."

"Ain't that Charity and Lee-Bet?"

"Yes."

"Ain't that yo mama, Caroline?"

"Yes, ma'am."

Lovingly she looks at herself as a creature of paints.

"You ain't tell me you had painted none of us." She looks some more. Looking enamored, enraptured, and tender.

"This is too beautiful," she whispers.

"Tell me how much you want for this now," she says greedily, like she's been starving all her life for just this, like she'd drive a truck through me to get it.

"Well, what do you think?" I say to Aint Kit. I'm sounding to myself like my mother at her most tentative. I had half planned to give *Figs* to Mama.

"Don't you think we should check with Miss Julienne or somebody who knows about pricing?" Leona poses the question. She has an idea of what I should sell *Figs* for, but she's got too much sense to say so in front of Aint Kit. My aunt has the look of pirates in her eyes. But that changes after Leona gets in the business.

"Well, we don't have to discuss figures now," Kit acts offended. "How many times do I have to tell you, Maggie, when you talk money talk, it's supposed to be in private. You supposed to talk low." She bats her eyelashes rapidly, dismissing all but *Figs* from her sight. "If you got your paintings stored away okay, now we can go downstairs and hang this up."

"Would you like me to carry that for you, ma'am?" Moses reaches for *Figs*, which Aint Kit is carting awkwardly.

"That won't be necessary." She declines his proffered assistance. Moses looks offended now.

I say, "Aint Kit, why don't you let Moses carry that down for you? Your back is bothering you."

Aint Kit is torn between her early "Oh, my aching back" and her new claim on *Figs*. Reluctantly, she lets Moses take the canvas. "Be careful how you tote that down these stairs."

All the way down the stairs, she sends to Moses over her shoulder, "Don't damage that now," "That's costing me," and "Look out for the turn right now."

This is the order of descent: Aint Kit, Moses, me, Leona, and Essie. Leona and Essie are a whispering caboose. Counting off the crazy rumbling of Aint Kit, the engine of our adventure in acquisition and denial.

In the front hall again, Aint Kit instructs Moses to set *Figs* by the mantel. Then she sends me to the kitchen for hammer and nails. She stands watch over her treasure. When I return, she goes in search of a gold chain to hang the heavy canvas on. She doesn't care that it's not framed properly. She wants her beauty in a hurry. "I can do that later on," she says.

Aint Kit has a floor safe under her bed. Her bedroom is just above the living room, where we're sitting and trying not to make comments about her. I just shake my head when my friends look at me with questioning eyes. There's scraping and bumping and pounding going on overhead. Like tumblers doing tumbling competitions. I surmise my Aint Kit is moving her bed and pulling up floorboards, then spinning that dial on her safe until it gives a soft click like a cherub doing knee bends, or a rattlesnake assassinated before it can find a tune for premeditated murder. A broken warning.

Anything could be in that safe. Insurance policies from husbands. Deeds to confiscated lands. I wouldn't be surprised if my Aint Kit had a deed to an Indian reservation. She is so proud of her Indian ancestry. When I asked her who it was exactly in our family who was Indian, and what tribe he or she came from, she rattled off a lot of pretty names. My daddy just said we were Blackfoot. Blackface. Blackbehind and Blackskin. Then he laughed his ah-ho laugh. Like he knew a bigger joke than that about life.

Aint Kit told Bay that she keeps Bay's adoption papers in her safe. But Bay says she doesn't, because she looked in the safe for them. Bay can crack anybody's combination. She has a gift for opening things. People's heads included.

Aint Kit keeps marriage licenses in her keeping place. But she doesn't keep any divorce papers. Bay says that's because she doesn't have any. Bay looked. Aint Kit keeps stocks and bonds, and a tiny rosary she said the beads were made of the teeth of all her stillborn babies who were born dead with heads full of teeth. When I was little she showed me and it made me have nightmares. Like miniature icicles those teeth on silver string that ended in a cross she said was made from the melted-down handle of a pearl-butt derringer her gambler husband killed a man with.

I dreamed that rosary when I was a little girl. I prayed that rosary all night long so many nights I began to dread sleep. Till Mama made me tell what made me avoid bedtime besides the love of old movies and an early predilection for rambling through the quiet house looking for ghosts and squashing roaches that gave a party on the kitchen floor when the lights were turned off.

Mama hit the ceiling when I told her what Aint Kit had told me about her rosary. That very minute she called Aint Kit on the kitchen phone. I was sitting at the kitchen table, dark circles under my dark eyes, eating oatmeal with bacon bits sprinkled on top and thick canned milk circling the cereal the way I liked it. Little lumps of sugar surprises in the oatmeal.

Mama on the phone. Madaddy in the bed he'd just gone back to because he'd worked overtime. It must have been near Christmas. He worked double shifts to buy the Christmas clothes and toys and fruit and nuts. Christmas and Easter were when we got clothes. Not fall for school because we wore uniforms, like I was wearing my blue jumper and starched white blouse, white ankle socks, and loafers, sitting at the table. Spoon in hand. My feet not touching the floor. Swinging like a hanged man.

Madaddy told Mama to just set Kit straight. "Set her straight, Ca'line," he'd yelled over me.

"She yo sister, Sam."

"And I know her!" Then he stomped on bare feet back to bed.

Aint Kit was at home. Her day off from the hospital.

"Kit?" my mother said into the mouthpiece. Then she stood up a little straighter to make her voice firmer. "What's this you been telling Maggie about a rosary made out of babies' teeth?"

Mama didn't say anything for a long time. Just looking at me nibbling on a bacon bit. Then she said, "Kit, I know you have lost children and I'm blessed to have so many, but right now my baby got dark marks under her eyes cause she scared to sleep for the nightmares you gave her with that rosary."

Mama didn't say anything for a while, just looking at me with my top lip and nose in a glass of milk. My eyes, over the whitewashed glass, looking back at her.

"Okay. Okay," Mama said finally, and real disgusted. "Just don't tell my child any more stories. Okay?" Mama had been bending to hang up, now she stood straight up again. Furious. "I'll tell her about my mama when she needs to know. What you specializing in—nightmares to children?"

Mama had her mouth open to say something else, but she didn't. She clamped her mouth shut just letting some hot uhhh-hmmmms slide through like razor blades so hot they red. "Well, you have a nice day then. Good-bye." Mama said.

Then she looked at me. She was breathing fast and deep. Her voice turning soft like a tissue paper falling on my eyelids. "Hurry up and eat your breakfast, sugar. Mama take you to first grade. Kit ain't got no babies' teeth on no string."

Everything was all right because I knew my mama would save me from the truth. Those were the teeth of babies on that rosary. Teeth like little ovals of ice. The way I would imagine ovaries later on when I read *Growing Up and Liking It*, the little blue book the sanitary people put out. I remember teeth and ovaries and not liking it at all.

Aint Kit probably has that book in her safe too. Because she holds the strangest things so dear. I know the stub from the first hotel room she shared with a man is in there (when Whitefolks let Blackpeople stay in Northern hotels). And the label from the wine bottle they shared. And postcards she never sent anybody from Las Vegas and Niagara Falls, though she wrote messages to each and every one on the back about the good time she was having and wishing everyone was there.

Aint Kit comes down the stairs. She's carrying a thick gold chain in one hand, and dangling a silver rosary of babies' teeth in the other. The teeth click together when she walks into the room. She hands the gold chain to Moses, saying, "Here. You can hammer this chain onto the back and hang the picture off it." She doesn't mind his help. She's supervising.

My eyes transfixed, I say, "Aint Kit, is that what I think you have in your hand?"

She gathers the teeth into her palms and cups them there, moving her fingers until the teeth click together like castanets.

"This is very precious to me, Magdalena. You know that. That's why I'm giving this to you." With a grand gesture she drops the rosary into my hand.

But both my hands are fists and I won't loose them. She pries open my fingers to make me take the nightmare rosary. And I giggle and wail at the same time like the nervous, frightened schoolgirl I am once the teeth settle in my palm.

"What can I do with this, Aint Kit?"

Aint Kit looks at Moses out the corner of her eye. He's hammering the chain into the back of the canvas and is missing all of this. Leona and Essie keep minding Moses's business. They aren't paying any attention to Aint Kit and me either.

"This is protection," Aint Kit says, so low you'd think she was following her own advice about the way to talk about money. "This rosary will keep you safe from bad influences. So next time you won't follow no Malcolm X elements into no university building." She's talking about the Takeover of April 1968.

"I wasn't following up behind anybody, Aint Kit. I went because I decided."

"Well, this rosary will help you with yo decisions. When you got this in your hands, I know God listens."

I look at the barbaric string in my hand. "How you know he doesn't turn his head the other way?" I mutter.

Aint Kit is aiming instructions at Moses. Moses is standing on a stepladder taking down a portrait of blue-tinted, big-eyed waifs with Dondi haircuts gathered around the open grave of a sparrow that one of the melancholic waifs is holding. The grieving urchins cry platinum tears that are raised from the canvas. The background is black velour. The sentiment of the scene is so fake, so put-up, I can't look at it without wanting to crack up.

Leona makes a comment about those big-eyed waifs having a vast extended family. Ubiquitous. Begging for tears in a world we can find so much more to cry for.

Next Moses places my painting on the nail and Aint Kit tells him to step down so she can see if it's crooked or not. It is. She says. And she climbs up the ladder and positions the painting just so. We don't notice any difference between her fixing and Moses's.

I almost cry when my painting is at last in the place above Aint Kit's mantel. Feelings tumble inside me. I don't have a name for them. They have to do with Mimosa, Arbor Avenue, which turns into Plenty, Eden, and the distances between them. They have to do with Great Zimbabwe, the EARTH, and the high-rises Moses and Essie grew up in. They have to do with Silence and Sarah Mahalia Lincoln Dancer, who keeps her head in her own hands, even after death by decapitation. I can taste a figlike taste of a longing in my mouth as I look at my painting of the Grace women—my mother, my grandmother, and aunts.

I don't know if it's my own hunger or each one of theirs that fills my mouth. My hand is so tight on the rosary that when I open it there are tooth prints.

Aint Kit is more hospitable to Moses now that her newly acquired treasure is in place. She offers him a sandwich, but he says we must be going. And Essie and Leona are so anxious to space they're fidgeting.

Aint Kit tries to entice us with promises of fresh greens and chicken. She brags that she grows her own vegetables and asks when was the last time we had collards just come from the ground, so I don't say anything. But Moses with something to brag about at last says his mother has a vegetable garden.

"Where's that?" Aint Kit is keen. Back to being a snob.

Moses having won a portion of her respect by being such a willing worker is not as intimidated by her, or he's so glad to be leaving her house he doesn't care about her good opinion.

"My mother keeps a little vegetable garden on the porch outside her front door. She's got a tomato plant on the railing on our floor. I live in the project up north." Now that he's said that, he has to say more. "Yeah, we growing everything in them 'jects. Kids. Hair on my daddy's head. He was going bald. And she growin greens and beans and tomatoes and stuff like that in a garden on a vacant lot."

Noting the belligerence in Moses's tone, Essie and Leona look away, fussing with their hats, coats, and gloves.

Aint Kit tries to be agreeable. "That's really nice she grows food. Cuts down on your grocery bills so much."

Sparks are coming out of Moses's eyes by now and he glares at Aint Kit. Essie and Leona get in a big hurry and kind of propel Moses to the door and out.

They wait for me in the car. I can see Moses fuming through the car window.

"Two poor people don't need to be together, Maggie. You need somebody with some cash money." Aint Kit is being very kind. She's whispering regretfully.

"You had all the rich husbands, Aint Kit. Ain't no more left for me."

"Get on way from me with your sassy mouth!" She has to laugh while she shoos me away. "Thank you for my painting. It is just beautiful." She snatches me back close to her and turns her cheek for the kiss I always owe her. Obediently, I peck her cheek.

Her friendly yelling follows me down the steps. "Y'all be good now . . . Take care of yoself—come on back and see me sometime." Her blue negligee swirls around her like long wisps of smoke and her nightgown lifts to uncover fur-trimmed glass slippers like Cinderella's.

In the backseat I lean over Moses and wave to the woman in blue. Essie and Leona wave too. Moses cocks his head in a single-gesture salute.

Leona backs out of the driveway. Aint Kit is hollering. "Bay gone—so you my daughter now!" I wince out a smile.

Aint Kit's starving dogs sound like a pack of wolves on the edge of the camp light waiting for the fire to go out so they can break loose and tear somebody limb from limb. I slip my rosary into my pocket, knowing full well that's the only payment I'll get from Aint Kit for my painting.

The ride back to Eden is strained. Moses doesn't talk much. He won't hold hands with me when I offer him mine in thanks. He tells Leona to let him out at Sleeping Cats Station. Ashamed and not wanting us to watch him walk down that concrete path into his building. A path with little patches of grass on either side of it, like the way to a maximum-security prison. I want to ask him why he'd never told me about his mother's garden. Why I hadn't seen it. Or why he hadn't introduced me to his mother, but had introduced me to his friends. Instead, I just say, "Aint Kit gets on everybody's nerves. My daddy says she's always been like that." Like that: salt and sugar and ground-up glass.

The wind nearly blows Moses back in the car when he tries to get out. It balloons his jacket out around him as he zips it and peers back into the car at me, slamming the car door at the same time. I watch him doubling his stride, running to keep a good pace against the willful Hawk.

On the last part of the ride, Essie starts dreaming. "Miss Kit knows how to live," Essie enthuses. "She knows how to get what she wants." Leona looks at my face in the rearview mirror. Essie says the strangest things. Neither one of us says anything, so Essie says, "I'd like a big house like that. Only in a nice suburb. So I could be a model for kids to strive after."

She turns around to talk to me alone because Leona is concentrating so hard on traffic. "I mean, I know Miss Kit got a lot of junky stuff in her house. I wouldn't buy it. But she knows how to get what she wants. I can respect that." She turns back around and Leona cuts the engine. We are parked in front of the Sweet Flats. Home away from home again.

✦

Leona's gone to Blood Island to a set and after-set. She is annoyed because I told her I didn't expect any payment from Aint Kit for my painting. I didn't forget the storage fee. I didn't show her my rosary. I slipped it into my dresser drawer. Leona is irritated because Essie wouldn't go to the dance lest she run into William and his bride. Leona said William and Rhonda didn't own Blood Island, but Essie still wouldn't go. Peeved with us both, Leona left us. She was really beautiful in a yellow miniskirt and matching sweater, with big, dangling earrings that chatter louder than teeth. She's been practicing the new dance called the yoke. You shrug your shoulders, swing your arms, and hitch up your legs like you're trying to throw something off your back.

Leona does the yoke magnificently. Poised like a Baule sculpture, goddess of whatever there is to be goddess of.

Now it's just Essie and me.

Essie is afraid of ghosts.

One fear builds itself on another.

Soon after Essie was raped by Antonio Silkey, so soon the injuries to her girl body were not yet healed, and Essie still trembled and shrieked at the sound of footsteps behind her, a greater fear climbed on the shoulders of the one that stood above her bed.

Essie's grandmother, whom she called Mama, who raised Essie when Fredonia was too economically and emotionally ill-equipped to do so, died of kidney failure. Essie tells us how she cried unceasingly for three days after this. How she fled in terror from the funeral parlor and the shiny powder-blue casket in which her grandmother's body lay. How she fled after Fredonia held her by the shoulders and whispered that she must kiss the stiff powdered visage of her grandmother. Essie ran from the

132

room. She hurried home and hid in the closet and cried for three days longer.

Fredonia, drowning in her own grief, could not coax her out for food or anything. Finally, Woody broke down the closet door and brought Essie out. They took her to the doctor. After the force-feeding of juices and broths, the doctor gave Essie tranquilizers so she could sleep. Because, he said, "sleep is the healer." So, with the assistance of pills, Essie slept. And in her drug-induced peace she avoided the visitation of her grandmother's ghost. Because that visit was what she feared and wanted the most.

Facing her grandmother's ghost would have been facing her total abandonment. The last good-bye, loosing the insatiable longings of loss. But Essie had neither words nor understanding of this. She simply said she was afraid of ghosts.

She repeats that now when I tell her about my grandmother Sarah Mahalia Dancer, who walks down Old Letha Road with her head in her hand.

Now that William has wed Rhonda, Essie realizes their future together (which she has expended days dreaming on and draping in imaginary conversation, children, houses, meals eaten together, wars fought and won, sexual bliss exchanged and magnified) will never be. This impossible future haunts her. And the sympathetic and I-told-you-so looks of the bloods on the Island make mischief like poltergeists in her head.

So Essie had told me how she fears ghosts, and I sit on her bed with her and tell her about my grandmother who is a well-known ghost, albeit anonymous. What I have not yet told Leona. I don't know why not. I tell Essie to alleviate some of her misery. At worst it is a charming story.

She does stop crying to ask me, "Have you ever seen her, Maggie?" Her eyes round as the gold wire-rim glasses William wears, and larger.

"No," I answer. "But I want to."

"Why you want to see that dead woman?" Essie asks accusingly. She shivers a little under the bedcovers.

"I don't know. I guess I know she's got something to tell me."

"You just want something unusual to paint." Essie acts angry. "She better not come up in this room." She threatens me. Looks stern. And turns her face to the wall and her back to me.

Then I think I know why my grandmother has not come to me, even though I've prayed for her. There is a presence that bars her entry. And maybe some of the fear in Essie is in me too. After all, I don't know what to do with my troublesome life. Other than the work of my hands, I don't know what to do. And that scares me.

Lazarus

A baby-faced giant comes from outer space. His huge metallic boots leave deep dents in the earth. He steps on a row of houses on Arbor Avenue and leaves them a jumble of splintered toothpicks. He demolishes all of Mimosa: tombstones topple under his boots. The inhabitants of this Arbor Avenue–Mimosa land run, terrorized and grief-stricken, to the only safe place. A large brown school building several stories high. We run to the basement, thinking he cannot smash us or step on us if we are underground. But he follows us, attracted to the fluttering of our clothing as we race away, attracted to the soft tumble of our limbs as we scurry. He tears a hole in the building that I know is Eden, and peers down at us in the basement. We scramble to far, dark corners beyond his grasp. When he is busy worrying us to show ourselves (will he eat us? like a Cyclops or like Grendel?), some of us slip further down into the darkness into a subbasement of the school. I among them. Some distance from the building, we come up from the subbasement into a clear field, where we rally to fight the baby-faced giant. He comes for us and we are ready. I aim the cannon, a sweet cylinder, at him. Fire comes out the mouth of the cannon. The weapon shaped like a paintbrush with wheels—the flame is a bristle of color. In the dark heavens an eye opens; we have the power to kill the giant, to send him back to his origins. The eye winks and calls to the giant. We are poised in battle and here the dream ends, in turmoil and the possibility of victory.

Innocent men turn into werewolves at the time of the full moon. I think now their fangs and fur and muzzles and claws, the lift of their heels off the ground, and the crouch of their spines is a nightmare released from troubled, grieving hearts. Because I dream such terrible dreams according to the fullness of the moon, I know how real nightmares are. Divisions blur, and I walk around Blood Island, nicknamed for a horror movie. I walk around with the awareness of nightmare heavy inside me.

This dream was born in mid-December 1969. The week before the night police raided the apartment of Ted Harris, a Black Panther leader on the Left Side of the City. Lazarus made the trip to see the spot where Ted Harris and Archie Ferguson were murdered. These Panthers were young as us bloods in For Bloods Only. Their deaths were sudden and bloody. The walls of the apartment perforated with gunshots. A barrage of fire.

I didn't know Ted Harris. I didn't know Archie Ferguson. I didn't work in the Breakfast Program, to which Leona's daddy contributed money to feed the hungry children in all the cities. I didn't go with Lazarus the times he went to talk to Ted Harris and came back talking about his down-to-earth style, the fire of the brother's soul, and the intelligence and the vitality of him. I didn't work with Lazarus when he worked with other Panthers, even traveling to the West Coast. He was teaching people about their right to be free from hunger and oppression. I was painting pictures.

Suddenly, the murders of Ted Harris and Archie Ferguson brought everything home to us. The walls of Eden press in.

Lazarus, my brother, is brokenhearted over the losses of Ted and Archie. When I go home to Arbor Avenue, he won't come out of his room. Mama, all her anxiety and fear for Lazarus's Panther activities vindicated, has said all that she can say to him.

"He's just sitting there, staring at the ceiling. Maggie, see if you can get him to eat some soup." She gives me a bowl of chicken and stars. I walk slowly so as not to splash any stars or the flakes of meat, not to spill the hot, healing broth.

I bump the door with my foot, but Lazarus doesn't tell me to come in. I do anyway.

He looks at me as I stand in the doorway. Then he looks up at the ceiling. A cigarette burns down in an ashtray by the bed, a Lucky Strike. He is swathed in the smoke that dims this room.

I used to sleep in the room with him. Then I discovered I belonged with girls and women, and my oldest brother, Sam Jr., left his cot in the corner of the dining room to share this room with Littleson who is Lazarus now. Then Uncle Blackstrap came and took over the boys' room for a while, till he got sick and moved away. But I guess Uncle Blackstrap moved away before he moved out of the house on Arbor Avenue. He grew distant—always looking beyond us. His attention turned to his inner scenario. As if he'd taken the furniture he'd reconstructed and repaired, the tools of his trade, his snowball scraper and his bottles of colored juice, and stored them in some hidden place behind some big, awkward, and grotesque piece of furnishing.

Sometime after Charlotte, as Miss Rose said, "moved down south with a wig on her head and a baby in her belly," Uncle Blackstrap moved back in with us. He had left his third wife. Or she had "turned him out," as Miss Rose said.

Littleson, who was Lazarus by then, and I had forgiven him for his accidental murder of our kitten, MySun, years before. He, without paying attention, stepped on our yellow ball of mewing sun. We had revised our accusatory eyes to see him as he had been to us. A big, generous man with crafty hands and genuine eyes that seemed to melt on us children because he held us in such warm regard. We remembered the rainbow snowballs in the summer, the miraculous trash of autumn and winter that he resurrected into worthy gifts for us, jewel boxes and scooters, bicycles and hand mixers.

We leaned over the stair railing like the confetti-dropping hordes welcoming home the victor, the dark hero of our candy bars we had always known him to carry. Head bowed, he came up the stairs with a big cardboard box full of his fortune in his muscular arms.

The smiles that flew up to our faces at the sight of him spread their wings to sail down upon his close-cropped head like a delicate crown.

Suddenly, he lifted his recently ordained head and we saw the grimness of his countenance. He saw us too, and the grim set of his unfamiliar face twisted into a scowl.

The smile birds bent back wings and died on our faces.

The stranger finished the stairs and pushed his way into the house. A corner of cardboard almost stuck me in the eye. Lazarus whistled. Blackstrap did not open his mouth to anyone, but we, at least Lazarus and I, knew that if and when he did speak, it would be in a language guttural and coarse like the German soldiers we heard in old war movies.

He moved in.

Miss Rose said that he had "lost his mind. Lord have mercy!" Our mama said that he was a Black Muslim.

"Blackstrap the Black Muslim," our father chuckled to himself one Saturday, then went on twisting the knuckles of the pipes that leaked under the kitchen sink.

"Blue-eyed devils," Uncle Blackstrap mumbled to himself in the kitchen when he assumed that he was alone. I was lurking in the doorway. Watching him. He prepared terrible sandwich meals out of brown rye bread, lettuce, mayonnaise, peanut butter, sardines with all the oil dripped over the sandwich surface, and banana circles on top. Sometimes he prepared bowls of pale navy bean soup to supplement his marvelous sandwiches. He laughed and whispered over his food. He devoured it all with relish, after saying a grace with his palms up and hands apart. He devoured his new knowledge and religion with eagerness and hunger. He called his god Allah and his prophet Master Elijah Muhammad.

Those evenings after homework when we children gathered around the sometimey, secondhand television set, he stalked in our line of vision. He clicked the television into silent submission.

"Watching them blue-eyed devils," he'd growl at us like a dark bulldog.

When Caroline or Sam sat with us, he'd simply stand in the center of the room and glower at us all, broodingly, resentfully, with no trace of his prior self in those looks.

Later he would hurry to the room that he shared with Sam Jr. and Lazarus, who used to be Littleson. He was Joseph 3X. Who used to be Lazarus Dancer. Who used to be our Uncle Blackstrap. Everything was private with this stranger, even his newspapers that screamed at us when we peeked at them, MUHAMMAD SPEAKS. Lazarus Littleson, who was privy to that little room, said that he spread the newspaper on his cot and feverishly read by lamplight. The sandwiches and soup collided in his stomach, and he would shift his weight from one hip to the other to release the invisible clouds of gas that slid out of him.

Littleson who said that he was Lazarus would enter their shared bedroom on some pretend mission or another, then rummage through his drawers for a figment of his imagination while he watched our ex–Uncle Blackstrap out the corner of his eye. Uncle Blackstrap would snort and swallow phlegm and swallow the news and prophecies from Elijah Muhammad. Then Lazarus Littleson would stumble drunkenly out the doorway, stagger across the living room, and fall across the couch, gasping, "Oxygen! Oxygen!"

At bedtime he would stubbornly refuse to enter the "stink hole."

"It's too thick in there to sleep, Mama!" he'd cry. She let him spread his bedclothes over the couch.

When Junior came home from his job at the gas station, he would undress in the dark that was so odiferous it made his eyes water. But the smell of gasoline on his hands and in his clothes cloaked the pungency of the smell.

The weary Junior would fall into the bed and proceed to sleep with one eye ajar, for at midnight the ex–Uncle Blackstrap would sit up in bed and unfold from the swaddle of the bedclothes a long, cunningly sharp knife. The edge of the blade winked and whispered in the moonlight while Joseph 3X caressed the curvaceous edge.

Junior, shivering in a cold sweat, in need of a bathroom, would practice sleeping with both eyes open from midnight to dawn, when the stranger with garlic on his breath, and another language in his mouth and eyes, would gently wrap the knife in cloth and slide it under his pillow. At daybreak the Black Muslim rose and stood above Sam Jr.'s head the room was so tiny. Reciting murky, strange Muslim prayers. At that time Sam Jr. would pray in English for salvation, deliverance. The alien chants would cease. Then the tight-cropped black head would meet the white pillowcase.

And Junior would fall into a terror-induced sleep just when Lazarus who was Littleson was rising to deliver papers.

After several weeks, when Sam Jr. collapsed over his breakfast from nervous exhaustion, he unrolled his story before our mother. She sent us off to school, dragged our father from his bed two hours before his official rising time after working the three to eleven shift, kept Sam Jr. home from school, and told him to sleep on top of the covers of our parents' just-made bed.

That morning my parents went shopping for another sofa bed and a cabinet, which they strapped to the top of the Ford and took home with them. In the dining room they moved the table from the center of the room and set up a temporary bedroom for their two sons on one side of the room. They removed the boys' clothing and effects from the bedroom and relocated them in the shiny coppery cabinet. On a final trip to the now single cell, Caroline climbed across ex-Blackstrap's cot and threw the window wide open so that crisp, winter air rushed into her face and past her, sweeping out old odors where it ran. Then Sam Grace ran his hand under the pillow and removed the big murderous knife.

No one knew what Madaddy did with the knife. And Joseph 3X, when he found himself with a private cell, snorted and wordlessly went out to purchase a dead bolt lock for his door.

Months went by and we lost memory of the first Uncle Blackstrap, with his eyes that melted you and the candy bars up his sleeves. Our Uncle Blackstrap was a Black Muslim who chanted to himself about blue-eyed devils, who ate sandwiches for the insane and the flatulent, who followed the prophet who chatted with God on a street corner. This prophet not only predicted the rise of the Blackman, he required close-cropped hair from men, and discreetly sleek hair of the women who moved like silence in long skirts. Of all was demanded an unceasing industry, a dogmatic courtesy, a grave restraint that sprinkled their conversation with "Yes, sir!" and "Yes, ma'am."

The ex-Blackstrap, Joseph 3X, who had always been industrious, tripled his industry and began to plan a larger business for himself. He would no longer haul his trash in carts with wobbly wheels; he would purchase a truck. And he did.

Joy leaped out of his eyes and he walked with a skip. Lazarus called it the Muslim strut. We liked the new Blackstrap when he was this happy, at least I did. He offered us, Lazarus and me, a taste of his navy bean soup. Lazarus said, "No, thank you." But I nodded my head at the good shine in his eyes.

I tasted the dish and found it so delicious that I sat down to eat it. We ate the pale soup with dark crackers. I was bold enough to ask him why he ate such light soup if he was a Black Muslim. Wasn't everything supposed to be black, or brown at least? He said that Allah had told the Messenger that such beans were permitted.

I finished my bean soup and accepted a large slice of his bean pie. It was a new ecstasy for me, more sufficient than candy bars. I hummed while I gobbled it down. Then we washed our hands together. And Uncle Blackstrap, Joseph 3X, patted me on my head and went back to work, fixing things that other people had thrown away.

Lazarus, in his new bedroom, looked up from his book to survey my satiated state, growled at me, "Don't come near me, stinking bean pod."

But something went wrong. After two weeks the truck for which Joseph 3X had given up his savings to the Brothers Klein died in the alley behind our house. There was nothing that Uncle Blackstrap with his considerable skill could do to revive it.

He left the house spitting words between his teeth. I could make out furious speeches about the "deceitful blue-eyed devils."

The next time I saw his face it was on the second page of the newspaper, scowling beneath the headline NEGRO FANATIC IN SHOOTING SPREE AT AUTO DEALER'S. The story went on to describe our uncle as a disgruntled member of a militant Black sect who had launched an unprovoked attack upon two auto dealers in the auto district of the city. A similar shooting spree had occurred at another dealer's in the recent past, wherein two men had been killed. The Klein Brothers had been prepared. When the angry Blackman (then called a Negro) had reached into his pocket for his service revolver, all those present had fallen to the floor out of the line of fire. The service revolver had rung out fire.

The story mentioned an accusation of fraud that the "disgruntled customer" had made. A truck that he had purchased, had paid for in full, was dysfunctional after two weeks, and the warranty did not cover the repairs. The alleged assailant was identified as Lazarus Joseph Dancer, who identified himself as Joseph 3X of the Nation of Islam. The Nation of Islam disavowed all knowledge of and relationship to this member. His affiliation with the temple had ended three months before in suspension over some infraction that remained unnamed.

The Nation said, "This violent malcontent in no way represents the philosophy or actions of the Nation of Islam."

My father said that even if Blackstrap was not a Black Muslim he was a Dancer forever. He went down to the station house with a group of Dancers and Graces—brothers, sisters, and cousins—to post bond.

Uncle Blackstrap went from jail to a mental hospital, where he rested his rage. When we visited him, Mama, Madaddy, and the Grace children, he introduced us to a Whitewoman with flyaway hair and a soft smile. He said that she was his friend. She smiled at us toothlessly and shyly. Mama slipped Uncle Blackstrap some change for the vending machines. And Lazarus brought him a deluxe candy bar. I hadn't thought to bring bean pie. Like I would have known where to buy it. So we left him sitting in a lawn chair with the fire gone out of him. A propped-up ash smiling at a Whitewoman who did not comb her hair, children who brought candy, and a sister and brother-in-law who brought news of family, encouragement, and censure. "Did you have to shoot 'em up?" He didn't answer. I remember how he had seemed to burn, and burn.

And when I remembered his burning that ended in his suspended animation, I felt a fluttering dread for Lazarus. Lazarus who is my brother. Lazarus who is burning.

"Those cigarettes will kill you." That's all I can think to say to Lazarus who used to be Littleson.

He looks at me with a mixture of horrible disgust and pity at my inanity. "I'm going to die anyway."

I stand there, feeling loose in the limbs, as if all I have to do is let go of the bowl and saucer and watch the chicken bits, and watch the tiny stars, and watch a messy soup broth go all over everything. Then I'd be right with Lazarus. Then I'd be feeling what he's feeling.

I don't do that. I act like my mother and set the soup down. Stub out his cigarette and jack up the window a little bit. I slide a copy of Mao's *Red Book* under the window. It's not that big. Cold air slides in and swirls inside the smoke-filled room. Dislodging the thick dimness and cooling the soup at the same time.

I sit on the bed beside my brother, touching his side a little; he moves over a little. "Eat your soup before it gets cold," I order him, in just the way he'd boss me around when I played war and marines with him instead of reading Nancy Drew like I wanted to. I hold the bowl out to him. He looks me in the eye. What is in his eyes is all the nightmare from my dreams.

Finally, he takes the bowl from me and begins to swallow spoonfuls of broth. After a while, during which the tiny clinks of his spoon on the sides of the bowl were the only sounds in the room, he gives me the bowl back. He has foraged out all the chicken, but left some stars. I just sit there with my hands wrapped around the bowl, holding in the last of the warmth from the vessel.

Lazarus exhales noisily. Now I know he'll talk to me.

"You should have seen what they did to them, Maggie. You should have seen it." He is Littleson now. Younger than we are now, awe-stricken, and scared.

My brother is very handsome. His cheekbones perfectly constructed wedges layered over by a deep, smooth brown, interrupted only by a few ingrown hairs that make little bumps. Sometimes I've sliced the infected bumps with a razor and searched for the hair that curled back into the skin. Lots of Blackmen have the problem with ingrown hairs. He told me. Lovers and barbers, wives and mothers and sisters have to go inside their skin and look for the little black hairs that have grown back too deeply.

Our ministrations are more than the pampering of vanity (though that is a part of our mission). Our meticulous razor slice and excavations are acts of healing and prevention, primitive though they be. I told Lazarus he should grow a beard, so that the hair on his face can just grow freely, not be cut back and turn into itself. But he doesn't like beards. His always grow so ragged and uneven. They require attention he does not want to give to a little thing like hair.

Lazarus doesn't wear a beard now. He looks boyish. He is clean-shaven, and he is beautiful. I scared myself imagining his face torn and covered in blood. His body ripped apart by bullet wounds. Like the two young men who were killed. Right now someone is weeping for them. Someone is weeping beyond repair.

"You know that's what the Panthers tried to tell people." Lazarus is Lazarus, and his voice is gruff and hoarse from cigarettes. He lights one now. His mouth full of smoke coming out with the words, "They tried to tell people that the police aren't about serving and protecting

Blackpeople. The pigs are about containing us. They're about maintaining the status quo for the select few who run this country and everybody in it. Racism, economic deprivation, are parts of their machine.

"The Panthers don't strike first. We strike back. Only we didn't have a chance to defend ourselves!" Usually I fidget when Lazarus talks like an editorial in the Panther paper. But Lazarus has always had the most expressive eyes. His eyes I'm not artist enough to paint yet. An anguish from his bowels, his heart muscle, his finger joints wells up in his eyes. And I know that every, everything he says is true.

"You know what?" I say. "Remember after Eddie died, how we went to see Aunt Silence and Grandmama then?"

"We not kids anymore, Maggie." Lazarus is reading my mind before I do.

"Why not, Littleson?" I call him by his old name. "What's there to do right now? You not running away. You got to think. This room ain't it."

"I don't believe in no ghosts, Maggie," he warns me.

"Maybe they believe in you." My posing of this makes it surer than I feel now.

Lazarus is talking feverishly. "I don't believe in God either. Honest to God."

This is a lie. But the next is true. "I don't believe in nothing but power and guns cause they can take people off. Good people off. Wipe them away like a piece of snot."

"Lazarus, if you go to Mimosa, I'll go with you."

He just shakes his head and lights another cigarette.

✦

It is the third time I've seen *The Battle of Algiers*. This time I don't cry at the end. When the black screen goes white with images and the first reel unfolds, I start. I dare not look at Leona and Essie all squinched up in their pea jackets beside me. Every seat is filled in the small auditorium in the political science building.

Grungy-looking students with rippling, dancing hair and young assistant professors who won't get tenure walk up and down the aisle, the Vietnam War pushing their shoulders down. The weight of protest.

144

The movie is cosponsored by FBO, SDS, and some other groups. It is midnight.

The black-and-white film scrambles over us: a noisily relentless group of children roll a drunk man down the street, getting him out of the way of the Revolution. Like the urchins in *Suddenly, Last Summer* who ate the poet-parasite on the beach. Like hungry birds eating a turtle.

Children carry bombs through the narrow alleyways. A boy dies like a man. A woman fights like a strong woman. Revolutionaries hide explosives in long, loose robes. They strike and disappear into thick air. While fire blossoms out of rifles.

Things start blurring not just in my tear-crowded eyes but in my head: the dark, fugitive fighters, the stoic Algerian child impassively waiting on his appointment with Monsignor Death. Death in the dim, humid room. No different from my brother Lazarus in that tiny, smoke-swaddled room. Did Ted Harris and Archie Ferguson wait, even as they slept?

I start rummaging for a Kleenex, and Leona pushes a ball of toilet tissue into my fist. The room we're in feels smaller now, overcrowded and heavy with breathing. "I'm not the only one." I think, "Remember that, stupid." The scream of my own blood pounds in my ears. The sounds of guns. This is not a movie now. This is a war we are watching. In war there are many funerals.

Around the room, we feel the weight of the bodies.

When the film is over and we walk out the building onto the new snow of Eden, nobody's talking. Above us is an adumbrated sky, a wish for stars, and a moon like moonseed fruit, so dark we cannot see it. Beneath our boots is the gaudy, spangled snow. We tramp through it like refugees, like refugees from burial and extinction.

Leona breaks the silence first. Her words coming into the cold like minor ghosts in ectoplasm. "The lines were drawn so sharply. They all did it together. They were willing to give up everything. Everybody. Even the children."

Steve Rainey is behind us, silent as a shadow. His blood must be coursing close to his skin, reddening him. His eyes, suffused with energy, shine like the moon we're missing. His irises are dark and luminous.

"We're not serious enough," he says.

I beg to differ. "Ted Harris and Archie Ferguson were serious," I say.

"And they are stone-cold dead!" Essie stops dead in her tracks. Steve sidesteps her neatly; he anticipates sudden changes, abrupt moves. "You interested in being dead, Steve Rainey?" she challenges him.

"I'm just interested in being serious, sister," Steve says simply and softly.

"That's dead," Essie spits. And picks up her pace again.

Leona and I look after her. It is two o'clock in the gloomy, cold morning. The street is deserted, isolated and insular with snow. Around the streetlight on the corner we cast long shadows on the new snow; our Afros make our heads heavy. Our legs are long like deer. We look like chiaroscuro cartoons of ourselves, like angry militant stereotypes who newly populate TV. Redundant and declamatory. Not like us.

Steve walks with us back to the dorm. And it's not about yearning after Leona. It's because the four of us are floating in a dark, heavy moment, breathing from one tube. Watching the development of exquisite fingers—knuckles and nails; the expansion of lungs, and the molding of four hearts, the projection of divine-celled brain, the profusion of hair on our heads and between our legs, because we are to be born old and odd.

And I know Lazarus is in this moment, Sam Jr., and my six sisters, my parents and Silence, even Aint Kit and Grandmama and them. Dancers and Graces, and Moses, who says he loves me, and Christmas and Elder and the bloods of Blood Island, all of us. Hanging in the amniotic fluid of prebirth. Lingering in the ectoplasmic ether after death.

Cars come down that lonely, snowy road that divides this campus. Down the road the wind swirls snow into shapes and shapes. Almost human, I think. They must be souls. A restless swirl in history.

✦

I. B. K. Turner has organized a symposium on the Movement. Eden University is funding it as a gesture of goodwill. The university looks good. Black scholars, activists, artists, and writers gather and exchange ideas. At a dance on the last night, FBO turns out in full regalia. We dance the yoke, jerking oppression off our shoulders.

146

Older people stand on the edges of the dance floor the way my parents surveyed us at our parties at home. The older intellectuals talk about African survivals in the way we move. I. B. K. Turner smiles at Leona and Essie dancing with some dudes.

"What is this, Magdalena?" he asks me, as if I were an authority. I'm sipping red punch on the sidelines with him.

"It's called the yoke."

"Ah, the yoke."

"You know, like what we carry from one generation to the next," I crack, thinking of Lazarus and maybe me too.

He looks at me. "Well, Daughter of Sisyphus, Miss Sisyphus, it only gets heavier and lighter at the same time. It's a paradox. We must keep shrugging it off—like—." He nods at the dancers. We smile. For a moment. Then I see Trixia in a transparent top, anxious for attention, which she gets. Mouths fall open. Eyes widen or wrinkle in laughter. Her breasts under the sheer fabric are like half-gallon jugs. Russell Garner can't take his eyes off her. Her breasts bobbing up and down as she dances with him, he who cannot dance. He smiles goofy, real goofy. She acts like she's the original African Queen behind her veiled boobs. The thought of her embarrasses me, so I turn away. I don't know why I feel so sorry for her.

That night I dream Lazarus is nursing at the breast of a woman who is almost my mother, but she is darker, like me. Once Madaddy told us a story of a man on a horse, going by a cemetery. The man heard a baby cry, so he searched among the gravestones and found the crying baby. He put the baby behind him on the horse's back and kept on riding. In the darkness just before dawn he heard the scrape of feet against the ground. He looked around and down and saw long man legs hanging from the horse's flank. The feet touching the ground. Scraping the ground as the horse trotted along toward day. By the time the darkness was through, the baby was an old man. In my dream, as in the story, Lazarus, a lap baby, sucks at the tit of a woman who is almost my mama. The longer he sucks, the longer his legs grow, until he is fully grown. Older than I know him now.

Lazarus hasn't written me one letter from Mimosa. I've written him five, and sent them to Aunt Silence. Mama talks to him on the telephone from Miss Rose's house. The police keep coming to the house on Arbor Avenue asking Mama and Madaddy questions about his whereabouts and activities. All of us haven't heard from him. Which is not exactly a lie. Lazarus doesn't call us.

My oldest brother, Sam Jr., is a policeman. His captain questioned him about Lazarus, and Sam Jr. came up clean. Because he really doesn't know where Lazarus is. I don't know either. No one will tell me. But I dreamed Lazarus was in Mimosa, so it must be so. And I send my letters to Aunt Silence.

Aunt Silence told Mama to tell the police to ask Aint Kit where Lazarus is. She'd have a good cover story. Mama said she told Aunt Silence the police are trained to recognize science fiction.

Lazarus hasn't done anything to run away from. He was never close to Ted Harris. The police only want to ask him questions about his Panther friends and their activities. The Panthers fed some hungry children breakfast and talked against the system. They offered people services to help them. Medical. Legal. Community organizing. They made poor Black people think about why they worked so hard and stayed so poor. They talked about community self-defense. "Arm yourself or harm yourself," the Panther paper said. They armed themselves and the police and federal government showed them what they had for them.

But Lazarus said it wasn't the secret arsenal the Panthers had that the government said was so dangerous. That the FBI, from J. Edgar Hoover on down, wanted to wipe out. Not just Ted Harris and Archie Ferguson. What about Fred Hampton? It was the things that Fred Hampton and the others said. It was the way people listened to him that was so dangerous. At the end of his talks Hampton would cup a hand behind his ear and then he'd say he was listening to the heartbeat of the people. The people would go wild, clapping hands and stomping feet. It was the heartbeat the government had to stop. So Lazarus says they must have drugged Fred Hampton (there must have been an inside man) and shot him while he slept. "Each one teach one," the Panthers said. I don't know how many people they taught just by dying.

✦

Something terrible has happened in Mimosa. Aint Kit is the one who knows. The Chinese man who owns the store on the corner of Chinaman's Store and Old Letha Road has shot his wife in the head.

The ambulance came and took her bloody corpse away. The blood spouted wild from her temple to her ankles. Staining the white sheet that covered her. In Mimosa, ambulance attendants don't know about the big plastic bags you drop people in like they do in Vietnam on television. The police took the murderer husband away. Aint Kit said you should have seen his eyes—like dark stars that had blown up inside his head. His eyes nothing but scattered dust. She says his eyes probably looked like when he discovered his wife had a Black lover. He didn't shoot the boyfriend because he couldn't find him, but with those eyes he could have. The woman is dead. And he is in the jailhouse or crazy house, one or both. His educated nephew has come from California to take over the store. Or sell it.

Aint Kit tells me all of this over the phone one Sunday morning when I made the mistake of answering the phone. After she finishes her gruesome tale of jealousy and bloody murder, she asks me if I heard from my brother Lazarus. I tell her, "Nope." This is the truth. I don't tell her about my dream of Lazarus and Grandmama Mahalia.

"Well," Aint Kit is winding down. Her probing unsuccessful. She gives one last college try. "I don't guess Littleson gone run up on any of this Chinese-nigger shit. Long as them people been living in Mimosa with us you'd think they'd learn to sing the blues about the backdoor man like we do, instead of knifing or shooting each other like we do. That ain't nothing but the wrong thing they copied from colored folks. And she was a nice, little polite woman always give you matches whether you bought cigarettes or not. I imagine she got tired of sitting up under that man watching him count money or read the newspaper. They say her boyfriend was old Mr. Smiling Brown LeRoy. How she ever find him I do not know. But he always work hard, drive a nice car, and tip his hat at you. They say he was up at that store two, three times a day buying this, that, and the other. He buy a dozen eggs and get them on three different trips."

She pauses and sighs and I roll my eyes around in my head in misery and impatience, so Leona knows I'm talking or listening to my Aint Kit.

Leona, clumsy in her blue nightgown, stumbles out the room, holding her stomach, laughing.

Aint Kit sighs again, "I'm glad you say Littleson ain't down there, because he just the age of that Mr. C.'s nephew and I'd hate to see him take up with somebody like that. That's too much violence."

"That boy can't help what his uncle or his auntie did, Aint Kit," I say.

"I know. I know. But if you'd seen his eyes, you'd know that man was loco."

"Did you see his eyes?"

"Naw, but they told me about them."

I'm shaking my head now. I say, "Plus I know Lazarus wouldn't judge anybody by the crazy people in their family because he got too many crazy people in his own family."

Aint Kit laughs a deep, big old laugh. She thinks I'm talking about everybody but her. I wonder if the Chinese man did kill his wife, and if his wife did have a Black lover. I wonder what part of the story is Aint Kit. Sometimes she tells the truth.

Aint Kit tells me to stay out of trouble up here in the university, call her sometime, cause she lonely with no Bay. And let her know if I hear from Littleson, whom she refuses to call Lazarus.

Now I can hear the chapel bells chiming. Dim and sweet in the distance. But I stay in bed, under the covers. Safe in my warm cocoon. Why would I get up? To go someplace to kill somebody? To go and watch someone else die? To pray to a drowsy God?

✦

Always I think of when I was little, no matter how prepared I was, on the morning of a test I used to wish for all wishing was worth that I could jump across time. Just take one step across an invisible chasm, with my eyes closed, then open my eyes and be on the other side. Like in slavery when lovers jumped over a broom and arrived after one cosmic and free step to the state of matrimony. A true and free state even owners of people couldn't erase, even though they tore people apart and sent them away from each other.

In I. B. K. Turner's class we read about Sunni Ali, the magician-warrior of Songhai who could disappear from one moment and arrive at another moment. He surprised his enemies that way.

It's a new decade. 1970. And I want to sense some magic in the turning of time, but I'm too wrapped up in dread. I want to jump over a broomstick and step down happy and free; I want to say a magic chant and disappear from this grieving place where men are shot to death in the head twice. But I stay in bed. I'm stuck in Eden in 1970, and even though I don't go anywhere, things go from bad to worse. The treaty the university signed with FBO is as good as the United States treaties with the Indians. And Vietnam keeps getting closer. Like one country, war-torn and muddy, was picked up and set down in Hollywood to be televised nightly on the news. It's so unreal. But I know real death.

Honeybabe's husband is coming home. One day. The guilt and shame and questions are in his letters now, and Honeybabe tells us what he's written. "I don't want to die here in this little hole that is somebody else's. My soul would never rest. I want out of this man's army. When I see little kids who either want to kill me or come to me, I think of the babies I haven't yet planted in you. And why am I here? For what? For my country? That's a laugh. When did that coldhearted bitch ever care about my black ass? When I checked out the number of bloods over here, it set me to thinking. Sometimes it's half bloods. Ain't we ten, twelve percent of the population? Will the coldhearted bitch have a banquet prepared for me when I get home? Because I am coming home. You think I'd let myself die here? I'm too mean to die. I don't do nothing but love you, baby . . ." There Honeybabe stops reading and she says the rest is private. She reads and rereads, then she folds the letter and refolds it in the same place.

✦

C.C. is someone else now. Because he's learned his lessons. I'm someone else now. I know this without looking in the mirror. My senior year in high school the U.S. State Department sent for me. My history teacher chose me and another girl to go to a big, plush hotel downtown to hear the story of the United States and Vietnam. When we got there on that rainy day, late and awkward in our black galoshes and shiny brown skin, untying our plastic rain scarves to the shiny black pressed hair underneath, in our neat little dresses, we were the only ones there. The only Blackstudents, except for a beige boy who talked in the careful, open-mouthed way of suburbia, the accent heavy. He kept not looking at us as we sat in the big hotel conference room on red, thick, cushy chairs that made me think of Napoléon and the courts of the French empire before Bastille Day. Some Whitemen told us about America and honor and Communism and Asia. They gave us glossy folders fat with papers that had dates and promises on them. I was very impressed. Even though the woman from the State Department acted like we were two cases of mistaken identity and she didn't want to give us two Blackgirls from the all-girl Catholic school what she'd been so careful to reverently hand to the others, I was still impressed by our nation's sense of honor, the responsibilities of democracy.

But now I know the tiny seed of resentment I would not sow properly. Those lessons weren't designed for us two Blackgirls. Those stories weren't meant to be told to us. I looked around the room at the constellation of little white stars twinkling around us. These were the ones the U.S. government was wishing on. They were the future leaders.

I am not the same Magdalena now. That room is light-years ago. I wish I were now in that place then. I'd truly be unwelcome. Now in Eden the future leaders are rallying in the meadow before the Dark Shadows Library, protesting that promised and honored war because all that was a lie you tell children to put them to sleep.

✦

"What do you want, Maggie?" Moses asks me, sounding all amazed. He's leaning on the counter in the lobby of Wyndam-Allyn. He can do that now that Mrs. Sorenson has retired. There's a new dorm mother. A young woman, the bride of an assistant dean. She's more permissive. Everything else is too. The freshwomen in Wyndam-Allyn don't have curfews. They come and go as they please. Without signing in and out in the big book on the counter. It's not there anymore. The only thing the same is me. And I'm not the same person. I still work the switchboard here sometimes when no one else can or will.

After I get through buzzing Evelyn Padalitas's room, and asking her caller to hold, I answer Moses's question. He's still staring at me, looking impatient.

"What's wrong with you, Moses?" I ask him. He came up here with an attitude. Pissed off that I was working and he had to find me at Wyndam-Allyn instead of the Sweet Flats.

"Why something got to be wrong with me?"

"Why something got to be wrong with me and you the one acting surly?" I ask him back. Something is the matter with me, but I'm not acting like it.

He spins through the pages of a yearbook they leave in the lobby. "You have a drawing in here."

"William sent it to them without my permission." It's a pen-and-ink portrait of Malcolm X, Martin Luther King, and the rest of Blood Island. Fannie Lou Hamer is in a window. Moses studies it, while I talk into my little talkpiece.

"Good evening, Wyndam-Allyn. May I help you?" Just like a courteous robot. I buzz somebody and look at him again.

"My letter came today," Moses announces. Everything's a declaration today. Even questions.

"What letter?"

"I'm in the army now."

I just look at him. The switchboard blinks. But I don't answer.

"I guess I'll go to Vietnam and get killed."

"You planning on dying?" I'm mad at him for getting drafted. I'm scared.

"My old lady says at least I'll get a regular paycheck in the army. She looks on the bright side of things. Who knows? Hey, me, I go to 'Nam, lose an arm or a leg, they give me money for college. Square deal. I might go here. It costs an arm and a leg, don't it?" He squints up at the staid portrait of the alcoholic husband of the patron of this building. Moses's expression is cynical and wounded. I answer the switchboard and mess up. I say hello, just like I'm answering the phone at home and the kids are arguing in the background. Now I'm flustered. "Hold. Please." I get it together and go into my robot mode.

Moses starts talking again. "You know why they call it boot camp?"

I shake my head so I don't have to talk and start crying by mistake.

"Cause it's mostly boots in there." He pauses for my response. When I look blank, he calls me tardy. "You tardy, Magdalena. Boots. Bloods. Spooks. Coons. Splibs. Darkies. Niggers. Negroes. Afro-Americans. A million names for us."

Moses is just talking now in his bitter, ironic way. And I don't know whether to laugh or cry.

"Could you go to Canada?" I suggest in a tiny voice, so desperate I don't know it.

"M.G., look at me. Look in my eyes. What do you see? Go on and say it. A little Black nigger trying to hypnotize me."

"I don't get it."

"In other words, Magdalena Grace, we are both Black in case you forgot going to school up here—"

"Don't start." Maybe that's why I never fell all the way in love with Moses. My going to Eden means too much to him. Maybe that's what held me back.

"Just listen! Rich White boys can run away from home and stay in Canada for a while, then they can come back home."

"How do you know that, Moses?"

"I know it. Let's just say I know it. Whereas I, on the other hand, go to Canada and am unemployed and a vagrant. I wind up in a Canadian prison instead of an American one. You hear about that brother that hijacked that plane to Cuba?"

"You going to Cuba, Moses?"

"Naw, girl, I'm just saying."

"Then what are you saying for?"

"I am too dark to go to Cuba. You and me, Black Pearl, we too black for all these mulatto militants."

"Who gives a care?"

"Naw, M.G., for real. I read about it in that thang that come out of California you was reading. *Soulbook* or something. A dark-skinned

154

brother from here went to Cuba and he say they way color struck. Let's say you the darkest one in your family, right. You the last in everything." Moses launches into an oral essay on caste, color consciousness throughout the Black world. I read the article too. I can't help but think about how easily Moses would perform in the classrooms of Eden. He is a man in love with ideas, in love with talking. Then he looks at me in a disgruntled kind of way. "A man wants a woman he can teach."

"It's not my fault," I want to say. Why didn't some grammar school teacher in an overcrowded classroom on the western side years ago recognize this Black boy, head shaped like a perfect avocado, and eyes layered in stark white and inquisitive dark? Recognize who he might have been? I feel heavy with the luck of my circumstance. Religiously, yet with detachment, I watch his face while he explains to me about race and class, money and war, meaning and death, and why he must sleep with me tonight.

✦

Moses walks around looking doomed, his eyes cast down, searching for his fate. I feel so bad for him, I don't want to send him off to the jungle without something to hold on to. So I give him me. Finally, I say, "Okay. Okay, Moses."

And it is a mad tussle in the dorm room when Essie and Leona are at the movies. He climbs on top of me and opens me. His weight almost smothers me. I cry because it hurts. He pauses. He says my initials, "M.G.," like he always does. "You're mine," he says.

I go on with it, following him, but deep inside, deeper than he is in me, I am not and never will be his.

✦

There are goings-on in Eden that I'm not in on. Quietly Steve pled guilty to arson and was expelled from Eden. Sentencing later. (His lawyer is still clouding the issue of his guilt. Saying he is crazy with a hero complex. Saying he is claiming credit for a crime he did not commit. It is not like the building actually burned. It was scorched.)

I am dreaming in a dream so tangible the images float off the screen, exaggerated and sensible as African sculpture—mimesis at midpoint. Where real joins surreal and is alive in body and spirit.

A window breaks. Someone throws a bright, bright torch. Maybe a Molotov cocktail. And a building turns into a huge fire, blazing up to the cartoon full moon. "No more war," a voice floats out of the dream.

First thing in the morning my father's voice gruff, deep, and gritty knocks the "No more war" out of my head. He says, "They talking on the TV about that fire you all had up there in Eden. It wasn't that building from Sa-ooo-di Arabia, was it?" He's talking about the glass-domed administration building.

"It was another one."

"That boy that did it has been sentenced to a psychiatric hospital. They didn't say his name. At least I didn't hear it."

When had Steve Rainey been sentenced and so quickly?

"Y'all ain't up there burning things down again?" The inquiry is keen.

I say no. And my daddy chuckles good-naturedly like Santa Claus's alter ego. "I told Caroline you wouldn't be that foolish. To be involved in nothing like that."

I make a guilty noise about what I've felt like doing, close enough to a reassuring giggle to soothe his too-stern-to-be-worried mind. He's relieved and wants to tell me a story, so he begins.

He launches into Aint Kit and what he told her to set her straight about some fabulous fib she's spread throughout the family. Her story is about Lazarus, how he's wanted by the FBI, and how Littleson was in the apartment with Fred Hampton and Mark Clark, but left because she called him up and asked him to come feed her dogs because she was too sick to do it. The truth is Lazarus was never at Fred Hampton's apartment, had met Fred Hampton once, gone to several of his speeches; Lazarus was a Panther and was at home that night in our city. Madaddy says Aint Kit says the Black Panthers are just an ordinary street gang who dress in gang black leather jackets and Frenchmen-style berets cocked ace deuce on the sides of their heads and held there by extortion and coercion. Madaddy says he explained to her how the

156

Panthers believed in an economic program. Economics was their thing. It was the root of all evil. He'd read about it in the Panther newspaper. He was sitting right at that dining room table where I used to do my homework. He and Mama were sitting there and he was telling her what the Panthers were about. He's read *Muhammad Speaks* too, and they had a different angle on the economics, but he knew enough about them from Uncle Blackstrap's bad involvement with the Black Muslims. Madaddy says he can appreciate the ideology of the Black Panthers.

"How you know the Panthers didn't burn down this building up here?" When I ask him a question like this, Aint Kit or Aunt Silence will say, "Girl, you ain't nothing but the devil." Egging people on.

"Well—ahhh—I'll tell you, Maggie Lena, that's not stated in their program. Their, ah, aim is to raise the consciousness of the masses so as to generate a mass movement to change this old bird around. That burning down a building, that sound like something mischievous (mischeevious) one of them youngsters up there would do."

"How do you know I didn't do it?" I ask him.

He laughs real jolly and long. When his big mirth is spent, he answers, "You better not had did that."

✦

White receipt ribbons with blue policy numbers curl and twist from the torn linoleum tabletop to the worn linoleum floor of my mother's friend Miss Rose's kitchen. Hope and luck are in the choice and arrangement of the blue gangster-lottery numbers. The luckless laughter of Eddie-the-boy-who-died hangs and spirals in the corners. Some nights he taps on the pots and pans a code that keeps his mother company, even when the memory of the man he will never be hurts her behind the eyes. She keeps busy with the contraband numbers. Her fingers efficient and cold-blooded on the adding machine that eats dreams.

My cousin Bay knows the numbers that talk in dreams. She looks them up in her magic dream book. Three-six-nine is Shit Alley, she tells me when I am a little, little girl. I remember that easily and mix it with the rhyme with jump double Dutch to:

Three-six-nine the goose drank wine,
The monkey played the fiddle
On the streetcar line.
The line broke.
The monkey got choked.
And they all went to heaven
But the sanctified folk.

We sang creative religious intolerance or retribution. Sam Jr., my brother, would sing that song at us while we jumped . . . "And they all went to heaven, but the Whitefolks." Then he'd laugh and walk away, happy that he'd hipped us to Judgment Day. But that judgment is a long way off. And Steve Rainey's judgment is here. Three-six-nine is the number I'm thinking of as we crowd into the basement of Blood Island. Three-six-nine. This is Shit Alley. And we're in trouble. Trouble hugs around us like smelly water that gives you a fever. It comes out of you like bad breath and body odor. There's nowhere to run. Outside, the university grounds are thick with the mud of a weeping spring.

Sherman is a reporter for a paper in the City. He gave up his graduate studies in mathematics and was recruited into a news training program to report on Black Affairs (does that include sexual liaisons?) after he sold those taped interviews of the participants of the building Takeover in April 1968. He's almost a stranger. The two years seem so long ago. He's not connected to us anymore by more than a tenuous string of memories. His eyes are inscrutable gems, cold and thin. His hair is now more meticulous than ever. His nails are buffed. He takes out a notepad, and fiddles in his pocket. Leona hunches me and says, "I'll bet he's got one of those new little tape recorders. Taking it all down."

Even if I had the gift to read souls, I couldn't read his. Something in him shifts and waffles like an image on disquiet water. He wants an exclusive on the new arson of the university building and the whereabouts of William and Steve, who are allegedly implicated in the fire. Trixia, a ready and willing interviewee, is careful to claim ignorance. Which isn't difficult.

Yvonne Christmas looks real tired. She's only around campus now for meetings and organizing. She's writing her dissertation on theories of African socialism. She's been to the Continent and must go back. Her hair is long and braided with early gray running through the braids. Her skin is deeper than the African sun. There are tiny lines around her eyes. Her eyes are grieved. The new Central Committee of FBO defers to her. She calls our meeting together three times. The chaos of voices breaks loose again, then again. Then quiet settles into a stall like restless horses. Horses. Yes. Muscular and balking with energy.

Hamla asks the first question when Yvonne opens the floor. "We want to know what's happening. Why are the police questioning people about Will and Steve? We know the Leopold Building was torched. And that's all we know. We only know what we read in the newspaper."

Some snickers like the whinny of horses when Hamla brings in the newspapers. Some eye rolling Sherman's way because he's now a member of the press.

Yvonne nods like she can understand where Hamla is coming from. It's Elder Levergate who answers. He looks as tired as Yvonne Christmas. His hair is all messed up, and his clothes look slept in. His voice is that kind of low and powerful that doesn't have to ask for attention. (Men are lucky. Or is it just luck? . . . Anyway. It started with Adam naming things. Their voices call the world to order. Right.) He starts slow. Ruminating. Pulling in the reins of confusion.

"Too many of us are too young to remember Malcolm's words. You may have never heard him say, 'Freedom by any means necessary.' It doesn't matter if you heard it directly or not. History is still history. One thing about the past: it doesn't change. It only resonates into the present and future. Malcolm's statement was a difficult truth that a lot of people repeat, but fail to internalize." He pulls away from the back wall where he was leaning against a poster of John Carlos and Tommie Smith, the Olympic runners with their fists in the air. (We weren't there to see them do that, but that is ours too. I painted it so I can keep it forever.)

Cletus the Elder stands up straight now. Looking into each of our faces. It feels like fifteen minutes pass, but it can only be that many seconds.

"We've been through a lot together up here. Sometimes I see us as the Africans aboard the *Amistad*, headed for a more sophisticated slavery, but daring and honorable and desperate enough to seize the ship and turn it around to our homeland. Our place of self-determination.

"We've been through a lot up here. We seized a building, in honorable protest against an institution that failed to protect and affirm us as we, in all our humanity, demand. We've wrestled promises out of the powers that be. And those of us who've continued to care and struggle know those promises go not kept. The promise of Black Studies. Not kept. The promise of an excellent and useful exploration of our culture, our historical reality, our imperatives, which are in turn the past and future and present of America itself. Because this nation itself is a part of our past. And we are a part of its present and future.

"Some of you have heard the cry of genocide and . . ."

He goes on and on; I think his chest will break open and a flock of moths, like tiny, winged ghosts, will fly out of him. He is telling us how important we are, and how important it is we strive to achieve even small victories of more Black students and more Black faculty and Black Studies. We have to strive to live as honorable and complete human beings with a sense of mission.

Some people are losing patience and just want the facts, like Joe Friday, the dog-faced monotone-growling sergeant on *Dragnet*. A grumble spreads. Then an unidentified voice yells from a crowd in a corner, a cluster of people gathered behind a table where we've eaten pizza, played bid whist, and asked spirits to tell us news through the Ouija board. The voice yells, "What about William and Steve?" And another voice adds, "What about the police?"

And Trixia asks, "Was William sentenced too?"

Hamla asks, "Was William found guilty?" Then Hamla asks everybody to be quiet, but Trixia asks again if William and Steve were sentenced. Leona asks her why she's got to know that now. And Trixia says she wants to ask them what they've done and what they expect us to do about it, and in order to do that she has to know where they are.

Yvonne says, "Another building was torched by someone, so the university came down hard on Steve."

"But where is he?" Trixia asks.

Cletus the Elder snaps at Trixia, "Why do you keep asking? They're not hiding."

"Cause I ain't risking nothing for nobody. Especially over something I didn't know nothing about."

Cletus the Elder says, "They're somewhere loose in the universe."

"Just like you," I add for Trixia not to hear but feel as people around her act irritated with her. Especially Leona, Essie, and me.

Christmas asks for quiet again. And Cletus the Elder looks at Trixia and asks her what she'd do if she found out somebody did something for her good and their own and it was something by any means necessary.

Now Trixia won't answer. She just purses her lips and looks indignant. I'd forgotten we used to call these meetings Indignation Meetings. There was a man in a City in the early part of this century, they used to call him Indignation Jones, because he enjoyed these kinds of meetings where everybody's talking and wounded and scared and angry. I hate these meetings. My stomach is twirling and somersaulting. I try to quit clenching my teeth. My jaw aches.

Then I say, "But Steve Rainey didn't do it."

And Cletus the Elder says, "We know."

It's raining full force outside and the air makes a thick, moist net around us, as if a superior invisible spider were weaving us into this silken and vulnerable moment.

Cletus the Elder says so gently nothing breaks, "But what if he did the first? Don't we owe him something?"

Not one of us can answer Cletus Levergate's question. Doubt and confusion twitch around the room. Trixia just opens her eyes real wide and mumbles loud enough for everybody to hear, "I just want to know if William and Steve are on this Blood Island?"

"If they're hiding, why don't you go seek?" Leona cracks.

✦

Eden University is offering a five-hundred-dollar reward for information on the whereabouts of William Gregory Satterfield and Stephen Gabriel Rainey. They haven't put out any poster for them like WANTED DEAD OR ALIVE, just little notices tacked up on the bulletin boards in all of the dorms.

Essie is taking this whole thing in a most peculiar fashion. She blames everything on Rhonda.

Essie sits on the side of her bed, braiding her hair with a vengeance. It is so long now she has to put bobby pins in to hold each finished braid in place. Her mouth is full of pins, sticking out like barbs on a barbed wire fence. "See, if stupid Rhonda had given him some support, this would never have happened." She pulls out a pin from her mouth and plants it in her hair.

"She probably still doesn't know anything about what was going down. She said she didn't when I saw her yesterday. She's so stupid. She should have known when somebody torched that building that the heat would come down on William and Steve. Now her daddy the big shot is flying in to see her. Maybe he's going to see William too, if she knows where her husband is."

Another peculiar scenario happens. William goes to his law school classes for three days before he's arrested coming out of Contracts. He's questioned and released on his own recognizance. Soon after that Steve Rainey is rearrested in his cubby hole apartment off campus. The police wrestle the handcuffs over his gloved wrists. His gloved hands hang out of the metal rings. Johnnie Mae's boyfriend, a premed student, collects the five-hundred-dollar reward and assurances that he'll be admitted to the Eden University Medical School. He'll save lots of lives. Lots.

No one has seen Steve Rainey except for Hamla (who is on the Central Committee), Cletus, and William and the lawyer. My daddy got the tense wrong. No one had been sentenced. There was a lot of confusion about the sentencing because a radio commentator had speculated that whoever burned the first building did the second and must be crazy and therefore should be sent to a psychiatric hospital. So all of Blood Island had been in an uproar over misinformation that turned out to be true because Steve was sentenced to a psychiatric hospital and not jail. Thank God. Or Rhonda's daddy. I don't say Rhonda was good for something or Essie would have boiled me in oil. William was exonerated because he'd tried to stop Steve and Steve had overpowered him. That's the story. The story is, Steve burned down the building because he did not get a scholarship he'd applied for. But we all knew Steve would have gotten that scholarship next year. He was a straight-A student in the five-year engineering program. Oh, Steve Rainey!

This is the way things go. None of us is the same. Changes upon changes. We are burdened with a baggage we can't name, so we only talk about it sporadically. We have reached the impasse. And the passageway is shadowed with risks, reprisals, and consequences.

Essie, Leona, and I have come to visit Steve. We are sitting in the open visitor's lobby, where men and women in gowns wander through, hair brushed severely, and bumming cigarettes. Newspapers rolled under their arms. One woman, no teeth in her mouth, hair standing all over her head, brushed that way, walks around whispering, "Earthquake!" and touching every wall. Like a doomed survivor in the aftermath of a disaster. We simply look. And wait for the earth to tremble.

When Steve appears in the lobby, the earth does tremble. It is Leona who breaks down. He embraces her first. Then Essie and me he takes into one fierce, sloppy hug that hikes up Essie's miniskirt so high her blue tights bottoms show.

We all sit down on the circular bench, while the patients and other visitors mill around us, like tigers in *Little Black Sambo* who chase each other around the tree, tail in mouth, and mouth in tail, until they're spent into exhausted butter. This is the trick of my mind. Sunlight pools around us.

Leona has a way of making herself ask difficult questions. "How are you, Stephen?" she asks. He just shakes his head. We all fall silent. Sinking into the sunlight. Steve peers at us, and shakes his wrist. We all look at the patchwork of skin on his hands. He decides to play it light, I guess.

"So what's happening?" he asks us. And we tell him, "Nothin' much." Just school and stuff. Right now school is out. The whole campus has struck in protest against the War. There are barricades across the road that divides the sides of Eden. We can walk across the street now like children crossing a bridge. There's no danger of getting hit.

Steve thinks this is funny. "I ain't there so you closed the place down."

"It wasn't us," Essie says. "We support it, though. It's everybody. Everybody's against this war."

"How's your boy in the 'Nam, Maggie?" Steve asks me.

"I don't know."

"You mean you ain't been sending him cookies regularly?"

"He just quit writing me. He must have quit me."

"I guess the jungle rot got in his brain. Brain rot. He must be crazy to quit you."

All of us look embarrassed when Steve says *crazy*. I'm blushing for more than one reason. Blood's in my face, and water's in my eyes and thick in my throat. "How are your hands, Steve Rainey? Almost healed?" I can only whisper. All of us hypnotized by the remaining discoloring.

He's still talking in a casual tone. "They're good. Good. You know they had to operate on them twice. They took strips from my back. Grafted them on. I don't miss 'em off my back. No skin off my back." He giggles at his macabre joke. "I just look like a slave who got flogged." He dances his fingers for us. "They may not ever have full dexterity. I lost my fingerprints, though. I'm a man with no fingerprints." He sounds delighted.

"You can have mine," I want to say. But settle for linking my right fingers with his left ones. Leona takes his other hand.

We sit that way for a good while.

Then Essie says real bitterly, "What did William lose?"

Nobody says a word about that.

When visiting hours are over, Steve kisses us each in turn on the corners of our trembling mouths.

"Will's a good brother," he tells Essie.

The next week we visit him again, but he will not see us. We linger on the outskirts of the buildings, not knowing what to do with ourselves. There are still no classes at Eden. And we have no appetite for books anyway. We'd just as soon have school stay closed forever. Then we could hang around in this moment between rebellion and despair. And there'd be no tomorrow to answer to.

The hospital is a big, open estate of low, scattered cottages spaced around the central building where the lobby and offices are. We're surprised when William comes out of the lobby door.

"Look who's here," Essie says with no surprise, even though she must be feeling it. William doesn't have time to unwrinkle his face, or wipe the tears from his face, or rub the tears out of his red eyes. He doesn't have time to shake the rhythm of his weeping out of his shoulders, so we catch him at it. When he discovers us, he doesn't bother to hide anything. He looks at us, and keeps on going to his car. He just sits in it, still crying.

We go to Leona's car and sit. We don't cry with William. We just sit till Leona tells Essie, "Why don't you go and see about William?"

Essie acts like she doesn't hear.

Leona and I look at each other, helplessly.

William's car pulls off. Leona's follows it down the long, thin road, through the trees and out onto the highway.

I imagine Steve Rainey busy making cradles with short string and emptying churches out of his almost-engineer hands. In the madhouse, growing more sane. He plays with his own mind, explores math problems, reads scores of books, and clips items of interest from the daily and weekly newspapers with his dull kindergarten scissors. The attendants watch him. At night they steal the two stones he'd found on his walks around the institution. They will not let him smoke, unless they watch. He must have no fire around him. No access to fire.

I can see him scissoring the newspapers and gluing clippings into an album. He places the reports on the investigations into the murders of Fred Hampton and Mark Clark in another city, Ted Harris and Archie Ferguson in ours on a page beside the student strikes at Eden, the news of Leona's selection to study architecture in Rome for a year, the brief notices about a man named Treemont Stone who is part charisma, part mystery.

Steve saves all the letters we write, but he doesn't answer them.

He threads his discolored fingers with short string, sits on his narrow cot with his back to the gray wall. His young, exuberant spirit walks with us down the gray-white paths that loop between the hidden roots of the trees of Eden and open onto the wide, central road that brings the City to us.

While one of him retraces our steps as we gather in the meadow for the speeches against the War, another one of him sinks into his narrow bed and ponders the import of Treemont Stone, who is a hope, who is a promise.

6

Seeing Eyes

On the street he had a habit of walking up to strangers and flinging his little arms around their legs.

"Hiiiiii!" he hollered like a country relative at a family reunion.

Women carrying shopping bags with their shoes and a change of clothing inside just stood in their tracks, stunned by such a show of affection. They lingered. Making him their own. Letting go, he'd stand by the iron fence in front of his family's house; holding on to a post with one tiny hand, he'd swing one leg back and forth. His short pants taking in air. Shirtless, his torso was brown and lean. Tiny nipples like curled seeds.

"What's your name?" the women would lean down and ask.

"Twee," he replied, smiling and swinging. Then he switched legs.

"Three? That's how old you are! Not your name, baby." The voices of these women, ascending in disbelief, were loving anyway. He nodded, meaning that "Twee" was his name, but he was so agreeable they thought he agreed with them. He wasn't three yet. He could have told them that. But his mother was more interesting.

"There my mama. There my mama," he pointed down the street where a blind woman sat with a girl standing beside her. The girl was eighteen or so, in a cotton print dress.

"Oh, she's pretty. Your mama's pretty. Bye now!" Reluctantly, and still stunned by the boy who was adorable, the women walked away.

He did the same thing to men. He stretched his little arms wide to get a pants leg inside his arms. "Hiiiiiii!" One time when he did that a man on one leg started to cry. He picked him up, balancing himself on his crutch. Lifted the skinny toddler high above his head. And held him there like a plane in slow motion for the longest time. So long the girl in the cotton print dress came running. The man let the boy down. "Twee" sat on the curb, swinging those legs in short pants.

"What's his name?" the man asked wonderingly, wishing he were his.

"Montie," the girl replied, snatching the boy up and positioning him on her hip.

"Twee," the little boy contradicted her.

The one-legged man reached in his pocket and brought out three quarters. He gave them to the little boy. "Twee" put all three in his mouth.

"Montie!" the girl fussed. "That's nasty!"

At this rebuke, the boy grinned and opened his mouth wide. Her fingers fit into his mouth, removed the coins. He swung both legs. Happy to be embodied.

His mother had given him more than quarters.

He was born blind in a little town where his mother was visiting a pregnant cousin. His blindness was a double loss. There were so many beautiful sights to behold. Have you seen—women in white veils and dresses washing their feet in a doorway at dusk, toothless men with lighted eyes under beat-up hats, black girls in clean white panties playing in a yard with blue and yellow flowers near the gate, tiny red flowers bursting on a stalk, flies so happy to be alive they land anywhere, water flat and heavy, quiet as stone swallowing a sun in a circle that drew no bounds? Boys in single file walking in the prints their father made in the mud in the rainy season. The quiet water slipping in behind them, soft on their heels, swallowing what marks they made. So they made new ones. Running ahead of the man, alongside him, then behind.

Beauty is in the eye of the beholder. That is what his mother said. And beauty is in the beheld.

Was that what he was thinking one day when he was ten and on his way home from school and came across the woman crying on the corner? He was in the middle of *The Man in the Iron Mask* and he wanted to finish it. His head hot with swords, agile men, and women in skirts round as globes. He had to help the woman in distress or lose his burgeoning notion of his own heroism. Gallantry. He had muscles. He loved to admire them in the bathroom mirror while his sister, Vivian, threatened him unless he got out instantly.

In the privacy of the bathroom he stood amid porcelain and clean towels contemplating the hard knobs that pushed up out of his upper arms. Touching them in the way his mother picked up plums in the market.

The woman wouldn't tell him what was wrong, but she went with him to see his father. Everyone came to see his father sooner or later. She told his father what had happened to her that made her cry so. She had been the victim of a pigeon drop. They had taken all her money. She had given it over to them.

This is what he remembered best. What his father said to the crying woman. "Go on and cry because you're shocked and surprised and poorer than you were. Be glad they didn't kill you or someone you love." He touched her shoulder. "Cry too long and something else will come in their place."

Then it was years later and he was on the roof of the church, standing like a man. The ground way below. He was on the edge and he wasn't afraid. The only things he feared were ridicule and the absence of his father's respect. The kids at school called him a German shepherd. They called him Seeing Eye. Most times they said it with affection. But, sometimes, with the spite of derision. Or envy. His parents poured love all over him like sunshine. His sister brushed his hair.

Some women wondered aloud after church if he was kept on a leash too tight, and if he would run wild one day. Other boys jumped roofs. Other boys smoked cigarettes in alleys. But he was Seeing Eye.

In the twilight, standing on the edge of the roof, he wasn't anybody's boy. He could feel himself as the haze set in—he was hazy, and who would make fun of this time of day? He was thinking of nothing. He was standing, inching closer to the edge, and thinking about nothing. It was just when a thought was about to occur to him that the woman burst out of the side door of the house next door to the church. She was naked; her full flat breasts slung low, and between her legs a white mouse or a squab. He couldn't make it out. She startled him and he was much too high up.

He rubbed his eyes to get the mouse out, the squab. His hurried movements rocked his balance and he started to slide.

"No!" his mother screamed loud enough to stop descent, the draw of gravity, but it wasn't enough. And his legs were unsteady and his feet slippery. He shot over the side, clawing in the air. He grabbed the gutters, the top ledge of a window. His legs swung—free, unencumbered by weight or support from the side, traveling a great distance into nowhere.

She was calling his name.

He turned his head to look at her. His arms at full length. He couldn't look long, a blind woman, naked, so grieved by something her pubic hair had turned white, her body moving as if guided by sound, into the church basement, up with a ladder. And how could she have known where it was? And how could she have lifted it and navigated it up those steps and around that corner and leaned it against the wall so that the top rung hit the boy at his hip. It was a long ladder, metal and heavy.

Over his shoulder he could hear a train go by, and he wished he were on it. Not dangling, limp, waiting for his mother to haul a ladder closer to his feet. He was swinging, but not too wide—he'd blow himself away, his legs clambered.

She crooned, "Hold on, just a little bit longer."

He was hanging on to the side of the church, at loose ends. Time itself was turning to a slow wind in which the world unwound around him (the railroad tracks atop the cement overpass trembled as a train went by, the countless houses with narrow doors that stayed open or shut, the drawn blinds behind which women cut the extra fat off sides of salt pork, and men hammered nails into the window frames so the window would go up no higher than a baby's head, teeth sat in glasses of water, and children ate sugar sandwiches on the day before groceries were made, yesterday's stew was today's soup, and the girl sold crochet sets to help pay her rent, the baby said Dada, and the retarded girl kept stacking checkers, stacking the colors separately with the red ones a taller tower, the man slapped his wife and dared her to cry, and the wife seasoned his food differently, boys pitched pennies and children played one, two, three, red light, homework got harder, and comic books easier). He understood the desperation in the voices of people who came to see his father as a stand-in for God. Now the muscles in his arms were more than physical adornment and appealing. He needed himself. In the way everybody needs himself. Without himself he would die.

So while his mother tried to move the ladder to him, he moved himself downward. He became as a spider, drawing his legs up toward his center, fixing his fingers into the corners of stones, balling his feet, grabbing with his toes. He inched downward, looking down only to find another place to hold on to. His breathing was a whistle, a single thread. Down and down he inched his way. At the window, he stopped and fitted himself inside the sill. Praying it would open and he could leap onto the altar. But it was shut and he'd rather break a leg than break a window.

Crawling out of the window frame, he slipped and skidded sideways down the stones. The stones scraped the skin off the side of his face, and the impact made his teeth bleed, but he clung to something, and in the end slid to the ground, and landed on his own two feet.

He walked his naked mother back to the house and upstairs to the bathroom, where the vision of him, about to be lost, had disturbed her bath. In a bubble like a tenuous crystal ball, she'd seen him falling, even though she couldn't see. Now the water was ice-cold. She put on her robe and looked at him without looking.

"I ought to beat your butt," she said. And she was shaking so she must have meant it. And he could feel what her shaking meant. Her minor trembling as of a body about to fly apart from the inside. The held-in fear. Now he could feel the place where she'd held him in. The secret in her heart in which he was held. He felt what she felt when she knew he was teetering at a great height, about to fall. And once he felt he could see her. Her insides. How an emptiness swelled up in her chest and opened into a wide vacuum when she thought he was lost. Now her face ran downward, defeated by the years of gravity. And her hair got wayward and went in every direction like she'd never seen the beauty shop. He could see her and he was sorry.

So he was her "seeing eyes" who felt and saw, leading her gently, her hand on his shoulder. Or her hand in his. Sometimes his buddies teased him and said he was his mama's dog. A seeing eye. But it didn't work because there was no shame in this for him. "She don't treat me like no dog. And she don't love me like I'm a dog. I'm her son," he said.

171

It could have been worse. She could have led him to believe that he owed her service for the rest of his life. But it wasn't like that. He gave what he liked to her. Leading her by the hand past the smell of roses pushing out of the fence of a front yard, walking her past the church where berries fell down freely on the sidewalk while the roots and trunk of the tree were caged behind a fence. The branches broke free, and, with the generosity of freedom, colored the walk. Sometimes people said he was walking his mother; sometimes they said she was walking him. He could hear the asides. And he knew both were true. She was walking him; attentive to each sound (the shift of wind, the car backfire, the hand slap of girls in a game; the rhythmic strike of the double Dutch rope, the distinct language of species of birds), so she taught him to pay attention to minute engagements of life. The implicit vibrancies that do justice to the total.

"It's an orange, son," she would say. "If you open it just right and peel away the thin white membrane, the segments fall open and away. Then you can coax them back together and fit the rind around it and it is separate and whole again and you can open it again and enjoy it, piece by piece. So you peel away the thin white membrane that separates you from individual things and you can know each one and each one will know you."

So he listened. And he saw the way he'd seen that night when he saw her in her white robe over her articulate nakedness.

The man on the corner, he could see him. The light spinning out of him. His teeth yellow and the bottom row bent. His mouth grimacing open in a smile as he made change for him, giving him the newspaper he would read to his mother. The man's hands stained, every knuckle beaten and ashy, the underpolish of flesh dazzling. What was meant to be. The man bent and picked up a newspaper, broke and curved it in his hands. His motion fluid and spiked with élan. Repeating this motion, he waved the next paper and rushed to a car. Accepted the quarter that shone like a silver dollar. Light jumping out of the man. Iridescent and indigenously glamorous in his hand-me-down clothes. The half-broken cuffs of his pants. The rough dry shirt and tarnished wool suit coat. Then he ran back into place and dropped the quarter, stooped like a burnished beast, a cramped angel, electricity riding out of him. Now lightning, primal and blessed, struck the boy's eyes and it shorted out and struck out, lucid and arching, sinuous and sublime. Bouncing back and rattling him and through his body and his mother's body. Everything hurt and the boy kept quiet, but his mother gasped for air. Mother and child now in the man's skin. Bending, stopping, accepting, smiling, working. The man sat and thought. His eyelids half closed, blinking like a sleepy lion, drowsy with the idea of pursuing his momentary meat, while something infinite inside him masticated the fleshy part of the Milky Way.

Then a woman, heavy as molasses, Brer Rabbit Syrup, Alaga. The color of molasses ran for the bus. Her limbs moving out discordantly, flailing away from her big body. In a gray cloth coat. A broken jar of molasses. "Wait!" Desperate and alive. Flourishing like blood and thorns in the air.

And the bus driver, his olive, mustached face, scowling and numb with monotony, waited the engine till the wounded woman reached the door of the bus. He shut the door then, as she stepped down from the curb. Looked her hard in the wounded, dark, broken angel face and smirked a spiteful victory. Then he cut the street in two with the big, empty bus.

This time the boy gasped. And didn't answer his mother when she asked what happened. He was watching the woman's hands drop down. The unspoken exclamation filling her open mouth. Her body, a salted wound. Her eyes flew open. Hurt through him. Pleading, she asked his mother who couldn't see, "Did you see that dirty dog?"

The boy answered, "I saw."

"They don't do them white ladies like that."

His mother spoke then. "They tell on 'em."

"I didn't do nothin' to him. Why he do me like that?"

"Ain' no tellin," his mother said. Whipping her thigh with the newspaper she'd just bought.

The woman looked at the boy then. Her face heart shaped and brown encased in the numinous scrim. "Buses just like men. Another be along in about two thousand years." This is bitter.

"Now you sayin Jesus the only man." The blind woman standing on the corner laughed.

The woman laughed then. "You right."

"I remember the number," the boy said. "You can write it in. He was mean to you."

173

The woman shifted inside her shoulder and sucked on her eyetooth.

"Gimme that number, baby. I'mma sho tell somebody something."

They stood with her like two guards, the woman and her son, until the next bus came. By then they were laughing good and sucking on jokes until the bus slid up and rocked a little like a big, gray cradle when it halted, and the doors opened by electric magic.

Then walking home, stepping over earthworms and cracks, sauntering through a path of familiar and original sounds, he listened to his mother's breathing, the soft undercurrent her body created in the air. He was thinking. He was thinking. "I once was blind, but now I see." And he had no idea why.

✳

When he was a grown man and his father had been dead awhile, his sister, Vivian, had told him the story of how he'd been born blind and his mother had given him the gift of her eyes. But there had been betrayal in the gift. She had given her infant son one of her corneas and the doctor took both of them. Vivian told the story of Mercy and Jeremiah Stone.

When Mercy awakened, she could not see her awakening. Everything was still the black dream and remained so. She would never again see the crooks in the slim arms of the tree that stood outside her hospital-room window. Her roommates disappeared. The nurses. She could only see her son, and saw him by his sounds—the cooing, the yawns, the gurgles, the burps, the restless cries of hunger. But him—he would never know a hunger to see. He would never know what it meant to be blind. And she was blind. Had been blinded by a capricious hand, but for years she had seen the world. They could not take Memory. The very taste of colors. She realized that after her howling and screams sank into sedated slumber. And her thrashing had been stilled by strong restraints. When her husband came to her room, she wept. He was worn-out from weeping and the beating he'd given the doctor, who never knew who hit him. The cavalier doctor was a patient. His head broken open by a two-by-four, then stitched and bandaged in his own operating room by a surgeon who hated to do the job for a man who'd played a whimsical, malicious god. And the man of God, husband to a blind woman now, had wielded

174

that two-by-four with all his might and God's wrath. The surgeon slept for days, and awakened a changed man. And all his life Treemont Stone knew there was much for him to see, and even more for him to do in a world where colors ran from grim grit to magnificent awakening.

Meanwhile, all through his boyhood, before he went off to college so young, leading his mother was natural. He was twelve or thirteen shopping with her in Sears, Roebuck and Co. Vivian bought a bag of warm Spanish peanuts. He ate them one by one as they strolled the aisles, his mother stopping to touch things and ask questions. He was unwrapping a peanut and popping it in his mouth when he saw her—a little biddy girl. "She's adorable!" Vivian cooed, for at this time she wanted a little girl of her own, was in a nesting mood with her husband.

A little brown girl with a roundish face, with a white bow propped in a braid on the side of her head.

"Yeah," he said, "she's a real angel and she's probably full of the devil."

"Hush," the enchanted Vivian said.

But he noticed how the little girl stood in the sunlight streaming in through a window as if she belonged there, and stared at him and his blind mother as if she were dreaming them with her eyes open.

7

Providential Ways

Leona and I come down on the bus because she's been to Rome in books and no longer wants to do what the Romans do. I told her about the elaborate stone cities of West Africa in the fourteenth century, how they were leveled by the Invaders. I. B. K. Turner told us and offered us proof. Then Leona really had no appetite for Roman edifices that still stand after centuries of their adventures in other people's worlds. We feel very adventurous, riding Greyhound from the City in the North to Atlanta. We talk about the Freedom Riders. The way we remember them. Riding from Washington, D.C., to a town in Alabama where they were beaten and torn apart by mobs. (Mean mobs like the flying monkeys in the *Wizard of Oz* we Grace kids hated so when they tore the insides out of the Scarecrow and threw his straw guts hither and yon. He wanted a brain, and ended up with a piece of paper that hypnotized him into intelligence. Is that all an education is?)

That was barely ten years ago, when SNCC students came down from Nashville to take up the freedom ride from Alabama into Jackson, Mississippi. They went into Jackson singing freedom songs a cappella. In Jackson they were herded into the terminal. Straight through it. And right into the paddy wagon. They went to jail, then to the penitentiary for sixty days' hard labor.

One kangaroo court sits inside the pouch of another; is mother to another. A mother with a cigar-smoking babe in her bag. During the

1968 Democratic Convention in Chicago police beat a lot of antiwar protesters all upside the head and arrested them just like they were Black. Leona and I are traveling and talking about the conspiracy trial of Bobby Seale and the Chicago Seven. I've painted a picture: Bobby Seale, the one Black defendant, the Chicago Eighth, bound and gagged before a blind judge.

The business Leona and I laugh over is the young White radical who testified to his group's attempt to levitate the Pentagon. Levitating the Pentagon is against the law. Leona thinks the whole idea is pretty dumb. She guffaws in her Black way. It makes perfect sense to me, because I believe or want to believe. I never could get the straight of what to do with the Pentagon after it was levitating like a chair or a heavily made-up blonde magician's assistant in sequins. Leona and I whoop it up over what to do with the Pentagon. Carry it to the Atlantic and drop it in with the bones of Africans? Or keep lifting until not only its body but its consciousness was raised? Or leave the Pentagon suspended in midair?

The last alternative I find most appealing . . . Or the ocean. Then I tell Leona, "Maybe we should save the Pentagon in case there's an alien invasion and we have to strategize a worldwide defense." I can hardly get it out I'm laughing so hard.

"Capture some aliens and put them on trial," Leona cracks.

All the while the Chicago Eight, then Seven, trial was going on, we danced the push-pull—hard, rhythmic thrusts from the pelvis. Two partners facing each other. At the time Leona said that dance could tell you who was a virgin. Virgins went roundabout. The rest went straight at it, in simulation of a sex act. That's what we thought the dance was about. Coy, civilized sex. But now we've figured it all out. It was about the shove and wane of power. Push and backlash. Giving some and getting harder back. Everything fits together. Even us, riding this Greyhound bus to an ASAP (Autonomous Senate of African People) in Georgia. We fit in. We remember as the wheels roll over highways for hours and hours. We've worked for this journey all summer long. Saving our money for the bus fare and hotel. Some members from FBO are coming down in cars, but Lee and I like the idea of being free and making our own time.

Bay is picking us up in Atlanta and driving us to Mimosa. She hasn't got a husband now, so she's free as the wind. Or a hurricane.

178

Leona counts her money again, and checks her ledger, where she keeps track of what each of us spends so we can be sure for the thirteenth time of where we stand. Right now we're sitting in the thick of things because the toilet has broken and the stink floods the bus. We gag like Bobby Seale, light incense real quick, and keep on talking. About Yvonne Christmas now and how she was a Freedom Rider. Our hotel is right across from the bus station. Leona, who doesn't believe in magic, interprets this as a fortuitous sign. Even the geography is set up our way.

I've never stayed in a hotel before. Leona acts like a world traveler because she is when we check in. The bellhops are all invisible, so we carry our bags to the elevator. Leona has the key. Not only have I not stayed in a hotel before, I haven't been in too many. The time I went to the brainwashing seminar sponsored by the U.S. State Department. And the fleeting memory of my high school prom. That's it.

The lobby is big and modern with uncomplicated furnishings and a family of potted plants all around it. We try not to bump into anything or anybody. The place is crowded with clusters of people, some of them I've seen on TV. Blackpeople from all over the country have descended upon Atlanta to resolve the crisis of the Black intellectual, and the situation of the Black race. Activists, scholars, artists, Black professionals, ministers of every kind, laypeople, all working on a Black World Agenda–U.S.A. All wondering in an unspoken and sometimes spoken way who will be the One. There are impressive-looking people here, and we don't want to appear country or naive.

The elevator door opens and four or five good-looking brothers fall out. "Party. Party. Paaaaaarty," is the first thing out of their mouths. "You pretty sisters here for the conference?" one of them asks us. After we nod, he tells us the room number and the time of the party tonight. Then they move on out the lobby, and Leona and I take the elevator to our floor.

In the little box going up, we bend over, carrying our bags and laughing. "Paaaarty. Paaaaaarty. Party." We mimic the man.

Leona and I get along. The little comedies of gesture and stance, the nuances of tone and phrasing, the absurdity of behavior and desire—all break us up into the hidden mystery of the moment. A cause for hilarity.

The insides of my mouth taste sweet. And my moist eyes see every-thing through a happy haze.

Leona's mother has made her a dress. A sea swirl of blue and green, a hooded caftan that floats over her as she moves. She models it for me before she hangs it up. I show her mine that Honeybabe has given me—sunset-sunrise colors. We put away our belongings. Lining the dresser tops with bottles and jars. Decorating the closet with colorful summer outfits.

We take turns showering and changing. Leona goes first. I sit on the bed and dream awhile.

When it's my turn, I savor the swift spray of the water all over my body. Then I enjoy the cushy towel that laps up the water. "If my Aint Kit were here," I holler to Leona, "this towel would go into her collection." It has AMERICANA HOTEL printed in bold letters, brown on cream.

I brush my eyebrows with a little brush my sister Honeybabe gave me. I put on my sister Pearl's earrings. Little beaded ropes that dangle against each other on each ear.

Leona glides gold into her earlobes.

The smell of the road between North and South, the smell of the Greyhound, are off our bodies. Anticipation fills our nostrils.

"Miss Grace,"—Leona flares her nostrils, working herself into being more outrageous than usual—"are you ready for the future of the race, the world, and the universe?"

Leona thinks big.

One day in Eden after Steve Rainey was expelled I found her lying on her bed in our room, in perfect repose, her eyes wide open. I didn't say anything to her. Just put my paints down and carried my junk into my room. She sat up in the bed and just looked at me.

"Magdalena," she said. And I knew this was important because she called me all in my name. And her tone was asking for something. "Have you ever thought about the stars?"

"You mean like Russell Garner?" Russell the astronomy student.

"No," she said. "Not exactly."

"You mean like astrology," I said, thinking of the time Essie and I went to that restaurant to talk stars and love and came out with Trixia and them into the late night of streetlights and hate.

"No, not exactly that," Leona said, and propped her hands behind her head and lay down again. I went and sat at the foot of her bed, waiting for her to tell me.

"You mean like *Star Trek*?" I asked, being a little silly. Enjoying this game.

"No, not exactly that either, Lieutenant Uhura." She calls me that sometimes, ever since I began working switchboard at Wyndam-Allyn.

She sighed and furrowed her carefully shaped brows. Like a blackbird hunching its wings. "I mean like God. The universe is so big, so wide, and all its little big parts keep moving out—" She sounds urgent and scared. "The whole thing gets bigger and bigger."

Fear is contagious. "Is that what you been thinking about?" I wonder about her. Leona always amazes me. Imagine that. Lying in bed and watching the universe.

"Yeh. It's real scary that something can be so big, beyond comprehension."

I think about the night I stole a candy bar. About the pact I made with heaven to always try to live big.

Leona says, "That's what I been doing, just lying here and trying to figure out where I fit in the vast scheme of things." Then she came out with the stunner, in that calm, decisive manner of hers.

"I'm not going to continue studying architecture," she announced quietly. "I'm going into my father's businesses and work with them."

I didn't ask her why or why not. I waited for her to tell me. But she didn't that day. Not until this bus ride to Atlanta.

Essie wouldn't come with us. She's not with us anymore either. At least I can't feel her presence. And I can't imagine the inside of her head anymore. But I know something crucial is going on. Ever since we saw William at the hospital where Steve is. Ever since that. And ever since the strike ended and everybody got T grades (for "time-out"), the only time in the history of Eden that grade's been given. Though I'm sure people took time out before, just not the whole school at the same time.

Leona offered to help Essie get a job at one of her father's restaurants, but Essie declined. The way she said NO was nice-nasty. Something about niggers and barbecue. Leona was too through.

✦

Then I was too through when Essie informed me that I could never be an artist. This is what happened.

Late one dorm night Essie has said even if it hurt her to say so, "Maggie, great artists have to suffer and you haven't really suffered enough. Look at your life—you got a mother and father and sisters and brothers. So you should just be as good as you can be and maybe teach art. Like your mother said. That's a good idea. Maybe you'll discover the next Picasso or Michelangelo. I hope you're not taking this the wrong way." She pursed her lips and looked consoling.

"Which way is that?" I wish I could take back the story of my grandmother from out of her miserable head. But it's probably gone already. She's forgotten it by now.

Somewhere in those geographies on the bus I told Leona the most important story I have. So important I cannot say why it's important. I just know it. Like Leona knows the Universe is a humongous beast of souls and solar systems, but doesn't know where she fits in. I know that story of my ancestress, but I do not know what I mean to it. Leona didn't say anything. Her mouth was half-open. Like a pause.

Nothing is bad luck. Lee and I don't take it. The noon sun is shining now. The hotel next to the bus station is miles from the campus where the conference takes place. We set out on foot. We talk about the Montgomery Bus Boycott. How could we complain when we put it like that? We've been walking a mile or two. We're at a bend in a highway, curving toward campus, when a car slows down and stops just ahead of us. Hamla sticks her head out the window. William and two other brothers (underclassmen) are in the car with them.

"You all want a ride?" Hamla hollers.

Years ago my sister Pearl sat on the radiator in the kitchen, the same hot seat sad, pretty Charlotte sat on and cried over the life that was beginning in her belly and ending in her head. Pearl sat there and cried for what she couldn't have. She wanted to go to college in Atlanta, to Spelman College. I was hanging around the stove, turning eyes off and on, watching my sister cry. I knew she was thinking of *American Bandstand* and dancing with college boys who were wearing neat suits and collegiate haircuts like newly mown lawns. Those boys would be the leaders of the Negro race like Martin Luther King Jr. Those boys.

And Pearl would live in a dorm full of women just like her. But Pearl got a scholarship and work-study at the Catholic women's college in the hostile White outskirts of the City. So she had to go there instead. Instead of taking out loans and stuff. Madaddy and Mama couldn't afford to send her to Atlanta. Plus, it's so far away. That's what Mama said. "It's so far away." Pearl cried just like Charlotte and I knew she was crying about *American Bandstand* and Negro boys with the future of the race in their suit pockets, and dancing in their feet. And Pearl cried over money.

So Atlanta for me is a city of lost dream. And it's the city of history. Sherman burnt it down. I like that part. Confederate soldiers shrieking and on fire. Scarlett O'Hara wandering dazed and dirty through the burning mess of human flesh and gray uniforms. I'd rewrite the ending and set her aflame. Before I'd actually wept real tears for that fake romance because I believe in two hearts that beat in unison and all that music that I listened to as a little girl. Now I am studying war.

One time I went with Littleson before he was Lazarus on his new paper route. Feeling brave and manly to be dressing in the near dark. He stuck his chest out. Mama got up a half hour after him in the dark. I sneaked out, lying to Littleson that Mama said I could go. We went to the little storefront room and picked up the papers, rolled them up, and piled them into a laundry bag and put the bag on the wagon Uncle Blackstrap made for Littleson. Then we marched like soldiers into the day.

Littleson would toss those papers in graceful arcs onto front porches and against side doors. Others he stuck into mail slots. He was acting real important like he was delivering yesterday before tomorrow came. It was man's work. I wanted to be a paperboy. And Littleson wanted that too, in those days I was his personal sister.

What I remember most (besides this longing to throw the news upside people's houses) were the little streets where the houses were smaller than the houses on Arbor Avenue. Dainty streets not much wider than the pages of a storybook. Streets populated with houses only one or two stories high, lined with young trees. When I got home later that morning Mama told me I had no business going with Littleson. It was too dangerous for a girl. So that dream was knocked out of my head. Yet the memory of close, dainty streets was not. I couldn't imagine belligerent ice babies living on streets like that. I couldn't imagine them there then.

Leona and I walk down a street like that, having turned off from the main thoroughfare that Hamla and William let us out on. We'd thanked them and told them we'd check with them later on. They had plans, so they followed them. We wanted to walk around and find our own way to the events of the day. Maybe in our nonprescribed journeying we'd wander up on someone who was not lost, and who had the directions to the future. And he would be the someone we had been waiting for.

⁑

Registration is going on at tables in the building whose name we recognize from the program the organizing committee mailed to us. We sign our names, pay our money, and pick up our informational packets. Then Leona says, "Let's eat." Because tall, sleek women can eat bushels of food and still be tall and sleek. Certain things are in the genes.

Leona's writing down how much money we spent on sandwiches and strawberry pop, the same brand I drink in Mimosa. They don't have that brand in the City Up North (or Up South like John Olorun calls it in one of his poems).

There are Blackpeople everywhere. Some we recognize from *Negro Digest* magazine; it's *Black World* now. Some from *Ebony*. Some from *Jet*. There are smiles and boisterous greetings. "Habari gani" and "Hey, there." "What it be?" I can see auras hanging around heads that I will paint. I am smiling. "Stop taking pictures, Miss Grace," Leona says. "Look who's coming."

Simba, the painter, strolls over to us. He's sipping juice through a straw from a bottle. "Hey, my sister, Sister African Queen," he's talking to Leona. He passes his tongue over his lips. This grosses me out. He doesn't see me and I'm glad. He's scoping Leona. "I see you made it down here to the folks for your for-real edjumacashun."

Leona, who is never wan, gives wan assent.

"You know the Studio Museum was purchasing my portrait of you for its permanent collection, but some Negro entrepreneur got a hold of it first."

"Yeah," Leona says, not telling Simba the Negro entrepreneur is her daddy. Mr. Pryor puts the picture in the main dining room of his

184

restaurant. He tells all his customers which is his daughter. The most beautiful one. Leona doesn't have to tell me he says this. I've met Mr. Pryor more than once. Leona is all he talks about.

Simba keeps on. "But it was cool. It was cool. We have to feed the consciousness of the masses."

"You have to feed yourself too," Leona smiles. "I bug Maggie all the time about getting paid for her work, and not giving it away."

"Huh," Simba looks confused. "Oh, yeah, yeah." Then he notices me. "Sister Maggie, how's your artwork coming along? You need to get with some of these master craftsmen and really study." Somebody catches his eye right then and he promises to check on us later on.

"Ugh," she says after he's gone.

Leona is chewing gum serenely and shaking her head to get the bad dream of him out.

"He'd be great if he wasn't so stupid acting. Acting stupid takes a lot of creative energy," I say.

I look innocent. "It does, Leona. It takes a lot of energy."

✦

I can imagine Mississippi. I cannot imagine Georgia. Mississippi has a wild streak. A meanness that caused a pickup driver to run Lazarus Littleson and me off the road in broad daylight. I remember that day and that bright sun and the dust that rose up in the wake of the truck to clog our noses and scratch at our eyes, and made Littleson mutter a long string of cusswords, while I just coughed out an attempt.

Excitement filled me all through a workshop on People's Art, even if Simba talked too much and the other panelists were men except for one woman, who wore her art on her back, wearable art. At dusk we go down Hunter, a lively section near campus. There are a few bars, nightclubs, and eateries. People are out having a good time. Mostly just regular people trying to get rid of the grueling workweek in a few hours of fun. Everything is warm and raunchy like the good times my neighbors had at the Butterfly Inn down the street from my house on Arbor Avenue.

Somewhere we make a wrong turn, and find ourselves near a housing development. I've never imagined them before in Atlanta. I knew they were there, but I never imagined. I've seen brothers poised like stalagmites and stalactites at the mouth of the cave of the City, but never dreamed men could be like that here. Little boys race through the spaces between the buildings. Blind alleys I cannot see too far into. Little girls sit on doorsteps with dolls with spearlike breasts and masses of blonde hair.

Leona and I don't talk much. I think she's thinking about stars. I'm thinking about ice babies. And I'm thinking about painting pictures that thaw them out, and I'm thinking about what if our dream of revolutionary change doesn't happen. What if we can't change things? What then? What about the ice babies? What about the Ice Makers?

On the other side of the seesaw of my workshop enthusiasm is an awful possibility. Soon we'll be in Mimosa and Lazarus I know now for sure is there. What will he make of all my workshop talk about protracted struggle and People's Art? My brother who has blood in his eyes. My brother blind with blood.

I am thinking about Steve Rainey and his flirtation with fire. Thinking how quickly fire goes out. But it is not necessarily the worst solution.

In our hotel room Leona and I are just girls in a hotel room for the first time. We figure we can survive off of our chicken sandwiches for the day, but we must have something to drink. I go for the ice, sticking my arm down into the cold jaws of the machine and scooping up piles of ice like my Uncle Blackstrap scooped ice on those summer days when he was the snowball man walking up the streets near Arbor, selling the sweet snowballs we'd suck the juice off then eat the ice. I eat ice now on my way back to the room. Leona has picked up the pop.

Sometimes you're not dreaming and you know things anyway. This time, as we braid our hair and put on nightclothes and go to sleep laughing, this time I know we'll be old women laughing about how young we were that time in Atlanta when we thought club soda was soda pop and almost choked on it. That's what happened. It was a bitter drink, sparkling in the throat like glass.

✦

Hamla's come to stay in our hotel room. She hasn't got a place to stay. She's been staying all night at parties and changing clothes like Superman in phone booths and washrooms. We went to dinner with Hamla and William. William ordered ham hocks, chitterlings, and greens with fatback floating on top like white rafts. Hamla, who is into health food, asked him how he was going to off the pig when the pig was offing him. Which is exactly why William ordered three kinds of pig in the first place. He refuses to follow fads or party lines. Or so he says. Leona said later he has to follow Rhonda's orders and that's enough.

William asked us about Essie. He didn't ask how she was doing. Only what.

Leona told him Essie was working and babysitting her younger brothers and sisters. He started acting very authoritative. "I worry about that sister. I hope she doesn't get sucked down into that life. She's come a long way."

Leona hunches me. Her knuckles digging into my thigh under the table.

Then Hamla asked the question that earned her the invitation to stay with us.

"I heard Rhonda is going to have another baby. Are congratulations in order?"

William looked embarrassed to death.

Later on, when Hamla mentioned she didn't have a place to stay, I was the one who issued the invitation. I know Hamla better than Leona does. Or I remember her when.

After dinner Hamla went to another party; she didn't invite us. She comes to the room in the wee hours, knocks at the door. Leona opens it and Hamla comes in with her shoes in her hand, musk coming off her body and the smell of whiskey coming out of her mouth. She climbs into bed with me. So I can smell her in my sleep.

It is morning and we leave her still sleeping. It's the last day of the conference and the major event is scheduled for evening. A gala of speakers and performances, later dancing.

We are at Stone Mountain with a brother from South Africa and Simba, who is still trying to lay a rap on Leona. The brother from South Africa is a poet in exile from his homeland. A big, round-faced man with fine scars on his cheeks and temples. We take pictures, the four of us, at Stone Mountain. Confederate heroes etched in stone loom in the background.

Stone Mountain is gray granite. The biggest piece of exposed granite on the planet. The poet from South Africa tells us. He has studied America. Just as he has studied his homeland. He asks me where I'm from (after Africa, that is). When I say Mississippi, he knows about that too. Mississippi and Alabama came out of Georgia. Georgia is the youngest of the thirteen original colonies. He says he knows all this American minutiae because he likes to read encyclopedias. He and my brother Lazarus would get along fine. Comparing encyclopedias.

Littleson undertook to read the encyclopedia set from *A* to *Z*. Our Mimosa summer he was reading *U*. United States and Uruguay and Universe. And Unions.

Brother Information from South Africa says granite is a mystery to scientists. No one is sure from whence it came. Or exactly what it is. However, rocks containing more than twenty percent of dark minerals aren't really granite. They are something else. Granite was used extensively for building and paving until macadam and concrete. After World War II granite came back into favor on building facings and the curbs of highways. Granite has always been used for tombstones. As long as people die, and other people decorate burial grounds, there's a market for granite.

I can see it now. This Stone Mountain with the faces of Stonewall Jackson, Jefferson Davis, and Robert E. Lee is a huge, ominous tombstone. A big lump of misery on an otherwise lovely landscape. Their own Wall of Disrespect to Persons of African Ancestry. The Children of the Enslaved. We stand with our backsides to the faces of the Confederacy, scowl, and take pictures.

There's no romance in this outing other than Simba with his big crush on Leona. Over the afternoon, he gives it up a minute and we are just friends. At least he and Leona are. He tells us how he dreams of carving out the faces of our Messiahs in stone one day, but he doesn't know who all to carve. The poet from South Africa takes my hand and we walk back to Simba's car. The South African, Tambo, is telling me how granite is mined. How diamonds are mined in South Africa. In his country the Blackmen who are miners come up out of the dark, stand in rows, and dance a boot dance, shaking the diamond dust from their bodies and boots.

Simba and his friend have to go meet a man about some business. That's what Simba says when they drop us off at the campus where they first picked us up.

We're walking on that diminutive street again, feeling happier than ever because of our sightseeing adventure. Then I see Hamla walking on the other side of the street. At first I don't want to recognize her. She's wearing my one good dress. Sun rises and sets on her.

I clear my throat, "Leona . . ." But Leona has eyes of her own.

"Maggie, that girl has got on your best dress."

I don't say anything because it's my fault. I invited Hamla and vampires can't come in unless you invite them.

Leona runs across the street. I don't want to go, but I follow.

Hamla is explaining, "I slept in my clothes. They were all wrinkled."

"There was an iron."

Hamla is acting mad at Leona for making such a big thing about this. "It was hanging there," she says.

"I want my dress," I say.

"Now?" Hamla incredulous.

"Come back to the hotel. Yeah. Now."

"I have something to do now. I'll meet you there."

"Now," Leona hisses. "I'll snatch you bald and naked, Miss Thing. Here and now."

"Goddamn, Leona." Hamla is exasperated. She'll probably write a poem about Leona.

"On second thought," Leona says, "meet us there. I don't want to embarrass ASAP and I don't want to look at you in Maggie's one good dress."

When you put it that way, it is my one good dress. Meant for a gala.

"Thank you." Hamla sugarcoats Leona's reprieve of her.

She shows up a half hour later at the hotel. Leona answers the door. I just sit on the bed, trying to keep from apologizing for the twentieth time, because not only has Hamla worn my one good dress, she's discarded Leona's onto the floor. It was too long. Leona folds the dress her mother made her and puts it in a drawer. She'll wear something else festive and elegant.

I put on a black T-shirt with white letters that shout UHURU ASAP.

We are children who've stayed too long at a party, whose mama has come to get them. Sleep burns our eyes. Our mouths contorted with yawns. What a mama Bay is! She's always been wild. This time she left her marriage in a tailspin. And ended in a crash. Hank was left in the wreckage.

Henry's name used to be a player. It's a curse now. And Aint Kit is anathema. I didn't know things were so bad. Bay picks us up in the morning. Ready to be gone.

Last night we watched the players of the National Black Theatre in their flowing robes, chanting and swirling and chanting, "We are money. We are money." And they were not telling us we are dollar bills. We are the essence of what is valuable in heaven and on earth. We are God's money and our own. When Bay asks, "So how was it?" I try to think of words to tell her about our being God's spending change and His gold and about Stone Mountain and how there were sparks that flinted between the two ideas. I try to tell Bay but she's not really listening.

She can sink her teeth, however, into the story of Hamla and the Best Dress.

"You shoulda kicked that cow's ass," Bay snarls. She yanks on that rage for many miles.

I didn't think it would be this way when Bay offered to pick us up in Atlanta and take us to Mimosa. I didn't know we'd have to pay such strict attention to her unhappiness. The time of the conference was mostly a good dream, but I can't tell her about it, and Leona is being quiet. There was a man with the brightest smile you'd ever see dressed in a white suit on the stage that last night. Someone behind us said he talked just like Malcolm X. He was a minister of Elijah Muhammad's faith. Then someone behind us paused and said tentatively, "He used to be an actor." The question they didn't ask behind us was the question I turned over in my heart. "Is he another hero to hang our hearts on like a Christmas tree? Is he another soldier to lead us into bloodless or bloody battle? Is he for real?"

Bay starts telling us about Aint Kit, about her latest capers. It's Aint Kit from Atlanta through Alabama to Memphis. In Memphis we miss the turnoff for Highway 61; outside the city we take a wrong road and wind up making a wide arc west. Bay keeps talking about how scenic this route is. But I can tell she's nervous about getting lost in an area she knows so well. She's talking fast and darting glances at her rearview mirror. Leona, in the backseat, is looking polite. That's how I know she'd rather be on the bus. She could stretch her legs too.

We wind up across the river from Mimosa. We start following a road lined on one side by a big barbed wire fence. Hulking hangars loom in the distance, set far back into a field.

"What state are we in?" Leona asks. The borders sit tight like families at funerals.

"Mississippi, I guess." I look at Bay.

"We're in Arkansas." Bay is short because we aren't home.

"Is that a prison?" Leona asks about the barbed wire.

Bay looks over the hangars. "That's not a prison. I don't guess. They put Chinese people there during the Big War."

Dusk is sitting on us. I squint into the silklike late afternoon. "Wasn't that the Japanese they put in concentration camps?"

"Yeah," Bay says. "Sho you right. It was the Japanese. They came all the way from California. Mama and them was talking about that."

When she says "Mama," I don't know if she means Gussie or Aint Kit. I don't dare ask.

✦

By the time we hit Mimosa, it's deep night. Bay comes into town from the highway. Bypassing Old Letha Road, going all the way around. We slide into the drive beside the house. The headlights splashing through the darkness. I can see curtains ripple at the bedroom window.

As soon as the car crunches into place over the tiny rocks, the back door is flung open. Aint Kit is standing in it with a twelve-gauge shotgun in her hands. It's near 'bout big as she is. My mouth turns to club soda. Bay gets out the car with her hands up. We follow suit.

"Goddamn, Mama, what you doing here?" she hollers.

We can hear Aunt Silence in her house. "I told you it was them, Kit. My goodness."

Then Aunt Silence is in the doorway next to Aint Kit. "Y'all come on in. Leave them bags. Son and Hoo'll get them."

191

"Who's Who?" Bay demands as she stomps over the little weeds around the house. We follow her. I guess Littleson Lazarus is Son. But who is Who?

Aunt Silence hugs us one at a time. And Aint Kit hugs Leona and me. Nothing but a wounded scowl for Bay, who doesn't care anyway. Bay asks Aunt Silence again who Who is? But she doesn't get a chance to answer before he does.

He's a young Chinese man standing next to Lazarus in the dining room. "My name is Ed Hoo. You can call me Eddie."

So this is the relative from California who came to Mimosa after the murder. He's handsome in a movie star kind of way. Black black hair and dark eyes shining. He moves gracefully. He and Son (who is Littleson and Lazarus) bring in our bags.

Bay is polite now, before a guest who is out of our race. I know she wants to ask what Ed Hoo is doing here. When I was a girl in Mimosa with Littleson that summer, we saw the Chinese boy and girl playing in the yard behind the store. They waved at us and we waved back at them. But they never came outside of the yard, and we never went in. Mama went to school with Chinese kids. She was friends with a Chinese girl named Anne. She named Anne Perpetua after her long-ago friend.

Hoo and Lazarus put our bags in the bedroom and they go back to the living room, where they've been talking. Did I get a hug from my brother? Did I get a decent hello? Did the bear? That's what my mama would say. Did the bear?

He and Ed Hoo are talking about something called tai chi chuan, which sounds like a drink with umbrellas or a beautiful woman with imprisoned feet and a mincing walk.

"Who's Tai Chi?" Leona asks me. Just like I know. After I eavesdrop for a while I tell her, "A system of exercise and meditation." Then I repeat what Ed Hoo said: "Martial arts are like checking accounts. Tai chi is like a savings account." I wonder what's saved. I keep listening and watching Leona as she inspects my aunt's house.

She's interested in everything. Looking hard at the china in the cabinets. The heavy old furniture. The ancient pictures of ancestors on the walls. The punch bowl on the buffet where Aunt Silence has thrown a handful of loose nails and screws.

"You girls come in the kitchen and get yourselves something to eat," Aunt Silence says. Bay's already sitting down with a plate. Smothered chicken, rice and gravy, greens and corn bread.

Nobody has to invite us twice. And we don't have to write the cost of the meal in Leona's notebook.

I'm fixing plates for Leona and me. You'd think we'd be tired of chicken by now. That's what we ate at the conference. But this is different. My Aunt Silence wrung these chickens' necks with her bare hands. They come from my Aunt Charity and her husband Ike's farm. Aunt Silence tells me how she went to visit her mother out in the country, and they gave her those chickens. She brought them home squawking. And she wrung their necks and chopped off their heads in honor of us.

Aint Kit is in the bedroom being real quiet. By herself. I'm a little worried because she's like a little kid—you'd better worry if she's quiet. I think her feelings are hurt because Bay's not happy to see her. So she acts wounded first, before Bay has a chance to act wounded. It's easier to act wounded than guilty. If you're guilty you have to do something about it.

What we've heard in the car from Atlanta to Mimosa is how Aint Kit gave the first snip in the coming apart of Bay's marriage. The second wedding was a rip in the seam the couple could never repair.

Bay blames Aint Kit. Kit gave Henry the bill for the wedding reception. It was hell over money after that. Even a generous man has a limit, if he's not a fool. Henry wouldn't let Bay buy anything. Bay went back to work so she could have her own money, and he wanted to be in charge of spending that too. Bay said that meant he was a fool.

"Men are real fine-tuned," Bay says. It takes only one insult to wreck their machinery for life. They can't get over tiny things.

In the dining room Leona and I sit across from Bay, whose back is to the living room wall. She's listening to Lazarus and Eddie Hoo and eating gravy. Finished with everything else, she went back for gravy and white bread.

"I wonder if that tai chi anything like kung fu. Hank used to like that. We went to see Bruce Lee and them Chinese movies together. In fact he like that kung fu so much he tried to pull some on me. But I nailed him with a kitchen chair." Bay's meandering in her marriage, humorously, so we'll laugh. "Girl, you should have seen him after I bonked him upside the head. He was weaving around like he was drunk, and you know he never touched a drop, not even at the second wedding, then he just fell out on that little rug I stitched up in the dream house. Fell out on that rug like one of them bearskins in front of a fireplace. Wasn't nothing to that chair in my hand but some kindling."

Aint Kit is in her doorway. Her head cocked to one side. Trouble in her uneven stance. "I wasn't there, was I, Bay?"

"What that mean, Kit?" Bay's not calling her adopted mama Mama right now.

Aint Kit starts talking loud. "I just want everybody to know I wasn't there when you criminal-assaulted your husband. So I'm not responsible for it."

The talk in the living room goes quiet and I can hear chairs scraping. Somebody taking leave. The door closes softly.

Bay slams her white Wonder bread down into the plate of gravy. It splashes a little. Gravy.

"You plant the seed then you don't want for me to call the tree after you? Kiss my ass." It's not a direction, this "kiss my ass." More an exclamation.

"Don't bring your vulgar mouth in this house. In front of these college girls." Aint Kit snaps her mouth shut like a pocketbook.

I can't look at Leona. I can feel her next to me, cleaning her plate. Too embarrassed to stop eating. "Let's go get some more greens," I whisper to Leona to get her out of here.

"Magdalena, I want witnesses. Stay right here." Aint Kit lays her hand on the air so nobody dares move.

Aunt Silence countermands the order. "Kit, it's too late in the evening for some mess. You two save it for your privacy."

Aint Kit sputters, "She brought the whole family in it. I'm defending my reputation."

"What reputation?" Bay says. "For intruding and making up and carrying tales? I bet you ain't tell Aunt Leah-Bethel how you dogged her all over the City about that young man that used to stay with her a while back."

Aunt Silence starts laughing now. Good and hard. "Treemont? Everybody knows what a good worker he was."

Bay says spitefully, "Kit swears he was working in your bed."

Aint Kit looks real nervous now, like one of her stories has come to life on her.

"Lee-Bet, I ain't said no such a thing. No such a thing. I was just worried he was after your property or something." The skin around Aint Kit's eyes is tight. She looks like she wants to jump out of her skin and go somewhere else.

"Bay, ain't no never mind." Aunt Silence waves it all away. "I quit worrying about somebody scandalizing my name a loooooooong time ago. What am I supposed to do about it—snatch every lie out of every mouth? You just clear up your mess with your mother and leave me out of it." Aunt Silence goes back into the kitchen.

Lazarus hollers from the living room, "Good night, ladies." And the front door closes again. Then I see him through the dining room window. He's in the side yard. Doing a strange dance. It's slow like a dragon careful of its tail. It's graceful like a bird dropping through layers of air and cloud.

I haven't told him about the ASAP conference and the agenda for Black Unity. I haven't asked him what else he's been doing in Mimosa all these months, besides talking to the Chinese dude from California about tai chi chuan. And doing the slow-motion dragon dance.

I ask Leona if she's ready to go to bed. Or should I say *couch*, because Aunt Silence has a let-out couch now and that's where we're sleeping.

Leona and I sleep as late as movie stars. We get up to a grim peace in the morning. Everybody has gone clattering about their separate lives. In my sleep I could hear them bumping around. One time I half awakened and peered through the curtains to see Lazarus and Hoo dancing like shadows at dawn. Like two wild dark swans for whom I had made sweaters in my sleep, and they were midway changing to my beautiful brothers in a magic tale. I fell back to sleep in a deeper sleep and woke up again to wonder if I'd dreamed them.

I'm in the kitchen boiling fresh eggs, praying I'm not cooking a chicken fetus alive. That's a hazard of farm-fresh eggs. Now those roosterless eggs we get in the City pose no danger of such a shock. Don't pose much danger of taste either. I make oven toast and Lipton's tea.

Just as we sit down to breakfast, Aint Kit comes through the door. She's got unripe persimmons in her pockets and pecans in her hands. The pecans are still in their pods like heavy little brown coats. The pods haven't curled back yet, exposing the nut like a dark hard teardrop. But Aint Kit hasn't the patience to wait for someone else's time. She needs now. Having lost all but things, she needs more things—unripe persimmons, premature pecans.

"How you feeling this morning?" Aint Kit asks us, helping herself to the hot tea brewing in the white kettle Mama sent Aunt Silence for Christmas.

Aint Kit sits with us.

This morning the sun has no pity. Aint Kit, who has eluded time and wrinkles, is caught in the light. Her face that has always been the same to me shows an aging. Sudden.

"Ugh," Leona growls and spits into her napkin. She's just beheaded a chicken fetus. I've cut my eggs into quarters in early dissection. I thought Leona knew about real eggs.

"I shoulda told you," I commiserate.

"Sure shoulda," Aint Kit agrees. "Quick! Wash your mouth out."

"Drink some tea," I command when Leona comes back from the sink.

"Eat one of these." Aint Kit offers her an early persimmon.

"That'll make her sick," I protest.

"It'll get that dead chicken out of her mouth. It's good and bitter."

When Aint Kit says "dead chicken," Leona grabs the persimmon and nibbles at it.

"You taking Littleson back with you?" Aint Kit asks. "Yo mama says ain't nobody asked about him for a while."

"He never did anything." This comes out of me so violently my toast jumps on the plate.

"That's what your mama told them. I told them that too when they come to my house asking all them crooked questions about your brother. I told them they better hightail it offa my property before I turn my big dogs loose on 'em. They lit out of there."

I sip my tea throughout Aint Kit's account of her encounter with the plainclothesmen. I wonder if it happened, and if so, how it actually happened. Maybe it's true. These are outlandish times.

They are plump and long necked like those African beauties with bracelets on their necks. The necks long and nervous. And their bodies are too. Nervous. Jumping straight up and flapping at the sound of our approach. They scream and flail the air, running without reason. They tickle Aint Kit. The feathers. Without touching her. We're still in the car. All this nervous homage outside. "Charity and Ike don't need no dog. Do they, Maggie?"

"Uh-huh," I agree.

"Maybe I ought to carry me a pair of them chick guineas back with me to guard my property."

"And get arrested for disturbing the peace."

We're leaning on the car, looking at grass, fields, and fowl. The commotion keeps resuscitating itself at our every gesture. Our laughter enflames the multitudinous birds. So, heralded by guineas, we tread free feathers and hanging shrieks to the house. Aint Kit, Leona, and me.

We've arrived at an inconvenient time. Lunch or dinner on this farm is over and Grandmama Patsy is watching her stories. After our greetings and introduction of my friend from college, we fit into the rhythms of the house. Consequently, when Aint Kit starts talking, Aunt Charity says, "My stories are on." And sits in a stubborn style with her chin up and her eyes straight ahead. She's concentrating on not listening to her sister, even though she can hear her very well and remember a recent lie that Kit made up on the spur of the moment, that her son in the army was court-martialed and is in the federal prison at Leavenworth. This cold shoulder puts Aint Kit's shoulders low.

During a commercial, Aunt Charity gets up and cuts Leona and me each a big hunk of caramel cake. She pours us coffee and says we can have milk and sugar. She looks at her sister coolly. "Kit, you can have some cake and eat it too. You know you want to." Aint Kit takes the cake.

"Marshall coming out the service soon. Isn't he, Charity?" she says by way of apology, attempting to clean up her lie.

Charity is the oldest, thin as a penny and penny colored too. She's in a stingy mood. (I don't know exactly what Aint Kit said Marshall was court-martialed for, but if I start to imagine, it could take me anywhere.)

The only relenting Charity will do is this: "Maggie might want to see Ike. He feeding the poultry. Mama be ready to visit in a little while after she get done with her nap."

This is a lie. Grandmama can take her nap, watch her stories, and give you an update while listening to news any day. I've started to imagine. I think this is a ruse to get Leona and me out the house while Aunt Charity gets Aint Kit told about that flash in the pan lie Aint Kit told Bay. Another one. Aint Kit says Aunt Charity was feeding Grandmama arsenic and Valium in her grits. Keeping her doped up so she could have her Social Security money. Suppressing her appetite so she wouldn't eat much.

Pearl told me that Aunt Charity called Aint Kit and told her just what she'd heard she said.

All Aint Kit, taken aback by the direct honesty and hurt in her older sister's voice, could say was, "Did I say that?" according to Pearl in the most fake-innocent way. With a naughty little giggle to boot.

Today, I surmise, the giggle to boot didn't get anywhere with Charity. I guess she gone do like Madaddy did when he put that lock on the phone and you couldn't dial out. Put a stop to this mess once and for all.

At one time Uncle Ike and Aunt Charity's farm was four times its present size, but it was his father's then, even though they worked it. His father had three other children and he left three-quarters to them.

Each in turn sold his inheritance to the same man, who was a company, a corporate body in and of himself.

But a quarter of a birthright is better than a disinheritance, and the farm is populated by fowl of every class, subclass, genus. Chickens, pigeons and doves, guinea hens, geese, turkeys tame and wild, and a pair of peacocks who walk in the assumption of beauty, keeping up a terrible duet. Sounds like their necks are stretched with iron prongs. They wander away from each other, then call after like Jeanette MacDonald and Nelson Eddy. "When I'm calling you-uuu-uuuuu." Their waste left behind their mincing steps like great globs of chocolate ice cream. That first summer Littleson and I were here, I wouldn't eat Fudgsicles for a year after.

I always laugh at the geese, who remind me of desperate children. Look! They all go leftward. Necks pulled out, each head pointing the one way, and then they go there. They mill around like spectators after a game. Then look! They all flock to the right. Honking all the way. I just start laughing and laughing at the sight of this. Leona says they are pitiful. One brain between them and it don't work good.

Now I know they remind me of the Marx Brothers, tuxedos pulled open, strutting into a major stupidity. Then I see geese smoking cigars and I laugh all the more. Lee looks quizzical, but I don't even try to explain the silliness I entertain myself with.

But what adds to the laugh is a delight. How do they all know to stay so close and go the same right way?

The peacocks yodel like lost lovers, the geese honk like jeeps, chickens squawk and complain, and the doves and pigeons coo like somebody who's just smoked reefer. I step carefully through the yard to the place they are housed. Leaving behind Leona, who is living a *Lassie* rerun, pretending she is Timmy's mother, sprinkling corn meticulously like a little girl letting go of flower petals, one by one.

Uncle Ike, his hat broken down on his head, the brim sharp to one side of his head, stands smiling and smoking a Kool. Two packs a day he's been smoking for years. So his voice, when it drives out of his throat like a truck, sounds like wheels on a gravel road. He's so dark his skin looks like smoke, shiny with the sun shining on it. And his eyes have caught fire with something deliriously happy. His smile opens doors. His body thin enough in his blue overalls to slip through on a beam of sunlight.

"Caution. Else you step in some stink," he throws over at me like a ventriloquist. You'd think a tree had spoken. Rock doves coo at the sound of his heavy, eight-wheeler voice. Laden with regard.

He and Aunt Charity wanted to keep me for my smile when I was a child. But Madaddy said no and Mama asked me if I wanted to stay with them. Knowing I'd throw my arms around her waist and holler protest at the invitation. Not only were they not Sam and Caroline, they were old. Even Ike and Charity's children are almost as old as my daddy and mama.

Ike is so gentle anything wild would eat off his eyelids and he would let it. So it's a paradox to hear the Uncles laud the level aim of his rifle. Uncle Ike killed a Whiteman and nobody had the nerve to take him in. People like him are a mystery to me. How is it certain death and systemic dishonor draw a circle around them and do not trespass?

"He don't bother nobody," Aunt Charity said when I asked about what I'd overheard.

"What that Whiteman do?" I asked.

And Aunt Charity said, "It's only ten commandments. Must a been one a 'em he crossed on."

I went through them in my head. (Blasphemed? Lied? Stole? Coveted? Killed? Dishonored? Disremembered?) This was a useless exercise, because sin was so general and usually tiny like the specks you raked your conscience for before confession in the small room with a veil between you and forgiveness.

You cannot put a pigeon in a new house just like that. The wood will make him sick. That's what Ike says when he explains the care and feeding of his many breeds. You have to grind up their droppings and spread the meal over the floor. The way our father spread his anger around the house, and if we stepped on it and made a sound—in movement or disgust—we were dead meat.

Now Uncle Ike mixes his own meal for each breed of pigeon. The batches separate in barrels labeled by name: Laugher (who hides the laughing in its throat when it's scared), Archangel, Ice, Barb, King and Mondain and Carneau and Chinese Fat Shan Blue (for squabs to serve in the finest restaurants), Wild Rock, Columbia Guinea, and Flying Tippler. He mixes so much meal, so much mineral, so much gravel.

His favorite is the black Egyptian Tumbler, a pair of which he keeps in big empty pots that hang from the ceiling in the barn. Each morning he watches them turn somersaults in the air above their clay resting places. He drinks black coffee and watches them, a black whirl, dashing and extravagant.

He used to have more breeds, but they died out or he sold them to showmen and gamblers. The Hungarian Giant House and Giant Mallorquina Runt killed their own breed over time. The weight of the mother's heavy body breaking eggs in the nest. Smothering squabs. Observing these murders Silence learned how to sit on eggs and listen to silence. Uncle Ike didn't have to tell her what to do, and if he had he wouldn't have because his speech is sparse.

He speaks when you don't expect him to. Like his mind is a field infused with blue, and suddenly a burst of sound, a deep rustle, or a fleet movement like the drop of an eyelash. That is what his talking is like. I don't believe he's ever loud-talked anybody in his life, which is long, like the last echo from the 1900s. In age he is midway between Grand-mama and Aunt Charity. Seventy, eighty, or so. But he doesn't seem so old as that. If that's old. Funny. Old seems less and less old and more lucky.

I'm trying to follow his life now. To find out how he wound up with so many wings underfoot. But a year is a rustle. And a decade the drop of an eyelash on his face.

"Look like I couldn't stay here no mo'. Nothing to keep me. I just set out to see the ocean. That's what I callt it. But I just went somewhere because I could go somewhere. Cotched a train. Then cotched another one. Walked. Worked. Scratched on a back door one time I was so hungry and cold. Lady gave me something wrapped in newspaper. I read the paper and ate the corn bread and sweet potato she give me. It was a story in there about a man who raised pigeons. Had his picture in the paper. He look like a pigeon too. White guy. Had a loooong nose made like a tunnel with a curve on the end just befo' you see daylight." He stops talking abruptly. Fowl doo on his boots. His hands powdery with mixing the many feeds for each breed of bird.

He is looking at his hands in a surprised kind of way. His heavy eyebrows shooting up at the sight of such hands attached to him—able, dexterous hands that have fine-line wrinkles inside a natural smoothness. Like snakeskin he can crawl out of and grow again. Start over fresh from the outside.

"When you go out in the field look for guinea eggs. They lay 'em out there. That's how I know a guinea is touchy 'bout they freedom."

I think he's trying to get rid of me in a roundabout way.

"What do they look like, Uncle Ike?" I'm certain I won't see one, because I'm not going. I'd rather get in his business.

His mind is long, blue grasses again and no sound stirs them. Holy Week, that Saturday, the Parks gave an Easter egg hunt. A thousand children would gather in a field named after a president. Jumping up and down like rabbits and rabbettes, as Sam Jr. dubbed them. Most of us in our playclothes. A weekend morning so we were still fresh, no food marks, and grass tattoos in the fabric. The girls' braids and bangs still flat. Vaseline still glistening on the scrubbed skin. This was a special time and a few dressed for Easter before it came. The girls in petticoats and stick-out dresses with pink satin sashes and white socks that ended in a border of ruffled lace at the ankles. Like frilly white manacles. Patent leather shoes for the wet grass and pits of mud that appeared unexpectedly but usually around the base of the bushes.

The Park Lady would stand with a megaphone in hand, lift it to her lips, and say, "Quiet, boys and girls. You have your instructions. Okay. Ready. Set. Search."

And we would zip like desperate little wood creatures after a bitter, long winter.

I peeked into bushes, parting the branches like prickly curtains. Circled the roots of trees, staring up into crevices. I didn't find not one egg, but once, I reached for something colored like a painting in dark blue and yellow in the deep wishbone of a bush, but another pair of hands, the same brown as mine, covered over it. The bushes shook like a ghost was dressing amid leaves.

"Guinea eggs are speckled," Uncle Ike says.

The next question I ask is caged in legend. I start, "Aint Kit said—" He slides me a look, just as I knew he would. I keep on. "She said you killed a Whiteman." I can't keep the longing nudge out. (Oh, please, say you did kill a Whiteman. And you a Blackman not to be messed with.)

It doesn't work. He doesn't answer. So I move to something else immediate and accelerant, looking not at him, but at a dove, brushing its breast with the tip of its beak. Curled exquisitely like a plump interrogative mark in a mesh stall.

"Littleson is scared to go home with me."

"They got something on him?"

"NO. But they make up things. They pay people to make up things."

"That ain't new."

"I know," I say, proud to agree with him based upon what I've learned on Blood Island.

The dove looks up at us, extends her wings, races with herself behind the mesh wire.

Now we're both in high grass. Thinking is lost balls. I feel bound, like I must be loosed. I get up from my perch too close to him, move closer to that dove that stops her traveling now and observes me with the ember eyes of pigeons. I know that look. It doesn't last. They fly away.

"I never killed a man. That Whiteboy fell out the tree ahead a me. I tole him I seen a passenger pigeon. So there he go. I knew it wouldn't gone be there. But he had to see. And I had to see if he seed. So he went up and I went up higher. And he got to grabbing after something tryin to get up higher than I was. And he fell down and cracked his head wide open. I climbed down and seed him bleedin, breath knocked out of him, and I flew. That's when I went north and went to Ohio and saw the passenger pigeon in a cage up there."

"You went to see the ocean then?"

"That was later on. Once I worked at the pigeon farm I came back down here and start my own place. Things just come to me. So they come and I raised 'em. Sometimes I pretend I work for a Whiteman and I can buy the breeds I want then. But I work for it. The rest I work for till I get it."

He says this to say his life is simple. He is not the outlaw I have imagined. He is not the murderer the Uncles laud. He says this to say shut up and be quiet and let me work. He doesn't talk anymore, looks up now and then from his task like a man in prayer looking at his surroundings in surprise.

"Them stories over," he announces without looking at a watch. Maybe it's the sunlight that has walked past the door to the pigeon house by now. The measure of light in which some people can read time. He's happy about this time. His gravelly voice lifted and his demeanor free of me and what he could tell me if it could be told. Or maybe he's just shy because he's a country man and I'm a college girl. But he's no mystic farmer. He keeps his own books, drives his racing birds and squabs to the railroad crossing, where they're loaded on and sent to the starting points or end points. Maybe they travel far. To the ocean. Over it. Maybe.

This is what it's like trying to talk to a man. After a while they drop their heads and smooth their chests, and are very busy about their hearts. You can't get anything out of them, during that private bathing in thoughts, that discreet inspection of plumage and coat. And his bits of story, combed out of his breast, are over. I can't get a word in edgewise this reticence.

Aunt Charity is standing at the table, pouring coffee from the small silver coffeepot that stays on the stove like a nonambulatory boarder.

"What were you and Ike talking about?" She looks up happily. The coffee smoking in the cup. The pot back on its iron bed like Grandmama Patsy in hers.

"Passenger pigeons," I synopsize incompletely.

"Oh, they all dead now." Any fact sounds happy coming from her. "Otherwise Ike would have one right out there. Under his eyes."

At the window over the sink now, I'm looking out. "Where's Leona?"

"Talking to Mama."

I come in the bedroom on the complexity of a continuing drama.

"You seen the new stories?" she asks as I enter. *One Life to Live* and now *All My Children*.

I nod that I know.

"They got colored on 'em. That girl—" she points at the blank screen—"Carla-Clara, who look White. I knew she was colored. I knew it. I tole Charity and Ike she colored." She is pleased to have known instantaneously what was clear in protracted revelation. (Protracted as in long drawn out as in struggle. Yvonne Christmas said once we are not used to protracted struggle.) But what's the difference between an instant and a season?

Time is a hopscotch game for Grandmama. She can skip over one and two and throw her rock into Sky Blue. Remembers the details of 1927, the deluge in which farms bobbed away like miniature tugboats in a bathtub. Trees treaded water. And rescue came by canoe, but she's not remembering that now. Instead she remembers twice Vikki, who's got an extra self named Nikki. The second one is a bad girl. So the bad girl takes the good girl to taverns and the arms of strange men, because the father of good and bad, Victor Lord, was no good and real rich.

Leona laughs all through this Vikki-Nikki and Carla-Clara, who real light and her mama, Sadie-Sarah, is dark and big and good. Carla-Clara is passing for White. In this day and age.

"Just like *Imitation of Life*," Grandmama Patsy says. "You see that?"

We nod like kindergarteners. She, in that sweet doll voice from the weathered body of a doll that's been worked like a mule, tells us both versions.

"We gotta go, Grandmama." I try to cushion our exit.

"Well, go on then," she says, grumpy and sad and happy at once.

Aint Kit has left us. We are stranded. The car that brought us here is gone.

Leona and I don't stand close to each other. I go back into the house and she goes to the edge of the field to steam. How do people imagine vacation? I should have come alone. Suffered through my own bad trip.

One look at my face and Uncle Ike says, "I got to run into Letha. Can go the other way too."

When she hears his truck, my friend comes quick to hitch this ride. And Grandmama Patsy gets out of bed for a brief, pain-shot walk to the front porch. She and her daughter—they wave.

Aunt Charity has put on her glasses that from the distance look like the surface of a river. Light on top, too much water underneath, the glint with a wave on it. "Tell Kit I say call me."

The engine of the pickup truck is loud. I talk loud. "I can't—"

"Tell KATHERINE I say call me."

I guess she thinks people can hear a legal name better. I nod like a pilot who understands the sign language of aircraft mechanics on the ground.

The ride is quiet. Only the truck talking and Uncle Ike, moving gravel through a whistle. We are no longer stranded, so I begin my defense.

"Aint Kit don't lie all the time." This is not to him or Leona, intentionally.

"That's because she don't talk all the time," Uncle Ike replies, mildly amazed that I hadn't figured it out.

✦

Leona is bored. She is too quiet, like a baby in the next room getting into something. It's my fault. I was born here. Out of all the places we dreamed of at Eden, Mimosa is not one Leona had in mind. Downtown Mimosa is about as exciting as lettuce. That's where Uncle Ike has dropped us off, having to get to Letha before the store closes.

Here the buildings don't have such big ideas; there are no high-rises like spectacular prisons the brothers at the EARTH would deem concentration camps. There is a certain grandness in the columns that hold up the front of the library and the municipal building. White and gray, respectively. They have a certain bulk to them, unlike the other buildings, which are low, closer to the ground. They would comfort by the absence of too much stature if we knew we were welcome or wanted to be. The five-and-dime, the photographer's studio, the furniture store, the women's dress shop, all lined up like a scene from a town on *The Twilight Zone*. There's a terrible secret you can never get out—or you're doomed to watch yourself in childhood die over and over—or some writer in a study with a fireplace thought this scene up at his Dictaphone. The dresses in the dress shop window would have been ugly when I was born. They're uglier now. Especially when I compare them to Leona's yellow mini and my royal-blue dress.

We linger at the window of the photographer's studio. Look at the framed photos of rosy-pink faces, uncomfortable and smiling in polyester dress clothes. The hair hammered on. It's as if they were framed inside something that caught them. Like a mousetrap.

There's no sign of the Revolution here. Here fires do not seem possible. Smoke rising out of the incineration of houses passes over. Traveling like my grandmama says rain does. Where does it go? I wonder. The smoldering hurt. The blood-borne disquiet. Imagine the KKK on *The Andy Griffith Show*. Barney Fife (thin as a spaghetti noodle, his Adam's apple a knot in the noodle) as the Grand Dragon of Mayberry. That's the kind of imagination you have to have to be Black and twenty in 1970 in Mimosa, Mississippi. Instinct fine-tuned to pick up what holds the surface together. It is the way I remember it from our summer here years ago. And probably the way it was when I came out of my mother, twenty years ago in the house on Chinaman's Store. The midwife cleaned me and put me on a pillow, where I cried and slept and waited for the hands, the breast, the milk, and a humming over my head.

Bay says Mimosa's changed. She's eaten often at the lunch counter downtown. The food wasn't that good till they got a new cook. But the concept was good. There are one or two Black clerks in the five-and-dime. A tenuous movement toward a show of equity. These remarkable signs are like tentative steps onto a tightrope—the rest of us stand below with our mouths open in amazement, in wonder, in fear of the inevitability of gravity as we know it.

Natural hair is here in force and Leona and I aren't alone. Some brothers, look like they're in high school, pull up in a black car. "Hey, Soul Sisters!" They salute us.

That sounds real to us. They're three or four years younger than we are. Their black Afro picks jammed into the breast pockets of their shirts. Everything about them neat. Up north, I can guess John Olorun and them at Great Zimbabwe are in sandals. These brothers have on shiny black shoes that tie with black shoelaces, dark socks, and dark pants and white and blue shirts, both of them. They are boy-thin. They look like new matchsticks.

"Hey, I ain't never seen you two gorgeous sisters befo'. How'd I miss you and I'm still breathing?" The taller of the two, he is Mr. Suave, though both of them are gangly. His smile, hefted up from way inside his chest, is more open than any at Eden.

Leona decides to answer this greeting. "We don't live here." Her boredom has only slightly diminished. It's still underneath.

"I was born here." That's me. I look at the pick in his pocket. At Eden we hide them. "But I didn't stay."

"At first I thought you were cheerleaders from George Washington Carver High." He's still looking at Leona. Admiring her long legs.

"A cheerleader?" Leona bursts out laughing.

Mr. Suave won't give in to crestfallen. He's sturdier than I first thought. He's Leona's height. Their eyes are even. "Carver High has the most beautiful cheerleaders in the state." All the while that smile, like a lamp you can't unplug. "My name is Ralph Collins and this is Leon Doolittle."

"Is it true?" I ask Leon Doolittle. "You do little?"

"As little as possible. I believe in efficiency."

We're standing on the street all this time. Very few passersby. Not much shopping going on today. Yet even though the street is vacant—a few trees, a few birds, not any pigeons—and clean, I start rubbing the nape of my neck and looking around. But the windows are blank, the blinds at midway, and no door opens to let anyone out.

In some way Leona has conveyed our station in life: we are in college. Instead of deflating the attentions of our high school suitors, it's increased them.

207

"I saw that on television. Didn't y'all take over a building?" Ralph's whole head is like a lamp now, beaming out of his mouth and eyes like a jack-o'-lantern. "I'm going to Tougaloo. We don't have to take no building. It's already ours."

"You own it, right? They killing Blackfolks at Jackson State. But your president is Black and every single trustee is Black. And even if it is Black, that doesn't make it revolutionary and designed to help you earn your freedom." That's Leona.

"You sound like the Last Poets. Don't she sound like the Last Poets, Ralph? Niggahs—awh, niggahs, niggahs are scared of rev-o-lu-tion."

They cut out the musical "niggahs" when somebody's mother comes out of one of the stores. She's thin, neat in a shirtwaist, brown-skinned and hair like a panther's skin, pressed sleek and black. We watch the tail end of her farewell, "Goodnight, Mr. Weatherby. I'll see you early." She turns toward us and I think she'd be sophisticated, if she didn't have cross-eyes.

Out of range of the store, she uncrosses her eyes. "Hi!" she says, sounding friendly, tired, and pent up.

"Hey, Muh Dear," says Ralph. "These two young ladies need a sight-seeing tour of our fair city."

Her interest piqued, Muh Dear whips her panther-skin hair around in our direction. She studies us smilingly while Ralph tells everything he knows about us. He's a talker. Both boys prance in place, ready to go and take us with them.

Muh Dear is Ruby Collins. "Y'all have to come on by the house for a minute so these young men can drop me off. My feet hurt. My deodorant is wearing off. I'm justa sweatin. And I'm thirsty. Weatherby's is air-conditioned, but I'm not." She talks and tries not to look us up and down at the same time. They wear their skirts longer down here. Ours get shorter when we slide into the backseat. She leans her head back against the front seat upholstery. "Wooooooo!" She sighs and turns around to look at us. "Integration wears your nerves thin," she snaps.

"The Blackwoman has always worked in close proximity to Whites," Leon Doolittle sounds like he's quoting an article in *Ebony* magazine. A caption under a photo of a Black maid serving iced tea to a governor's wife or a movie star of faded dimension.

"And we all had thin nerves," Ruby shoots back at him, ducking her head the other way to pin him with the authority of experience.

She's talking to us again. "We live over past Highway 1. On the other side. They've built a lot of new stores and restaurants out along the interstate. Downtown is dying. Aaaa, me. Weatherby's losing money, so they hired colored to keep the colored dollar. We're very loyal people."

The car is quiet. We're all looking out the window.

We pass a funeral home and a rice-packaging plant.

"There's the famous rice!" I exclaim. Dumb of me to have never considered something so simple as how rice gets in a package. Then, I figure, if they package rice here, they must grow it nearby. And that never crossed my mind before. What the EARTH was talking about. After the Revolution it would be easier to live from scratch than try to control an infinite number of factories even though we work them now. Of course EARTH would say it'll all be gone. The grad students would talk about controlling the means of production. Even rice is complicated.

"Further down on that road," Miss Ruby points, "is the soybean plant, if that interests you. I worked there for quite a while, but the dust stirred up my asthma. They told me I didn't want to work. It was all in my mind. They refused me disability—listen at me, sound just as grouchy. It is the end of the day and my feet hurt and I got to cook dinner for these boys."

"Never mind, Aunt Ruby. We'll take them to the Sunflower Café or something."

"You ain't goin in no juke joint."

"It's nice."

"Don't you go there."

That's how we wind up in Miss Ruby Collins's house for dinner. Especially after she learned my last name is Grace. Kin to Miss Leah-Bethel.

"I worship that woman. Here, take her one of my pies."

"Mama, you told me that was my pie."

"You ought to be glad to give Miss Leah-Bethel Grace of the Mississippi Freedom Democratic Party the food out of yo mouth. That woman laid her body down for you." Tucking the edges of the pie with foil, she keeps repeating herself. "Laid her body down. You better remember that."

Outside the bungalow, at the black car again, the night coming. "Ask her if she remember me. Ruby. Used to follow her home from church. Be sure and tell her I know my Providential policy has lapsed, but I'm working again, and my husband is still at the soybean plant, so I'm ready to get caught up. Be sure you tell her now."

She's standing in her sky-blue house shoes, haloed in the headlights of the car. Smiling, arms crossed in front of her, holding back the weariness she tries to hide in relentless hospitality. I think she is happy. Now she can go to bed and sleep until her husband comes home. She'll talk to him in her sleep, until he says something that wakes her up. Then she'll get up and put his food on the table. Did she leave it in the oven?

We're sitting inside her black car, stomach tight with fried chicken, crowder peas, corn bread, and okra. My mind is up to its old tricks—I paint her as a ruby, the jewel itself; the light from way inside pushing through the lustrous dark. She is not foreign to me. I've known her all my life. When she got to the City, she was the same, only walked faster, talked faster. Developed a craft to get ahead. Met somebody or came with him from home. Went to church on Sunday and met a peace of mind. Had a husband or didn't. Birthed children. Got on the waiting list for the Homes because the rents were reasonable and the rooms concrete and modern and not a hovel. Till something better came along. Locked the door. Watched TV. Sewed. Talked on the phone. Read mysteries and romances. Helped with homework. Served in the Women's Club. Fixed dinner, washed dishes, and worried. Went to work. Worked hard. Maybe moved out of the Homes. Maybe stayed.

When I met her I recognized a vernacular decency, ordinary as grass, consequently unremarked. Her dream is medium-sized, not easily sat-isfied, but not so big someone must take a gun to it. Though, odd as it is to me and Leona, men have taken guns to it, come riding six white horses or more, carrying guns to shoot down the simplest aspiration. Why should it be an aspiration? Working at Weatherby's is a big thing. But the fee is in her aching feet, nerves thinned by suspicion and conde-scension from her coworkers and owners, and a general tiredness after work. And if that's not the worst that comes of being the First Black Sales Clerk in Downtown Mimosa, then she's number one without a whimper.

She makes half the salary of the other clerks and does twice the work.

When Ralph and Leon take us past the mission church, white stucco Spanish hacienda style, I tell Leona that's where I was baptized. That's my story.

"I'd like to meet my godmother, but she's dead now."

"I would have just liked to have seen my father's face," she says in her Leona way.

This gives me pause. My mouth locks open and I can't close it to make words. She laughs a little to watch me thunderstruck.

"I never told you? That's right. August Pryor is my stepfather. He adopted me. My father died when I was in my mother's womb. He was working in a factory or something and a piece of machinery fell on him. They say they couldn't get it off of him. If they tried. He was a foreman over some White guys. They weren't thrilled."

"So they let him suffer and die."

"Suffer and die. That's what everybody does, isn't it?"

"That's so sad." My voice, I can hear, sounds like gravy, all thick and over everything.

"Yeah. He was from Arkansas. That's kinda why I wanted us to come here. It's all the same. But it's not."

She waits for me to dispute this, but I don't. This is my story.

"I'm going to visit his grave sometime." This promise is pensive, already denied by her love for Augustus Pryor.

In the front seat, the boys haven't heard us. They've been talking loud about sports: Kareem Abdul-Jabbar, Muhammad Ali, Gale Sayers. When we tell them we saw Lew Alcindor in a game against Eden, they say, "Who's that?"

So, now I know a name is something you wear.

"Kareem, Jones, Kareem is Lew Alcindor."

An African name. That would be beautiful, but my mother named me on her own. And Grace I wouldn't mind feeling. So I'm stuck.

"What was your father's name?" I ask Leona.

She has her head leaned back. "Thomas," she says, her mouth moving. Blinking one time.

"Thomas."

"Thomas L. Register."

"Leona Register." I taste that.

"Leona Register! Awh, Daddy, bring home the bacon! Give me the check so I can make this house note. Rest yourself, darling. Do you still like your eggs sunny-side up! Hey! Hey! Hey!" She's in another life.

"Leona," Leon says, looking goofy eyed. "We belong together. Leon and Leona. You can be whoever you want to be."

"I'm gone be that anyway."

He's so smitten he doesn't mind the rebuff.

✦

"Did I tell you about the time Sam Jr. and Honeybabe almost made you a Popsicle?" Aunt Silence asks me. She is sipping from a glass of soothing springwater she gets by the jug in Georgia. Bay picked up gallons for her. She's been drinking this water for a long time. Right now drinking and telling me the stories that tell me who I am.

"No, ma'am," I say to the Popsicle story.

"This was about nine months or so after I came back from the hospital. You were a little biddy thing, still walking like a bird the way you lift your legs straight up, pick up yo feet from the floor."

This pleases me. Aunt Silence remembering so particularly my ways as a child. I feel special.

"When I was in my own little world like I used to be in those days and I was walking in the shared yard between Mama's, my house, and yo daddy's—you all's house. Hunting pecans I believe I call myself doing. Don't ask me why I call myself doin that. There was plenty other things to be doing. It was spring I think it was and them pecans would have been on the ground a long time. They was probably rotten. Or else you kids woulda been done picked 'em up and ate 'em all up. I guess I was lookin for pecans. So I was lookin down nowhere near the pecan tree and soon looked up to find myself under y'all's kitchen window. So I remember shadin my eyes like I was lookin at the sun and starin into yo mama's kitchen.

"Sure enough, I saw Honeybabe and Sam Jr. just as busy as you please taking all the racks out yo mama's 'frigerator. I thought they was good kids helping they mama while she was at work. Well, when they had all

212

the racks stacked neatly beside the 'frigerator, they wiped it out and here come you. Laughing. Just laughing cause you was playin. Honeybabe picked you up, while Sam Jr. holt the door open and they was grinnin like funeral parlor directors. You know our cousin Hilliard is a funeral parlor director. You should see that foolish grin. Especially when somebody be dead and the family carrying on.

"Do you know them fools, Honeybabe and Sam Jr., put you in that 'frigerator? And you sat down like you was having yo picture took, with yo rag doll my mama made for you in yo hands. You was laughin. Pearl and Littleson was in the room. I could hear them callin Honey. So she and Sam went to see what they was screamin so for, and they closed the door on you. Pretty little smiling you. Look like a baby angel walking and sittin insteada flyin and floatin.

"I kept lookin for one of them to come back and get you. It couldna been longer than a minute. But all of a sudden I got so scared. My heart was beatin in my eyes. All in my throat and chest so loud I flung those hollow pecans out of my hands and went flyin through the back door. Almost pulled the screen door off its hinge. Then I flung open the 'frigerator door and you was still sittin up in there smiling like you was waiting to have yo picture took.

"But you opened yo arms for me to pick you up and you said, 'Lee Bee,' cause that was what you called me then when you couldn't say my name. That was enough for me. That was enough for me. I took you away from there. I fried you some green tomatoes. When the other kids come looking for you and something to eat, I wouldn't give them none and I wouldn't give them you. I wouldn't give you to nobody till Caroline came to get you. I tole her they tried to freeze you and she whipped them foolish kids all out in the yard. Then she came back and I gave you up. That day was so nice with you I didn't feel like being quite so lost in my mind. Yeah, like I told you and Littleson that time, it was Silence that saved me, listening to the Silence, and you called me Silence after that. But before that having somebody else to save brought me to myself the resta the way."

By the time Aunt Silence finishes the story of my near demise, Lazarus, Leona, and I are wallowing on the couch and floor, holding our sides, crying-laughing, and whooping it up. I don't know quite why the refrigerator episode tickles us so. Maybe we're laughing at how casually, accidentally, my life defeated death. I was a goner, but for a little coincidence.

"You have to believe in Providence," Aunt Silence says, shaking her head in satisfaction with the Lord.

"What do you call it when Providence doesn't work?" Lazarus asks. Now he looks old and sad and wistful and cynical.

Aunt Silence doesn't act like she likes answering, but she does: "I think they call it God's will or Devil's work one."

"Don't you wonder sometimes?" asks Lazarus, standing at the window, searching into the night.

"Wonder about what?" Aunt Silence asks so he'll say and know himself.

"The nature of Providence. Ted Harris and Archie Ferguson died in a pool of blood. They shot them in the head, both of them. Someone must have given them drugs to make them sleep like that, because Ted was serious and understood our oppressors. The blood soaked through the mattress. The walls were perforated with bullet holes like a sponge but the walls couldn't hold that blood . . . I can still see it in my head."

"You think I can't see, Son? I wasn't there, but I can see it. You know people like to say Jesus died for our sins. Jesus was murdered. He was unnaturally murdered. Do you understand me?"

Lazarus is still looking into the dark beyond the lamplight. Leona and me looking at Aunt Silence's face, the play of wordless language vibrating around her. She's sitting right near the lamp, but she's turned so her face is half lit and half hidden. She purses her lips delicately, then she asks as if the words for her asking were already inadequate. "Who else do you see?" Aunt Silence asks Lazarus, my brother. Lazarus keeps looking past the porch light into a swelling night under a full moon. "I keep seeing a man running alongside of the road and he's being chased. And they almost catch him, but they don't."

"It's Providence that saved him," Aunt Silence says, and the words are sure as a rock in your palm. She's got her feet up, and she's sitting in the rocker that doesn't move. She's too still for anything to move beyond the light. "You mean to tell me you read them letters, Son, and you still don't know."

I do not know what my aunt is talking about. Lazarus doesn't answer and we each sit for a while without anybody opening a mouth. Then Leona and I start telling Lazarus about Atlanta. He keeps searching out the window, not like he's looking out against something, but like he's looking for something. Aunt Silence rocks now, going back and forth, not taking her eyes from Lazarus's back. Leona's looking at Lazarus and I'm looking at Aunt Silence. There's something we don't know about, Leona and me. I ask about these letters Lazarus is supposed to have read.

Lazarus won't tell me. He just looks out the window. Maybe he's looking for Bay, who's gone to her mother, Gussie's, house. Or maybe he's looking for Aint Kit, who's gone God knows where. Most likely to see Grandmama Patsy and Aunt Charity, where she will cry and throw herself on the mercy of the court of feminine familial authority.

Lazarus doesn't look like he's about to move, so Leona and I pull out the let-out couch and stretch across it with our clothes on.

Aunt Silence is telling us a story like we're little biddy children. We become like little girls, Leona and me, sprawled languorously across the couch bed. Lazarus acting like Littleson suddenly goes and switches off the light. Leona and I look at each other. I reach to turn the lamp back on. Aunt Silence stops me. "It's a full moon. You'd be amazed at what you can see on a night like this. Did Ike tell you about that Whiteman he killed on a night bright like this?"

By the window, I can hear Lazarus sigh and choke a little. He sounds so sad. I forgive his rudeness, and leave my pique and follow Aunt Silence into the story of the Mississippi Freedom Democratic Party. We don't need any light because her voice glows in the dark when she talks about her friend Mrs. Fannie Lou Hamer. That's what she calls her— Mrs. Fannie Lou Hamer. And how Mrs. Fannie talked so clearly and beautifully about the Democratic Party in 1964. That President Lyndon Baines Johnson got worried and made a speech on TV so he could cut her talk off the air waves. The moral beauty of that woman, her sharp mother wit, "Why it was a change power!" Aunt Silence says.

A communal farm owned by the people who work it—that's my Aunt Silence's dream. Already she has turned over the profits from the truck she owns that carries workers to the Whiteman's fields. The communal farm is the idea that has turned Aint Kit cold because Aunt Silence wants to donate the sale of her property and some other Grace land toward purchase of a vast communally owned farm. Aint Kit won't hear of giving land away. She says, "Lee-Bet sound like she need to be examined in that hospital for the funny-headed people."

Aunt Silence is quiet for a while, having unwoven all her dreams for us. After a while the quiet thickens like a roux. She's sleep. Next to me, Leona is snoring softly.

"Your friend sounds like a monster in the woods." Lazarus chuckles; his mean mood has drifted somewhere in the spreading of a red-gold fan of secrets. He glances over at Leona. "She don't look like no monster, though."

"Leona. Leona," I whisper urgently. "Stop snoring." I jab her in the ribs. She jumps and closes her mouth, then sleeps silently the way Lazarus sleeps.

It's me and Lazarus like it was when it was me and Littleson. Neither of us saying anything for a while.

"Is Mr. Hoo going to stay down here?" I ask him.

"I don't think so. He's trying to sell the store so he can go back to California and finish graduate school."

"What's he studying?"

"Astrophysics."

"Oh." Another Russell Garner. I hope not.

"He's doing mathematical computations on the creation of the Universe. When energy jumped into matter, the temperature dropped ten to the eighteenth power or something like that."

"That's cool," I say.

"Ha-ha," Lazarus says. "You remember when you thought Chinese people came over on slave ships?" He's talking easily now, remembering what I remember. "That wasn't all that stupid for a little kid. Some of them were kidnapped to work on the railroads for just about nothing. Others came willingly to work for peanuts. They called them yellow niggers. At least you were wondering about things like that. It was the Indians (some say the Mexicans) who left the tamales people eat around here. Where'd the Indians go? Inside of us."

We don't talk for a long time after this. I feel like I'm nine years old, my breasts like little Christmas bulbs. Lazarus is eleven. Now he's looking up and out the window to the encyclopedia of stars. Suddenly, he asks me, "You want to see the letters I was talking about?"

"Sure," I say, careful not to sound overly curious like a kid sister.

"These are letters from Treemont Stone." He hands me a packet of letters all addressed to Mrs. Leah Rudolph, care of general delivery, Mimosa, Mississippi.

"Leah Rudolph. This ain't you." I inspect the neatly addressed missives.

"Just read," Lazarus orders, like a lifeboat captain exhorts survivors to row if they want to keep living.

I read.

I read for hours that are outside of time. The clock says I begin around nine thirty and finish at eleven thirty. My head is brimming. Lazarus is watching me when I look up from the pages at last. It's like coming out of a spell. Everything is blurry.

"I used to think it was all just a story. About her," Lazarus says. "Now I want to see for myself."

"Who is this Treemont?"

"The letters tell you that," he answers by dismissing. Then he asks me, impatiently as always, "You going to go with me to Old Letha Road? You're the only one I'd ask."

"Why me?"

"Come on now, Maggie? I've been twice by myself. I just want to go one more time before I space this place."

"So you're coming home with me for sure?"

"Yeah, I'm coming home." It's a grumpy concession, but it's what I want.

"Okay, then." I jump out of bed and slide on my shoes.

I shake Leona and call her name. When she stirs, I ask her if she wants to go for a drive in the country. She mumbles unintelligibly.

"I guess that's no," Lazarus interprets my friend's sleep talk.

It's colder than I've ever thought it could be in Mississippi this time of year. I almost hate to leave the car—parked in a dark spot between bushes.

We're crazy, Lazarus and me. Scurrying like rabbits down this Mississippi road in 1970, while moonlight tries to catch us. No friendly whistling of tired working men threads through this night as it did sometimes in my childhood nights. We're walking fast, then running, then walking again. What is real is exaggerated and heightened. My breath comes in pants. I can see it in the air. Lazarus exhales a cloud. I want to write in it words from the letters of Treemont Stone.

"There she was like a saving tree to me, against the flood of human and inhumane events. As if she'd been there a thousand years, or only several hundred, or possibly forever. I know now in clarifying retrospection she is what the ancients would have called the Tree of Life. Like a great baobab with her roots in the air—" His words jump in my head. Without knowing his voice, I know it. His voice could be coming out of Lazarus's mouth. I know Lazarus is listening to it now.

Listening. I'm panting to keep up with my brother. Our mission is like any adventure from our past, like rising before dawn to sneak out of the house before Mama knew I was going with Littleson to do boy's work. Mama would skin me alive with a few quiet words of chastisement, admonishment after the act. What would we say to anyone who chances along this chancy road this time of night? Lazarus has a gun.

"I hope no cars come along," I pant.

"We'll duck behind something." Lazarus is looking attentively down the road. For some sign.

We stop for a minute. I bend over and catch my breath.

"If you did tai chi you wouldn't get winded so fast," my brother says.

"If I wasn't out here with you I wouldn't get winded at all," I snap. But it's not a sharp retort, just something you say to your brother when you like being in his company. More than anything I want to see her, she who Treemont Stone saw.

"What do you suppose he looks like?" I wonder to Lazarus.

"He? Who?" He's ready to move again.

"That man."

"What man?" Pause. "Treemont Stone? I don't know. Don't care, either." He's lying.

"I do."

He looks at me in disgust, but he doesn't have time to say anything because a car's coming and he shoves me in front of him down a ditch and over a clump of bushes. The car goes by so fast the leaves rustle and crackle. A fine moisture coats each leaf.

"It is cold," I say. "I hope I don't catch pneumonia running up behind you."

Lazarus looks out through the leaves.

"I hope I don't catch a death of cold," I grumble, just to be saying words, even though words fail.

We go back onto the road. When we arrive after another mile, we argue over the place.

"This is the place." Lazarus is sure.

"This is not the place Aunt Silence brought me."

"Aunt Silence don't know everything."

"How come everybody wrong but you?"

"Because I know."

"How you know there's not more than one place to see her?"

We wait in the place my brother has chosen. Leaving the road again, we settle ourselves among the bushes. I hug myself hard to keep warm. We look out. There is no one. Except the moon. After we've been poised in the night silence for a long time, the moon starts to be someone. A familiar face.

"There's Mr. Moon," I say, as if it just came out. Lazarus looks up.

"Do you believe them turkeys walked on the moon?" he asks me.

"I think so. Do you?"

"I don't know." He considers. "I guess so. If a dead Blackwoman can walk around this world with her head in her hand, then two live Whitemen can walk around on the moon. I guess."

I guess. "The moon belongs to the people. That's what Treemont Stone said he saw scrawled on a wall. He likes wall art. Composed at night. Graffiti. The truth on any wall." I like him.

We wait and watch all night long. I don't try to talk anymore to Lazarus. He's cracking his knuckles like Grandmama Patsy used to break twigs to put into her wood-burning stove when we were little in Mimosa. At first his knuckle cracking irritates me and I start to tell him to stop, but I don't. That sound mixes in with all the other sounds, tiny rustles, little throbs in the grass, infinitesimal stirrings in the earth. The darkness is so lovely I could cry.

The cold primes us for wakefulness. I can see something, see it with my third eye. All the colors I will ever work in this great blackness. The shapes of this earth are magical.

My brother speaks and his voice sounds dry and old. "I can't believe they died for nothing. It feels like it sometimes, but there must be——"

I don't know who Lazarus is talking about right now. Instead I ask if that was him early this morning doing that weird dance with Ed Hoo.

It was. They were doing tai chi chuan exercises, putting the tiger back on the mountain.

I haven't dreamed that either, but I know. So I say, "She's not coming tonight, Lazarus, not tonight."

It is as if our mama or Madaddy has called our names. In the dimness we rise together and walk down the road.

✦

Bay is staying in Mimosa awhile with her mother, Gussie. She's spent most of our visit over that house where she was born, in which she lived for a few days. She and Aint Kit don't have much to say to each other. They make half circles in the room as they walk around each other. Aint Kit is going to fly home, so she's leaving after us. Leona, Lazarus, and I will travel the highway; Lazarus driving Bay's car. Bay insists. She wants Lazarus home that bad.

When she turns over her keys to him, she wishes him good luck.

"If I was lucky I'd be a girl and not get caught up in the draft." He's bobbing a little, talking this nonsense. He'd die as a girl. To let Bay know her faith in him is not wasted, he tells us his plans. "I'm going back to school, though. Psychology. The mind. That's what I'm studying. How to harness all the mind power." He turns to Aunt Silence, who's standing on the front porch looking on. "I'm going to look up this Treemont Stone man." She just nods over and over.

The day is clear and warm. We're all standing in the sun. Leona hoods her eyes with her hands so she can see who's coming down the street. It's Ed Hoo. He smiles and speaks to all of us as he walks under the arch of the crepe myrtle and joins us in the front yard. He and Lazarus round the house and go into the backyard to do those tai chi chuan exercises together one last time.

Nosy me, I follow Aunt Silence into the house, just so I can watch Lazarus and Ed Hoo do their dance through the kitchen window. Leona goes with Bay to the grocery store. Aint Kit feels a sick attack and has to lie down. Aunt Silence is fixing us lunch and making a feast for us to eat on the road, down Highway 61 and beyond, driving along that trail of blues.

They are like two young trees, an ash, a sumac, learning new tricks against gravity and density. They stand with their feet apart, their spines straight, half sitting, half standing. Slowly they lift their arms, the grace of wings collected in the curve of their arms. This dance my brother and Mr. Hoo do, weightless as astronauts on the moon.

Aunt Silence and I are looking at them through the half-open window when Aint Kit comes up behind us. She's wearing one of her silk negligees, a pale swirl, a froth. She squeezes in beside us so she can see. "That looks pretty, don't it?" Aint Kit's mouth makes an O. "What they call that one?" she asks Aunt Silence. This asking is a rare thing. A truce.

"Oh, I don't know. I think they call it putting the tiger back on the mountain. Got that doggone tiger and hoisting him back up on the mountain." Her eyes glisten in the sunlight that comes at us through the window. She beams, really beams.

Aint Kit has the last word. "Look like they moving that mountain to me. Picking it up. Just picking it up." Then Aint Kit gets in the middle of the kitchen floor and spreads her legs, and half squats in her pale, foamy negligee. "I got it." She flaps her arms and the material flares down.

Aunt Silence laughs, "Kit, you ought to quit."

"Naw, Lee-Bet. This it. I got it."

She looks like she did when I was a little girl staying at her house overnight and burst in on her in the bathroom. She is squatting over the stool. Never letting her buttocks touch the porcelain or the fuzzy furlike cover over the seat. Making water. Now she's moving the mountain and Aunt Silence is laughing sweetly at her sister's high jinks. The men are still dancing like dragon angels.

"Go head, Maggie, try it," Aunt Silence encourages me. So I try it. Slowly.

Awkwardly, I try to lift that mountain.

Riding in the twilight, headed for the City, I lean back and the memory of Aunt Silence's voice hangs in my ear. She is telling me a Mimosa mystery story.

One night driving by the church she saw sacks of flour come dancing out of Mt. Tabor Church. Sacks of flour got religion. Come together and going out to spread the Word.

Sitting in her chair like a delighted sack of bones and blood, muscle and something more, a prayer away from an angel, she says, "If a sack of flour can sing and dance like a man, then a woman can be a woman and a man can be a man. You better believe it."

Everything Is All Right

Lazarus is home. But he didn't get up to see Star of Bethlehem Missionary Baptist Church burning down during the night. Bright red flames and gray and black smoke rolling into the black sky. He didn't watch as I watched the building where at Saturday morning Youth Club meetings Lazarus was boy president and Jeannie was girl president and I was vice-president of everybody. We were unofficially Baptist then, so now I mourn what my father has told us remained. The church gutted of everything that could burn. Choir robes, and ministerial gowns, and Bibles and hymnals. The tiny communion cups we marveled over as children melted down into little lumps, and the funeral parlor fans curled into spade-black feathers, disintegrating to touch. In the night we poured out of the house like a private stash of black pepper. All but Lazarus, who slept through it all because there was nothing for us to fear.

In the morning he just said something about Malcolm X being right: integrating into America is like integrating into a burning house. It's not like that, though. What is it we want? Something so simple I see it in the ruins of this familiar church. Expectancy. Remuneration. Comfort. Justice. The singing from a hundred Sundays, a month of Sundays, hovers here, and the quiet of the ruins is cruel. This was an accident, a fault in wiring, the fire captain said. His slicker shiny and crackly. The boots authoritative. And if the product of blameless devastation is so cruel, then every evil end, planned and carried out, is a burden of grief almost beyond human endurance.

In the burned-out church I know what it is to miss four little girls. This is a fleet grief washing over me and I think of my brother and his Panther friends. What that room looked like. Blood. Like fire but immutable in itself; not only in effect. A mattress soaked in so much blood you wonder if somebody else came and gave there. Bodies opened up offering the last gift besides breath.

Lazarus says he's put blood behind him. He is after minds. He's met a man he won't tell me too much about. That means he must be fine. And brothers don't tell their sisters about men who are too fine. At least mine doesn't. I don't know why. What he says is, "The brother has a mind, Maggie."

His eyes have lights in them again, and I think maybe Littleson is back. You know. Optimistic. Daring.

The wind is still high when he collects his textbooks and other papers and hits the door. I'm still standing on the stoop, so I notice he doesn't notice the gutless church. Nor does he imagine the old singing because he's doing that under his breath.

"Is he anything like Huey?" I put a lot of interest in my voice, so my brother will think I'm thinking of a wing-backed chair and an arrogantly seated man with hot eyes and a tam on his head. I've heard that in person he is gentle. Some old intelligence guides me with Lazarus, "Keep it light. Keep it light."

Lazarus really considers this. His mouth stern and eyes searching the ground for coherence. "It's funny, Maggie. I heard a musician talking about something like this once. He said you know you are playing as yourself when critics name four or five different people your work is like but they still can't get to all of your style. In some ways he's like Malcolm. He's quick and intense. Then he's like Martin Luther King because he's always trying to talk morality, to lift up this mysterious core inside of everybody. There's some Fred in him too. How he's so devoted to organized action. He doesn't just love the People. He's in love with the People. Like Ted Harris and Archie Ferguson and all the other workers. He wants the People to exert their will for their own good. And the brother has a mind like Du Bois. Always booking. Reading law or something. And then the brother is just a brother. Talking stuff. Got an eye for the sisters. But this is the weird part. He reminds me of Aunt Silence sometimes. The way he can sit real still for a long time. And come up with something profound or just a way of seeing something that was right there. Sometimes he comes up smiling. It makes me proud, you know, to think he got that still action from our auntie. Doesn't make me feel like a beggar, like he's giving it all. He acts like it comes from us too."

Then his mind jumps to the church, charred and inert.

"They may as well tear the frame down and build a liquor store. Same thing." He still hasn't forgiven God for standing on high while those men went in on his sleeping comrades.

I can't argue with solid conviction against him. Where was God in the slave ship? And where on the plantation, in the fields, under the sun that crashed down on bodies? And where at the lynching tree? There's a joke. Who said it? "If he did that to His Son, what you think He'll do to you?" So was God in the darkness of Ted Harris's room when the police came in with Death on their minds? Was God on the balcony beside King? Was God in the Audubon Ballroom, descending like a dove Audubon drew? Or was he on the other side of the Universe blowing up stars, leaving holes that only He could go inside?

Did Medgar Evers crawl, bleeding, toward the front door of his house while a disinterested angel sat on the curb watching the carload of assassins career away? Do angels nap or preen before mirrors of grace always? Looking at the burned Star of Bethlehem, I wonder. At a loss. Sitting on the stoop in front of the Grace house. The end of August promising the possibility of Eden. More hassles. More useless hassles. That's not where I am now. Not Eden.

When I think of the severe classrooms and the students and teachers who have never been here to Arbor, never known or loved who I've known and loved, Eden is not enough. Not even FBO is enough. Not while there's so much blood. Nothing is right. And that includes me. Jesus used to be my best friend. I loved the moment in the temple when He whipped the money-changers out. And the Beatitudes. Blessed are the meek for they shall inherit the earth. That's why Mama taught us such nice manners. I guess. Being meek could get you stolen from your land or your land stolen from you.

The way I feel now the best person for me to see is an atheist. I. B. K. Turner wants me to help him. He says he doesn't believe in our God. He believes in something else. I'm not sure of what he means. People say a lot of things. Like Moses Outlaw swore he'd write me every day. I thought a man named Moses would write, at least a tablet. But if I got a letter from him, Richard Nixon, Tricky Dick, did. It would have said, "Here. Take my place. You're welcome to it." Then I got the letter.

Inside I. B. K. Turner's house is quiet. The only sound the clug-clug of the aquarium. It is big like a small square sea held in glass. Like the one in *For Love of Ivy* in Sidney Poitier's apartment. Wide-eyed Abbey Lincoln with her bright, wary smile couldn't believe the piranha. She was so in love with Sidney, the businessman by day, gambler by night, she didn't heed his warning.

"I'm a piranha." He promised her he'd left a trail of (lovesick female) bodies strewn about the road. Leona and me, sitting in the induced midnight of the movie house, both kicked our feet up and whispered how we'd love our bodies strewn behind him. He was too fine. Dark as the movie house and talking in that island accent that's always there underneath.

The same accent as Professor Turner, different island, only Professor I. B. K. Turner was educated in the British system, so his accent sits like a tablespoon of honey at the bottom of a cup of black Ceylon tea, brewed awhile.

The small fish dance, flit in the transparent atmosphere like heavy flecks of light.

Essie is a better typist. She got so much practice typing William's papers. I told him that. Not the William part. But he just said Christmas recommended me, and I was the one with the smile who asked such interesting questions in class. His wife usually types his papers, but she's sick and he is inundated. Inundated. He used that word so much in class I looked it up.

From this I surmise that wives maintain the earth's axis. When Mrs. Person got sick, her husband's brother died, and the church burned down. Mrs. Turner's sick and the professor is flooded.

He doesn't look it. His dry, white hair, which has not seen or felt a barber, flew out from his head and is suspended there by the force of his mind. His eyes, the searching eyes, look at me now.

He gestures to a chair with a back cushioned in a pastel brocade print. The armrests curved and narrow as a young girl's ankles. "Sit down. Sit down."

He sits on the couch, facing me. Takes out his pipe. And puts his feet in the soft slippers on the coffee table. This tells me his wife really is sick.

"Tell me about Atlanta," he says as if I hadn't told him before in the course of the year.

I do and it's exciting again. Mimosa blooms. And feathers fly.

He seems happy about my trip. Vicariously. "Those events sound grand, Magdalene." That's what he calls me—Magdalene. "I would have loved attending the symposia, but paper has enslaved me. I am in bondage to the necessities of wood pulp and a failing mind."

"And an ailing wife," I think. I say, "Your mind's not failing."

"No? We'll agree to this, then. I think the same thoughts, and generate new ideas, but I do it in double the time."

"If I help you type, you can think some more."

"That is my hope."

He slaps his knee as if to command his body to get up quickly. He does. I follow him into the next room, separated from the living room by French doors that don't close. I can still hear the regular gulp of the aquarium.

The shortest paper is on the ANC, its role in the rising revolution in South Africa. The longer paper on the aftermath of the Nigerian civil war. The only thing I remember about that is a picture of a starving child. His body a bone wrapped in thin skin. There are letters as well, concerning a grandniece, and a cousin, trade unionists in South Africa, and *dependista* theorists in Chile and Brazil, permissions to reprint poems and short stories, and responses to requests to lecture on the Negritude poets and the Harlem Renaissance.

I. B. K. was there as a young man. A peculiar student, newly arrived from his island, devoted to Garvey and Du Bois, even though they hated each other. A curiosity, then, who synthesized ideas and added his own. After a short stay in the States, he traveled to England, where he completed his education in the chilly climate of the British Isles.

I type hunched over, tense with the desire to do a good job, and please I. B. K. and contribute to history at the same time. Even if only in an ancillary way.

I type until Professor Turner asks me to perform a different task.

"Close the door," she says. "And lock it." Her hair is spread out across two pillows. Parted in the center, it looks like straw, most of it gray, some of it black. Her eyes were closed, now they're open. She gives me a left-sided smile.

"I'm sorry you're not feeling well," I say politely.

"I'm well enough to be sick when I feel like it," she says. Reaching for the tray. Her hands are bone, yellow skin and purple veins. Big hands. She looks pleased by the careful arrangement of food on dishes, and dishes and flower on tray.

"Thank you, miss," she murmurs.

I stand at attention, one hand inside the other's palm.

"Sit down, please."

I do.

"How old are you, Magdalena Grace?"

"I'm twenty."

"When I was twenty, I was married to Dr. Turner. We were expecting children. Multitudes. We received one." She piles the marmalade of mango onto toast. Eats like a wolf with narrow intensity. Nourishing herself. When what's left of the chicken is a bone, and the last grain of rice has vanished, and the peas passed away, she begins the cucumber sandwiches, and sips the strong tea lightened with cream.

"Dr. Turner is a good husband. But it's important that I take to my bed occasionally. In order that he may do for me what I do for him. Otherwise he will fly away, because his thoughts are clouds. They have powerful drift." She explains things to me as a science teacher explains the laws of physics.

"You're not sick?" I ask, trying not to sound retarded.

"Not exactly. Everybody needs time. B.K., his heart is pure; he doesn't consider personal need. Neither mine nor his own. I remember. So I ail when he must be slower. I am sick so he won't be sick. We're husband and wife, you know."

"He's not resting now."

"He's in the kitchen, isn't he?"

"Yes."

"Cooking, stirring in pots?"

"Yes."

"Then he'll wash every dish I've used one by one."

I nod.

"He will do this very slowly. Each dish like a year. And his mind will be slow. And his body tied to one task."

I nod again.

"That's rest for him for a day or two. He can't stir up too many new ideas and run his mind to a rag developing these thoughts and interpretations. It's rest for him and for me as well. I don't feel like typing, and don't you type too fast. Then he will fall back on himself. And typing frustrates him. He'll rest."

She takes out a Harlequin romance from a drawer by her bedside. There are many other books of that kind, paperback, pastel covers of White maidens. On this one a blonde with rosy skin and a sheik and caravan as background. Hostage wife or something like that. In the drawer I see *Love's Paradise*.

"Go slowly today, and don't let him know you're a smart girl. He'll burn up your mind with his ideas and projects. You have your own preoccupations, I'm sure." She settles into her pillows and means to be finished with me. I, however, am too intrigued to leave her in peace.

"What are you reading?" I ask redundantly.

"Don't you know?" She sweeps open her drawer. Waves her hand like a wand. "These are the prelude to this flat, this room, this bed in which I have slept with one man for over fifty years. It was romance that brought me here. Don't you know romance, young Magdalena?"

Somehow I think not. I think about the letter Moses wrote me a while ago.

Dear M.G.,

How are you? I am fine. The weather here is hot as the middle of Hell. But as bad as it is something good happened to me. I don't know how to tell you this. So I'll just say it. I met someone. She makes me feel like a king. She can sit on her hair!

Maggie, I have been thinking about our relationship. A man likes a woman he can teach. I can't teach you. I can teach her everything. You even taught me the salad fork. You taught me I can use the G.I. Bill after I get out of this place. Hell, I'll always appreciate you, M.G. You gave me a lot. I hope we'll stay in contact.

Truly yours,
Moses

I never wrote him back. I cried one day, then put the letter away and Moses too. Moses never did see the Promised Land, did he? That was my romance. There was more to love than that, wasn't there?

"What do you mean?" I ask Mrs. Turner so she'll give me her version of romance.

"I loved B.K. from the moment I first saw him. I knew I would be his wife. The air of expectancy made the world crack open like a hen's egg. The yolk was bright and the clear whites clung to everything, hung over trees, and fruit stands, and Her Majesty, the Ocean. Even the moon was covered."

I'm thinking Mrs. Turner has read a lot of those love books. Pearl and I used to trade them, turning the pages quickly, sighing in the same spots, like listening to an album by Smokey Robinson. And the radio spinning down blue ecstasies into the dishwater in which I could see my fortune of bliss. The truth is I have read and heard about romance. It is hearsay and clever propaganda. That's what I guess I've thought without thinking about it. Until now. I assumed love was waiting for me. Or I was waiting for him. Moses was a stand-in.

"What is romance?" Her thin face puckers as if she were tasting a mango and a lime at once. She asks and she answers because she knows I don't know. "A little dream you share with another. Usually a prelude to tedium, but for me a prologue to a life with a man romantic by nature. Who dreams dreams with millions. Little dreams and large dreams. And so he dreams an earth-changing dream that makes him more romantic to me, B.K., my husband, my hero!" She's missed her calling. She should have been onstage. All elegant dialogue and swaying hands.

This is screwy. She's in the bed, but she's not sick. He's waiting on her hand and foot. And he's her hero. Yet really he seems happy and so does she playing this silly pretense, so he can play devoted servant husband.

"Are there more like your husband in these books?" I pick up *A Man and a Woman*, turn it over in my hands. The man and woman on the cover are alabaster with a crop of corn silk for hair.

"Occasionally. I while away the hours when he's in his dreams with others."

"Don't you have dreams?" I want to tell her she's a brown Katharine Hepburn. Thinking she's a movie addict too.

"Yes." This is so simple she smiles. "I dream what he dreams because he has such good dreams that they are my own. I am active in clubs and organizations."

"But to do things?"

"I do do things. He does what he does and I do other things. There are enough things in this one place for twenty people to do. I make lists. Do you?"

I shake my head.

"No lists? But then you can't check things off. I see now why you are here. Why the typewriter broke. It was ordained that we speak." She doesn't sound like an atheist. I ask her.

"I am what you call Episcopalian. B. K. is savagely human."

Now I notice how she and her husband talk kind of alike. In an old-fashioned way, stiff as if the thoughts had starch in them, and melodious so the words catch breath and swing up and down. Like bright, starched dresses the talk is pretty.

They talk like people in books. That's it. This house is stuffed with books. Hers in the bedside table. Silly books that don't amount to anything beyond the pleasure of an hour or two. For me four. It takes me four hours to read a romance. And when it's over, the lie hovers like a dream you wish you could put back in your head. With people who look like you. And happy endings.

Dr. and Mrs. Turner are not a lie. Even though when I return to the kitchen with her finished tray, he asks me how she's feeling.

"Fine."

"But she is sick, you know." He sounds sad.

I don't say anything, putting the dishes into the still-soapy water. He uses too much soap. Too much Dove.

"She's told you she isn't sick, but she is," he repeats.

"What's the matter with her?" I don't know who to believe.

"Her heart ails. She tires and she must rest."

I finish the dishes. Me. Who normally hates to wash dishes. But each dish is an adventure. A part of this screwy story of I. B. K. and his wife. The gold rims on the saucers like the wedding band each wears. Third finger, left hand.

"I can finish typing now, if the machine is ready."

To the contrary, it is truly broken now, because Dr. Turner, historian, man of letters, and social theoretician, has no gift for the mechanical. Now the keys are locked against the paper. Jammed. He says I can help him file. So I begin that. Putting letters from four years ago into folders.

It is easy to work in this house. It is so quiet. The phone rings, but I. B. K. Turner answers it before it rings twice and disturbs his sick-healthy wife. There is no sound from the bedroom. I imagine her reading about the sheik and his hostage Englishwoman. A two-hundred-page story of tension, release, tension, and ecstasy. I wonder if Dr. Turner's bride would have so much to say about romance if they'd had more than one child. The one they had neither talks about. I don't know whether it's dead or living. Oh, the house is often filled with students and even grad students at I. B. K.'s feet. He has work and the love and respect of many students and scholars. She has this house, which belongs to Eden, having left a house in the East. More than anything they have each other. In their weird, protective charade of sickness and tenderness, they are careful with each other. And if a heart is anything it is a muscle of vulnerability and power, music and short silences that break into a pounding.

I heard once—Elder said it—I. B. K. could have been prime minister of the island of his birth. He'd been away for decades, first learning, then teaching, to return upon the acquisition of independence. By then a former student of his had come to power, a man who had long encouraged him to come home, and this man rather liked power and rather liked the sunlight of glory he basked in outside of I. B. K.'s shadow. It's true, Elder said, some people need you when they need you, then hate you if they don't. That's the way it can be with student and teacher. So Turner had left because rumor had it his ex-student had experienced a change in philosophy. That happens when a man sits in the pocket of a fruit company.

Bits and pieces of his life Dr. Turner scattered throughout his lectures. His mother was a laundress, one of many, to the governor's palace, his father a fisherman. Barefoot he walked to an edge of the island and skirted it. Knowing that would always be his way. He climbed the rocks of a promontory and stepped off into a salt-heavy blue.

"Dive into the world," he told us then. "Dive!"

He was agitated with the exhortation, his eyes staring through us, past us. I wondered how anyone he had taught could have turned on him. I wonder now as I hear him open the door behind me, tiptoe in, and speak tenderly to the woman.

Someone is at the door, and the man laughing softly in the bedroom with his bride cannot hear it. At least I think not. I get up, folder in my hand, and he comes out. His movements purposeful, appointed.

"I'm expecting someone." He smiles at me.

At the door, around the corner, I hear jovial slapping through jackets. Names sung. Though I cannot make them out. These rooms by now are so suffused with the marriage, the presence of intimacy in the everyday-ness of objects, the repetitive swallow of the aquarium, I feel poised, at the edge of a moment of departure.

Once, after class, Professor Turner remembered. In his boyhood he went down to the beach and watched his father work, mending the net so the fish would not slip through, back into that infinite blue. He watched his father's fingers, calloused and ashen, work. Once the net was sealed, he was happy. Later, another day, he saw the men toss the mesh over the side of the boat. Like a huge, heavy scarf. Then pulling it up, heavy and rounded with jumpy, nervous fish. Euphoric fish, the air slicing through them like silver, dying in the ever-mended nets.

Last year, after he could accept gifts from students, I gave Dr. Turner a pen and ink of dark men casting out nets. It was a small thing. Not much bigger than a postcard. A detailed piece. The facial expressions of the men, stern and hopeful, though tinily described. It was the beauty in the smallness of feature, he said, that made him humble to receive a gift. He said the imagination and hand that could take excruciating care with the merest detail delighted him. I was embarrassed to be so appreciated. Most people don't know the sweat and concentration that go into even the tiniest art. He asked to see more of my work. He bought *Gold*. But I don't see it anyplace here.

I can't see the guest who's been so warmly welcomed. Can only catch the louder exclamations that rise out of a murmur. I. B. K. comes into eye range. Jacket in hand. Not his own. He drapes this over the radiator, then turns and goes back to the seats by the front door, which I cannot see.

The invisible men keep talking. I keep filing letters. Each letter from a person I've read about, miraculous as notes stuffed in gin bottles and given to the open sea for transport, arriving at another given place at a given moment, such as this. Piles of letters and carbon responses at my feet. How fortuitous the machine jammed! Professor Turner wanted to add more letters and provoke some others. I wonder if it is possible to answer every letter, phone call, glance, kiss that's sent your way. I wonder if everybody answers everything or if someone special comes and you answer. Like what was it that brought Essie and Leona and me together? It was a bureaucratic decision that placed us in the same room, but what was it that kept us friends? Even when Essie is strange. What if it had been Essie, Leona, and Trixia? Then what? Or Leona, Essie, and Hamla? How would things have turned out? Leona's changing majors and needs more classes to graduate; Essie's at Eden over the summer in the six-year premed, med-school program, and me, I don't know what to do. Maybe if Trixia had been my roommate she'd have stolen Moses (that's a laugh!) instead of some unknown Asian girl. I don't think Trixia would have trespassed, because roommates have a loyalty. Christmas says twenty years from now we'll still be loyal to the women we lived with. I can't imagine why now.

If I had guessed or considered a visitor, I wouldn't have worn what I have on—pink kneesocks, a jean skirt, and a pink blouse; my hair held flat in front by a wide pink sash that frames my face, making it rounder, more babyfied. I'm almost twenty-one. I have history. School is wearisome and useless to me. Devoid of reality. I am restless like one of the guinea hens in Uncle Ike and Aunt Charity's yard. I have no eggs of my own. But I brood. And if I had eggs I would not drop them on command into a man-made nest, but like the guinea hens go off into the field. This is the way I draw and paint—alone.

Soon I won't be always painting alone. Simba invited me to join some people working on a wall, a mural. Like the Hallelujah Wall from 1967. Funny. As the blood flows and people fall, the walls celebrating what they stood for go up. When I told Aunt Silence about my new project, she sounded pleased.

Then she commented in her wry way, "As many Blackpeople who've died in this land, we could build a wall like the one in China."

I'm the only girl. The only woman on the Wall. Simba's in charge and he has a theory he keeps spouting like a fountain in the park. "In order to be great, a woman has to be a lesbian. The rest of these sisters crying on canvas like Billie Holiday," he says. "It's okay if you're not great, Magdalena. We don't have time to linger in solitude like monks," he says. "That stuff is for the birds," he says. "They already free."

His condescension reminds me of the grad student who asked me who would need art during the Revolution. Then I started this dialogue in my head.

"Who did Beauty ever hurt?" asks one voice.

"Who did Beauty ever feed?" asks another.

"Me! It fed me!" I answer.

But I don't count because that may be only my individualistic heart that asks this, and I shun it as a traitor to the Revolution. I shame myself before the tribunal of myself. Medgar, Malcolm, Fred, four girls—all the dead gave life, and what am I giving?

Professor Turner has given fifty years, half a century. Now he's giving counsel to some stranger. When I offered to give this time to the Turners, he refused, insisted on paying me.

My earlier polite refusal of nourishments has backed up on me. My stomach is growling. It would growl just as Dr. Turner goes by.

He is extra happy and makes a joke. "The tigress has roared. It must be dinnertime."

At my rising to assist him, he turns me back. In the living room the stereo goes on. When it's Ellington, I think of Jeannie and her boyfriend Lamarc swinging through the air, their bodies arched and flying up, given impetus by each other. Is it possible two people stretch and snap like rubber bands to fly across the room, hit the floor in a sharp clap of electrified joy? They said they were jitterbuggers that day. There was a contest at their school. We were in high school then. And we wound up going different paths. That little bit of time seems a generation ago and I have nothing to verify that I have witnessed so much. I go into the bathroom beside the kitchen, reapply lipstick (pink) and blush (pink). Unhappy with my youth. I look younger today than I did the first semester at Eden. Maybe then I tried to act old, or felt older. I thought I knew stuff. Now I know I don't. Last night I saw for myself: even fire dances.

When I'm ready, I take over from Professor Turner, against his wishes. I'm being paid to help. My mama would die to know I let him serve me. I spoon the curried chicken (saffron-yellow and spicy with apples and potatoes and onions) into a dish, the rice, the peas. Make a salad of spinach, tomatoes, and goat cheese. His special dish he takes care of himself. Chunks of dark meat, honeyed and greasy and saucy.

He forks the last over. "This doesn't agree with Madame, but it agrees with me."

"What is it?"

"Taste and see, Magdalene. After you ask what it is, taste and see."

Perhaps the same is true of people, especially of men. This one is brown-skinned, in the range of color of burnt honey. About six feet tall or a little over. Modest Afro and neat mustache. A neater beard. A goatee it is. Nothing like that umbrella of hair William used to walk under. It was Sam Jr. who taught me to run a make on a man. An art student, anyway, is trained to observe. So I see I. B. K.'s guest, and I wonder who he is. Trying not to look too hard. He looks so familiar I keep rummaging in my memory trying to know. I have lived in the City most of my life, and have stared into a million faces over time, like swift mirrors of a moment in time. The days like one long bus ride, looking out through a window while one moment recedes and another approaches.

To tell the truth, I look at my plate a lot because I'm hungry and I'm shy and I need to fill my stomach to quiet the moths that flutter around the light that burns inside me. Every time I look up, he is looking. Sometimes at me. He has a poised stare, a still regard, without shame or judgment.

Suddenly, breaking this regard, he gives Professor Turner an earnest study, but his tone is casual, "You could go back—"

I. B. K. swallows the goat he has been chewing on. Wipes his fingers. The cloth napkins don't glue to the sticky grease the way paper ones do. His wife insists on cloth napkins. She washes and presses and folds each one like paper airplanes.

"I am as the belle of the ball who loves to dance, but must be asked to dance. It is sadly unfair. If she dances on her own, she would cause scandal and outrage. I am coy and must be asked to dance. Even before this, I must be invited to the ball. Poor Cinderella! With no fairy godmother."

The Visitor seems to accept this. I do. Having stood around at enough FBO dances. Waiting to dance and waiting. And then somebody from another campus comes up walking and looking like Norman Bates in dark glasses. *Psycho*. I do not dare refuse. And it's a pleasant enough dance with a stiff whose mind is not on you. On some other girl he's too scared to ask. On himself and his misery. Yet there are dances with brothers who are just brothers. You like each one and even keep up. Laugh at the close of the record.

I wonder if it matters who asks him to dance. So I ask I. B. K. just that.

The Visitor looks from me to I. B. K. I'm studying my teacher's face. Finally, he says, "Yes." It matters who asks him to dance with them. It matters.

When I. B. K. makes the joke about dancing with the devil, doing the multinational tango, he looks at me, ready to portion his smile, but I don't look at him. The Visitor still smiles, but he doesn't include me. Or he includes me impartially, the way sunlight spreads itself thin. But I know light and I know certain locales are favorite places. I feel favored just being here. Just when I start to swell up with being especially here, I notice what I hadn't noticed I've been noticing since the new arrival.

237

Nobody has said the Visitor's name. Professor Turner has called my name. But the man has remained Anonymous, like that dude who's written so many songs and poems.

What's even more peculiar is I think I. B. K. thinks I know this man. And odd as it seems, the man acts like he knows me. He doesn't ask me my name. Right? It's not rude, though, like those people who don't say your name because they don't think you're important enough to have a name. Like you a rock or an orange. At Eden, it was true what the bloods said: I didn't have a name. Oh, hell, no. Not in the rooms or on the grounds of Eden; nothing born or built there said my name. And if I tell the truth at the bottom of the red falls of my heart, what huffs and shoots back up, then no one has ever said my name as who I am. The truth aside from being a Grace, or somebody's daughter, somebody's sister. Not Essie. Not Leona. Not Moses. I wonder if a woman can go her whole life with no one saying her name because no one knows it. Like that essay by James Baldwin. Dumb of me, romantic, and impractical. I don't know this visiting man. And I don't know his name.

Professor Turner is talking about his little shack house on his island home, how he and his wife, Isabella, used to go there summers and Christmas break. No island, he says, is an idyll, and there was sorrow in the riotous beauty. Amazing how the inequality of Nature's work and man's business tore at the heart and spun the mind into despair or outrage. The poverty of the island astonished him. Shocked him to his core. The makeshift shanties.

The mean living eked out amid natural abundance. The colonial governance supplanted by corporate rule. The exuberance and vitality of the people in their element in the markets. So many kinds of flowers sunlight lay stunned on them, then fell back onto the ocean until it shone more blue than the deepest sorrow or joy.

"It's still beautiful," the guest reassures him.

"Well, my son, only if you say so. And you say everyone gave you a welcome tree?"

I wonder what a welcome tree is. Is it planted upon one's arrival? Do its limbs go around your neck as in Hawaii, placed by a woman in a moving skirt?

The guest is describing the quiet of the island now; the weird silence before the hurricane that skirted the island by fifty miles, but sent a deluge and a battalion of winds that almost lifted the house from its foundation. It is his description of the solid silence that descended from the trees and rose from the earth that does it.

This time when he smiles at me and keeps on talking, I smile back. The air is light in my chest.

Then he starts talking directly to me. "My father sent me to I. B. K. when I went away to college. He was the only one at that place who made any sense to me. Later I came across others before they ran some of them away. It was too many of the Black White men who deemed it their right and duty to rule Blackpeople, instead of leading through service, leading by doing. The law school was crackerjack then, so I studied there, then went out into the world." He is offering me a portion of his life, this stranger who is not a stranger to me.

"You graduated law," I. B. K. corrects him. "Passed the bar."

"Yeah, well, the wheels of the law turn too slow sometimes. The turning of the wheel so slow each turn seems imperceptible."

"Magdalena is taking her own sweet time to graduate," I. B. K. scolds me on the sly.

"You're an artist," the man says. Already he knows a part of my name without my telling him. My whole body feels lighter, as if I float toward him.

Professor Turner excuses himself and goes to the back.

Encouraged, I look directly at the man. "I want to be a part of the Revolution," I say.

"What will you kill with—sweetness?" he smiles gently.

Professor Turner comes back. He is holding *Gold* up for the guest to behold.

"Magdalena created this!" Dr. Turner exclaims.

The man contemplates *Gold*, his brow wrinkling. His smile broadening.

"Magdalena, your work is luminous." Then he says, "You are luminous."

I smile shyly.

Outside it is dark. I'd assumed I'd call Lazarus or Pearl or Honeybabe and whine if my work kept me too late. Professor Turner promised me a ride home when I got to his house. Now his wife is sound asleep. Now I know how it's going to be. The new man who Professor Turner tells me is Treemont Stone ("Oh, I assumed you knew, Magdalene.") is going to take me home to Mama, Madaddy, and every Grace this side of Eden. Like a little baby child. Home to Mama. Oh, wouldn't you, wouldn't you know? The kneesocks itch all up my legs.

It is quiet. I sit beside him still as an artist's model who used to perch on stools in the studio at Eden. A turned head remained so for an hour, hands casually draped on the thigh stayed. Neither one of us speaks for a long time. I don't want to assume familiarity, thinking maybe I have pictured him so often in my head that I thought I knew him when I didn't. Not really.

Finally, I say, "Why didn't I. B. K. go home? He'd have won."

"His wife has a condition." He doesn't say anything to spell it out. So I figure I'm not supposed to know. He must figure this is strange, so he takes his eyes off the road for a second to glance at me. Then he says, "A married man can't do what a free man can."

"Like what?"

"What did I just say?"

"You were talking in a generality like there were a million and one things. Then you just named one."

"You wanna know a million?"

"I might."

He's got a nice laugh. He uses it to fill the car. Then he says, "Like take you for a long ride home. I mean this ride would last years and years. A lifetime. A century or two."

I don't say anything because I kinda wish it would.

The night is fertile. White seeds peek out of the earth of the sky. The moon is the base of a tree, or an onion parting the soil.

Or the many stars are torn leaves of hot, white, shining trees that bloom so deeply in heaven we cannot see them. Or the trees of heaven were burned down or up and all that remains are the still-burning fragments of bright trees that cover the sky by day and by night. Looking up through the windshield of Treemont Stone's car, I imagine this. And if I imagine it, given skill and time I can hold it on canvas. At least be close. Have it at my fingertips.

I don't know where this comes from, me with my arms crossed and head against the seat. My eyes full of heaven. I think of I. B. K. and his people. "Do people go from one oppressor to another? I wonder." This doesn't fit into my dream of the Revolution.

"We don't have to," he says. Then he reaches and turns on the radio, abruptly. The sound of Stevie Wonder singing "Uptight." Unexpectedly we start singing together and our voices fit into the song happily, wondrously. "Baby, everything is all right, uptight, outtasight . . ."

Still in pink kneesocks, but in a nightgown, I lie down beside my sister Anne Perpetua and dream. The house still noisy with the TV in the next room and nobody watching it. It isn't that late. I just want to be alone so soon after I'd come face-to-face with him. Funny. I didn't rush to the phone to tell Leona or Essie.

＊

I can hear Anne whimpering beside me, her mouth slightly open. Anne of the Commandments. Ten now, and having periods instead of putting them on the ends of other people's sentences. Mean and moody with cramps. Whimpering.

In the window I see the last of the flowers, stripped and tenacious. Bits of color caught in a big breath. Cold. The moon, what I can see, isn't the same moon that rode over Treemont Stone's car. Nothing is the same. Not even me.

I close my eyes and try to hold his face on my eyelids. The old movie on TV and my sister whimpering are the only sounds.

He said, "I've seen you before, you know." That's what he said.

I didn't say, "But have you looked for me the way I've looked for you?" Why would I have said that? Other than it sounds so good, like a line from a black-and-white movie where men and women wear hats, the brims cutting into their eyes.

In my head then memory, movie, wish, and dream running all at once.

Now a dream.

"Oh, my little chickadee," he murmurs.

"My quail," he says.

"My little turtledove."

My breast in the palm of his hand, plump and quivering like a plump bird with one eye and no mouth, so it needs one. He bends and I think he's listening to my heart deep inside the turtledove, but it's the mouth he gives me, a tongue. Cupping the brown dove in his hands.

ASANTE

Silk was standing and sunning himself in the glow of a trash-can fire. In the distance he could see a crowd approaching. He heard the low music of voices lacing through the field bright with excitement. He saw the flash of curtains like the wings of moths along the boulevard. The neighborhood was watching the progress of the people. Silk squinted up the street at the group. He looked for his mother's face and the face of his younger brother. Stared for a long time, but saw no one that he knew he knew. Then, shrugging, he squatted and took another wrinkled wax-papered ham sandwich from his torn coat pocket. He sniffed it, enjoying the juicy smell of ham. He opened the sandwich and looked at the pink meat inside the soft, white Wonder bread slices.

He worked a little, bought a little. He could put that in a bottle and drink it. The rest slid by him. Life was cold. And he was cold. All the time.

He was chewing with satisfaction, easing the weird swirl in his stomach, wishing for something to drink. Maybe a red cream soda he used to like when he was a boy. Red cream soda made him think of blood and girls when he was a boy. Before he died.

He was gobbling the last of the sandwich, his eyes misting because his mouth was too full and because he was catching a cold. It was colder than it had been, like someone had opened a door on the outside. The people had crossed the street and were approaching the glare of his private campfire.

Then they all disappeared, except for one man.

Silk blinked and shook his head. But the man, who was young as he'd been before he died, just stood in the aura of the fire—flames licked like obedient animals at his jacket sleeves. Silk stood shakily on his unbalanced legs. The cold fell away. The warm wrestled it away. Then the warm grabbed him and wouldn't let him loose and he was weeping.

Weeping from way inside himself, holding himself, as if he were holding he own dead body as a dead boy and weeping over him.

He wiped his eyes. He was walking with the people who had come again. He was a part of the throng, no longer an outsider, an outcast. He smiled lopsidedly and walked as straight as he could on his twisted leg.

"Craziest thing" was how he described it to his mother, who didn't care how it had happened as long as it had happened. "It was like I was in this movie, Mama. Technicolor. Cinemascope. Big colors all over everything. And the shape of the man on the horse be long. I'm telling you it was outtasight. Then I stepped through the movie and I came out on the other side. Different. More real than any movie. Because it wasn't a movie. That's the only way I can describe it. I came out on the other side of the minute I met this dude alive. I came out alive and ready."

He opened his name in a different way. Not just Antonio. But Chaka. Chaka Antonio Silky.

With a new name he discovered he had new gifts, a natural affinity for remembering things spoken (gossip, rumor, prophecy, dates, snide remarks, innuendo, and romantic raps). So he was the griot who told Lazarus, my brother, about Treemont Stone after Mimosa, after the ghost on Old Letha Road, after Silence, and after thirty-nine dollars and a bus ticket to the City in his pocket. The trip to the bus station Miss Leah-Bethel made to take him away, leaving from Greenville, because he's spent his time in anonymity and had to leave that way too. On the way the drive up Old Letha Road, along which they'd stopped when they got to the piece of road around where he'd almost died. He got out of the car. Walked around in the bright, soft daylight. Miss Leah-Bethel paid him no mind; she spent her time picking the wild greens that she recognized from the days she was in love with the things of this earth.

Those days when the shoots and vines showed her their tender parts, and in reading these she read her own fragility and endurance. He'd performed a private rite under a tree near the spot where he remembered. But Chaka wouldn't say what he'd done, because Treemont Stone hadn't told him.

The way Chaka told it she needed a fixing-up man. Miss Blue Nile. Someone to keep the club looking good because the blues deserved a happy home. A room came with the job. That's how he'd first stumbled in. He saw the sign tucked in a window. It was around the corner from Roscoe's and just above the basement club. When she asked him if he wanted a room and a steady part-time job, he said that was all he needed.

Five o'clock the next morning he started in the bowels of the club—the washrooms.

Something began then, in the bowels of a blues club.

Tearing walls down and building them up new gives a man a chance to think with his hands. Layers once removed, he can look in and see the bones of a building, the rotten wood, the scampering insects. He knows what he has to do.

That's how Treemont Stone knew what he had to do with everything he had seen and learned in his journeying. Everywhere was the Underground Railroad and he had to be a freedom guide.

✦

Chaka, I've figured out, can't believe anyone can love him, although he has a mother and brothers who do. When I give him my reluctant attention, he gets all awkward because somebody is listening to him. His arms jerk and his feet make blurry footprints in the dust around the Wall where I am working. He's sitting on a crate watching me paint, working hard at being lovable by telling everything he knows. I look at him out of the corner of my eye. I have a hard time with him because of Essie. I've never mentioned him to her. He is no friend of mine. He's a hang-around, a member of the Community.

For Chaka, knowledge must be love. I don't know exactly how he came up with this equation. His mind used to be ice. He told me that when I wasn't looking at him. That's the way people used to look at him, he told me. Like they knew he was a human iceberg. Only showing the cap of his violence, while a thousand felonies crashed underneath. But, since Tree and ASANTE, he'd found out about books. And when he told people what the books told him, for once their eyes on him were less wary, less unforgiving. Even though the sisters were still distant. He read more so he'd have more to tell and more warming gazes waiting for him after they got through with his limp and his twisted walk. His injury sinister and eccentric; he dragged his crimes behind him. He dragged the broken boy he'd been behind him. Sometimes his walk tangled in the screams of girls. The girls he'd raped when he was a boy before he was sent away to die then released on a technicality of justice. Or was it mercy that sent him back to the Homes again to be found by Treemont Stone and redeemed?

Chaka told me what he'd read about the history of the Homes. I didn't say anything. Just kept on working.

He began with the War because History, he says, jumps out of the belly of war. Change is a kind of afterbirth. In the 1940s when hopeful Black veterans and their families, immediate and distant, surged into the City, the City fathers got nervous about the amount of city space Negroes would take. The housing commission had to make plans for the future.

Strangely enough, he said, the commissioner at that time was a woman.

"Why is that strange?" I asked, ready to fight for women. Ain't I a woman?

He didn't answer. Kept talking.

She was a daughter of one of the Seven Sisters colleges.

She proposed scattered-site public housing throughout the City. Sweet. Neat rows of one- and two-story houses for anybody, placed in any neighborhood, poor, wealthy, or fair to middling.

"When she came up with this bright idea, they didn't fire her right away. Her family had money and more connections than Union Station, ya dig?"

"So what they do?" I ask, stirring paint and looking at the Wall where I will make my mark.

"Ignored her. The same way Mr. Rochester ignored his loony wife in the attic and kept on laying his rap on Jane Eyre."

When I laugh against my will, he casts his eyes down for a moment, then grins at me, astonished that I find him so witty. I am astonished too, though I know him by now. At first reluctantly. My responses to him terse, detached. Till finally, he said, "What must I do? Just tell me and I'll do it. Because there's nothing I can undo. Nothin' I can undo." Since then I've observed him in the present. A disciple of Treemont Stone. I've never brought up his past. Most of the other sisters act like he is air. But I see him. I haven't told Essie I have seen him, though I've seen her mother many times by now. Each time, her hair is different.

✦

I almost don't recognize her without the wig. Her own hair is an Afro, sculpted by trained hands. No gray. With the help of a bottle. She has on a nice, sky-blue polyester pantsuit. Like Mary Tyler Moore. She's stacked, built up good at the bust and hips. I didn't notice before how pretty she is. Instead of just being in a hurry, she looks efficient. A paper bag curled in her hand. I spot her waiting at the curb for us as we pull around the corner. She knows everybody in the neighborhood and she waves.

We pull up and she smiles. The unshielded pleasure at our arrival, disarming and happy. Tree is driving, but he gets out to open the passenger door. I get out to change seats.

"Good morning, Mrs. Constance," I say.

"Well, I know you! Girl, you going to the bank with us?" Her voice sounds like a rush of water, subversive and urgent.

"Yes, ma'am. I sure am."

"Well, good. Just keep the 'ma'am.' I am Madame Treasurer. As soon as I get rid of Woody, I'm gonna be Mademoiselle Treasurer. Can you dig that?"

I thought they were divorced, but I don't ask her.

"That plant he was at moved to the suburbs. Ask him if he wanna go a hundred miles each way to work every day and take a pay cut. He tried it, but the car broke down too many times. Didn't make enough for

247

anything new. He is many things, but lazy ain't one of them. So when he get something steady again, I'm gone put him out."

Tree is out of the car, holding the door for each of us. She moves with a happy flourish. The small courtesy a heady gesture that makes her lift her head up higher.

In the front seat she is a queen, gracious and affable. "I didn't know you knew my daughter's friend, Brother Treemont," she says.

"Yes, ma'am."

"Essie's at school. She got a job at a hospital."

"She's so busy we barely see each other," I say. But that's not the complete case. Only part.

"I don't see her much either and I'm her mother. At least that's what they told me at the hospital and I was so doped up they coulda pulled a switch on me." She turns in her seat and cocks her head to the side like a gun. Talking to me. "You think so?"

"You two look alike." I verify the relationship.

This is for Tree. "You wouldn't think I could have a daughter in college, would you?" she asks.

"No. Sure wouldn't."

This sits right with her. She bounces back against the seat. Pleased with being alive and looking so good and being here and going where she's going. "Turn up there," she points. She could be in the driver's seat.

Something good is in her and she can't stop talking. "It's wonderful what the residents can do if we all pull together. Buildings not much more than ten years old and falling apart. They do us so bad because poor people got to have a place to stay. Or stay on the street. But we are taking our destiny into our own hands. Ain't that right, Brother Treemont Stone."

"You asking me? I just go where you tell me, Madame Treasurer."

"I like that. Our destiny is in our hands. And they have the rent money after they make the repairs. And we are going to manage our own buildings too. They can try to be an absentee landlord. That's over, baby. Ain't that right, Treemont Stone?"

"Yes, ma'am."

"I know it's right."

"They have the perfect person for treasurer, Miss Fredonia." That's me. Telling the truth.

"Girl, don't you know it? I have never been funny with the money. Anybody can tell you that. I am straight up about the cash. That's why it's going in the bank, so the bank can sit on it. I know it's the truth because one time I got some money from a friendamine, and he wrote me a check. I took the check to the bank and they said they had to hold my money for ten days. TEN DAYS. MY MONEY. Girl, don't-ya-know I took that check to another friendamine own a business, and he cashed it for me no questions asked. They say love don't love nobody. The bank don't love nobody. And I want this money sat on like a full suitcase. Cause next thing you know when things are goin good somebody will get a attitude and wanna lie and say I took their money. Then I have to whip somebody's ass. You don't know, Maggie, we right right now, but look, if we ain't gone turn around and be wrong when it's good and sweet. It's like a love affair. All nice and sweet at first, then it be bitter as black coffee. Wake yo ass up too. But we wanna keep this good feelin' goin, gotta hold on to this feelin'."

I'm thinking I've heard of Miss Fredonia when she's been wrong. But now I know she's right. And this is the way it should have always been. She, capable and fierce, in command. Treemont calls this the Beautiful Time, when the people rise as tall as trees and rustle with the winds of transformation. It sounds better when he says it. The Winds of Change. I've heard it before. But I never sat behind a woman who is now a great tree.

When I ask, neither one can tell the same story of the rent strikes at the Homes. He says the people who are fed up had a meeting and he was invited because they knew he read law. She says some people went to a meeting and heard Treemont Stone speak in person about autonomy and self-determination. They had a meeting.

The Homes men and women have a plan. They talked about two things. (1) How to blow it all up and live in tents until they could find something else or agitate the City into constructing smaller buildings and spreading them out so people aren't all on top of each other. One family of high-rise projects leading into another into another for miles and miles. (2) Strike and fight for better management and demand to manage the Homes themselves.

Miss Fredonia lays it out like that: one, two.

"Essie think now that I got my hair in the natural, I'm gone get rid of my wigs. She thinks hair mean Black Power cause she got so much of it. She got that from her daddy. He had some hair. That girl he married combing it now. But hair is like a dress or a suit to me. It's something you put on depending upon the occasion. Now, this, Treemont'll tell you, is a serious occasion. Money is plain talk. So I got my 'fro. We doing like Aretha say. 'Taking care of the TCB.' Taking care of the taking care of business! Heyyyyyyy! Essie didn't call you to tell you?"

Like a child on her way to her birthday party she can't stop talking. So much talk adding up to so much happiness. Pulling her along like a rope through a thicket, into a dazzle of sunlight. She reports the course of Treemont Stone. How he began speaking at his father's church, then a community center. His reputation as a speaker spread. But his reputation as a doer spread before that. He helped organize a community free clinic. The doctor was a medicine man by day and a blues guitar man by night. Shaman they called him. Treemont's talking and listening skills pulled people in, pulled people around him. Another doctor. Two nurses. He helped organize a Sunday supper and Wednesday supper out of the community center, where anybody could get a free meal. He talked August Pryor and Roscoe and other restaurant owners into donating leftovers and surplus. He coaxed people into giving. He could talk a rabbit out of his tail and ask to share the good luck! That's what people said. He could talk a bird out of its wings. Or just one of them. His talk caused people to talk about him. And his actions made them love him. He urged people to grow gardens shaped like Africa and give a portion to the elderly who could no longer grow their own vegetables. He read law for sons and daughters who were in trouble. Then he talked three lawyers into doing pro bono work. He could talk the best out of people.

When he visited me at the Wall, I swore I painted better. He would stand and watch me paint, saying little. One day he said, "I can see your soul. You are so full of love."

I felt my face go warm. My hands trembled a little.

"I'm sorry," he said. "I didn't mean to distract you. That's Fannie Lou Hamer." He nodded toward the face I was creating.

"Yes," I said. "She's one of my heroes."

"Mine too," he said. "Her and Miss Leah-Bethel Grace."

"I know her," I said.

"I know you do," he said. "You look a little bit like her."

"Really?" I turned to look at him.

"It's the eyes, I think. Dreamer eyes."

Then he said, "Gotta go. See ya later, Magdalena."

The next time he was at the Wall I was not there. It was evening and trouble was brewing. When a Maniac Apostle member (people said his gang received money from the government) shot into a group of children gathered in front of the Wall of Honor, trying to land a bullet on a rival gang member, Treemont shielded a girl and boy, giving his own back for bullets. But he wound up unscathed. The children were untouched. The Wall of Honor was dishonored with bullet holes. We incorporated the bullet holes into the mural.

Things had a way of not happening to Treemont Stone. When he was in the war he wrote his father, Reverend Jeremiah Stone, about it. Not mentioning it to anyone else, but word got out.

> Dear Dad,
>
> I hope this missive finds you and Big Sis well. I am well, in spite of it all. Mosquitoes here are big as Cadillacs. They suck your blood like Bram Stoker's Dracula. I'll be glad to get out of somebody else's war. As I fumble through the jungle that idea becomes clear to me.
>
> I told you about the Incident. Yes, I did walk through what was later found to be a minefield. My buddy followed behind me safely. Papa, my whole body was praying across that booby-trapped area. I sweat the 27th Psalm—the Lord is my light and my salvation. In the time of trouble he shall hide me. And the 23rd Psalm. Mama must have been with me too watching over me.
>
> Your loving son,
> Treemont

They gave him a medal for bravery. He gave it to his father. He tells me a piece of the story, making it seem the least of events. It was just another time Death passed him by.

It is a garden where plums burst out of their skins, and scarlet apples pull branches toward the earth. Mangoes and oranges turn up as big as the heads of newborns. Everything is sweet. The air laden with invitation and surprise. I was walking with him. "These fruits are insufficient," he says. So he reaches up into a dark sky and picks a star. It fits into the palm of his hand like a starfish, but it is fruit, light pulsing out of it. It does not burn his hand. He tells me to taste it and I do. It is so sweet it makes me cry and grieve for the rest of my life.

This is the dream I tell him after we've come in. I recognize his apartment above the Blue Nile. When I ask if the DeadandBuried still meet here, he says no. Most of them are gone now. They died in threes. It's funny how movie stars and relatives and people you admire die in threes.

"Is that right?" He's on the couch, pulling me next to him.

"You miss them?" I ask, already knowing.

"That I do."

We just sit, quiet as the books and paper and mail that take up so much space. Enough music from downstairs, flowing through the floorboards. The phone is off the hook, the receiver hidden under the couch pillow. The lamp is low and the overhead off. We just sit.

There is a lot I think about I could ask him, but I don't feel like thinking about it now. Steve Rainey and Chaka Antonio Silky, the women and men of ASANTE. Why he's so careful, always looking over his shoulder, even when he's looking straight ahead, moving forward and looking back. I've noticed the way his eyes sweep up toward the curve in a stairwell and down toward the rise in another when he comes out of my apartment or another. Sometimes, on his way to a meeting, he pretends like he's sightseeing and explores new approaches, driving real fast. Yet when he's with the people, the bona fide people, he is open to a fault. That is why Miss Fredonia has taken so to him. He doesn't look down or up with the people. He looks straight ahead. He looks into people.

He looks at me, spinning me so that I'm sitting inside his embrace. His shoes are off and he holds me with his knees. He has something in mind and I don't feel any panic. As he looks I look back into his clean smooth face. The hint of a goatee. The eyes like bright stones, small painted eggs marked at the center, the place to enter.

We're just sitting there, looking at each other, being quiet, when sounds come up from the floor below. And the floor trembles with the blues.

> *Gypsy woman told my mama, before I was born*
> *You got a boy child comin, gonna be a son of a gun.*
> *Gonna make these pretty women jump and shout*
> *And the world will only know what it's all about.*

We laugh. "Is that for you?" I ask.

At first he starts to say no. Then he sings with the song:

> *And I'm the hoochie coochie man*
> *Everybody knows I am.*

We really laugh then, enjoying ourselves.

"You scared?" he asks. He pops a mint.

"Uh uhn," I murmur. "I know you got me."

Then we pay the music no mind and let it sweep around us. We just kiss and kiss and kiss. His tongue tastes like Life Savers. Then my mouth.

Funny about the body. The body in studio I can look at and know it is beautiful, obedient to the line and curve of it, remarking on what is supple or flat or muscular. But this body of this man is a mystery to me. The arms, muscles hard and roped with veins. These are the arms that hold me tight. Hold me to the chest that houses the heart that punches out time. Faster now as clothes fly and tumble and kisses multiply tender as the ghosts of moths on my mouth, my nose, my cheeks, my eyelids, my throat, my breasts.

Naked, I am incomplete, momentarily. Half limp and driven to let in some missing portion of myself I never missed before not even with Moses. With Moses three times we did it, he did it to me. I was absent, just watching, letting him. With Tree I answer, alive and anxious to please. When I see Treemont, a light comes out of his body or his soul

253

and circles him. And I feel like light. Hot. Surrendering to flesh. But just when I give up, relaxed and surrendered on the couch, the bristles biting into my back, any resistance gone, my mind washed and glistening in the dark of itself, I hear him calling my name. I know I am the answer he whispers for, the drum his heart beats faster after. Without what I have, something of his is lost. Without this final part locked in place, the rest of him is rudderless, for a moment at least, forever I like to think when I think but I'm not thinking now.

"Hold on," he says. Suddenly, he scoops me up and takes me to his bed. Safe in his arms. I can hear his heart pounding. No, I feel his heart pounding.

Finally, the bed creaks and we settle into place, wrestling and kissing. He parts me and puts himself in me and pushes and pushes and eases and pushes and rocks and I go with him. But dim in the distance we've traveled away into our bodies. I hear it—a plank holding up the mattress. It's a wonder we don't cave in and tumble down like following the stroke of lightning or good luck. I think I am sounding amazed about the lightning—how swiftly it travels, what it does to your body. Wondering which one of us was hit, and who passed it to the other—we trembled, each limb alive with the current. He dives into me and he dives into me. I hold his sweat-slick back. Hold on. Lightning strikes again. Then he says, "I love you, Magdalena Grace."

I say, "I love you, Treemont Stone." Seriously, like I am marrying him.

Children and people in love like stories before bedtime. He tells me his like a song from another room—in snatches. He tells me fragments and bits beginning with the time he left Mimosa and came back to the City. How his father loaned him money after he started working part-time at the Blue Nile. His mother loaned him enough money to buy three abandoned buildings and he started working on them. Restoring them. He sold one restored building to two schoolteachers. He paid his father back and had money to begin his organizing. The people were used to him by then. They knew him. He knew how to talk to people like they had some sense. He talked to them like he had some sense.

The rest of his life comes in different times. While I'm washing dishes and he's drying or the other way around. Or sitting on his couch or mine in the apartment I share with Katherine Pearl, who is a nurse with her eye on the building he is restoring. Sometimes he tells me his story when he visits me at HoneySounds, the record shop C.C., Honeybabe's husband, owns. Tree buys enough records to pay my salary. That's what C.C. says. But he's lying. Tree hardly stops by. He's too busy. When he does come in, I play Marvin Gaye's "What's Going On" for him. He hums and whistles it around his apartment

The day soon after I met him at Dr. Turner's house a story. I noticed his hands. I was sitting on the scaffold, with my legs hanging down. Like a child on a swing, only I was one in a man-sized shirt and jeans. My mouth and throat full of air like I'd just swung down on a holler. I popped an apple slice in my mouth. I was looking at the red of the apple, working on Malcolm's face. Using two colors, red and yellow, I mixed his hair. And the sunlight jumped down from the sky and bobbed up and down just where he was standing. But I saw the hands. The strength in them. I heard his voice. "You do beautiful work, Magdalena Grace."

Suddenly my stomach was emptier than it was and I wished I had brought more than a stupid apple. I was hot and my hands got too busy. He wove around a little restlessly, awkwardly. Maybe I surprised him because I wasn't cheezing. But I was too nervous for smiles. He'd jumped right out of a daydream into real life. Real life is paint that gets under your fingernails, on your work clothes, and in hair hidden under what Mama calls a rag.

"Do you know where I can find Simba?" he asked. Was he really looking for Simba?

"No. I sure don't." That's all I said, and went on grinding on that apple, while the wheels in my head ground to a halt. One thing I know, bad as I used to talk about Trixia, man-crazy girl at Eden, if somebody like him approached her, she'd know what to say to him. Then I was starving, eating that apple.

He wouldn't leave.

I couldn't leave this Wall of Honor unattended with our supplies all out in the open. The paint-stand brushes fair trade for anybody. Aint Kit told us about her neighbor who went out in her backyard to pick some flowers from her garden for her dining-room table centerpiece; when the woman came back inside, it couldn't have been a good five minutes she was outside in her backyard. She came back in the house and all her furniture was gone. Ev-e-ry-thing. Even the pot of greens she was cooking on the stove. The only trace the police could find was a trail of ham hocks plucked clean. All of this occurred within five minutes. So I couldn't leave, or Simba would have had a fit like he had a fit one day when he found out I had been staying late by myself to work on the Wall or bringing unauthorized personnel around the work site.

"You know what somebody told me?" Simba stirred some color that morning.

"No." I answered short like I usually answer him.

He was serious, so he talked high in his nose. "Somebody told me you almost got attacked last night. Somebody woulda snatched all your good womanhood if your boyfriend hadn't been hanging around here again watching over you."

"Nobody was here with me."

"Awh, come on, Maggie. That old brother on the corner say he saw you and him. That brother sell the melons said he saw you and your little boyfriend. But if you wanna play dumb, okay. Just don't be bringing no unauthorized personnel around here. Dude might have something up his sleeve. Be walking off with all our supplies. Might be walking off with items undetected as yet. Might be some slick crook. Who is he?"

One late night in Eden, William asked me the same thing. We were standing on the steps of Blood Island. "Who was that dude I saw you walking with?"

I was by myself. That's what I told him.

He said, "Yeah, uh-huh, Magdalena. You got a man off campus and the Negro real shy. Must be married and making that creep."

Simba pretends like he's so worried about me alone or with an imaginary man. Did he tell me when they were coming back from wherever they went to work on this doggone wall? I be taking orders like a waitress and keeping it all straight. Who don't eat meat and who do. Who want juice and who want pop. Who wants hamburgers and who wants just fries. And I don't mind being nice to people. But when they never show consideration? When I hand them stuff and they grunt and don't thank me. I tell them my name ain't Stepinfetchit. Then they call me Caldonia and Sapphire.

It was hot and I was hungry. "They never tell me nothing." That's what I said to Treemont, who was still a stranger then.

"Well, shame on them," he said. "Mistreating you like that."

"Yeah, just cause I'm a woman." I might as well have said "girl."

"That's counterrevolutionary. Uhhhhhmp. Uhhhhhmp. Uhmmmmp," he said just like he was real old.

"You want to go with me?" he asked like a kid. I could see how wide his shoulders were. Wider than the first time I saw him. Shoulders were my fascination then.

"I can't," I said. Then I got scared that he would go without me and the red of the brush I was painting with would be less red. Because everything woke up when he turned up again. The trees—monkey cigar (like the one next to our Grace house on Arbor) and tree of heaven— blazed and stank. The spine of each life like a skeleton. Or one of those Halloween suits that turn to green neon bones when you turn off the regular light and turn on the black light. You can see infinitesimal specks of lint like living moles on your clothes. In your hair. Your teeth gleam.

From two blocks away I could smell the first ribs of the day smoking in the sauce at Roscoe's. The smoke from that faulty chimney made signals in the day.

"Can you read smoke signals?" I looked at Treemont Stone sideways through my eyelashes. Coy as any geisha.

"Yeah." His chuckle was dark as charcoal. "I can read smoke signals. Run. Call the fire department."

I rubbed the juice from my apple on my jeans and looked at him. I was standing next to him. That's when I really found out he fit just right.

"You think Roscoe's will ever get its ventilation fixed?" I asked, just to be talking to him.

"Place probably burn down before they do that. If they fix it, he claims the ribs won't taste right."

We laughed. He went on, "We're a peculiar people. Last year when our sister Angela Davis was in hiding, the cops nabbed a sister about your height. (He looked at me. I could tell he measured me correctly at five two.) She was brown-skinned, about your color, and they called it in as the arrest of Angela Yvonne Davis, who, as you know, is five six and light-skinned. When they walked her out the building, a crowd had gathered but nobody protested. Everybody looked. One brother squinted real hard and said, "How they manage to shrink her down like that? How they get her tan that deep?"

"You're making that up?" I laughed.

"No. I'm not. If I could make stuff up I'd be J. Edgar Hoover or an informant for the FBI or somebody very high up in the CIA. You've got a sense of humor. I like that. I'll bet you hoped those White kids would levitate the Pentagon."

"How did you know?"

"Everybody's got limitations," he smiled. "That's why I take measurements."

✦

Now the music is drifting up from the Blue Nile. "I love my butterfly so sweet so neat."

"Sweet little butterfly," he murmurs down into my ear. "Butterfly."

And I spread my wings.

And we fly.

10

The Hallelujah Wall

Shout hallelujah
In the pagan place
In the poisoned atmosphere
Shout hallelujah
At the Hallelujah Wall
Here the air is clear.
Right here.
Saints and chump-change sinners
Spinners of destiny,
Styles and silhouettes.
Children whose black blood was blasphemed
And names profaned
Join in the circle of our Black Jubilation.
In our ancestral attitude.
Blessed be those who bled.
In the holds of ships.
In the fields.
In the cities.
Remember us and rejoice.
Be sanctified in the power.
Black Art revives!
Asante! Asante! Asante!

This is Hamla Lamumba, poet-priestess, performing before the finished Wall. It's been seven weeks since we began. Working quick and sure because early in the year the Wall of Honor has been ravaged by a fire of unknown origins. We began a new mural on the side of a building bequeathed to ASANTE by the D and B Benevolent Society. I painted again my own portion. Painted it more beautifully, with greater confidence and inspiration and the grace one receives when retrieving what is lost. We've ground our axes and ground them as fine as Jean Charlot said of our political and otherwise art. In seven weeks. Hamla says seven is a magical number. Seven days for Creation and seven weeks to make the mural. Looking at her, thinking how pretty she is in her own African print dress, I'm also thinking, "Seven days to make the world. That's why it's in such bad shape." But she's all mystical and I dare not crack. I can relate to her generous euphoria. She's in love. I am too. But she's in love with Alhamisi. Father EARTH who intimidated us when we were freshmen at Eden and came back into the City to be taught our Blackness by men who hated us.

Sometimes when you see somebody grinning, wide and fast, shaking with excitement, worshipping everything, their voice light and tight, and their eyes overwhelmed from the inside, then you know something's wrong. Especially if her wrist has an Ace bandage on it.

"What happened to your hand?" I ask Hamla.

"Have you seen Alhamisi?" she replies.

She lives with him. But her parents don't know. She keeps some things in a graduate student's dorm room. Checks on her room once a week, gets some things, and splits. Into the City. To Alhamisi. Who looks like her daddy.

At first she told me things, when she called me trying to convince me to come back to Eden. I listened. Hamla said Alhamisi said the problem with Hamla was she was one of them brainwashed Eden babes. Knocking back birth control pills on the sly. Rejecting the life he had for her. Acting just as dumb. And her the daughter of a social worker and a dermatologist. A bourgie brat. She acted dumb as any Whitegirl because she liked it when he tightened her up. Set her back on the right track. She liked it. Yeah, she said he said he knew she liked it because she told him she liked it and she had to tell me she had told him she liked it because she did like it. It was so good she begged him not to stop. When she was under him, he repeated, when she was under him, she nodded out after the ecstasy. And she lay where he put her. She said he said uh-huh that's how he understood what she needed. And deep in her womanhood (he liked to say that—her womanhood—as a synonym for her vagina), deep in her womanhood she knew he was right and she was wrong about everything and anything.

And when I tried to suggest that maybe she was right sometimes and he was wrong, she told me I thought Treemont was perfect.

"What if I do?" I said.

"He ain't no better than Alhamisi. At least Alhamisi ain't no janitor."

I'm swelling and getting hot like a bean in boiling water.

"Alhamisi says he don't trust the brother because he might be FBI. Don't nobody know that much about him."

"He grew up here."

"Does that mean he ain't a pig?"

"I can't believe this."

"Maggie, your brother is a policeman."

"And your father is a dermatologist. Maybe you secretly White and got a color transplant."

"That's not funny, Maggie, because Alhamisi told me we have to be careful."

"Who does Alhamisi trust, Hamla?"

"He trusts himself."

"And you."

"I have to earn his trust. He is into serious business."

Now Hamla seems to have forgotten that charge against Treemont. She's in this quick pain and I can't get close to her. She's open only to the big intimacy of the party. She smiles and says *asante sana* when people praise her poem for the Hallelujah Wall. I wonder what Alhamisi thinks about her saying the word *asante*, the Kiswahili thank-you and the name of Tree's organization. Hamla's going to get it.

For weeks after the mural was done and weeks before this day word of mouth spread about the unveiling of the entire piece. This gathering is like the block parties we used to have on Arbor Avenue. The entire neighborhood came out. Women danced with boys and men danced with little girls. The loss of balloons was a happiness. Our neighborhood, colored and convivial, floating out of itself into the rest of the City. In the evening the short blasts of cherry bombs, the fumes and the exciting fire. My brothers, Sam Jr. and Littleson, and the older boys sent rockets into the night sky, fireworks that burst into brilliant pieces as if they were our own brief stars.

At the curbside, my Uncle Blackstrap sold snowballs, till he ran out of ice, then he sold the syrup diluted with water in the cone-shaped cups.

In the morning the watermelon man parked in the alley. By noon his horse-drawn wagon was empty. And his horse, named Desdemona, who was a tired mare, pranced in place like a foal.

One block-party time, late at night, when the street was well littered and looking lived on, before the boys went around picking paper up and before the women took the leftover chicken and slaw and spaghetti and cake back into their own kitchens, and the men cleaned the pits, Madaddy brought out his harmonica. He made that harmonica moan and sing right in front of our house. Then he sang. A song no one knew.

"What's that song he singing?" Miss Rose asked my mama. This was before Eddie died and Miss Rose was more attuned to sudden strokes of beauty. "It sound nice."

"Some old blues song," my brother Sam Jr. said over his shoulder as he dipped to pick up the dirty paper cones from the gutter. "He made it up. Sound like something he made up." Sam Jr. was a teenager then and the worst thing he could say about something was it didn't come from a store. Nobody punched a time clock to earn money for my father's song. Or so we thought.

The song was about paying dues. It was short and my daddy didn't do an encore. He embarrassed us so. What if the women next door went home to their kitchens and laughed at him? How could we survive such secret laughter? The men would whoop into the engines of half-dead cars or the dirty grills of barbecue pits, so that the haughty mirth echoed back at them. All of them would be laughing at the blues inside themselves. But they weren't laughing, and they loved the song, for itself or for the joy of the moment. They clapped and called out to our daddy, Sam Grace, affirmatively. They lifted themselves on his song.

We wouldn't clap for him. We wanted him to shut up and be at work and give somebody a whipping so we could recognize him. He quit singing and playing that harmonica.

Have you ever heard a harmonica? Even after the playing is over the atmosphere sustains the notes, rolls them round and round till they have a momentum all their own. Then they keep rolling over you like moonlight or like shadow.

The day of the Wall is like one of those block parties. The remaining musicians from Great Zimbabwe and some others, a few Eden people, and students from other colleges and universities, high schools, and grammar schools, some Graces (my father at work or he would have whipped out his harmonica and Tree would have egged him on because he likes my daddy and his strict ways), scores of Blackfolks from that neighborhood and this one, poets and artists, scholars and activists, all gather in front of the Hallelujah Wall. The marketplace merchants of Great Zimbabwe set up tables and sell their handcrafted wares, and people buy jewelry and fabric and art pieces homemade or imported from Africa. Leona's daddy sent a truck with a big sign on the side. BEEF RIBS. "Beef" underlined. Nowadays we don't like any kind of pig.

I am so happy I could float, be diffused like oxygen through the moment. Each face in my face. My face in each face. I haven't seen Tree today, but it doesn't matter because he's here anyway. I didn't expect to see Steve, but he's here. And some people ask when Treemont Stone got a beard. Steve doesn't answer. Just smiles.

I talked to Aunt Silence about Steve, how he's changed since getting out of the hospital. She said she could understand him in her way.

"He's not the same anymore, and nobody acts the same with him anymore. And some people shouldn't act the same anyway because they want to get away with murder because they hurt."

When I see him, he's the same with me. Like now.

"Hey, Maggie. This is beautiful." He does a slow turn like a drunk man at a surprise birthday party. Nods again. "This is beautiful." His eyes on the Wall, shining with delight.

"Can I tell you the parts I painted?" I ask for singular appreciation.

He looks without my telling him where to look. "I always know you, Maggie. Don't I?"

"Never failed me yet."

"Never will." He looks at me and smiles through all that beard that makes him look older. I guess that's what it is that constructs a distance of years between us. For some reason I feel innocent. More innocent than I am with Tree, who is older, even if he's not an old man. You've seen those paintings, haven't you? The man or woman has a mist of sadness around them? Suffering makes their faces tender and lovely: there is something so sweet when you look at them, you almost want to cry. If I painted Steve Rainey, I'd paint him in a mist of an anguish so sublime it makes your eyes water to look at.

Steve doesn't get around much. The time in the hospital has brought a change. He is dead sober, like somebody who's sworn off liquor, dead sober most of the time. Some minutes, though, when we're talking, he's Steve Rainey again. That's when I'm sure the earth revolves around the sun and the moon orbits the earth and water will quench thirst. Otherwise, to see his new face is to know life can trick you.

"You ever hear from William?" I asked him one day soon after his return. We were sitting in HoneySounds, waiting for the Isley Brothers to stop singing "It's Your Thing." Steve had studied the words with his keen sobriety and found them individualistic and counterrevolutionary. "It's your thing. Do what you wanna do. / I can't tell you, who to sock it to." I like the beat and it's easy to dance to.

Steve said, "People have to do more than what they wanna do."

I didn't say anything. He listened some more. The same words over and over.

"You can't just do what you wanna do. The world would be exactly what it is."

Stupid me, I chose then to ask about William.

"In law school." That's the short answer he gave.

"Do y'all talk?"

"Every now and then."

"That's how often I talk to Essie."

"Why is that?"

I can't say exactly. It hurts to consider knowing. A cloudy pain in my body.

"She must not be talking to me either."

"You're okay."

"Because I was in the crazy house? So I must be crazy forever. The brother with the kinky hair and mind. Oh, wow!" He smiles, but not happily. Limply. "Sometimes I think about that night and wonder if I was. I wonder if it was worth the rest of my life. Maybe I got carried away for nothing much. I believed everything we said. But there ain't no change at Eden. One more Black teacher. And even if there were more change, would it be worth my life? The War is still going on. The next time I give my life for something, it's gonna mean something. It's going to matter."

"I hate to hear you sound so bitter." The cloudy pain is heavy now, holding some of this regret.

"I'm not bitter, Maggie. I just grew up the hard way. I want justice. The Old Testament wasn't wrong. An eye for an eye. A tooth for a tooth. And a life for a life. So when I give now, it's for justice."

I don't know what this means exactly. "You taking up a collection?"

"Hell, naw. I collected enough misery." His macabre humor causes bitter delight that breaks up his face. So he laughs. Not like he used to, but a laugh with corners in it, sharp edges, hidden spikes.

"You sound like that man on *Dracula* be standing at the bottom of the steps in the hold of the ship Dracula arrives on. Everybody else on board is dead and he so crazy he loves death. When the people discover him, he just laughing. Then he start eating flies, graduates to moths and rats and stuff." This is supposed to be funny. And he finds it hilarious.

"Eden U. can have that effect on a brother," he says drily.

I don't know why Steve still hides from people, working so quietly for ASANTE, researching, and running the old-fashioned printing press, which must be difficult because his fingertips are so smooth, without prints, difficult to hold the tiny letters to make the words and line them up on the plates. But I told him once that difficulty was his delight. He told me that I was right.

It is Steve Rainey Essie Witherspoon walks up to, not me. "Hello, stranger," she says like that record by Barbara Lewis. Her voice is so strained and so pointedly directed away from me, I don't enter into the finish of the song like we would have only a few years ago, Essie and me and Leona: "Shoo bop, sshoo-bop, my baby, oooh / It seems like a mighty long time."

When I say, "Hi, Essie," she doesn't say a thing.

Not to me. For Steve there is a hug, which he receives with a puzzled look, his eyes staring into mine.

"I'm so happy you're out of the hospital. How long you been out? Are you going back to school?"

"Not to Eden. Maybe Paradise."

"Where's Paradise?" Essie asks.

"I don't know. Could be right here," he says. "Feels like it."

Essie's smile starts to wobble, and she looks around Steve nervously, not wanting to look at me, but looking anyway, for some straight answers. Not wanting to align herself with the man who's talking in mysteries in a way he must have learned in the head hospital, she turns to me. Because she is sure hostility is sane, and unsure whether Steve is. I know he is.

"I had to see what you been working on so hard." She studies the wall for a long time like a teacher going over a poor test paper.

The last time I saw Essie was at Yvonne Christmas's going-away party. It was a weird day. I was working on the wall and Simba didn't want me to leave. They'd all started treating me funny when they found out I was "being seen around town" with Treemont Stone. This didn't surprise me because Simba told me one time about some man I was hanging around with, seen with me at the Wall. And at that time there was nobody. He said more than one person saw the man who waited for me while I worked.

Simba was acting strange I think because I was no longer his girl-painter-cum-waitress fetching dinners and stuff from Roscoe's or some nearby eatery. The day of the parting Treemont Stone came to see me, and after that I was Hester Prynne in an Afro. All the brothers had their mouths tooted out. They liked him. They worked with him on other things. They didn't like him liking me. I figured that out.

I saw Essie soon after, excited to have seen her mother's new Afro and been witness to the birth of the rent strike. But Essie just asked me if I'd seen Steve. The answer, yes. Then she asked if I knew a man named Silky.

"Chaka," I said.

"They're one and the same, Magdalena."

Uncomfortable, because her voice was so harsh, I waited for her to speak. She wouldn't.

"He's not a friend of mine, Essie. We work with some of the same people."

"My own mother. Yeah, he work with her too. My own mother."

"I've never seen him with her. She works with Treemont Stone and so does he."

"Treemont Stone. The latest in the line of jackleg Black leaders hustling a shot on the six o'clock news."

"Do you know him?"

"What's there to know? If he's lucky he get himself killed and his name will live forever."

"I can't believe you!"

"Believe me, Maggie. Believe me."

That's what she said that day. Today she looks at the Wall.

The Wall does not belong to us. But no one has wanted it for five years. It's just a wall with an armpit of beams. We cleared the space around it. Raked and pulled up a multitude of weeds that pulled back, away from us, driving themselves into the earth. Hungry to survive this attack of beauty. We usurped their possession of the spot, and cleared the land for flowers.

ASANTE had done most of the interior work. We worked outside. Simba used to dream of planting trees. But he convinced himself and us that such permanence disregarded the imminence of Revolution, which disappointed me because I don't know why we must always wait to enjoy what delights. Sometimes I don't know. So like all of us who've labored on the Wall, I've told myself it was art to stir the blood I made, while secretly I whispered for art to ease and restore the heart.

The Wall, a mural of heroes, men and women, is beautiful and bold, the colors climbing off the surface, and bad, the stature of us pushing muscularly off the brick.

"Whatchusay!" Simba says every time he looks at it. Sounding like my daddy. "Whatchusay!"

I wait for what Essie will say, a part of me still wanting a word of praise.

"My mother could pick out the part I painted without my telling her." I say this but Essie doesn't try. In the dark of night, last night, my mother and father came and stood with Tree and me and watched the Wall, trying to name all the great Blackpeople looking out. My mother's favorite was King. My father's, Marcus Garvey.

"You shoulda had Haile Selassie up there with all them others. Oh, ho, ho. He turnt them lions loose on the Eye-talians. I read about them lions." Glory is bright as new dimes in his eyes.

And I can see him as I've seen him when he's told the story before. Sitting in the kitchen of the house in Mimosa, reading about a dark young soldier protecting his people and land. And more than anything, winning with the lions, great beasts straining to leap down upon mere mortals and swallow a head in one mouthful.

My father sees these victories when he looks at the Wall.

It is I who insisted on Fannie Lou Hamer next to Malcolm X. And that is where Simba and the brothers drew the line. No Silence. They never heard of her. Or if they did they didn't want to put too many women on the Wall. They didn't want to give the impression that we were a people pulled up on the apron strings of women. That would be a shame.

So there is Sojourner. And there is Harriet Tubman.

And here is Essie Witherspoon studying it all.

Noise is all around us, drummers and horn men, dancing girls with bodies on fire and bells on their ankles. We should be shouting, but we don't.

Essie says, "It's a lot of positive images up there." There's a rustle in her voice when she says this.

"Maybe the Wall, all this work, we help one person change and see and be better." I'm fishing. I can hear it in my own voice. So I quit begging and ask, "How's Moneeka?" I think I ask because she's somebody I had in heart as I painted. This Hallelujah Wall is for Essie's baton-twirling little sister and for my younger sisters, Anne and Frances, Ernestine and Shirley. For everybody.

Essie answers politely. "Still trying out hairdos. She wears an Afro on top of her head in a bunny tail. It's cute. You talk to Leona?" Her voice has begun to give like a tight belt loosening.

"She's here. Didn't you see her?"

"No," Essie tells me. "Nobody I know is here." She lifts her arm straight as an arrow. Her straight index finger is the arrowhead. She's pointing at Chaka. Chaka, standing a half a yard away. Looking at her.

He waits for her. She gets right up in his face.

"Remember me?" she asks him. Very polite. "Remember me?" It's less a question. "Remember me? Do you remember me?"

Chaka doesn't talk. He just stares straight ahead.

"I remember you." This is so heavy it drops to the ground between them. Chaka's face is coming apart.

"I remember you. You changed your name, but I know you. I remember you." She's all in his coming-apart face. She shoves the arrowhead finger into his chest. Right where his heart beats underneath.

"I don't forget," she says.

Chaka's mouth is open and he's drawing in air. I think he's going to fly apart like a propeller whirling so fast it flies off its pinnings.

"I can't forget." Her voice is muffled, as in a coat. She raises her right arm now and it's not an arrow, but an oar now. She slams him across the cheek. "Not ever." Her voice sounds like it's shredding her throat. "I can't forget." Shredding.

Chaka turns his other cheek. His whole face is wet. The tears just hold there. Not even from his eyes, but springing out of his face. He whispers, "Can you ever forgive me?"

The question ignites her and she explodes over him. Pummeling him. Kicking him. Two brothers and I pull her off him.

Chaka is crying and it's not the blows that did it. It's not. This weeping is older than the fresh wounds of Essie's scratches on his face, his pleated eyes, the blood-filled nostrils. He is crying over what he did to earn his injuries.

Two brothers, cooing softly into her face, take Essie across the street.

I start to follow, then I turn around to Chaka, wanting to tell him something. He's still standing there, looking across at Essie, waiting for another blow.

Chaka starts to lift himself inside. Pulling his stomach in, stiffening his back, backhanding the water off his face.

I turn to follow Essie. Out of the corner of my eye I see him. He looks like I've hit him. Struck him a wakening blow. He walks off. Wiping his face.

Essie's teeth are bared. She lunges at me. "What you come over here for? There go your friend."

"You are my friend, Essie," I say.

After the Takeover, Sherman graduated and took the tapes he'd made during the siege. He sold them for a large profit and gave a nominal sum to FBO. He was offered a job at a newspaper, even though journalism hadn't been his major. His training was on the job, and his instinct was there all along. He can smell a story. He walks right up to Essie and starts an interview. Questions about Chaka.

Essie tells him about Silk, who is Chaka now. Then she launches into Treemont Stone.

Some people standing around say, "Naw, naw. Don't do that, little sister."

But she does.

I say, "Essie, why don't you leave him out of this?" My voice is hot.

"I will not," she snaps. "I'm not going to leave him out. He put himself in when he took in that rapist. That criminal rapist. Call themselves ASANTE like they something. Even got my mama fooled." She points me out to Sherman, as if he wasn't there at Eden with both of us. As if we didn't have a history together. "She was defending the rapist."

"That's not exactly true." I care about Chaka as a redeemed brother. Hopefully redeemed. I don't care about Chaka personally. Not like I care about Essie. Even though we're at odds.

But Essie's a raging river not to be crossed and I feel awful that Chaka is not Silky anymore and is in ASANTE. And I am Essie's friend in spite of everything.

"Well, see, I don't think they should be allowed to fool the entire community. Talking about Antonio Silky is Chaka now. When does a snake grow wings?"

There are one hundred others in ASANTE, sixty men and forty women. All of them different. Students, lawyers, and laborers, teachers and bus drivers, secretaries—all kinds. Five ex-cons, who are some of the hardest workers.

"Essie," I'm still trying to talk to her. Trying to. "Essie, how long does Chaka have to pay?"

"Pay till he dies. Pay till he dies. Just like I do." She's through with me. I hear her.

"Okay," I say. "You're the judge. You got the right."

Sherman keeps asking questions. Essie keeps answering them. Sherman keeps writing in his notebook. Like one of the doctors from the Keep-You-Sick Clinic down south, writing down the symptoms of my great uncle's descent into death.

There's going to be the devil to pay. I'm sure of it. There's going to be hell to pay.

Day is disappearing, like a white mouse running into a hole. People scatter. Men roam around picking up after the festivities. I have to find Treemont. I start searching around the mural. I'm right up on it. I can pick out every stroke and dab I've put on this wall. The hours spent at this were the only gifts I thought I had. Now I'm tired. And nothing is enough. There it is, a twenty-foot-high, thirty-foot-wide kaleidoscope of dream, happenings and dramas, and heroes, women and men. I've helped make it. And it's not enough. I thought it would be. Each time I make a painting, I think, "This will be enough." But it is not. I cannot give Chaka someone else's forgiveness and nothing is enough to undo Essie's violation. And I cannot find Treemont. So I go home alone.

✦

The newspaper reads, ASANTE GANG VIOLENCE.

What happens is there is blood on the ground. Blood on the Wall. And the dead body of a boy from whom the blood runs. He is propped up against the Hallelujah Wall. If I could really look, past his open mouth, and fixed, empty eyes, I'd figure out if the knife is pinning his clothes to the wall and holding him up, or if the blade has torn its way through cloth, skin, muscle, bone, tissue, and blood to the other side and pinned him there. I could know, if I could really look at something beyond the open mouth and eyes in infinite, soundless, breathless snore, eyes in immutable, sightless gaze. He is a brown boy in a brown jacket, a maroon knit top, and wool pants. Blood draws me closer to see.

He's propped up just under Malcolm's chin, in contemplation. I make myself look, drawing closer and away from Treemont and the others. We are like some weird Nativity scene. Shepherds and kings inching closer to see. I can see his face now. The attractive heart shape, the high, high cheekbones (Chaka says he was called Apache because his cheekbones are like an Indian's. Sometimes they called him Geronimo because he said that when he ran like somebody jumping out of an airplane, the last syllable—mo—running behind him in a fast echo), the fleshy lower lip, and the mole on his cheek, and the small scars from cuts and burns. I study these particulars.

The newspaper reads, SUSPECTED GANG LEADER THREATENS GANG WAR.

Now Treemont is wrestling with a boy about sixteen, his Afro bushy and sculpted like a well-pruned bush. Tree has pinned the boy's arms tight to his sides. He's wrapped one arm around the boy's torso, holding the boy in place. Tree's other arm is around the boy's neck. He drags the boy by the neck, the way my grandmother Patsy would go out into her yard, choose a hen, and snatch her by the neck. Sometimes she took the chicken directly to the chopping block, other times she wrung the neck, snapped it with a twist of her wrist, then chopped off the head in a clean stroke.

I'm scared something will snap in Tree and he'll snap the boy's neck. The boy spits and claws like one of the feral cats Lazarus caught and terrorized. The man, my Treemont, pushes him down to one knee; the boy is facing the Wall and the dead body of the other boy, splattered with blood. Blood and paint of the mural disguising each other.

"Look at him," Treemont commands in the voice his father must have used in the pulpit. Soft rumbling thunder. "Do you see you?"

"I told you I didn't have nothing to do with this," the boy mumbles, closing his eyes like a little child so he won't have to see.

Treemont knows this is the truth. This boy didn't drive the knife through the other's heart and prop the body against the Hallelujah Wall. But when he heard about it, he snickered. Made a remark. Like, "He was a real hero. He made it on that wall." This was so cold it shook even Tree. To hear a boy dismiss another boy's life and death.

We stay there till the police and ambulance come. Then Tree goes to see the woman who isn't the mother of a living son anymore, the father who isn't the father of a living son anymore.

The newspaper describes the discovery of the murder at the Hallelujah Wall. The story describes Tree's wrestle with the boy as a warning from ASANTE to another gang. The story connects Stone and ASANTE to the death and gang activity in the area. The story quotes an unnamed source who claims the members of ASANTE are all criminals. One a convicted rapist, another a convicted arsonist and an ex-mental patient. Their leader a man named Treemont Stone. Their name ASANTE, a Swahili word for "thank you," experts called a subtle form of intimidation to extort money from shop owners and other businessmen in the area. ASANTE, the story said, was involved in the defacing of property, since the Hallelujah Wall had been painted on property owned by a corporation on the West Coast.

When I tell Mama and Madaddy the story isn't true, they say truth doesn't matter to Whitepeople. The point is that Treemont and ASANTE have been identified as outside the graces of the law. They'd hate to see somebody wind up dead or in jail, especially me or Lazarus. Treemont's name is Trouble now. My parents' fear descends on me like black doves, cooing, sheltering in those dark, thick wings, lithe and dependable, and smothering.

11

The Blue Nile

This is the road my father rode on his way into the City. It follows somewhat the Mississippi River, so this is our New Nile. And this is the road we came by after him. The car loaded down with a Mississippi life, so heavy the burdens and baggage the belly of the automobile drooped like a pregnant woman almost full term. Yet so light the dreams we floated on four worn wheels. We were not much more than babies then. I was the youngest, so I don't remember what the others do. My younger sisters had not even been born. The memory of the older siblings is history to me. A world of signs, a mist land to me, even though I could read early. I didn't experience the signs. I experience dreams. That is why Treemont Stone wakes me with the light to ask me what I've dreamed.

I do not always tell him.

Yesterday I told him I dreamed of my Aunt Silence. But I dreamed of the Blue Nile. I dreamed ghosts with gold in their mouths all along the banks of the Blue Nile. They bend over the bar. They lean against the blue walls that Treemont Stone painted. They holler, they hum, they growl just behind the blues singer on the bandstand that Treemont Stone built years ago in one of his lives. The women ghosts take off their wigs and stand under their natural hair, sweating and fanning themselves with their false headpieces like their kinswomen fanned themselves with funeral parlor fans at their funerals. I can see them. Here with us. I am not dreaming, but I am. But the dreams are so rapid now they pile up on each other all through the night; they push and sidle under the doorstep of day. They people the noontime: the dreams and the ghosts. So many of them I cannot count them for Treemont. They frighten me. Because they come for someone.

He tries to play it off. His interest. Stands combing his new beard in the mirror. It is a vain thing, a beard. Keeps a man looking in glass and touching himself. I tell him that.

He laughs. His teeth even and straight. So that laugh is a flash of delight for me. "It keeps me cautious," he says. Ruminating by stroking his facial hair. He pauses to consider a plan, brushing his small beard like the hair on a baby's head. Softly.

Winter is gone now. That is what the calendar says. But now I'm thinking we are in an episode of *The Twilight Zone*. The one where people are dying from the heat, and a sweating woman in her slip is desperate for water because water is almost gone. The sun is moving toward the earth. Or the earth is moving toward the sun. Whichever is moving, the earth is burning up. All the people burning, scorched. Then, in the end, we find it is a dream of delirium and the sweating woman dreamed the heat in a fever because the world is cold, a slow ice cube moving away from the sun or the sun moving away from it. And all the people are dying of the cold, under layers and layers of clothes and coats. Blowing into their hands, trying to restore the heat to their own hands.

This haunts me because I don't know where we are. The people are on fire, ready to take our destiny into our own hands. But there is a cold front, a massive cold front, that catches us off guard. And it is worse than the ice babies.

In the Homes, something was about to explode the day the sheriff's men came to evict Mrs. Fredonia Constance. I wasn't there, but I heard about it. How she told them this was a legitimate rent strike. The rent money was in an account at such and such bank (the Black one). They threw her out. All of her belongings in garbage bags or hauled out loose and unwrapped. She didn't know what hair to wear to protect herself. So she stood in her own hair, in her housecoat, screaming, denouncing the men who would do a woman this way.

Treemont Stone was out of town, but some people blamed him anyway. Even though Chaka and ten other brothers from ASANTE showed up in time to stop Essie's mama from being put outdoors.

There was a scuffle over a new toaster oven that Essie had bought her. The sheriff, in a dark-brown uniform, fell on the ground with Chaka on top of him and the toaster oven. That's how Chaka got shot. The sheriff said the gun went off. And Chaka got shot in the shoulder. A few inches lower and he would have been dead. When the onlookers, already full of sympathy for Mrs. Constance, saw blood, people had had enough for one working day. Then the fight started and the sheriff called in sixteen squad cars to contain the melee. Every able-bodied man on the scene was arrested. And the women carried Mrs. Fredonia Constance's belongings back into her concrete rooms. The sheriff hollered, "Halt!" but the women acted like they thought they heard "Go ahead!"

My father analyzed the situation best when he said, "All the law involved in it need to be drug out in the streets and hung." The same thing he said when Aunt Silence was beaten in Mimosa when she first tried to vote a while ago.

✦

Treemont pulls into a gas station, not the kind we are boycotting for exploiting in South Africa. Though he says we'd be hard-pressed to go to one that doesn't have dirty hands. I don't laugh; he thought I would, but I am not in the mood for laughing. He goes into the gas station store. I follow. We buy juice and chips. The town is Moody, in the southernmost part of the state. This is a long state and once we are free of it, I'll celebrate to see another lying welcome sign, even if it is further south and back to the open hostilities instead of clandestine. It doesn't matter: now the veiled is open-faced and the open-faced is veiled. This is one country. And there is nowhere to run, but we do.

The towns when we come to them are industrialized, but not hulking. I point to a gathering of lights in the distance, past the dark stretch of highway. "I bet Aint Kit could fit that whole town in her pocketbook."

He smiles, his head leaned back, resting while I drive. "We'd never find it again."

Pearl likes to tell the story of the day the weather changed while people watched. It was two in the afternoon and people were sauntering in shirtsleeves and light sweaters. The women had their legs out. The sun was lenient and bright. And the Hawk was sleeping with his wings close to his big sides. Then, Pearl said, she went around the corner, waiting for the light to change. And before the light changed the weather did. The Hawk woke up in a bad mood, flapping his huge wings and roaring. Skirts flew up and chill bumps jumped all over people's bodies. Girls in skirts stood still, holding their little skirts over their privates and screaming. Everybody ran for cover; while the Hawk pushed them back away from buildings or slammed them into the sides of buildings. Tearing purses off arms and unbuttoning men's shirts. Pearl had plenty of witnesses because everybody remembered where they were when the weather went from seventy-two degrees to twenty-eight degrees. Nobody could call her a lie.

A voice broke in my ear like a lightbulb. It was Aint Kit. Waking me up. It was pitch-dark in the apartment above HoneySounds and there was no music anywhere. I didn't hear the phone ring. He did. And handed it to me.

"Maggie," Aint Kit's voice was hoarse and jagged. "I ain't slept a wink all night."

"It's still nighttime, Aint Kit," I mumbled into the phone. Trying to pull the sheet up over my bare breasts, so she wouldn't see what he could.

"I'm paralyzed. I can't move a muscle." Her voice was urgent, aggrieved. "Bay, my own daughter, won't even come here and help me. Nobody in my entire family will come help me. I don't know what to do."

"Can you call the ambulance, Aint Kit?" I don't know if I should.

"Maggie." She's more spirited now. "The last time I went to the hospital them doctors did me so bad." Talking faster now. "They did me just like they did yo mama's uncle E.W. Just stood around that dying man, writing down his symptoms. And they was killing him." Indignant at the memory, she sounded better. Livelier.

I knew he could hear her. Some voices have that way of carrying even when they're whispers. The tension in the pinched tone wiggles like a wire in a little water. He could hear. He watched my face through half-closed eyes.

"Do you want me to come over there, Aint Kit?" Kinship is a form of obligation, but not always happy. I screwed up my face. He started to laugh, ducking under the cover, because the closest relative he has is a sister in California. All the rest who were close have died, except for the cousins scattered throughout the states.

"I'll see if I can get my friend to run me over there in a little while. Can you hold on till then?"

"I got to. Cause I don't know what else I'm gone do. I CAIN'T MOVE. You come on now."

"Okay," I said.

"Bye, bye, baby," she signed off.

With Aint Kit you never know. You never know if she's as bad off as she says or if it's all a ploy. One time I got Bay to go over there with me and Aint Kit was sitting in her sunroom eating cantaloupe just as well as she please. After leading me to believe that she was on her deathbed. Any Grace can tell you a tale of Aint Kit. And any Grace can tell a tale Aint Kit has told on them. I think that's it.

Pearl's told me the latest rumor Aint Kit has on me: I gave up Eden University for this no-good gangster. He's been in prison. Alcatraz. Now he supposed to be working for the people. I gave him the money I made from my fabulous painting. He lives off me. His name is Treemont Stone. His face was in the paper. You know he connected to gang activity. Ain't that something? Maddog Stone. He a human rabies carrier. He killed that boy over some dope and put him up against Maggie's Wall. And what she wanna waste her time on that piece of building ready to come down for nobody know but he musta put her up to that too. I have had three husbands and I know how a man can get. Don't like to see you do better. Sabotage what you do. Like that one useta shine his shoes on my good bath towels and the other used to eat his grits outta my good china that I keep in the cabinet and when I tole him about it he say he was company and I say you right cause you certainly not staying in here with your hat in your hand and grease around your mouth and grits scarring my good bowls.

"If she's paralyzed, how's she going to answer the door?" Treemont wanted to know.

279

The dogs were crazy with the darkness and the noises we'd made. Car doors closing, footsteps, the dance of our voices in the dim and lightening air. No one but us about.

Treemont sees everything. He chuckled at all the names on Aint Kit's bell.

It'd been a while since we rang. Inside the lights were on.

"I can pick the lock," he offered. A smirk on his face.

That would've been it. "She'd swear you were a gangster then."

So we waited. I put my ear to the door.

Standing in the lifting dark with Tree was a moment dipped in ink and imprinted on the round face of Time. Whorls and whorls of feeling. He was standing straight and I looked at him and gave a quick grin to avert any ill will directed toward him. But he was just curious, by then. We listened, and scattered minuscule sounds greeted us.

"She's coming," I said. I could hardly hear for the rough din of the starving dogs.

The door cracked and a weak exclamation issued out. "Uh, ooh, thank you, Jesus. I didn't die alone."

"Aint Kit?" I pushed open the door. She was up against the V between the wall and the open door. Standing stiff as a sarcophagus in a case.

"Miz Grace, are you all right?" Treemont reached out for her.

"Who are you?" she asked, suspicion quickening in her eyes. As if she didn't know.

I stood on the same formality she required. "Aunt Katherine, this is my friend, Mr. Treemont Stone."

"What kinda name is that?"

"Colored."

She liked that. "Ain't we good for some names? I know this woman, her last name was B-U-T-T and she named her son Chicken. For real." Suddenly, she is wan. "Can I lean on you, Mr. Tree?" She offered him her hand. Coy as a well-schooled debutante. She pulled away from her corner and walked with Treemont's help like the Mummy, dragging her stiff left leg behind her.

"Help me to the living room, would you please?" Her voice shot through with pain.

I turned on the floor lamp. It was new. A truly monstrous thing. A pseudo-owl on a perch stand. The eyes and mouth emitting light. The grotesque light grabbing the room.

She sat down in the wingback chair. He stood near her. He was seeing everything. Like he always does. My aunt's zoo of beauty. Oddly, then, I wanted to protect her. Her with her imaginative mouth and hungry ways. Her ridiculously assembled knickknacks. I didn't want him to laugh. Like we do when we hear somebody call somebody "a running-dog lackey of the military-industrial complex." He wouldn't laugh to her face, but later I didn't want him to say she wasn't worthy of grudging attention. And I didn't want her to shame me with a cruelty, with a hot little snub or snide remark. Worst of all a lie about me or a member of my immediate family.

She managed to get out, "How you like my house, Mr. Tree?"

He got the smile out quick, and I was happy he was a minister's son and the son of a woman who could give so much she baffled reason. "It's a wonder, Miz Grace."

"The ninth wonder of the world," I said. He looked at me. I looked at him and saw him again for the kind of man he is.

"I'm thinking about putting that owl lamp in the bay window. Keep the pigeons away. They keeping me up too much."

I didn't know pigeons even bothered neat little neighborhoods like hers. So I said, "I didn't know you had a pigeon problem, Aint Kit."

"Maggie, I got every kinda problem there is. Every problem."

"You feeling better now, Aint Kit?"

"Naw," she said, before I could ask good. "I'm scared it's going to come back on me. Worser than it was." She looked all around at the pink rug. "I was petrified."

"I don't know what come over me," she said like she just woke up from a trance. "I could not move a muscle. I was powerless over my own body. That's a terrible thing."

His eyes were full of compassion. "I imagine that's a pretty frightening feeling, Miz Grace."

"You can't even imagine how terrible it is." It was her disease and she would only share the details. "I could not have even dreamed this," she added.

Then Treemont couldn't take his eyes off the long-eared porcelain dogs the mantel. Madaddy said his sister is a real customer because she will buy anything. That's one of the reasons he says it.

"Maggie, turn on that gas over the fireplace," she ordered. "I got a chill."

I did her bidding. Soon, a fake fire burned inside fake logs. The heat was genuine.

"I been having them bad dreams again, Maggie," she confessed. She must have thought she'd mentioned them before. "I don't know what they about. They just come to me. Funny dreams like you and yo mama be having."

Tree sat on the couch with me. The plastic cover snapped and crackled.

"I'm worried about Bay." There's a finality in this. As if this were the cause of all things. She might have said, "I believe in God and He punishes."

She enumerates Bay's crimes. "She don't write me no letters. She don't call me on the phone. She don't send me no message by nobody come by here. She don't care about her own mother."

"She's all right. Or you would have heard from her. Aunt Leah-Bethel would have let you know."

"Lee-Bet don't tell me nothing. And down there stealing Mama and Papa's land for that old Freedom Farm. Just a bunch of no-counts trying to get something for nothing."

"I thought the communal farm was a great idea."

Aint Kit looked up in the ceiling for my common sense. I get it from my mama, she says without saying anything. She tried again.

"Everybody ain't decent, Maggie," she told me as if she's told me a thousand times before. She peered into my face, and the pain in hers was real. "People will hurt you and laugh." A quick glance at the man beside me. "Lee-Bet just let folks use her."

I left this alone. And Treemont didn't open his mouth. Just looked at her wonderingly. I know how he is now.

On television I've seen magicians in elaborate capes pulling rabbits out of hats; doves untangle their wings from sleeves and sweep upward, caught by the magician's hands. Aint Kit is the magician, and this next one was a rabbit held up by ears or dove jailed by the feet so it wouldn't travel.

"Whatever come of that young man you brought over here with you that time?" She slid a look at Treemont, who was staring at my painting above the fireplace. Staring with a smile on his face.

"Who? Moses?" I asked her back.

"Was that his name? I knew it was something from the Bible—Noah, Judas, Esau, or something like that." For some reason, having written off Moses, she turns to my Stone. "Your name is not from the Bible, is it, Mr. Tree?"

"My middle name is Michael. Treemont is the name of a town my mother visited once."

"Oh, you named Michael?" She glowed. "My husband was named Michael." I didn't know which one.

"I think I'm going to call you Mike. Like that oldest boy on *My Three Sons.*

"Just don't call me no-count," Treemont Michael Stone said, and grinned.

She claimed him then and he was in the family. Her muscles worked again. She stood up and sashayed into the hall, then she remembered her disability.

"Ooh, I was feeling so much better, but this leg giving out." She dragged her right leg then, into the kitchen. "Come on here while I fix you some breakfast."

She thawed one of her famous sweet potato pies. Put a pot of coffee on the stove. She was steady talking. Her Mike walked through her house, stopping at various artifacts. He acted like he was in a stunned state.

"Seeing is believing," I reminded him in a whisper. I've told him. But Aint Kit is a rare bird. You have to see her fly. And to really know her you have to keep your binoculars trained on her nest, study how desperately she collects bits of straw and rag and paper and shells and discards to construct some place for safety and solace.

He keeps looking and looking at a wall platter just heaping with martyrs, Malcolm X, Fred Hampton, Mark Clark, King, Kennedys, Chaney, Schwerner, Goodman, Evers, and Jesus Christ. A nouveau Last Supper with a waiting space.

"Don't let anybody eat off my face." He was kidding, but I didn't like it. Not that he imagined he belongs in the august company of the august dead, but that he could imagine himself dead. His eyes were afraid.

"You ain't dead."

It was a confident thing to say because who could say who was dead and who wouldn't be. There were only a few faces on the plate, but the faces of dead young men and women could fill all the dishes of a banquet table. We could have a feast of grief off of the faces.

Having seen Malcolm's face, who would have thought that he could die? Or King? Or further back, the Kennedy in Dallas with windswept hair? Dying is for people you've never seen. Or old people who haven't got anything better to do. Really, really, really old people. When Silence called after her house was bombed, it was her bravery I kept inside me. Not the fear. Grandmothers die of old age, or by accident on a road between Mimosa and Letha in semidarkness and with terrible consequences.

And young men die in jungles, their bodies locked in plastic bags like leftovers from a banquet. Maybe Moses. But even that is impersonal, not because I don't wonder and worry about Moses, but because that kind of ending is distant. The grief, when it comes, still comes home to the body and cracks it like an egg until the clear parts run out and the heavy yolk stays heavily pressing against the shell.

This is a renegade grief that leaves us gasping for air. The grief right here. Because Death has practiced works on us, and ended lives and stolen the last sweet from the starving.

How long did we struggle up for air? Miraculous humans who learned to live under the weight of water. Then to pull and tear the water back and glimpse the exquisite blue of sky, it was heady! To go under again now? That would be to drown.

I feel like I'm drowning now. Suddenly, my breath outside of me and I'm standing between the Contemporary Last Supper and Aint Kit fixing a breakfast of pie and coffee and eggs. I gasp, and what she's just said is so laughably amazing, neither one of them turns. Who wouldn't gasp?

She's talking. "You know something is up. I'm telling you something is up. That jar of worms is jumping."

"What jar of worms?" To be busy I began to butter bread on one side, knowing she liked hers buttered on two.

She looked at me. Amazed and hurt. How could I forget? "Them worms come out of that watermelon that man sold me while they was assassinating Martin Luther King in Memphis, Tennessee."

Treemont, banned from labor in Aint Kit's kitchen, leaned on the refrigerator. Listening. The only sound then was the refrigerator. It sounded alive. The constant growl of the cold machine keeping things the way they are. This is the newest kind that makes its own ice cubes, and just to show it off Aint Kit offered Tree some water.

She inserted a cup into a square hole and pressed ICE then WATER. That's what she got. Her joy was smug, barely contained. She held in her bottom lip, handed him the glass, and minced back over to the coffeepot on the stove. Modern as she is, she still likes her coffee cooked on the stove. Tastes better.

But it's keeping things that keeps her happiest. And Aint Kit keeps an icebox on the sunporch attached to her kitchen. An antique icebox, the kind men delivered ice in. It's doorless now, and full of flowering plants. Its open face is sideways to the new sunlight that came through the window, with the stirrings of the neighborhood. The dogs had quieted down. Gnawing on old bones. People were walking on the sidewalks, their steps sounded crisp or smooth like dancers over glass or cracked ice.

In the kitchen, I didn't want to move lest I bump into a corner of Aint Kit's fabrication. I supposed old Tree was satisfied she'd brought up that jar of worms.

"I thought you flushed away all them ole worms." I nudged her memory cautiously. She could usually remember the turns in her tune better than this.

"No. I started to," she corrected. "But I decided to save them for evidence. I figured they could probably tell me bad news."

I didn't open my mouth.

Treemont opened his. "May I see your jar of worms, Miz Grace?"

Only too pleased to oblige, she marched to the old icebox and reached way back into the back of the bottom where she used to store preserves when I was a little girl. Her movements were supple and well. But the sickness was over, excitement was in. She held up the jar of worms to the sunlight. They lay still in the mound of soil that cushioned the glass bottom of the jar. She shook the jar in the sunlight. Nothing woke.

"Aaaaaahhh, shit, Kit," she cursed herself. "Jesus-the-Gentile! These warning worms are dead. They dead and they ain't moving. Can't even use them for bait."

Against my judgment, Tree squeezed his hand in the jar. Sifting the dead soil. Stirring up nothing but dust ghosts. When he finished and his hands were dressed in dust, Aint Kit took the jar and turned it around and around in the sunlight.

✦

I want to go to a motel because I've never been to one. But he says no, we can make it if we go straight through. But at least we pull over to the side of the road. He is silent, contemplative, smoothing his brow to end the slow car of thought. A boxcar of inevitabilities. I think of Bertram and how he cried to go with us, but Tree said no. I, for the life of me, couldn't figure out why not. Charlotte seemed happy at the thought, grinning assent. Not because she's so eager to be rid of him, but the chance for her boy to spend time with Treemont Stone. I knew Tree was right, after I thought about it. We have to save Bertram.

Tree found Bertram jammed like a wishbone into a pile of rice. The snow was that deep. Some boys put him there. He was trying out a new walk as a gang member. The rival gang said they would dismember him, but the process was too complicated. They took off his gloves and jammed them in his mouth. They bound his hands with his shoelaces. They left him for dead in a high drift the City made as it swept a path clear with a snowplow.

Tree brought the ice baby home to my apartment across from Charlotte's. (She lived with Honeybabe until C.C. got home and they put together the money to buy HoneySounds. I was wrong and C.C. opted for music instead of hardware because hardware reminded him of war. I imagine the sound of the instruments slicing off his leg while he lay in a sweating, infected semicoma was enough machinery for one man's army. And one woman who had waited for him with pounding pulse and controlled hysteria bridled in confidence and wishful thinking was enough to share a house with. And Bay asked Honey then if she wasn't a little worried because Charlotte was lethally pretty. And Honey said no because if C.C. had something on his mind that wasn't her he ran the risk of losing two more legs. This was raunchy enough for the women to laugh over in the kitchen, and cause men listening in to blush. So by the grace of Honey and C.C. I live in one apartment and Charlotte in another above the music store in the neighborhood near the university of the City.) I didn't know what it was in his arms. Ice was broken like glass over the body. Like a shattered mirror. And with the ice was crystals— hard snow, as if a cross between granite and frost. His cap lost and the snow caught up in his hair like gravel. It wouldn't melt.

I opened the door wide, and Tree stumbled past me, moving fast. He headed for the bathroom and lay the boy in the tub. Quick to unravel the teenager from the wet and stiff coat. Then the T-shirt. Pants. Socks. Jockey shorts. (I looked away.) The warm water rose to cover him and Bertram lay with no mystique. Half frozen, thin as a wishbone, brittle from the cold. Whoever broke him in two could have made a wish: to be men one day.

Treemont, talking under his breath, took one foot into his hand.

"Maggie, get his hands."

I did. Rubbing his one hand between my two. So hard I could feel the veins shift and the bones resist. Then the other hand.

Then Tree rubbed his whole body. Bertram lay still, moving only as we pushed him until his life throbbed in our hands. The boy lay quiet, his mouth slack and eyes closed. Breathing differently now. Now we knew he was sleeping. We counted each breath like fairy godparents at the christening of a magical babe.

Treemont began to laugh. His hands dipping emptily into the clear water. His wrists and arms damp. He looked at Bertram and laughed again. "Brothers get some hair and think they're lions."

I brushed the hard frost from the hair on the boy's head, off his eyelashes. He stirred from either our touches or our laughter. Then Tree told him to step out of the tub and into a big towel. I looked away again. More vigorous rubbing until the skin glowed. Then a robe that Tree's sister had sent him one Christmas. Bertram was swallowed, lost in the love of the generous terry cloth. And Treemont guided him.

I fixed him steaming tea with hunks of lemon and spoonfuls of honey. He sipped through huge, swollen lips, still blue under the brown. He blew, sipped, and recited in snatches what had happened to him.

287

"Good thing they knew your head was too hard for a bullet. They just put you in an outdoor freezer like a dressed bird." Treemont sounded so pleasant, smiling so broadly at Bertram, I had to look twice.

Bertram was quick on the uptake. He mumbled through those monster lips that looked like they had little balloons in them.

"I ain't in no stupid gang, man. Mindin my own business. I ain't runnin from nothing." Bertram glared out of icy eyes.

"My father told me if you see a good fight, get in it." Tree.

"Yeah."

"Otherwise run."

"I ain't runnin from no punks." His boy body shivered with this. Was it the cold in his limbs and torso?

"Boy, a hard head cracks like an egg. Too bad you the best we have to offer life."

Bertram was torn between praise and rebuke. Hid his upper lip in the bottom.

"A good fight, Bertram. Keep yourself for the good fight. It's okay to talk your way out of something. It's okay to run. Then you can make your moment, or just stay alive to meet your moment." Tree's hands were clasped almost beseechingly. Then he loosed them and rared back in his chair beside the bed.

"You don't hear me, do you? You will later on. I believe you will. I know nobody is made up just the same. God ain't got no cookie cutter for making people. The world has never seen the likes of you before. And never will again. I've seen brothers similar to you, but they weren't you. We could search the earth and scan every star in the sky and never find you again. A woman from the other side saved my life. Saved me. And she said something that comes to me in different ways. Sometimes it sounds like 'Only You.' Or 'Own You.' Or 'I love you.' Or 'All love you.' Or 'I All Love.' Or 'I All Love You.' It's like it turns around in my mind and I hear it a different way echoing back. And each way means something to me. Each way made me stronger and impenetrable. Some men wanted to kill me. They were White men who wanted to kill me in the dark. I was so close to dying I could hear Death whispering in my ear. I was an eyelash away from dying. And I'm not afraid of dying now. She taught me in a way I can never repay. And I'll be good and goddamned if some other motherfucker is going to take me outta here. And if you choose to run up into Death's arms so you can be a man, the paradox is you will die a boy. Now get the hell outta Maggie's bed. You messin up her sheets."

I opened my mouth to say never mind, but Tree looked at me to keep quiet. I shut my mouth.

In his jockey shorts, oven dried, carrying his damp clothes in his arms, Bertram got up and walked. He stopped in the doorway and waited. Neither one of us said anything to him. Walking across the hall, he hollered back to us, "I'll see you all later on."

After that, he hung around HoneySounds, looking for Treemont Stone. When the newspapers came up with more stories about ASANTE being a gang, he was the only one who asked Tree directly about the story.

He was standing in my doorway looking like a little stick with tremors in it. Desolate and brash. "Hey, man, I thought you didn't go for no gangs."

"I don't."

"Can you read?"

"What do I look like to you?"

"A Black man with his feet on Maggie's cocktail table."

"Who do I look like to you?"

"Muhammad Ali." Bertram broke out grinning and Tree was on him.

This happened so often it became routine. The jabbing and dancing. I started something: faces and hands ablur and bodies bent and aimed like arrows. It was blue. This painting. The figures shifting in the foreground. A closed window framing the ice outside.

When I told Tree, "It's *Boxer Day*," he laughed. Gave it a tender scrutiny over my shoulder. My body was light, decisive.

"When you going to quit the Blue Nile?"

"As soon as I see Mockingbird July."

"Why?"

"Every man has a dream, woman."

"Yours is a hundred years old." Jealousy chooses hyperbole.

"It's all in the song."

"No wonder there's so many rumors about you. You cultivate mysteries."

"I'll tell you what. When we hit a minute that's got it all, I'm gonna say, 'Magdalena, this is Mockingbird July.'"

"You lyin."

"That's what I'll say." His eyes are shut then. But by then I know every shut eye ain't sleep. So I called him, but his breath was soft and even, and his body relaxed, innocent of turmoil. I covered him. Falling on him like a little rain, which I am now, because I dream shadows and cannot make them out. And when I do, I wish I could not.

✦

I'd catch Treemont Stone looking over his shoulder. The terrain plays out around him, thick and grotesque, lush as Mimosa, hard as the City, the tents in the deep distance. He is the image in the center. Panting chest, sweat, eyes alert, body poised, every pore listening for ambush, pursuit. He, in the middle of a thicket. And this time hounds, terrible and fleet with white teeth and white as Calypso, a nightmare dog from childhood. Hounds in the distance. The distance narrowing. And following the path of the hounds, the men heavy with guns and rifles. And in front of Treemont (It is Tree, isn't it?) thick, wild birds, quails, pigeons, rising up in skittish surprise in front of him. The hunters measuring the panic of the birds. The panic giving him away. The rifles. Then fire. I dream this.

✦

Not satisfied with the side of the road, he starts the engine and we search for the rest sign, and turn in. He goes to the corner, distant from the trucks that have stopped while on an interstate haul. The overhead lamp, wrapped in hard plastic, dipping down like a clear melon, its juice trying to find us.

He is curved around me like a blue man around a blue guitar. Picasso would have jumped at the chance. But Bearden has locked us together. Locked me in a man's arms. Me, sitting upright, like a caressed guitar. It is night. We are on our way to Mississippi to see Silence. A quick getaway. I am a guitar. My name must be Lucille. We can go through

Indianola on our way to Mimosa and look for the place B. B. King was born. If we have the time. Otherwise we can look for the place Treemont Stone almost died. Either way we can sing, "Everybody wants to know why I sing the blues."

I start to hum it under my breath. I like the part where B.B. sings with that funny bitterness Blackpeople do, "We gonna build some apartments for y'all."

✦

"Somebody oughta take a bulldozer and just mow down all that mess." Aint Kit pointed at her French Provincial television set. The image of the tents around the Homes filled the thirty-something-inch screen. I'd come to get some of my paintings to sell at an auction ASANTE was sponsoring for the people who got evicted. I'd already loaded the car. Aint Kit thinks of ways to make me stay. I could see the wheels spinning and rolling, disappearing under viaducts in her mind.

"It takes niggahs to bring down the propity values," Aint Kit observed. Her mouth tighter than ever.

"I think people just want to be treated like people," I said. The images on the screen were seductive. First, the tents and the people. Then, the mayor. After the people were evicted, they and others set up housekeeping where they'd been put. Outdoors.

Aint Kit was very annoyed with me. Because somebody demanding something that she suffered for takes the bread of vindication and self-congratulation out of her mouth. She sighed like she was setting down something heavy. Explained, "Maggie, when I come up here from Mimosa, I made my way. I made my way where there wasn't no way. I worked and didn't drop a litter of babies on the county for somebody to take care of."

"But shouldn't there be a way?"

"I'm telling you I made mine. Them women lay up on their asses, and open their legs and open their mouths like they baby birds waiting for they mammy to drop a worm in there. They just better fly like me."

"Women aren't the only ones who live there."

"If a man live there who work, he no-count!"

291

"Aint Kit, how can you say that!"

"A man don't get hisself in a predicament like that, and stay there," she snapped. Her voice thick and meaty as one of the hams she used to slice for sandwiches at the card parties she catered in her early days in the City. There is consolation in the recitation of memory; her voice is thin, shaved, when she goes on. "I used to stay in the public housing when I first come up from Mimose. Lots of peoples did. I used to stay right over there in the Tubman Homes on the Left Side. You don't remember that? You weren't born yet. Then you were in Mimose. I remember a picture of you in front of the house down south." Aint Kit loves to take pictures. Dark and stylish in heavy high heels, and a pompadour hairdo.

"It was a row house." Aint Kit was talking slower than usual. This was no lie. "I had me a pretty garden fulla flowers. Every kinda flower. The insurance man come by and he say, 'You're a regular florist, Miss Grace.' White men call you 'Miss' when you come up north. I had to get used to that. It didn't take me long. And when they didn't, I didn't answer until they did. I told him I was a horticulturist. It's like a manicurist for flowers. That's what one of them doctors at the hospital called me when I told him about my garden. I figure a medical doctor know more than an insurance man. I've seen doctors bring folks back from the dead. An insurance man ain't nothing but a legalized gambler. Betting yo money on when you gone kick the bucket. I told Lee-Bet that when she started in it. Well, I loved that little row house and kept it real nice and neat. I made Old Lazy Bay get up off her ass every day and mop them floors and get that dust off my furniture. She wash my good glasses so when the sunlight come through the window the whole house was full of rainbows. Pretty. Pretty. Oh, just pretty. I had my own rainbows. Bay used to sit around reading all kinds of books when I wasn't home and wouldn't have half did her cleaning right. I had to lock them books up. I had to teach her to work. You know, Gussie's people was kinda trifling. If they had moved up here, they be right over in them Homes today. I was working two jobs. So Bay had to keep the house spick-and-span or I'd spick-and-span her tail. I saved up my money and bought me that brick house over on Beulah. I rents that one out now." She couldn't keep the triumph out of that part of the telling. "Then I got my cash and bought this house." She surveyed the room from ceiling to four-inch-thick rug.

Fairly swelling with this material evidence of her victory over life and a Blackwoman's lot. "Nobody give this to me," she announced with a pride that was endearing, even when you didn't want her to be dear.

It pained my Aint Kit to think that somebody would get decent treatment without suffering as she had to get it. The possibility of the Homes' tenants' victory presented a crisis of faith. Her God is a bank loan officer. He gives not even the right to a blessing without proper collateral. He bestows no inalienable rights unless one has material assets.

Reverently, she watched a television commercial. Like a mother watching her sleeping infant, who will wake to make marvelous gestures, uncanny expressions. I could see her filing away the name of some new bit of business to spend her money on. She would have it. She probably wouldn't use it. Once she's got the name of a new kitchen device or feminine hygiene product locked into memory, she goes on a new tack that's oddly related to the old one. "Of course, Lee-Bet gone say folks suppose to get something for nothing. That's how she got tied up in that Liberation Farm business . . . You know that done fell through." She added this last like some thousand acres of land gave way and the people on them deservedly tumbled down into a pit.

"I tried to tell her, but you know you can't tell Lee-Bet nothing. She just as ignorant as a mole. Blind too." She gave me one of her quick looks. My displeasure warned her to switch the subject quick, lest I leave her. "Did I tell you my dogs dug up one of them ugly creatures and ate it?" Dexterously, she segued from Aunt Silence to moles, then, "You remember that little French poodle I had I called Snowy? They ate her too."

"Oh, no!" I cried. "They killed her?"

"Naw, they didn't kill her." She soothed me and sounded disappointed at the same time.

Then she socked it to me. "She had a heart attack. Po' thing. They started eating on her after she was dead."

"They must have been starving," I said before I could stop myself. Thus casting aspersions on my aunt.

She eyed me quick, shrugged, and pulled a sad, stern face. "I don't know why they did it. They wasn't hungry or nothing. Animals like people and they don't just go after something cause they hurt. I believe they ate her because she was so beautiful."

This was a doozy. Ate her cause she was beautiful. (Substitute "white.") I could hear Pearl whooping over that one.

Aint Kit said, "I used to keep her up so pretty. Had her toenails polished and her hair clipped and curled. She was white and used to dance around just like snow. I used to call her Snowy. 'Come here, Snowy,' I say. She was nervous. You have to talk to her real nice. She was so pretty and white and nervous, she used to pee on herself sometimes when she was happy or scared." Aint Kit summoned tears for Snowy, who was a little pee machine. "And them big old doggish brown hounds out there was chewin on her. Come up in the basement I forgot to lock the door and they jumped on her. Just so they could be pretty."

This was Aint Kit's story, which left her misting and pressing tissues against her tear ducts. She gulped back misery for Snowy. On TV the mayor was talking about a deadline for the Tent People. They had forty-eight hours. I was seeing Miss Fredonia Constance and all the other beautiful people who'd been fighting for the right to determine their own standards for living. My Aint Kit was crying for her Snowy. Her eyes glued to the tube.

Maybe it's guilt. Pearl told me another version of Aint Kit and Snowy. Pearl said, "That French dog was so nervous Aint Kit had to have her put on tranquilizers so she'd stop peeing on that pink rug. Aint Kit gave her too many and accidentally bumped the little b-b-b-b-bitch off!" Pearl loved it. She was holding her sides from laughter. "It was murder! Kit killed that silly high-fashion dog! Who's next?"

Aint Kit beckoned me to the kitchen. "I want to show you something. I ain't shown nobody else." I followed her. "I know Sam and them be saying I ain't telling the truth. So I got my evidence."

She bent down with her face thrust full inside the kitchen cabinet. I sat at the kitchen table watching her, thinking this better be good, because I have a million things to do. Aint Kit reached into the space and hoisted something heavy out. She staggered back a trifle from the weight of what was lying across her wrists. An oblong watermelon, long waisted and green. Its stem a curl like a pig's tail.

"Why'd you have that under the sink, Aint Kit?"

"Cause I didn't want to cut it by myself. I had to have me a witness. Or folks think I'm not tellin the truth."

I moved the napkin holder and the naked-butt babies salt and pepper shakers so there was enough room for the watermelon. Aint Kit laid it down like a dead body. It hit the table with a thud. She stepped back and looked at it. Her hands on her hips and the top of her dress bunched up. She jerked it down and kept looking at the watermelon like it was a bomb about to explode.

"He come by here this morning," she finally began.

"Who?"

"That watermelon man what come here that last time. I hadn't seen him since that last time he come down that alley."

I wanted to be somewhere else then, not sitting on the edge of Aint Kit's nightmare, waiting for it to take me in.

"I knowed y'all didn't really believe me when I tried to tell you about that other melon I bought from him. He was waiting over by the back gate and he was so ugly even the dogs wouldn't bark at him. He was looking like dust with some dusty clothes on. He made them old lips make a smile. Ooooh, and that smile, Maggie. I tried to act like he ain't scared me like he did. I said to him, 'I didn't hear no wagon and I didn't hear no truck coming down this alley. I didn't hear you callin. How people suppose to know you got anything for them?' That's what I let him know." She looked at me then. He said, "You know."

She looked at the melon. She looked at me. "Well, shut my mouth. I just looked at his old, ugly, bad-luck self. 'You know that other melon you brought last time a few years ago was just fulla worms?' I sure told him that. He said, 'You never know.' I said, 'You the one selling this shit. You suppose to know.' He liked that. He liked me to fight with him a little bit. Men like that. Like my husband, Sugar Bear, the prizefighter, he liked it when I talked tough back at him. He used to call me Kit T.C. Tough Customer. Kit T.C. The watermelon man smiled at me in that very same way. Like he liked what he saw. If he hadn't been entirely too ugly and put that bad melon off on me last time, I mighta had some talk for him. Oh, but he was hopelessly ugly. So I kept my distance.

"Shoot, I wouldn't get close to him till he reached up on the back of his wagon and picked up the watermelon and brought it to me. He was cradling it like a baby in his arms. He brought it right up to me to the back gate. I got close enough to take it from him. 'This one's on me,

Kitty.' You know that tickled me when he said that like he was Marshall Matt Dillon on *Gunsmoke* and I was Miss Kitty. At least she was making some money. He didn't look like Matt Dillon with his old cement self, though; he looked more like gun smoke. He slid that long, big melon into my arms like he was a doctor handing over my baby to me in the hospital.

"Ain't that strange? That sound like something old, stupid Lee-Bet would do. Just take something from a relative stranger. But it was free, so I went on and took it.

"He come tipping that old, raggedy gray hat at me. The brim look like somebody put some ridges in it with a fork just like they do pie-crusts. And then, you know what that ugly man did, Maggie? He smiled at me, and that smile was so pretty and so nice, it made me want to cry. I felt like my heart was unburdened and I was a real little girl."

She acted conflicted then. Drawing back her head and squinting so she could see what she remembered. Puzzled like a little girl. She kept on, gathering speed as she thought of refutation for her tale.

"It was so strange. The way his smile made me feel like I had every-thing, and didn't want nothing, Maggie. I started to cry and I reached down to wipe my eyes with the hem of my housedress. Naw, I was not trying to show him my panties. Lee-Bet and them is a dirty lie cause I never showed my panties to nobody but my husbands and my mama. But I was all involved in trying to hold on to that big old melon without dropping it on my sore foot and scooping up the bottom of my skirt so I could grab hold to it and wipe my crying eyes and I did all that and looked around and do you know he was gone? I don't know where he went."

"You didn't hear him pull away?" I asked.

"Naw, nothing. Do you hear me? I didn't hear nothing. Now I'm scared to open up this melon. Might be a big old snake curled up in here."

"Ain't no tellin." We'd been talking in near whispers. Like children in church.

Aint Kit pulled out a long butcher knife from a secret pocket behind the refrigerator. It was one of her weapons in her hiding place in case of burglars.

"Since you sitting right here, I'm going to cut this right now."

I didn't want her to.

I said, "Why don't we wait till somebody else comes. Why don't you bring it to the party tomorrow?"

Aint Kit heaved a sigh. It was relief, but she played it off as martyred disappointment. "Okay then, I guess I'll cut it tomorrow night. So everybody can see. And all them Doubting Thomases can get a good look. Cause I ain't growed no watermelon in my imagination. Yo mama gone be there?"

"Uh-huh."

"Yo daddy?"

"Uh-huh."

"Yo Michael? I mean Treemont."

"Uh-huh."

"Honeybabe, Pearl, and yo wild sisters?"

"They said they'd be there."

"I know Lazarus and Sam Jr. gone be there."

"Sure are."

"Honeybabe's husband with his crippled self."

"Yes."

"Yo friend. What that girl name?"

"Leona?"

"Naw, not the one with the money. The one with all that pretty hair."

"Essie?"

"Essie with the hair. Yes. Oh, she got some pretty, thick hair."

"Maybe."

"Didn't you tell me her mother was one of them organize that rent strike? She be there for her mama, see she don't get throwed out on her behine again."

"She might."

Then she looked at me and saw something there. "Y'all don't friend no more, do y'all?"

"Nope."

When I didn't add to this, she said, "That's the way it go."

✦

When I see Chaka I think of Essie. Her face in his like the back side of a mask. Her rage, his shame. Her vengeance, his self-rebuke. The absence of her forgiveness, a plenitude of menial tasks he performed without request. He brought stray dogs to the back door of the Blue Nile, picked the fleas from their coats, washed them till their coats shone, and he fed them, until Treemont asked him not to because there wasn't enough food for the animals. So Chaka took them to the SPCA. Stray dogs and cats. One time Chaka brought home a pigeon and put its sprained wing in a splint. He fed it crackers and cheese and the crumbs at the bottom of a bag of potato chips. When the pigeon cooed, he cooed back. The sound, dark and little, coming out of his throat, his Adam's apple floating up and down. They were twins then. The pigeon who could not fly, pinned up like a human with a broken arm, but worse. The man who could not be forgiven, locked to his crime, pinned in time to the moments of corruption and spite, while he wrestled toward redemption.

He told me the story of a lost girl at the parade. She was crying on the sidelines when he found her. He sent his nephew to find a policeman, who never arrived. Meanwhile he sat with the little girl on the curb until someone who knew her came along. I asked him why he hadn't just taken the little girl himself and helped her find her people. Chaka acted like he hadn't heard me. I repeated the question, and he got up and walked away from me.

When I asked Tree, he answered cryptically, "He couldn't walk with her. That's the way it is. And that's the way it should be."

So the next time I saw Chaka he told me about the angel. The one inside him. The angel looked like Essie because he knew her face. The other girls he didn't know. But he told me their voices—whimpering like torn kittens and shrieking like birds scaling the air inside a locked, windowless room—kept him awake nights. So he got up in the wee hours and finished some task he had finished already and began another. The only sleep the voices of the violated girls couldn't keep him from was the dying sleep, and even when that would come to him, he said he knew the voices were waiting for him on the other side of the river. And the angel that had the face and breasts of Essie Witherspoon and sometimes the body of a lion waved a golden machete-like sword.

That's what she was standing like, in Miss Fredonia Constance's apartment, soon after the eviction attempt, in the middle of the same living room I'd visited with her after King was murdered, all through grief riots, and the rage. Her arms were folded and she was leaning against the TV, observing people as they entered, placing footprints into the rug. Her eyes critical and her body language cold: arms locked across the heart, body jacked to one side in an attitude. Even her hair had an attitude—the huge Afro dipping over one eye, spreading away from her head, taking space. When more people had come in than she could stand, including me, she threw her hands down and stalked into the back bedroom, the one where Moneeka slept the sleep of a blue rose, the dark passages between the petals opening into light.

The room was full of people from ASANTE, Tree and Lazarus and Joanne Nzingha, Gloria, Luci. Chaka in jail and Steve in hiding. I followed Essie into the back room, even though I wasn't invited. I ignored the fact that nobody answered my light knock on the door.

She was sitting on the bed. Her attitude was not so fierce. Just sitting, like Essie. She looked at me and neither one of us spoke. I sat next to her on the bed; the mattress gave to our weight. I had to duck away from that hair of hers. That made me laugh.

"Do you remember the time that Whiteman asked you to move your hair to the side when we were at the movies?" I asked her, hoping memory would do it.

"Yeah, I braid my hair when I go now."

"That's courteous."

"Sometimes I braid it."

"I heard Chaka saved your mama from the sheriff."

"I heard that too."

"Does it matter to you?"

She stood up and went to the dresser, where she played with Moneeka's miniature bottles of perfume. Neat little cylinders with jagged sides. Her hair under lamplight making shadows across her face. "Nothing he could do would satisfy me, Maggie. I just want him to die and the buzzards eat out his eyeballs. That's all I got for him. No matter what niceties he performs."

"Oh, Essie!" It was a wail, a grunt, a hopeless sound tearing out of my gut and heart, given not just for this moment and the peace she will not consider, but given for Eden and the nights we stayed up late, dreaming with our eyes and mouths open, telling every dream.

"If he'd done it to you, would you love him? Ever?"

I couldn't say yes or no. I wouldn't.

"Would Mr. Treemont Stone?"

I looked at her.

"Steve Rainey don't count. He got messed up on his own. He live like a rabbit, hiding from people."

"He still works with ASANTE."

"His mind is bad. And Leona, Miss Barbecue Queen, has always taken care of Leona. It's you."

"Me? Who?"

She didn't answer. Just started talking about the money the doctors make in specialties.

"Is that what you're about?" I asked her. She didn't answer. I didn't ask her about her job at the hospital.

That's why Essie, even though her mother was a leader of the rent strike, didn't show up at the party at the Blue Nile that is sometimes called the Blue Rose.

My father wasn't a ghost, but he was leaning against the bar in the Blue Nile, as insouciant and familiar as the ghost of the blues. He had cut a step or two with a pretty girl. Mostly he'd done the Uncle Willie, which went out of style about six or seven years ago. The Uncle Willie was on its deathbed by the time I got to Eden. So you know that was a long time ago. But, funny, one time on Blood Island Cletus the Elder showed a film of West African dancers. We hollered out the names of our dances as they did them on the screen. The Africans lined up just like we do the line. Then they did the ancestors to our dances. The boogaloo. The Watusi. The chicken. The stomp. The yoke. The bird. The African twist. The popcorn. The Uncle Willie. "America," somebody said, "is the Land of a Thousand Dances that will not die."

I don't know how it is that we are immortal. Does one person remember, then demonstrate to another, then something in the moment awakes and everybody is dancing what one remembered? My father will not give up on the Uncle Willie, a dance alternating pigeon toes and slew feet with accompanying hand movements. It is inelegant and goofy, meant only for fun.

It fit in. From the stage some of the Blues All Stars yelled over to Madaddy, "That's it, Angelboy! Work it! All right now! You got it!" He Uncle Willied real hard then. Suddenly stopping, as if he'd caught himself.

At the bar I asked him about the name they'd called him, but he said it was a name for anybody. He sipped his sherry and his eyes looked all around; something in him appeased. On his head a ring-creased mark where his Clark Gable sat, before he set it on the bar in front of his glass. One hand on his hat. The other on his glass. As if he were a gentleman who's only come calling long enough to leave his card. On these occasions he is a gentleman, genial and decorous. My father with the belt for any transgression. Not with rebuke delivered from rebuke given him. Not then. He was relaxed and in his element. He ordered drinks for Mama and Aint Kit. He didn't ask me to help carry them because his hands were full. I offered.

I walked ahead of him through the smoky club. Wondering if he saw as I did. Like someone in a dream with hundreds of other people. The Blue Nile, a canvas like Picasso's *Guernica*, without the monsters in hiding. Like Romare Bearden's *Morning of the Rooster* but dark over the serenity, a veil over the miracle, like Hale Woodruff's *The Card Players* seated around a table looking laconic and regal, cigarette smoke coming from their fingers, gathered around a game of chance.

> *Everybody wants to know*
> *Why I sing the blues*
> *Yes, I say, everybody wanna know*
> *Why I sing the blues*
> *Well, I've been around a long time*
> *I really have paid my dues.*
>
> *When I first got the blues*
> *They brought me over on a ship*
> *Men were standing over me*
> *And a lot more with a whip.*

If Silence had been there I wondered what she would have made of the pigeon that flew through the window of the Blue Nile, flapping around wildly, then threw himself against the wall so hard he broke his own neck. Steve, out of hiding, took the body out and buried it just beside the steps that lead down into the Nile. I wondered what she would have made of the man with two hats, tall, and double dark, standing on the edge of the alley, looking up at me as I looked down at him from Tree's bedroom window. He tipped one of his hats to me. Smiled and shook his head. Then I heard the heavy clod of a horse pulling something. The tinkle of little metals, coming from behind the garage where he disappeared. The roll of wheels. Scraping.

And what would Silence have said about Chaka out of jail later that day, at my door with a bloody hand, holding his wrist with his clean hand? I asked him what happened and he said a dog bit him. The bite was deep and wide. I was washing it so I could inspect it good. It was a savage tear.

"I was on my way here," Chaka said. "I saw a big dog, look almost like a wolf. But hell, what I know about that? I ain't never seen one. It was his howling at the back door to Roscoe's that drew me. Howling up a storm. Didn't you hear it?"

"That dog bit you?" I was worried.

"Yeah. I was just trying to help him. I thought he was hungry."

"He was hungry enough to eat you."

"I had to pull my hand out of his teeth." Chaka sounded amazed, reliving this.

"You have to go get a shot," I said.

"I already been shot this season."

"That dog could have rabies!"

"Uh."

"Where is it?"

"It ran away."

"Did you see which way it went?"

"West."

"You got to tell the police."

"They probably be sorry it didn't tear up my face instead of my hand."

"I'll call my brother Sam. You like him, don't you? He's a policeman."

"Sam's okay."

That's how Chaka wound up at the hospital. And a dog with blood and flesh in his teeth wound up the fugitive my brother and Animal Control searched for all day. And if Aunt Silence had been there she would have said these events didn't augur well for a successful affair. And I'd have said, "We won't go through with it, then."

And she would have said, "That don't mean don't do it, Maggie. It just mean: watch! When we embarked upon our Liberation Farm, we knew the presence of a county full of hostile and money-grubbing cracker farmers and bankers and businessmen didn't augur well toward the success of our venture."

And I would say like a true niece of Aint Kit, "And it failed."

And Aunt Silence would say, "But they can never get us quite that way again. And better than that, better than that, Pretty Girl, we had a Paradise in our hands that we created on Mississippi ground. It didn't last a thousand years. But it lasted a little while. Give me a little while of heaven and I take sixty years of hell."

The quick and the mist commingled in the Blue Nile. I could hear them, see them. The mist, ghosts with gold in their mouths all along the banks of the Blue Nile, growled out of the throats of the blues singers. They bent over the bar. They leaned against the blue walls that Treemont Stone painted years ago. They hollered. They hummed. They shouted from the bandstand Treemont Stone built years ago in one of his lives. The women ghosts, mostly ladies, fanned themselves like Miss Fredonia, who kept threatening to take off her wig because the music made her warm.

They complained that the space was too small to hold them. This basement. The grave itself. The space too small to hold them. I could see them fanning with funeral parlor fans from Lovely Moments Mimosa Funeral Parlor, the same ones I know the DeadandBuried swept the air with at their mock service for the quick dead in the rooms above the Blue Nile. I could see them. Grumbling for the bread they'd never tasted. The wine they'd never drunk. Grumbling for these because they were born with the memory of it in their mouths—oh, a hundred, maybe, years ago. I wasn't dreaming when I saw them there. Maybe I was dreaming. But even if I was dreaming, even if I was crazy and saw them there—they were there.

Blues brimmed all around. The quick were telling the story we were living. Each person adding something on. I passed one table and heard about the sheriff who shot Chaka when Chaka tried to stop him from moving Miss Fredonia out.

I heard a man say, "We're gonna build
Some new apartments for y'all."

I passed another table and heard a part of the story of the day they came and moved out ten families. It was funny. Somebody said they didn't move Miss Fredonia out. And somebody else had circulated that curiosity as evidence that Miss Fredonia had been co-opted. After all, her daughter was doing so good in medicine. Then accusations flew through the air like the knives of a drunken circus performer, making an outline of knives around Fredonia Constance, but never striking her in the heart. Because she put herself outside.

One day Miss Fredonia Constance came home from work and saw two more families put out and their stuff on the cement walk in front of the Homes. That's when she said, "I'm sick of this shit." And went upstairs and packed her household up and moved all of her things downstairs to the street. Others followed into the heat. Better to remove yourself than wait for somebody to put you out. Better to get the jump on the Authorities.

When the cameras came, newsmen asked Mrs. Fredonia Constance why the rent-strikers had taken their strike outside and left the very apartments they were fighting to control.

Miss Fredonia proved highly photogenic in a large black Afro wig and gold hoop earrings. Succinct and articulate too. Her reply ran on all three channels, "We didn't have anything to lose. We wanted to be seen."

Tents blossomed around the Homes like hot-air balloons. It was midsummer then and children and birds were in plenitude. Let loose from a bondage of nests to the outdoors. They careened around touching each other and running or flying. Wherever they ran, they dropped something—crumbs, bitten pieces of apples. These the birds and pigeons scavenged. From the lake, a seagull flew inland, diving down to collect half-eaten morsels and take these back to the water. It was a hundred and two degrees in the shade of one of the tents. We had passed the temperature for murder. Treemont commandeered three first-floor apartments for toilets and kitchens. When the suddenly busy building managers padlocked the doors, Tree carefully picked the locks.

The small, round tables all over the Blue Nile were filled. Leona was seated at one with her new boyfriend. Bay and Hank kept her company together. Lovey-dovey. A loosome twosome. We said BayandHank in one breath because they were back together. Calling each other honey and darlin' all the time. Bay said they're together because they moved. To Letha. They bought a tiny house down south and bought an eating place down there called the Sunflower Café. At home they keep a party, moving to every festival in the state: catfish, cotton, blues, and magnolia. When I eavesdropped on their conversation, they were always talking about moving.

It didn't matter who was talking. They said, "Honey, I loved the way you fixed that fish just right."

They said, "Darlin', would you pour me another glass of that?"

They said, "Sweetheart, would you like some of this?"

They said, "Sugarplum, I like the way you wear your hair."

They said, "Honey, this is a nice event."

Then they looked around the room with four eyes that could have been two. Soft, shining eyes. Like dark marbles in glasses of champagne.

This was so until Bay got the happy blues and started to dance. It was a haughty dance, erotic and attitudinal, we were used to. The dance of feeling good and being bad. She was smiling and hollering out epigrams from way inside her throat. "Don't mess with the messer!" she yelled. All this pleased Hank at first. Then she pulled her wide dress tight across her behind, gathered the hem up in her hand, and lifted the bunch of material up to her thigh. She was stomping and swaying hard, doing a combination of the slop and the booty green.

"My name is Bay. But my real name is Trouble. Hey, hey now," like she was trying to get somebody's attention way 'cross town.

Every time she shook something she and Hank got more and more separate. Aint Kit started eggin her on. Got up from her chair with the mink stole slung over the back and started taking big steps toward Bay, shaking her behind, holding her head high.

This was a moment and Time waited for somebody to answer. The blues were going down in a solo by a blind man named Blind Potato Spellman. I could see. My parents were in the moment and my Uncle Lazarus and Aint Kit and Bay and Hank and Leona, and the boyfriend named James. And Tree and Lazarus, and my sisters scattered around the room, and Steve, hiding someplace in the building.

> Blind man on the corner
> Begging for a dime
> The rollers come and caught him
> And throw him in the jail for a crime
> I got the blues
> Mm, I'm singing my blues
> I've been around a long time
> Mm, I've really paid some dues.

Blind Potato wagged his head like a dog with fleas, casting off fleas, letting the air scratch his blues, and the music—rapid picks at the guitar, the let-loose growl climbing out of him away from his body and back into it through the air.

I knew about everything because right then I was born in knowing, squeezed into a brown paper bag that almost burst with water. That's what I thought. My grandmother, a member of the mist, all of herself was squeezed into a brown paper bag and the bag was untied at the neck and the water ran all over us.

"It's cold in here," my mother shivered and wrapped her arms around herself. Her nose was red like it is when she gets cold. Nobody else was cold, though. And everybody thought maybe she was coming down with something. Or having a hot flash. Only she thought it was cold.

Aint Kit, in a burst of generosity that would be legendary because she'd tell about it so much, offered Mama her mink stole. Mama looked at it like it was still alive. Tooth and claw. When it was on her shoulders, limp and languid in luxury and death, Mama still shivered and the mink stole shivered with her. Maybe on its own.

✦

Past Memphis, we climb down through the bottom of Tennessee into Mississippi. I'd be lying if I said I could tell the difference. But it seems like there is. For amusement we think up names for towns and cities in Mississippi, some of them real, some made up: Midnight, Cold Water, Alligator, Itta Bena, Mound Bayou (an all-Black town we went through on the way to Mimosa), Keep-a-Running, Long Rope, White Citizen, James Crow, Sharecropping, Bill of Rights, Spits in Your Eye, Long Time Crying, Tallulah, Holly Springs, Biloxi, and Ocean Springs and Exodus. My favorite is Long Time Crying, Mississippi. Treemont favors Spits in Your Eye. Neither one of us really likes Keep-a-Running.

✦

The box arrived at my address. A shoebox full of earth. A letter planted in the soil.

Dear Maggie,

You have been on my mind so much. I just want to see your face and see some of the beautiful things you paint. I have worried about you and this school business. Though I know there's more than one way to receive an education. Your mother worries that society will leave you behind if you are not a college-educated individual. The time is past when a Black woman could get by on doing laundry and baking corn bread in a white wom-an's kitchen. I confess I worry about you in this time of guns. I carried one so you wouldn't have to. And to stay alive. The man your grandmother tipped her special hat at would be a sight for sore eyes. I've been visited by her lately. I mentioned this to your mama, but you know she not gone tell that. Just keep it to herself and let it stew in her heart. She the silent type like you and Lazarus say I am too. I speak, when it suits me. I can wear words out like a red dress above the knees! Ask the Sher-iff Columbine. Or them kin of his that own the rice plant. Miss Ruby who work in the department store gives you her regards and she hopes you will see her perchance you come to Mimosa. Her presence in the store is a barricade to our actions. Before they hired her we were ready to boycott the establishment. So they hired one to keep our money. And we are loyal to the sight of one Black face. But as much money of ours they hiding under the floorboards of the First, there should be a multitude of Black faces at least waiting on people. If not accumulating capital. In these days since our farm died, I have searched my mind for the answer. Failure sits in my mouth like salt. Maybe that's why I seem to be failing to myself. I am gloomy, Maggie. Your Silence is not golden, but gloomy. I wish I had a pair of eyes to guide me through the sadness. Say you'll come and bring a friend and cheer me up. I worry about you.

Love,

Your Aunt Leah-Bethel

So we set out, Tree and me, in the darkness, the day after the Blue Nile. I kept looking at the letter. I'd kept it in my purse, where it seemed to whisper, "Hurry. Hurry. Leave this place. Hurry."

✦

Treemont was on the bandstand. The singing had ceased, and the dancing settled into the repetition of gestures, picks up the glass and sips, leans over to someone close, whispers something, the faces stretch and screw into a laughter that was tight because the faces were all turning one way, quiet because they were wise that something was about to happen. It was something soft, his voice soft, wandering without drive to exhort or incite. Wandering.

"Truth is just like the rain—it falls on everybody. The Just and the Unjust. When it falls on me it's all right because my name, a part of the name my mother gave me, is Tree. And I was raised to like the rain. I need the rain of truth. I been around and I have heard some things. Truth is I was born in the bed with a Blackwoman, so I know to whom I owe my life. I sat beside the pulpit of my father while he preached in a church enslaved Africans fled toward, hiding underground. I even heard them running in my sleep. And I remember one of my father's friends advising me to keep enough money to get out of town. You never know when you'll need it. Some people write things about me and they don't know me."

He stood there staring into the rush of light. Meditating. Then he bowed his head, raised it, and started talking again.

"I don't hate anybody. I don't even hate Whitepeople. Sometimes I feel sorry for them so busy doing the devil's work, or being scared like little children in a dark closet. But I'll tell you what I do hate. I'm a man, not a saint. I hate a lie. I hate what it builds up. What it lifts up from under rocks. What it builds up. I hate the lies this country tells. What a lie built up. I wanna tear a lie down. I wanna pull it down. Let justice build back up. The lie is: you and I have no singular value. The lie is that you and I are less because of who we were born as. And the lie is that any human heart was made to squander, usurp, destroy, or employ another for its own selfish, wicked ends.

"Don't let anybody lie to you. You know how some people do. Tell you the way it was, and it wasn't that way. Tell you the way it is, and it ain't that way either. Tell you you were this and you were never hungry, you were never property, you were never overworked and overlooked or unemployed, will tell you you were never called a bad name, tell you things were the same for you as everybody else. Tell you you were never separated from the ones you love. Then tell you the way things are is the way things have always been and you can't change a thing. Don't let nobody lie to you. Look you in the eye or look down on you and lie. You know we have been lied to. We know right here in this metropolis we've been lied to. They told you you couldn't make them listen to you. And you did. They are listening now. They are listening now as I speak with you. Trying to figure out how to stop listening and keep on lying. Trying to figure out how to keep things the way they are.

"But don't you let them. Don't let anybody sell you a pair of shoes too small for you and then you go out and wear them till they cripple you. Don't let nobody tell you what's good for you when you and this experience, your memory, has told you it is not. Don't let nobody look down on you and lie. And don't let them look out from the television studio and lie. If you were there and saw five hundred people, why would you believe it when they say it was one? They don't want you to know how big you are. Oh, we big. And we bad. And we leave a mighty footprint where we step.

309

"Don't change what you remember to please or feed somebody else, including that little chicken butt part of yourself that doesn't want to be a part of that big footprint. That lying little toe that is so scared of being stepped on. Scared of fulfilling its destiny to make you stand. Don't conspire against yourself. It's a bitter seed to sow—betraying yourself. Right follows right. Wrong follows wrong. You know that. And the mean part is, you can do right and somebody else's wrong will hound you, dog you like you a bone instead of a human being. But you still right.

"Don't worry about the wrong tomorrow has. If I stand up now, will I get fired? If I say no now, will they come for me? Now don't be no fool. But don't be nobody else's fool. When the call comes in, you know how to answer. Because you know what's right. Is it right to live in a place where you pay what little you have and somebody treat you like a hog supposed to wallow in a pen? That ain't right. Is it right for thousands of people to live together under the rule of other people who don't know a thing about them and don't care? Is it right for the police, who are supposed to serve and protect, to maim and kill because you are Black and poor? You know that's not right. Is it right for young men to turn their rage against each other? Is it right for young men to turn their rage against innocent girls and women? It's not right. Are we going to start being right tomorrow?

"Just do what you have to do today. Don't say I'll be a woman or a man tomorrow. Does a baby put off walking to keep on crawling? Stand up now. I know you can stand. I have seen you stand mighty in the tents that surround the Homes. When we stand together the way we've stood there, we can grab the sky. The West Africans tell a story of a time when people ate the sky. The sky was just above our heads and we could reach up and touch and grab hold of it and stuff our mouths with it. I believe because I have seen you, been with you. I believe the sky is just above our heads and we are reaching now. Can you feel it brushing your fingertips? Can't you make a fistful of it? Make a fist. Feed, clothe, shelter, educate each other. Care for each other. Work for each other. Demand your due from your work for others.

"I was born with a burden. I couldn't see. You have heard the story. My mother gave me the sight from her eyes. She did. She made the choice to give me sight, and they took the rest of hers. But she had another sight. I'm beginning to understand such a love that was tortured and left in blindness. But she was a woman, my mother, who saw with her heart and her mind. I've learned a tenth of that love for myself and nine-tenths for you. And tonight I am a full man."

Then slowly, so easily we barely noticed at first, he started running in place in low steps like he was going somewhere in a hurry. A solitary tear, or maybe a drop of sweat, was standing in his eye and it roared and cut when the light hit it.

"I just want to tell the truth tonight. I just wanna be straight up with you. I'm asking your permission to be straight with you. I'm gonna be, just because I'm an honest man."

"You ain't never lied, Brother Stone," Somebody shouted. "You ain't never . . ."

But Treemont cut him off. "I may have lied once or twice to myself, but I have never lied to you." Then he looked through the light to the place where we were. "I have never lied to you."

His body was quiet then, straight up. He took a deep breath and looked up at the ceiling, where the smoke had drifted like thin clouds, winsome vagaries that came from inside of us.

"Funny," he said. "I'm thinking of hide-and-seek. Remember the words of the song: '*Last night / night before / twenty-four robbers at my door / I got up / Let 'em in / Hit 'em in the head with a rolling pin.*'

"Children tell each other the truth. They sing it out with their mouths wide open. Use whatever you have to protect yourself and each other. Be not misled. Somebody can do your body in. But why would you make it easy? Ours is a good fight, and somebody wants to keep us down. Can't we name the names of those of us who have died for something as sweet as justice, something as tender as human dignity? Didn't we walk out into the icy atmosphere of this terrible land only to be met by a blast of wind so cold and insensitive it drove us blind and numb and frostbitten, till we had to let them cut off limbs in order to save the body? Sweet Mamas knew—when you go out into the cold, cover your ears or you will lose them, cover your head because it keeps the heat—and nobody has to tell you that something can hurt your body. You know it. And we are supposed to know. But don't let the fear of that stop you from the truth. When fear comes calling, like a robber, twenty-four robbers, I got a rolling pin—or something else—in my hand. But I don't need it. I have it, but I don't need it. My father was a minister. You may know his church. It's over there on the corner of Faith and Glory, on the other side of Misery and Degradation. And I'm not afraid of anybody now because he told me fear is a mist. Now I know and I can say huh! And the mist be gone. I've been through fear and I'm telling you it is a mist—a cloud that can try to tell you it's alive. But it's a lie.

"I'm not a fool. The devil doesn't ever die. The best I can do is say, 'Get thee behind me, Satan. Get to the past.' Then knock him down and move him out. Let a man come in. Ain't that what James Brown say? Let a man come in. Well, we, brothers and sisters, better come in doing more than the popcorn. But, really, what is our enemy going to do? Send something for me? I won't go. Send me a pile of money? I want only what is mine. I want what I earned or what was given to me out of love, but I don't even want that. Send me a woman? I got one who chose me without guile. I chose her. Send me power over other people? I don't even want it. Send me fame and notoriety? It's a trap. How can that many people know you? Somebody bound to get something wrong. You come in over the airwaves and dropping into people's homes and they think you a little doll they can dress up any way they want. Quit laughing. I know it's funny. We have to communicate with people. But what else the devil gone send? Send fear? Send a bullet? I feel like a bullet won't stop me. I feel that when I can feel you all with me. I know it won't stop you. I can take a bullet in my body and I know it won't stop you. They can tear my body apart and spread parts of me all around, down to the molecules. They won't stop anybody, unless we let it stop us. That's the truth. You heard that song Sonny Terry sing, 'Truth and Confidence'? I believe it. I have confidence in you. I know you. I know what you can do. I know what we must do. I know what we will do.

"I'm going to tell you a secret that I only tell my nearest and dearest, and because we been through something together, that's you. I met a ghost once. The woman saved my life. Stepped through time to save my life. You know what she told me? Naw, you don't know. You don't know because I ain't sure. Sometimes I think she said, 'Only you.' Sometimes I think she said, 'Own you.' Sometimes it's 'All you.' Don't worry about it. It's the same. We weren't sent here to be gods above each other. We were sent here for each other. In case you are asking now, 'What time is it? He been talking a long time now. I wonder what time it is,' I'm telling you it may look like night, but it is morning. May look like night for a long time. But it is morning. I'm telling you it's a damn good morning."

The clapping swelled up around him and the stage that he had built years ago. The applause so thick it was like musical smoke that engulfed us all. When it was impenetrable and interspersed with whistles while we all stood and stomped our feet and rattled our chairs, Alhamisi walked into the Blue Nile. Fresh from jail. His love affair with Hamla ended in blood. When he moved his third "wife" into the apartment, Hamla rebelled. This was at the same time the EARTH was breaking up, the members lost to their individual destinies, so Alhamisi was as heartbroken as he could be. The new woman gave him new heart in the strength of her admiration and sexual submission. For a long time Hamla looked like a pirate with a patch over her swollen, closed eye.

Alhamisi came through the doorway of the Blue Nile.

"Power," he said, and threw up a fist. It was not a beautiful gesture to me like when the brothers in the Olympics raised their fists and bowed their heads in reverent, serious defiance in 1968, a millennium ago.

Alhamisi got to our table just as Treemont did. "Alhamisi," Tree said his name. Lazarus mumbled something. I didn't say anything because I saw how bad he hurt Hamla. I held her hand as Steve Rainey took her to the hospital. Alhamisi hadn't spoken to Treemont Stone since he called Tree to bail him out of jail. I'd already described how Hamla looked, so Treemont had made up his mind. Treemont told Alhamisi he could not in good conscience come up with bail money and start a legal defense fund in his name. Alhamisi said he was a political prisoner. I was listening in the background. Alhamisi started yelling real loud over the phone. I could hear every word, even though I was deaf to his pain and confusion. This is what he, breathing in jackhammer rhythm, yelled so loud Tree held the phone away from his ear: "Let Liberation Law be my judge. Whiteman's law can't judge me. I don't live under no Whiteman's law. Treemont Stone, you faggot motherfucker, you ain't nothing but a flunky for hunky law. Whiteman's law can't comprehend my actions."

Treemont shoved the phone up under his mouth. "Common decency can't either. You beat her within an inch of her life. And you forced yourself on her."

"She my woman. I told her to shut her fat mouth up. She ain't shit but Emily Dickinson in blackface, laying around, writing them poems. Trying to tell me something. I told the woman when she moved in my house, my word was law. I told her that. She said she understood and she was serious about struggle. Then when the going get kind of rough the bitch gone nag me about some job. My job is the EARTH. She knew that when she come through my door, begging me to control her like a woman wants. Then when the deal go down, them three bitches conspire together and send her little Eden-educated ass to tell me I need to get a job because two of them pregnant and they can't work and Hamla can't take care of our household. Just like my grandmother and mother didn't pick some motherfucking cotton till they was ready to drop a baby then was back in the fields the next day at dawn. The bitches don't know shit about struggle. It's hard. I try to tell them. Hard as Hamla's goddamn head. She was the one asked for it. I had to straighten her out. Challenging my authority."

Treemont put his mouth on the receiver again. "Brother, you got a lot of mouth, but nothing coming out."

"You mean you ain't gone help me out, man?" Alhamisi tried to keep the pleading out of his voice, but it tagged his intonation.

"Can't do it, Alhamisi. I won't."

"You call yourself a brother. Brainwashed motherfucker with your tongue stuck up the Whiteman's ass. Shit-eating punk . . ." There were more obscenities, but I didn't hear them because Treemont didn't because he hung up the phone.

Alhamisi acted like he'd forgotten the bitter diatribe. He was clumsy and grinning like Louis Armstrong at each man. Like he just got off vacation in Jamaica, instead of home from jail. Everything was cool. He didn't say a word or give a nod to any woman in earshot or eye range.

Lazarus kept giving Treemont quick, perplexed looks. Chaka, walking by the table, stared at Alhamisi openly, watchfully. Steve Rainey stared away from him. Hamla trained her two eyes on him. They glittered with rage. In my head I could hear her voice as I looked at him.

"Look what that niggah did to me. Would you look, Maggie, because I can't see." Then she just burst into tears. I mean burst like a brown paper bag dropped out of a third-floor window, hitting the ground. I pitied her the day she said this. Once I thought we looked too much alike for anyone to see me as me. She must have felt the same way when she borrowed my dress and threw Leona's on the floor. Now I miss the innocence of our faces. I'd give anything to fix her sorrow for her "Hamla," I heard myself say. "Let's go outside and get some fresh air." Simultaneously, we stood.

"Where you going? I came here for you." Alhamisi opened his eyes real wide, and dropped his mouth on his last word.

Steve stood up. "Come, go with me, my ladies, while I cop a smoke." We started heading toward the door with Chaka behind us and Treemont left standing, facing off Alhamisi.

Alhamisi said, "What is this shit, man? You still haven't learned I have rights over my woman?"

"She ain't no animal you can put on a leash and drag around, Alhamisi. She is a grown woman. And she's not your woman. She's telling you in no uncertain terms she's not your woman and she's telling you if she were she wouldn't stay with you and let you beat on her. And I don't like speaking for her. She's already spoken eloquently for herself."

"We gone see how eloquent she is." He turned and headed for the door. I was at the door and could see him coming. Treemont right behind him at a leisurely, relentless pace.

"Get in the car, Hamla," Chaka ordered.

"I ain't getting in shit. I'm enjoying this party and who are you to tell me what to do?" Hamla's not taking orders from any man.

"I'm Nobody. And I'm sorry if I was bossing you. I'm just trying to stop this fool from hurting you anymore."

She was touched. She looked at him, then looked down. "Appreciate your concern." Then she said, "Steve, can I have a square?"

"Gonna smoke it in the car?"

"I promise."

He shook his pack until one cigarette jugged out. She reached for it, just as Alhamisi said, "I wasn't finished talking to you, Hamla baby."

"Yes, you were," Chaka said.

315

"Rapist punk, you ain't in it."

"I am," Steve Rainey said.

"I'm just trying to talk to my woman, Brother Rainey."

"I'm no longer your woman. I'm my own woman. And I say no. Just like I said it the other night and you acted like you didn't hear me. I'm telling you no."

"That's the one word you can't say to me, bitch." He was swinging on her as he said it, and Chaka caught his fist in the palm of his hand at Treemont's nod. Chaka pushed Alhamisi back away from Hamla and toward Treemont, who was at the door.

"There's a restraining order on you, Alhamisi. You're not supposed to be this close to her. She put the peace bond out on you herself."

"Don't tell me about Whiteman's law. You punk. You dead and buried, Treemont boy. You dead and buried six feet deep. You stepped on toes you didn't even know you were stepping on. Whiteman's law don't love you either. You dead and buried, Treemont Stone, brother."

"You oughta know about Whiteman's law, Alhamisi," Tree said. "They paid you enough."

✦

He's laughing. I'm talking about our days at Eden. Steve Rainey, he can't get over how he used to say, "What's happening?" two times all the time. Like he was twins in one body. An *ibeji* from Nigeria maybe. Figurines covered in cowrie shells. Two heads on connected bodies that are one body.

"Are the faces the same?" he asks.

"Close." In Nigerian art nothing is the same. Things resemble but are not exact. Same with God. I guess that's who they got the idea from. Before I knew, I used to believe I was flawed because even my eyebrows didn't match perfectly. Two wings. One broken. Then I learned to look.

This leads to something else funny that Treemont told me before he knew that I knew who he was talking about. The time Yvonne Christmas was arrested for the Fugitive Sister. Twenty agents swamped a restaurant. She was eating gumbo and had her napkin tucked in her collar.

316

When they brought her out, napkin collared and hair and eyes wild, a crowd had gathered. The people were saying, "That's the Fugitive."

"She don't look like she do in the paper."

"She's a pretty thing."

"How they manage to shrink her down like that?" one brother said to another brother, both of them squinting at five-foot-two Yvonne Christmas brought in for the five-foot-six Fugitive Sister.

Tree won't stop laughing. His whole body vibrating. The sound of him coming out like a deep rustle. When he laughs so long, I tell him Yvonne didn't laugh till she was out of the holding cell.

"How is the good sister?" He wipes his eyes, relishing in the retelling of the story.

"My friend 4-1-1 gave her an African name. Furaha means 'laughter' in Swahili. She needs to laugh more." I study him. "I like it when you laugh."

"I know you do."

Neither one of us is laughing now.

The City's poverty does not stab the eye like the sights we see as we turn off 61 and dip into the burrows of the countryside. Some shacks make you want to cry or close your eyes. This was Tree's idea to see what he saw before when he went searching for his life and almost found his death. He found his life anyway.

My sketch pad is on my lap and I am at work on my favorite subject.

"All this countryside to see and you sitting up looking at me." There is a certain embarrassed pleasure in this, but he directs my attention to dusty wonders. The little girl turning cartwheels with her little, limp dress flying down around her straight arms. The dress like wet petals and legs dark stalks at sixty-degree angles to each other. That's funny. She lands and tilts herself again like a windmill. Over and over. Until her legs are absolutely ashy and her braids stand up on their own. We idle for this show of comical events. Her exuberance cracking us up.

"What in the world . . . !" I say, sounding like Mama.

"She's just happy. Kinda nice." He watches her through a smile, so intent his observation I wonder what he's thinking.

"Aint Kit used to show her panties to boys"—I remember what I heard—"for money."

"This little girl is just glad."

He is so happy to have found her I begin to sketch her. So we don't budge for a while. He opens the shoebox and takes out a chicken drumstick. Between bites, he begins to talk about the little girl he doesn't know.

He chews the chicken Mama fried and packed with tenderness equal to the texture of the bird. He pinches a biscuit (so light they float, these biscuits tucked tightly into the box to keep them from moving away from us before we could hold them, like food in the astronauts' chambers, floating). There are slices of pound cake and apples. Not a shoebox exactly, a boot box, really, for a pair of my father's black buckle-up galoshes. Plenty of fried chicken and biscuits and cake and apples. And in the cooler, apples and oranges and potato salad (gone) and carrot salad, vegetable juice and wheat bread and bean pie from the Muslim restaurant. Once he starts eating chicken, Tree decides to eat everything that is left, so we get out of the car and ask the little girl if her mama and daddy would mind if we sat under her tree near the house. Not much grass there either. Just the generous seat of earth.

"Where is everybody?" I ask her.

She stops making like a windmill. We are what is interesting now.

"My mama and daddy at work. They choppin cotton. I'm too little. And I'm sick."

"You didn't look sick a while ago the way you were turning cartwheels all over the place." There's a teasing amusement in his voice.

"You ain't gotta act sick to be sick. Except for when yo mama come home." She was watching what was coming out of the shoebox and the cooler.

"You want some?" I ask. Treemont says she is too sick to eat.

"Uh uhnnn. I ain't too sick to eat." She proves this by devouring a chicken leg, thigh, breast, and wing, three biscuits, an apple, and an orange. At first she refused the cake in case it would upset her stomach. When pressed, she accepted it.

Her face is shaped like a heart.

"Who made this chicken." Not a question. A demand. She's kneeling on dusty knees. Her back real straight like a needle with a dress on.

"My mama. Why?" I answer her in the same tone.

"It's good!" This is a shocked commendation.

"Maggie, be sure and tell your mother that the food critic from off Highway 61 sends her regards." This little girl sure tickled him.

"Her name Maggie." She pointed at me. "What's yo name?" She points to Tree while she talks to him.

"Michael," he says. "My name is Michael. What's yours?"

"I'm not gone tell you."

"Why not?"

"You gone laugh at me."

"No, we won't."

I didn't say, "Speak for yourself." But I was thinking it.

"Okay, you can laugh."

"No, we won't laugh."

Miss Triangle Face takes a deep breath. Her eyes dart from one to the other of us. Grease around her mouth. A piece of chicken still in her hand. "My name is Mockingbird."

"Okay. What's your last name?"

"July. Mockingbird July. That's my name."

"Hey! You're my favorite singer."

"I know that," the little girl says.

"Were you named after her?"

"I wudn named after her. I was named *fa* her." This is emphatic.

"I see," Tree says, put in his place.

"You know what?" She's eating the cake now and is extra generous with confidences. "Everybody dead."

"Naw, baby."

"My mama say everybody dead."

"You're alive," Tree says.

"I know. But my mama said everybody dead. Grandpapa dead. Martin Luther King, he dead. And everybody. Goodman, Chaney, Schwerner, Medgar Evers, Viola Luipo, Nat Turner, all of them dead. Them four little girls in church. Them college students at Jackson State. The Walkin Lady told me. And my mama said so. They were listening to the radio and they dead up north."

"We come from up north," I tell her.

"They killt that man. They blew him up."

"Who?" Tree asked, very quietly.

"They killed him for everybody at the Nile."

"Mockingbird, you killing me."

"You can't kill me." She laughed and rolled around on the ground a little.

Happy again. Her replenished body ready with energy, she bobs when she talks. She points at Treemont. "He ain't dead. He ain't gone ever be dead." I think Miss Triangle Face got her eyes on my man.

"Oh, I am, huh?" I ask my rival.

"You might." She is coy. "He ain't gone be dead, though, unless he wanna be dead. He not dead."

"How do you know?" I ask the child with the full stomach.

The food is affecting her now. She's sleepy and yawns the answer. "The Walkin Lady told me. She told me to tell you you not dead."

"Thanks for the information, Miss July."

"Knock yourself out," she says, just before she follows her own advice. We sit on either side of her, like guardian angels, and watch her sleep.

Sunlight dances through leaf shadow. Each playing across her face like a lifetime of either-ors. This is too good to miss, the tender contemplation on his face as he watches her. The embryo she's drawn up into, like a dark question mark, quiet, quick only with breathing. I'm busy with my hands. To keep him still I ask him what he's thinking while he looks at her.

"I'm thinking about what her life's going to be like and what it ought to be like. What she deserves. She deserves to be able to spread out as far as she wants to and can. And I'm thinking about what in the hell she was talking about. The Dead. Everybody we left behind without saying good-bye. Just going because we were sent.

"I'm thinking about her and all the dances she'll invent. All the songs she'll sing that'll sound as beautiful as 'A Love Supreme.' There's so much life in her. Mockingbird July in the flesh. All these years I been hoping to meet her and here she is. Sleeping like an angel. Full of the devil. Maggie, you're here with me when I met Mockingbird July. That's all I got to say. You're with me. I know something bad happened, but we survived. Must be for a purpose."

He nudges Mockingbird July and urges her to wake up because we have to be on our way. She sits up and rubs the sleep deeper into her eyes. He helps her stand and walks her to the steps of her house. Watches her while she goes inside, still rubbing her eyes.

If you go along Highway 61 you will see the fenced-in fields of cotton and soybeans, gardens of okra and tomatoes and squash and onion and green and pole beans and greens. In some places wild onions grow and their aroma races to your eyes till you weep. Maybe it isn't the smell of onions at all, maybe it is just traveling 61, going back the way we came. Knowing how we left with everything on the car roof, strapped down, the trunk of the car roped around, and the insides stuffed with children and everything to carry. So he is driving us back to the place where I was born and we don't have much to carry. Traveling light. I drew that once: a sunrise hitting a certain street. The light visibly moving across the stones and the faces in the windows. Traveling. I wish now we'd come by train, so we could have traveled faster. Taken the train to Memphis, then caught the bus. And let the noises of petulant babies keep us up all night or day, the snoring of middle-aged men, the rustle of paper of a sojourner smoking away the anxiety of movement, the intimate murmur of the voices of travelers who have only met an hour before, life stories, wonderings, regrets stirred up by the rise of dust after moving wheels. But then we wouldn't have met Mockingbird July, junior version. And we would never have known everybody's dead. Or so she said.

When Treemont spots the row of watermelons, bellies pressed into the earth like soldiers during a bombing, I wish he didn't have such keen sight. We don't want to talk about Aint Kit's watermelon she got from the man in the wagon.

✦

Aint Kit said she was too scared to cut that watermelon. So she asked Madaddy to do it. She turned her brand-new eyelashes up at him as incentive. Attempting to look helpless to her brother. He shrugged his shoulders and shimmied his body a little bit like he was shaking himself awake. When he took the knife from her, he was looking handsome with expectancy, the way he must have looked when the troops went into Germany and he helped liberate the people from themselves.

Aint Kit did a choppy little dance of terror like a marionette on speed.

Madaddy drew an invisible line down the center of the melon. Then he laid the edge of the blade on the line at the curve of the melon. He pressed down (expelling a "Huh" from way inside his guts) and pulled the knife back in one stroke. The watermelon fell apart in perfect halves, but the perfection was lost on us. Something like smoke swelled from between the halves, leaving the blue meat of the fruit behind it. A gray body floated, then broke apart into infinite pieces, and the pieces were myriad eyes and wings and legs.

"Have mercy, Jesus!" Aint Kit screamed.

"Goodness gracious!" was Mama, and "Go'amighty!" Madaddy hollered.

The rest of us were speechless at the flies. Flies all around our heads, like huge swarming halos. They kept coming, even after Mama snatched up one melon half and my father another, while Bay and Hank batted the flies from their faces, from squeezed eyes and narrowed nostrils. Flies roamed above and around us, looking for openings. We ran.

People turned over chairs, getting out of the way of the flies. Aint Kit's fur stole hung off the back of a chair, unperturbed and dead. A line of drinks stood in a row on the bar, flies sipping. Sitting on the rims. The flies fanned out across the ceiling like a thundercloud, but the place was clear before the masses of them came down again. They were like a biblical swarm of locusts, hovering over the Nile.

I couldn't find Treemont and I was scared that something had happened to him or Steve, whom no one ever saw much anyway. How would we know? So scared I was calm and walked in a straight line and spoke in a straight line—I kept asking people if they'd seen Tree.

Lazarus and Leona appeared; her date had long been banished for stupidity. Lazarus said Treemont wanted me to go with him to take Leona home before her father sent the sheriff. ASANTE dispersed the crowd quietly, reassured. With a lot of laughter over Aint Kit and the watermelon with more flies than a dog has fleas. My brother said not to worry. My brother said not to weep. So I didn't. At least not until I got home to the apartment over HoneySounds and found Tree there and Steve with him, eating greens and corn bread at my table, where I'd picked the greens and stirred the corn bread batter. Eating fried perch and buffalo with hot sauce and drinking lemonade out of jelly jars. Neither one of them had on shoes. They'd sent Lazarus to bring me home. They had things to talk about. So they came here to where it was quiet. Bertram was right with them. From across the hall with some cha-cha he swiped from Charlotte, his mother. They spread this liberally over their greens. I was pissed off. I told Tree he had to be crazy to leave me and be here, relaxing.

He smiled. "It's not what it looks like," he said.

I sat down and ate with them. I was telling them about existentialism and Sartre and that play where hell was a room full of flies. They laughed some more about flies and Hell and all a regiment of flies ascending and descending could mean, what bad luck. Treemont looked at my *Book of Dreams* under "flies."

He read, "Flies. To dream of flies denotes sickness and contagious maladies."

"Nope," Steve deadpanned.

"Also that enemies surround you," Tree read. And we all fell quiet, even Bertram.

That's how Steve moved in. He'd stay with Charlotte and look after Bertram while Charlotte was at school or modeling in an evening show. Children he said he didn't mind. They didn't cause that quivering in the middle of his stomach he told me about. It came when he was around people who made him nervous.

He was sleeping on the let-out couch when we left. Lifting himself up in the half sleep in order to get up to help us load the car with the shoebox, my suitcase and overnight case, and Tree's duffel bag and backpack. Tree said, "Go back to sleep, man. We know you'll take good care of things."

Then we finished loading Aint Kit's dead third husband's car because Tree's was too unreliable for so long a journey. That's what he said. We planned to make it longer. To see everything we could see. Traveling quietly with only each other, even though Bertram begged to go and Mama gave me all kinds of instructions of what to tell Leah-Bethel by Lazarus, who delivered the car and the shoebox. Lazarus walked away quickly in the darkness, not even waving. We were traveling light.

The fields of Letha and Mimosa are most beautiful, or so it seems to me. Whatever is living and wants sun leaps toward it. Uncle Ike and

Aunt Charity's farm, hidden away, comes alive for me and I am giddy to dance through the squawking hens with Treemont. Eager to see him stroke the wings of the pigeons and doves. To write him love notes and strap them to the legs of homing pigeons and toss them in the air so they could sweep the brief distance to Silence's. And come down in a flurry of little rejoicings. The fields are beautiful and now Mimosa opens herself to us in a loving embrace. Like me when I reminisce about Eden when it was beautiful too. All of us students dancing in the green meadow, while the yellow caps of field flowers leapt up toward the sun. That was the time we closed down Eden. Students, Black and White. Everybody together dancing in the meadow because the government had gone too far across the sea and invaded Cambodia and students went on strike. The music in the meadow was big and everybody's hair was long. White students you never saw, conscientious commuters, came to dance. Hippies with flowers painted on their vests and jeans came dancing. Asian coeds in miniskirts, their hair sweeping like languid brooms. Bloods extravagantly Afroed, in jeans and minis, in dashikis and dangling earrings, were dancing. The PA was loud and sometimes you could not even make out the words except the important ones, "STOP THE WAR."

Then Eden was beautiful. That meadow.

"You're gonna have to go back. Sooner or later," Tree says. Trying to bring me down because I'm kneeling on the car seat pointing now at the old plantation, open for tours no one I know has ever taken.

"Shut up. I'm home."

"This is Africa?"

"Next best thing, Brother Stone," I grin at him.

He smiles the quiet smile that drives me to distraction and halfway across country to my aunt's.

He turns off the highway in the wrong direction.

"Old Letha Road is in the other way," I tell him.

"I know." He keeps on driving.

The Fields of Letha

"One, two, buckle my shoe." In the half-light even sound is halved and her quiet walk begins with the buckling of shoes. "Three, four, shut the door." She does. Quietly, considerate of the sleep of travelers, when it is she we have come for. "Five, six, pick up sticks." I see her in the yard, gathering kindling for the stove she still prefers to cook on. Even though she has another. Black, potbellied, reliable, and elementary. "Seven, eight, lay them straight." In a pile next to the door. "Nine, ten, the big fat hen" is in trouble because Aunt Silence has a hatchet in her free hand. She floats through the yard in the buckled-up nun shoes. Floats down quick and grabs and twists her big fat hen by the neck in one or two smooth gestures. This is a beautiful murder. Swift and necessary, with neither malice nor contempt. She has to fix fried chicken for breakfast. It is a special meal. We are here. Treemont Stone is alive.

I am close to sleep in her bed. Listening to her. Imagining what completes the tiny sounds that come from the back of the house and the yard where the few hens and one rooster promenade and putter like forgetful scientists testing the grains and crumbs scattered around their wired-in space. I listen to what is tiny because what is big is too much. Sorrow and panic squat over me. I wonder how it sets with Treemont in the front room, connected by a door. It was all right for Aunt Silence, Aint Kit, and me to crowd into one bed to keep each other brave and safe that time

Bay was in jail. But Tree and me aren't married and this is my aunt's house. Even more than my grandmother's. We slept apart, for a while. But pain was like a fever and I tossed, until, finally, I gave up on separation and tiptoed into the front bedroom and climbed into bed with Treemont. There I slept. My head fitting into his armpit as he lay with his hand tucked under his head.

Nothing was erotic, until I dozed and dreamed demons and he woke me up. Then he covered me and we defied loneliness in a rush. He lay his hand over my mouth, and I wondered how because my body had floated away and I watched him biting his bottom lip while his body shook with mine. He breathed like someone who's been dying of thirst and drinks a long drink of water in one swallow that is so many swallows it comes as one. The room was dark. No light slipped under the door because all the lights were out in the house on Chinaman's Store. Silence acted like she did not hear us as she softly rocked in her rocking chair. Sometimes she'd do as she did when I was a girl. She'd sit on the chair so perfectly balanced the runners did not sway. She'd seem to be sitting on eggs. Delicately. Nothing cracking. Nothing worried her then.

Nothing about her surprised Treemont because he had seen her that first time when she finished saving his life. She was like the woman who'd stopped the killers on the road. He'd do anything for her. It was he who drove to Georgia for her and brought back the cooling waters the wealthy Whitepeople purchased for their nerves. He got it for free at a spring where Silence told him he would find it. After Treemont was gone, Silence journeyed there again herself.

I can feel the soft warm of the black potbellied stove now. We are safe, I think. I think, "We are safe." But I know we are not safe and he will never be safe again. He hasn't said that all through the long journey, but I know.

I turn over on my side and smell the sheets. I can smell the Tide in them. The soft brown water of Mississippi only needs a little detergent. Up north the water is hard. The window is open, cool air coming in, morning air. Tree is out of bed.

"Stop kidding yourself," I tell myself. "You were never safe. None of you ever was. Sam and Caroline built a house. They thought it would keep out the cold. But the cold came through the thinnest fissures in the walls. The cold came through the windows, delicate with reflection. The windows were so thin you could see through them and see yourself at the same time. That's what happened. We saw through things and saw ourselves at the same time. And something cold killed somebody in the Blue Nile. Killed some possibilities. "This is worse. This is worse than the ice babies. This is a giant ice. It's smothering us."

I see myself now in a classroom, maybe first grade again. We are lined up in rows beside our wooden desks with the inkwells on the right-hand corner. But we don't use ink bottles. We use pencils, number 2. The yellow pencils rest in the grooves at the top of the desk. We are straight as those pencils. Our hands over our hearts. We say, "I pledge allegiance to the flag of the United States of America and to the republic for which it stands, one nation under God, indivisible, with liberty and justice for all."

The flag is killing us.

I think about the time I could have spit in that Whitegirl's face. Now I would. I would spit blood. And it wouldn't be enough. Because she was an overworked waitress with a bad attitude in a dive looking for somebody to sling her life like snot. It wouldn't be enough. This is bigger than her. Bigger. Bigger. An evil that grew up, pampered by generations and institutions. An evil with a bodyguard sent to search us out and kill us before we know who we are. A Herod evil that slays a thousand possibilities.

I don't have to tell Silence. Just as I don't have to tell her I haven't spent the whole night in her bed. She already knows. Still she defends the meaning of the flag. She said last night, "Even though a liar says what's true, it's still true."

I was on the phone. Treemont was pacing behind me, desperate to talk. Ready for the show.

I said, "Lazarus, is it true? Is Tree dead?"

"Sorry you had to find out the way you found out, Maggie."

"How'd it happen?"

"The building just blew up. The whole damned Blue Nile. The media say it was gang-related violence. But I guess we know who did it."

"I'm coming back."

"Maggie, that would be too hard on you. The memorial is in a week or so. Come then, Maggie. There wasn't enough left of him to ID the body. But they knew it was him because some people saw him go home at night. He was wearing his work clothes."

I can see Steve Rainey in that meticulous way of his. Removing any memory of himself from his body. He smiles as he looks at the tips of his fingers, smooth as rubber. He strokes his beard like Treemont Stone strokes his beard. Combs his hair like Treemont Stone's hair. Stephen Rainey. I see him before the mirror. Considering this simple gift: his given height, a tall man. Does he consider that he is young? In his twenties. Does he consider that we love him? Does he consider that he has already given more than he should have? Was that just crazy and this crazy too and his life wasted? But I am relieved that Stephen Rainey is dead. A little imp glee wild jumping up inside me, because he is the one. Steve is the one. Stephen Rainey is the one who was killed. Is the one who died. And Treemont Stone is alive. Then before I can breathe relief, I know that that is lame.

I put my head under the pillow now. So I can scream Steve Rainey's name over and over and over. Concentrating on the sound so I won't see the pictures of him and me and Leona and Essie in Eden. (Now he's running ahead of the car guiding us to Wyndam-Allyn. His long legs like stilts cutting through dusk.) That must have been two thousand years ago. It had to have been two thousand years ago. (Now his face is in front of mine and his lips brush my lips like a whisper.) I am screaming when Treemont comes to rock me.

He's saying, "Maggie, Maggie, Maggie." His voice tender with consolation.

Wrestling the pillow from my tight grasp, holding me until I come back to Mimosa, Mississippi, where he needs me because he's crying too.

The bedclothes look like a storm and we are two grieving children lost in the covers when Silence opens the door to behold us. "Breakfast is ready," she says to us. To Treemont she says, "You were prepared to die, weren't you? But you're not prepared to mourn. You wanted the easy part. But you didn't get it. Now we have to keep you alive. That boy knew what he was doing. He's dead now. Don't make him a fool."

All day long we play the TV and radio (a Black station in Memphis) for news of the murder of Treemont Stone. In the middle of the night is a sharp rap on the back door. We aren't surprised. We are up and talking and see the car pull up onto the gravel path. I look out the window over the kitchen sink. And Aunt Silence, with her rifle in hand, stands with her ear pressed to the door. Tree is on the side of the bed lying down. Somebody says something and Aunt Leah-Bethel says, "Oh!" and throws wide the door. Leona and Lazarus stand under the back-porch light. In blue jeans and dark jackets. They are the same height. They don't waste time. They tell me to come out to the car and help them get their bags. I go in my gown. Knowing I am a weary ghost in a hurry to beat time. In the backseat of the Volkswagen are Essie and Bertram. Bertram's eyes look like two big crystal balls filled with snow and a dark house in each.

"Well, I'll be!" is what I say. Sounding like Mama or Silence, astonished by the devotion of a child in love.

"Maggie, we come to save you!" Bertram squeezes out of the backseat.

"Shhhh!" Essie puts her finger to her lips. She shakes her head. He understands and, mute and jubilant, he flings his arms around me. His body like a little heater.

Essie gets out slowly. She is busy collecting luggage and little packages. So busy she cannot meet my eyes. Before I say anything sentimental or grateful, she says, "Leona asked me to come with her." She looks at me then and bats her eyes three times as if she were trying to make me disappear. After she does this, she's stronger and lifts two suitcases. Points her head toward the back door and marches.

Now I wish she hadn't come and Leona had left well enough alone.

My mind is on the space where Treemont Stone is hidden. When I come through the back door, they're all talking about the remains that I. B. K. Turner and Chaka would send to Tree's sister in California. I call to Tree to rise up from behind the bed and he does. Bertram runs to him. They fall down on the bed. Laughing.

"What about Steve's people?" Essie asks. She's sounding like she's in a courtroom. Cool and stern.

"He has an uncle out East." Tree is sitting on the couch. His hands clasped between his legs.

"I know that. I'm asking what about him."

"Well, what about him?" Treemont sounds testy.

"You're not going to tell him?"

"Tell him what, Essie?"

"His only living nephew isn't living anymore."

"Why would we do that, Essie? Now?" His voice is strained.

"If I have to tell you why, there's no point in me telling you."

Aunt Silence, who has heretofore been silent, cuts off the words that are building up to bitterness. "Why don't we let the travelers get the road off 'em and eat something before we talk. That okay?" This last for Essie, who is the model of civil belligerence.

I go into the bathroom while Leona washes her face and hands. I look up from the toilet. The only sound is me making water. "Why'd you bring Essie down here?"

"I brought her so she wouldn't blow it." Leona cuts me a glance full of fed up. She's tired, she says, of explaining herself to Essie. And she doesn't want to explain anything to me. But she does. "Miss Fredonia talked to Tree before y'all left. He stopped by her new apartment. So she knew he wasn't in the building. She didn't tell anybody but Essie. It just jumped out because she was so relieved that at least Treemont was among the living. If not our beloved Steve Rainey. Soon as she said it she told me she knew she'd confided in the wrong person. We were at the ASANTE place. Anyway, I asked Essie to come because she was so angry about Steve being dead. She's looking for somebody to blame. And of course since Tree is Chaka's savior, it must be his fault. So I brought her because I was scared she'd wreck Steve's plan. Okay? Steve must have known something bad was there, waiting."

It's not okay, but I say it is because I don't know what else to say. It'll have to be okay. I never thought the woman named Essie who was my friend could be my enemy. Though I guess Essie would say the same thing.

Leona looks in the mirror at her red eyes, pulling down the lower curve to see more. She sighs. I don't say anything. Then, her eyes focused on the face bowl, she rummages in her purse halfheartedly.

"You want some?" She offers me the little spigot of Visine.

I don't talk, so she does.

"So, okay, Dreamer. Did you dream this shit?"

I disavow.

"I keep trying to make it make sense. Why he had to die."

"Everybody dies, Leona."

"But do you remember how much fun we had before the fire? I keep thinking if Steve hadn't acted like he was crazy and taken the blame, he wouldn't have been so crazy when he came back. I don't know. Maybe it takes a crazy person to burn down a building in the first place. Maybe it takes a crazy person to know when a building's gonna blow up and go in anyway. Maybe you got to be a little off to do something so outlaw. Maybe he was just brave and selfless. Maybe he never had anybody, so he never—" Her head is back and she's dropping in the medicine. Blinking her eyes while they run.

"Maybe."

"He was in love with you, Maggie." Wet around her half-open eyes.

"Leona, everybody knows Steve liked you."

"He liked me, but he loved you."

"That ain't true."

"It is. He told me."

I'm breathing out of my mouth.

I don't want to look at her toweling her eyes now. Instead, looking at the patchwork linoleum, I ask, "Told you what?"

"He said you offered him your hands once and he believed you would have given him a hand. He said you always appreciated him." Her eyes are tortured. "I coulda been kinder. If I'd known time was so short."

"You never did anything mean to Steve, Leona."

"And I never did anything tender."

"Don't—"

"You listened. And he loved you."

"Oh, good grief." I sound like my mother.

"Naw. This ain't a good grief. Neither is Essie's."

It's not true about people being bent with grief. That's only a moment. Grief makes us walk straighter, holding it tight inside. An internal burden we compact and shove between the organs. Behind the heart it weighs like stones tied to a dead boy to hold him under the surface of the water. Against the bladder and sex organs, where it presses to be let go or be born. It climbs into the throat and threatens a scream, harsh and horrified. It makes pictures in the mind. Those ghost films that run in front of what is happening. Interjecting images of the dancing wonder. Leona holding his hand. The brother sleeping beside you with his arm around you, protecting. Didn't we lie down like black sheep and hope for a morning green and just and kind? Didn't we wander like lambs directly into the path of wolves because that wandering seemed the only way?

"Hair like lamb's wool." I do not think I've spoken out loud.

"He was crazy." Leona looks at me. Her mouth flat like the line on a heart monitor when somebody is dead. "He was crazy. He had to have known it would happen because he put on Treemont's clothes."

Guilt makes me cast my eyes down. I am glad it wasn't who they wanted.

"Treemont doesn't even carry a gun." I sound like a little girl, half sulky, half defensive. Leona looks at me.

"I've never seen it," I say.

Leona nods. "You know what my father says?" She half sits on the face bowl. "He says he thinks Mr. Hoover has put out a directive to kill anything Black that moves us together. Anything that looks like a Black Messiah has to go. I know Tree ain't into being no Messiah. But any organization that aims to unify and serve as the foundation for a mass movement has to be infiltrated. He says that's what happened to Garvey. And it worked fifty years ago. It can work now. Only then J. Edgar didn't have to pay anybody to kill niggahs. They are doing it wholesale. Murder was de facto. Now its de jure. I think he's right. My daddy didn't make money being dumb."

That is it. Exactly what Tree told me. And the truth is, Tree didn't have to tell me. Leona's offering verification.

Leona jerks herself off the porcelain. "Let's go see what's happening. Lazarus brought something."

Two bushy heads like black shrubs pore over double-sized pages. Lazarus and Treemont are sitting on the couch, searching a map. (Lazarus, who looks like me. Tree, who looks like a dead man.) Lazarus says something about a boat and safe passage for him. That's what sets me off.

"Who's going on a boat?"

Tree looks up at me. His face expressionless. But his eyes look like the dark in the basement my daddy used to walk into to fix the pipes that brought heat and water. His eyes. "I am," he answers me. His voice is steady, matter-of-fact.

Once, I was leaving the house, saying good-bye to everybody, starting with Mama and Madaddy, all my brothers, and sisters, I thought. Frances, the quiet sister, came running, "What about me? What about me, Maggie?" She was bereft and injured, standing at the head of the stairs, waiting for a kiss good-bye. And I gave it to her. Treemont does not kiss me now.

Me. I walk grief straight, back into the bedroom. What about me? Sitting on the bed. My mind blank. Trying not to explode.

He closes the door behind him. Stands with his back against the closed door.

"You know you can't go with me, Magdalena."

"I don't know that."

"You know."

This is his trick. To wait until some niggling thing inside me rises up and agrees. But I say no.

"No."

"I'd never forgive myself if something happened to you."

My voice is full of mucous. "And if I die of heartbreak."

"You won't do that."

"I won't? I won't?" Hollering now. It's traveling through the door into the living room, where I can hear somebody say something about they knew I would take it hard.

He's still standing at the door. Talking softer. "No. You won't die. You went into that building with the rest of the bloods before you knew me. You joined the Hallelujah Wall before you knew me. You worked before me. You made great art before me. You studied before me. You didn't search for justice after I told you to or showed you how to. You did that. I never made you you. You won't die if you stay. You might die if you go."

If love hurts bad enough it'll act just like a kind of hate. "Oh, no, brother man. You don't tell me how and where and when I will hurt. You don't mandate my misery, Mr. Biggification Negro man. You Mr. Social Justice, Mr. Race and Class Struggle, Mr. Self-Determination, and you gonna sit up like a monarch and choose where I go like I'm a package you bought at Sears."

I keep going. Somebody tries to open the door, but Mr. Stone won't move.

Aunt Leah-Bethel whispers through the door, "Maggie, please, don't—"

At the sound of her voice, he moves.

She stands in the middle of the floor and looks at one face, then the other.

He says slowly, "There's only arrangements for one person. Dead-andBuried made the choice." He looks at her, but talks to me.

"Arrangements can be changed," I say to my aunt.

She just looks at me, as if he weren't there. "Where'd you get that one from?"

"What?" I say, not to be distracted from my rage.

"Treemont Biggification Negro Man." Her stomach and shoulders start shaking and a smoky laugh comes out.

"Got it from a dream. A bad, bad dream I had."

"Ain't it nice the way she saved that up and turned it around so she could give it to you!" She's looking at Treemont and laughing her head off now. The smoky laugh a conflagration that catches first him, then me. We are laughing like fools, falling over our own bodies. And for a moment sorrow rolls away from the heart, eases off the bowels, and climbs out of the throat and finds a giddy flight.

Then it's over and my eyes are wet. To hold the top of my head on, I press down with my hands, my arms curved in front of my eyes so I don't have to see him. The one I've lost.

"What about me?" I say. "What about me?" whining and crying, like a little, hurt kid.

He doesn't even try to comfort me now. Neither does Silence. At first she fetches me water. He goes out of the room with her. When she returns with the water, she says, "If you go with him, they'll know he's not dead. And they'll look for both of you. Would you want that, Maggie? To ruin his only chance? And you'd mess up what Steve wanted too."

Right now, some selfish girl inside me doesn't care. I look at her and I don't say a word.

She leaves me and I look out the window, past the pink blossoms of the crepe myrtle, onto the gravel road. Past it and the streets of Mimosa is the Highway Blues Walked Down. A long way off is the City I don't want to go back to. The life before Treemont Stone. And what about his life? What's it going to be but running, pretending to be who he is not? I start up crying again, burying my face in a chenille spread so hard I make ridges on both cheeks and my eyelids too. And I don't budge when Bertram tips in to look at me and goes back to say, "She sleep."

✦

When I wake up I am sitting at the foot of her bed, my body is tight with ingratitude, and I can't keep sitting. I just go. Out the back door. Bertram, who's been fitting in corners, silent on the edge of the sofa, comes running behind me. Leona has taken Essie on a tour of the area, while Lazarus talks to Treemont about the details of their plan. I think, "Is it God or the devil in the details?" Treemont must memorize his route; then they'll eat the pages I.B.K. sent, ways to arrive safely and anonymously on his island, where I.B.K. will be waiting. He had decided to go home. Once there, offer Stone a refuge. And Stone will be Steve with all his papers. We know we should be calling him Steve now, but we don't have the heart to deceive ourselves. I called him Rainey, but the tears only crowded my eyes. Like now.

Different streets have different histories. The upkeep depending upon who is home and who went north looking for something better. In the house in which I was born people who were renting decided they didn't like the tree outside the front window. So they cut it down. The nuisance tree that took over fifty years to achieve its gorgeous maturity they hacked down. My father called down there and the man told him the tree got on his nerves. I am looking at where the tree used to be. Now the light shoots like a rocket through the window; and no leaves impede surveillance of the road where I walk and look into the house where I was born.

Bertram says, "You were born there, Maggie?" Knowing that it's so because I've told him before. Thinking this question will make me talk.

"Yes." My nose is stopped up.

Spinning on my heels a little bit, I turn and lead us across the street into the Chinese man's store. They sell eggs by ones and twos here. On the off chance we've forgotten to get enough from the farm or supermarket on the highway.

Ed Hoo went back to school in California. The man and woman behind the counter are his cousins. They've settled into a routine. She moves the purchases down the counter. He touches them and rings the register.

"Do you have newspapers?"

"Only one I got the one I'm reading. You can get one at the supermarket."

Because he's been so helpful, I have to buy something. Bertram picks out cookies and Popsicles for us to eat. The dainty Cokes to sip. We are on our way. Bertram is tagging along, sticking to me like tape. Because he can't hang around Treemont. We wander the streets like orphans.

The supermarket is Mighty Johns. That's what the sign says. Inside are fruits and vegetables grown on corporate farms. Colors and juices sealed in wax. Red apples with their bruises turned toward each other, pressing inward. Green, unripe bananas and lettuce circled in cellophane. Black eggplant with blue undertones. I think about getting some.

"What's them?" Bertram knocks against my elbow.

I hold up the big tube. "A Black militant squash."

"Yeah. Yeah." He wants to touch it.

"We're going to put it on TV."

"It need some hair."

"We'll dye some corn silk and tighten it up. It'll be real dangerous looking. They'll discover it and put it on TV. It'll be a militant pimp, gangster, anarchist, monarchist, who's the head of a voodoo cult that sticks pins in random Whitepeople till they die. It'll be a rapist cult leader who keeps a pet snake and a pet switchblade long as a butcher knife. This eggplant ain't got no program. This eggplant don't love nobody. This eggplant ain't got no desire for justice. This eggplant is a raging vegetable. He carry a book of matches and his mama is a rutabaga. They put her on TV to pray because that's all she can do and her prayers ain't like the big ole eggplant's fist. He ain't got no daddy. You ever heard of an eggplant with a daddy?"

"I ain't never heard a no eggplant."

"You see, Bertram, the militant eggplant is wanted by the FBI and the City Police because he said he wouldn't tolerate violence at the hands of others. He used to lie with his ear to the ground and dream. Because the ground is black like he is. And he used to dream about a field that rose up and touched the sky."

I'm just standing, looking at the eggplant, a tremor starting in my hands, when Bertram asks, "Maggie, you really want that eggplant?"

"No. Pick us some decent fruit. I'll go get what I came for."

Then I'm wandering the aisles for a box of sanitary napkins. Even though I'm late, I know it's coming because it's regular. You can always depend on blood. Yet when I try to remember when the last one showed, I can't. Too much has happened.

I put the blue box and little kit of tampons in the cart, expecting a heavy flow, like a break in a dam. What I expect when I think too long about Steve Rainey. This time, I want to tell Bertram the joke about the baby that was an eye, but I'm trying to keep from laughing in the store. My mind keeps going and I wonder if the Eye had a lid. Anything could fly into a naked Eye and set up an infection, so it can run snot or bloody clots. It could go blind, if Steve hadn't said it was born blind. A lady is coming up the aisle, so I cough to keep from laughing like a lunatic in lonely elation.

My private hilarity takes her in. It is Miss Ruby Collins. Refined in pearl earrings and a tan shift. Shiny brown pumps. She remembers me, even though I know my face is older with strain. And fear makes my eyes jump. She remembers me and asks after my other college girlfriend. The one in the tiny skirt. I know she's talking about Leona.

I tell her Leona is at my aunt's house. "They hired any more Black down at the store?" I'm talking like a Mimosan.

"Brought in some black nylon socks," she cracks, and puts on a disgusted face.

Is it the disgruntled angel in the look that makes me know we need her help? The aisle is empty. I ask her quick. Before someone sees us and thinks we are planning shoplifting or worse.

"Miss Ruby," I begin, searching her strong, friendly gaze, "you said one time if Miss Leah-Bethel Grace ever needed you, you'd help."

"Don't tell me nothing. Just tell me when," she says.

I tell her.

Bertram and I bring back yellow bananas (he said you have to know what you're looking for and keep digging until you find what you came after), apples, Vienna sausages in the small, neat cans, dried fruit, and nuts. He's carrying the bag and doesn't look around as we go through the arc of crepe myrtle, not even when we hear the sound of girls dancing a game that sails over the hedges.

"Hands up, touch a touch, touch a touch—"

Hands appear over the top of the hedges.

"Got a pain, touch a touch, touch a touch—"

We go over to watch them. Spying on their sassy play.

"Right here, touch a touch, touch a touch—"

The girls, lanky and limber, prepubescent, grab their stomachs.

"In my side, touch a touch, touch a touch."

He's so enthralled, neck craned over the hedges, a mischievous look on his face, I take the bag and leave him outside. I watch him through the screen door, till Tree comes from the back of the house.

"What's outside?" he asks. His voice a little tense.

"Just Bertram and true love."

"The girls next door?"

"You saw them?"

"I heard 'em. They sounded like angels. I thought they were coming for to carry me home."

I can't be flip. I can't ask where home is.

We just stand there. Somehow I have always known he would go. Some people live their entire lives in one place. Cells bound to cells. Or spiraling down to the center from one space. They tend their fields or flowerpots. Save pennies and photograph albums and stacks of seventy-eights and forty-fives. They stand under trees and hunt for fruit. It is their lot and they live there, looking back to the same clapboard houses, the same brown and gray stones, the same weeping willows, monkey cigar trees, ash, crabapple, and trees of heaven. Looking ahead to the same.

Some people travel. They make detours after accidents in the road. They keep on going and fall over sunsets and stumble into sunrises. They eat berries along the way and carry the stains with them. They search for roots and wild greens. They mark the trees they meet, hoping to find that way again. They try to remember the changes in space. They carry children on their backs. Or they leave them with people who stay. They travel light. They are connected to light in a curious way. Alone. They walk hand in hand with the light through the window they are walking by. Their only company the singing hands of flickering light.

A howl pushes up from inside me. I clamp my mouth closed and turn from the pretty sounds of girls chanting and Bertram attempting sophisticated flirtation. I head for the kitchen and take the fresh fruit from the bag. Leave the rest. Treemont has followed me. I hand him the bag.

"You should put this someplace."

He looks inside the bag. "Nice. Thank you." He doesn't say he doesn't eat Vienna sausages.

"Don't mention it." I pour myself lemonade.

He's leaning his arms on the sink, looking out the window at a fig tree or the outhouse. "ASANTE can't end because I'm gone. Everybody knows that."

"I never said ASANTE would end."

"It's going to be there when I get back."

"Am I going to be there when you get back?" I ask, spitefully.

"I don't know," he says sorrowfully. "Don't wait for me," he says. "You're Lieutenant Uhura, remember. You have worlds to explore."

"You're leaving. I'm not."

"The time's not right for me, Maggie. Something has to give. The people have to work it out. I'll be back."

"Garvey left America."

"Garvey got put out."

"W. E. B. Du Bois left."

"Yeah."

"Stokely left. Angela Davis took flight."

"Angela Davis didn't leave the country, Maggie. And Sister Angela Davis knew the charges against her. She could prove them false in a court of law. I just know I'm supposed to be dead. Didn't that little Mocking-bird girl say everybody's dead?"

"She said you weren't."

"Okay. I'm still here."

Footsteps stop him. Without finding out who it is coming through the front, he heads for the backyard, where the outhouse still stands like a border guard's post. When Lazarus hollers his new name, "Hey, Steve Rainey," he turns around and comes back in.

"You were gone hide there, man?" Lazarus hits him on the back. "That little shack will tumble down on you. Or that hole in the ground let loose some old stuff grab your breath from you."

They laugh then, the way men laugh. One funny thing leading into another. Time has crept into a slow measure of moments (stands still in the hourglass, shadow does not cross the sundial, and the clocks have lost their hands) since Steve Rainey died. This time in Mimosa is one long day. A dream walk.

Lazarus and Treemont are laughing like the time we were in the apartment over the Blue Nile. And Bertram was there, caught red-handed with a copy of *Jet* magazine with a swimsuited girl. He was studying the photograph in the centerfold, anticipating. The brothers and sisters from ASANTE were having fun after a meeting and rally.

Lazarus said, "What's that you got, Bertram?"

Bertram showed him.

Lazarus looked and looked perplexed, "You're supposed to have the magazine with the girls in it this early?"

"Yeah. Now I need to see the men—how big they get. So I'll know mine."

"You can have an airplane, don't mean nothing if you can't fly." That was Tree from a corner of the room, breaking it up with his dry deadpan.

"Maggie, can Treemont fly?" One of the nosy sisters from ASANTE wanted to know. I wouldn't tell her. I acted like I couldn't hear her.

When will we laugh like that again? Even harder when Treemont took Bertram's magazines from him. "You'll get to biology in high school," he said. We were all alive then.

I remember how I played dead with Moses over me once, asking me to give him the love he didn't really want. Soon I won't have to play. I

340

think about the farm Essie and Leona say John Olorun, the poet, and Hamla are talking about starting. Olorun was Hamla's final proof that she was through with Alhamisi, whom she won't call Alhamisi anymore but calls him by his slave name of Ogden. Essie and Leona say they will farm by day and write poems by night. Happy in the quiet of listening to vegetables grow. The blank noise of fruit falling. Happy for however long. Now I wish, but it's too late to wish because each wish is broken by the bone it was made on. The star it was hoped on. And Hamla and John Olorun's farm is not far enough to run to. If it happens at all.

Aunt Silence is stretched out on the couch watching TV. Sipping her relaxing Georgia springwater. Ever since we came she's been in her jeans, in case she has to run. I get out the big-toothed comb and start parting her coarse, thick hair. Side to side on each cleared line of scalp, I rake, until the dead skin loosens and the pores breathe. This causes her to exhale, relaxed. I line each part with Royal Crown hair oil. Wiping the excess grease onto her hair so that it has a sheen. In the kitchen, Essie and Leona are cooking mustards and turnips, corn bread, and baked hens from Uncle Ike's farm. They're not chicken hens. I think pigeons of some kind. Because I am my mother's daughter, I didn't ask. Once at Eden in the library, where I used to sit and read for hours about Africa, I read about the people of Ibadan, who during a war went to the caves above the city until it was safe to return to their homes. I don't know who it was they were fighting, defending themselves against, the British or a neighbor, but I remember in the cave they ate only pigeons and the eggs of pigeons, and fruit. Probably the pigeons were rock doves, but it sounds cannibalistic to say they ate doves, maybe because Whitepeople make so much of doves, and the Holy Ghost came down as a dove. Rock doves are brown with pretty markings, which means they are pigeons after all and that is what the people of Ibadan ate. And, standing here now, doing what I'm doing, a most ordinary act, I hope eating pigeons as our ancestors did in a time of war will save us. I would eat doves and be glad.

"Maggie, see who that at the door," my Aunt Silence mumbles in a drowsy reverie.

"I didn't hear anybody."

"He's here." She still doesn't open her eyes. "Ask him if it's something he's trying to buy."

That's what I ask him when he steps over the doorjamb to Silence's house, with his hat in his hand, trying so hard to appear civil.

He chuckles at the question—letting it ride into a big ha ho ho ho like he's Santa Claus. That's who he tries to look like, albeit beardless. "I sure would love to buy the smells coming out of that kitchen back there. You all got a plate for me?" He winks at me. Winks at me. And that shuts me up good. Flames burst up inside me. Face on fire, I step aside a little so he can see Miss Leah-Bethel Grace reclining.

"She's resting." I interpret for his eyes. My voice wooden.

He steps past me, ducking his ole head around my shoulder, bent like he's bobbing for apples. Sliding all the way into the house, he straightens and pulls up the chair at the foot of the couch.

My auntie still has her eyes closed. Mildly she acknowledges him. "What you know good, Sheriff Columbine, sir? Excuse me, while I'm resting my eyes. I got a terrible headache my niece here has been trying to relieve. You know how it is when you getting old and cain't do for yourself like you used to."

"Well, what I have to say should eliminate your pain, Leah." He offers this courteously enough, but it is the courtesy that slides down an assembly line. Manufactured. With tons and tons of Biggifying Pills that his father made before him. Watching him, an old Whiteman, sitting on the edge of my aunt's chair like he can't really bear to touch his bottom against the seat, he tries to swell. He clears his ringed throat and I see the invisible pills ease down his esophagus. He has to fortify himself against the recline of my aunt. At this point, she opens her eyes, halfway, regarding him in a half-shuttered look.

Ten years ago this same man beat my aunt. The knee that is turned now toward the couch, he shoved into her stomach. The meaty hands that now hang off the armrests he made fists and struck blows against the same head I just scratched. "You not law. God didn't make you law." She was lucky he hadn't broken her fingers prying them off the silver shield. Instead he'd grazed them, deeply, until they bled. This when she tried to vote. Before Freedom Summer.

He thinks these things are best forgotten. At least I think he thinks of them as he stares at her and tries to put congeniality in his looking. The looking is the evocation of friendship based upon the shared trials of the past. I guess I'm the one who's looking at him, so he looks at me. I am standing in the doorway that leads through the dining room into the kitchen, where Essie and Leona have stopped talking and sit listening.

Sheriff Columbine turns his head, trying to shake off my stare. "If it hadn't been for me the Klan would have killed your auntie years ago. I put in the call to her house. I saved her life. I was the one. Now if word of this was to get out, I'd be a dead man."

"Don't worry, Sheriff, even the KKK wouldn't believe that." That's Aunt Silence cool as mint.

"Things could have been a lot worse for you a while ago, Leah. And they could still be rough on you. New laws can't stop old ways. I think you know that."

"If the laws are enforced, might be different."

"Not without goodwill." He swallows another Biggifying Pill, but makes like it's a Belittling Pill. Jams a diamond smile on his face. "I'll be retiring as sheriff soon and upon the occasion of my retirement I'll be acting as an agent for the Danube Corporation. You may have heard they have made an offer to add your little farm to their holdings. They own the soybean factory in Letha. And my understanding of their hold-ings is they own the green beans and corn market down here."

"Does that include what I grow in my backyard?"

He laughs. "Haaa. Haaa. Hooo." His face stretched out of shape until I know he is uncomfortable with his own duplicity. Or maybe uncom-fortable with the need for it when he'd rather just take what's Silence's.

He keeps on in spite of himself. In spite of her white hair that shines so prettily he wants to touch it—he almost does. He keeps on looking at her in spite of her calm that makes him want to saw his teeth down to salt or keep his teeth and pistol-whip the hell out of her. He keeps on in spite of and because he remembers the woman ether he called the Midnight Rambler, the Midnight Special. And that mist Black woman had scared him so, he was ashamed to tell it. So he swallowed a Biggifying Pill and thought about money; swallowed another and thought about guns; swal-lowed, thought land; swallowed, thought legislature; swallowed, thought power and custom; swallowed, and felt his crotch.

"Sheriff," Aunt Leah-Bethel says finally, ready to rid her hair of this. "You can talk to our lawyers, sir. I'm not sure I'm the best person to discuss so much money. You and the Germans might beat me out of thousands."

"Wait, now, girl. We're not trying to beat you out of anything. This is an honest corporation."

"Since you say so."

He's easing off the chair when the car pulls onto the gravel road. I realize then that the sheriff hasn't parked anywhere near. He may have not even driven. That whoever comes inside now doesn't know who is here. I turn to go, but he stays me with a question.

"Where you goin in such a hurry?"

"Do the West Germans want to know what my niece is doin in my house?"

"You got a lot of visitors, Leah. The sheriff might want to know about all these comings and goings." The sheriff reminds her of his authority.

Essie and Leona didn't hear the car; the mixer was spinning cake batter. Lazarus and Treemont are at the back door before anyone can forestall them. I go to the door. Aunt Silence's voice comes over my shoulder.

"Tell your brother to get on in here. And leave them KKK sheets in the laundry."

A voice in my head says, "Play it off." "Don't be skittish." I decide if he sees and recognizes Treemont from the news I can kill the sheriff with the butcher knife Essie's been chopping onions with. I can put him in Leona's car and jam him into the trunk and drive down to the Gulf and put weights on his corpse and drop him into the Gulf of Mexico. Or I can bury him someplace in Tennessee. No one would ever find the body then. I could think of other ways to dispose of him. But thinking of these things is tiresome.

I am surprised that I think like this. I have considered murder. Bloody murder.

But it looks like I'm not going to have to save Tree because he didn't come in with Lazarus.

"What name do you go by, boy?" the sheriff asks my brother.

I hope Lazarus doesn't say, "The name my mama gave me." He doesn't. He says his given name.

"You ain't risen from the dead, have you, fella?"

My brother looks at my aunt. Her answering gaze is direct, steady and sweet, like berries in cream. Lazarus swallows then and I know he's swallowing pride because he looks at Leona then doesn't look, then tells the sheriff, "Ain't nobody risen from the dead since Easter Sunday. And we all know Jesus was a Whiteman like you, Sheriff. Not much chance of me rising. That's if I was dead. I don't like the idea of dying, that's why I try to stay away from the instruments of death: butcher knives, razors, pots of boiling acid, scalding grits and lye, and guns that set up in holsters like dogs begging for a Blackman's behind."

That is how my brother relaxes the sheriff and lulls him into leaving. Sheriff Columbine wants Aunt Leah-Bethel to consider the sale of the land to the West Germans. He can't keep his smile from being a smirk when he shakes hands with Lazarus, who must believe Jesus is blond and blue-eyed. Lazarus looks back at him with a little smile on his face.

"I was just advising your aunt on the sale of some farmland. I know a good company that will give her an honest price for it. They're into canned goods." Columbine pleads his case condescendingly before Lazarus the believer in White Jesus. Lazarus acts like his ally.

"Aunt Leah, you not about to throw good money after bad, are you?"

She is as dry as iron. "I like to see it fly."

"Watch butterflies," my brother snaps.

The sheriff laughs heartily. This whole scene is too funny.

Then Lazarus starts business chitchat. He tells the sheriff where we're from. How Aunt Leah's ailing brought us down.

"Your head bothering you again, Leah?" the lawman asks.

"Nothin' but the headache you giving me," she says mildly, so sweet it brings a smile to his lips.

The sheriff laughs his businessman laugh. It comes not from the belly or heart but somewhere around the Adam's apple.

"Heard you had a big noise up there where one of them militants got killed. Whole damn half a building blew up. The FBI report says he was killed by another militant group. Over some dope."

"Is that right?" Lazarus is cool.

"I would have liked to have had an older picture of that Stone fella. Look like a Nigra escape from custody a few years back. Knocked out two deputies."

"Didn't it come out a husband or boyfriend or something did that young White lady like that?"

"It was never proven." The sheriff has to hold his gun in his palm now. It's pointed down in the holster. He has to remind Silence that his word is law. "Like I was tellin you all. This Nigra musta been doped up on something because he knocked out two deputies and escaped from jail."

"Couldn't have been the same man, Sheriff Columbine. If it was, they both dead now," Silence says.

He laughs again. "You got that right, Leah. If it was the same man, his teeth were blown up right in his head. Nothing left of the skull. Ashes to ashes. The Bible says, 'He who lives by the sword, dies by the sword.'"

We all look at him then. Just look.

"Am I right, Leah?"

"Oh, the Bible says so much. And so do people. People say so much. Some still tell stories that never happened on me. What can you do?"

"I'm going to be getting along. Got to get me somethin to eat. You think about the things we discussed, Leah. And, son, Lazarus, you help her. Afternoon."

He slides his big feet and goes out the screen door sideways.

Little Bertram, who's been taking it all in, opens his mouth in disgust now. "He look like Mr. Potato Head."

"He got eyes. You see where he goes and who he asks questions, if any."

Bertram slips out the back door, making as much noise as an ant. At the same time Treemont throws back the curtain and comes from under the kitchen sink. A hiding place he made years ago.

Now Aunt Silence is on the bed, reading *Black World* magazine. Her hair tied in the two careful braids I made with fingers that trembled. Only the task bringing stillness. She says, "Old man Columbine knows them Germans want to build cars near the river for transport."

In Leona's little car it is Tree and me in back, and Essie, frowning, thinking real hard. Leona and Lazarus in front and Bertram squeezed between them on the floor. Nobody is talking. I won't look at this new Steve Rainey. His shoulders and thighs press against me. My hand looped in his, squeezed so tight it is numb now.

That is the way we ride into Uncle Ike and Aunt Charity's farm. Anonymous runaways on the edge of dusk. The birds are in their coops and only the watch bird, the guinea hen, squawks and flaps away from the wheels of the little car.

I get out of the car and go inside. As I knew he would be, Uncle Ike is gone. Has been gone two days. He is traveling in a wagon with his friend O.C., who sells watermelon off that wagon. Whatever is in season he travels with. His horse has died; now he drives a truck. He sells whatever off that truck. They should be at the Gulf now, waiting.

Aunt Charity is nervous. "I hope y'all ain't got into nothing you cain't get out of," she says, and pours coffee from that pot that sits on the back eye of the stove.

Grandmama Patsy says, "It's like the stories, Maggie. You think somebody gone and they come back every time."

"This ain't no story, Mama. This is real. Somebody could get killt."

I don't tell her somebody already got killed. What would be the point?

"Sheriff Columbine is a mean old sly peckerwood. I know the lady used to clean for him and his wife. His wife, she used to drink whiskey in her Coca-Cola. Stayed drunk. Don't know if he beat her, made her drink. Or she drink and he beat her. Both of 'em a mess. He greedy and he mean. I believe he wore the sheet too. But he don't need it. Just strap on the law and that be it. Be careful." She's drinking coffee now to stay awake until we get back, more coffee to stay awake until her husband returns days in the future.

"Let me see this bird who so valuable other people put they life on the chopping block for him."

I stand in the door and beckon for the runaway.

In the kitchen he stands under the scrutiny of old women.

Grandmama says, "Ta look at you, I can guess why women want to save you. Must be more to you than that or you wouldn't have these men running and ripping."

He smiles. "You don't think sisters see more?"

She looks at him a long time. Her glasses heavy and solid. Her eyes wavy behind the lenses. "Oh, they see more. Especially us old women."

He goes to her and holds both her hands. Squatting beside her chair. His back is bent in a curious repentance. They stay that way until, after a while, she is holding his hands.

She is the surprise. Her voice crackling. "Let some of them die for a change. You ain't no criminal. You ain't harmed nobody. You just defending your own."

"Mama, don't be inciting no riot or rebellion now."

"I ain't inciting nothing."

"Mama, if you live by the sword, you die by the sword."

"This handsome face ain't lived by no sword, Charity. I can see his eyes."

"Yo eyes might be deceiving you."

"No. They not. I got sense enough to know he ain't been down by the riverside, but he ain't lived by no sword either."

I didn't think anyone had told them, so it startles me when Aunt Charity pitches black coffee into the sink and says, "Who you think did that to that boy? The law, huh? North ain't no different from South. We like flies stuck to flypaper, walk a little, but we still on the same flypaper."

Up now, Treemont asks her if it's any use traveling, then.

"If you can move yo feet, why wouldn't you? If somebody can lift you up, you can fly."

"Yes, ma'am."

"I guess you flying. Here come a car."

These women who have never seen him before, but who have heard of him, kiss him, pulling at his arm, kneading something in the muscle. They go into the bedroom, leaving us alone. We look out of the window. I do. Because I can't look at his face anymore. I know it. He keeps looking at me. Without looking, I know who I am and what I'm feeling. The way he looks at me is the way I imagine you look at grief that's on its way. A dark-blue flower that opens, each petal creaking like a round little door, hinges alive and slow. A blue rose that finally is wide and wasting. Its edges tainted and withering, bruised and worn. All of this an outside thing because the rose breathes on its own. Wants to live. I think. This look. But it doesn't help. It only makes it harder for me to breathe. Through the window I can pick out anything. Concentrating so hard I can pick out a leaf on the tree across the yard. Study one leaf. Anything.

Anything. I'll look at it. If I don't have to study him. So I am first to note the roll of wheels and the double line of light that spreads coming from the direction away from town on the little road so old it was forgotten by all but Grandmama.

"Is it her?" he asks me.

"That's Miss Ruby Collins."

From the window we watch Lazarus and Leona loading his belongings into the trunk of Ruby Collins's car. The gun and ammo carefully stashed in a hidden place that looks innocent enough. He told me. He carries a gun after all.

"Maggie," he whispers to say more, but I don't want to hear it. So I run out the door and across the yard and into the field, where he follows me.

Kneeling, I'm not crying. Just staring at the sky through a window of tears. Thinking of an old dream.

He squats beside me. I don't turn to see. I can feel him.

When my mouth is full of tears and after I've swallowed half, I try to talk. "It's not fair."

My head won't stop shaking no. "It's not fair."

"Nobody told you it was fair. I never said it was."

"How can you just accept it then?"

"I don't know all of DeadandBuried's plans."

"Tell the people your story."

"From a prison cell? The people aren't ready."

"How do you know?"

"I know. I have to think, Maggie."

"While you're thinking, they'll be adding to the lies."

"But we'll be alive to tell the truth."

"I won't be alive."

"Maggie."

"I won't be dead, but I won't be alive, either."

"You're alive, Magdalena. Do whatever you do to be you. Go to the Sorbonne if you want to. Go back to Eden. Only when you marry, marry me. I can be selfish. I'll find you wherever you are." He puts my head on his chest and I listen to the quick, loud beat of his heart. We fall down into the grass. And he holds me to him like a promise. The grass bites through cloth and the air rushes over me. I can hear him breathing. "Only you, Maggie. Only you."

He lifts my chin and looks into my eyes. "Girl, I'm the son of Jeremiah and Mercy Stone. My mother sacrificed so that I could see. I can see past this deep night. Does Steve Rainey's sacrifice have a meaning? We have to make it have a meaning. I'll be coming back for you. I'm one man, but there will be many. But I am the man for you. And you are the woman for me. Only you, Magdalena. You."

✦

We have fifteen minutes' head start. It is dark now on Old Letha Road and the bald-headed moon looks for shoulders to right herself on; the light from her head touches our faces even inside the car. We look afraid, and I wish for my grandmother to come to us. Even though I know she won't. Once a dead woman saved his life. Once a man died for him. This time no single life is enough. Each of us would give some part of our own and risk the rest. Me and Bertram and Essie and Leona and Lazarus. And Uncle Ike and O.C. And Aunt Silence and Miss Ruby Collins. My family, Mama and Madaddy, and Sam Jr., who let us know the investigators were suspicious of a body so completely obliterated. Who let us know whatever he could tell. Miss Fredonia, Mr. Pryor, and C.C., and Honeybabe and ASANTE members who collected money for Tree's memorial. Finally, DeadandBuried members who gave Tree a pack of money to get out of town years ago and arranged safe passage. Anything can happen to a Blackman who stands for something.

Leona turns on the car radio and picks up gospel, a swell of sound. "Oh, Mary, don't you weep. Tell Martha don't you mourn . . . Pharaoh's army drowned in the Red Sea." It's Aretha with a choir beside her, singing from her *Amazing Grace* album.

Beside me, Bertram turns his head attentively. "Maggie, where's the Red Sea?"

I wanna say it's the Mississippi River. But I tell him the facts. I hope he doesn't ask me where the rock where Moses stood on is. Because I don't know.

Aretha sings my brother's name, "Lazarus!" Bertram doesn't ask why. He tilts his head and grins at me.

Headlights come up behind us.

"This is it," Lazarus says.

We each assume a position.

"Outta the car now," a voice demands.

We unfold our legs, hunch our backs, and crawl out of the Volkswagen. Sheriff Columbine himself stands before us. One man with a gun in his holster and a rifle in his car. But this spring night I can see good and I see the mountain of ice behind him. Glaciers that slid in on this hegemony. If we can get past him and just make it through this cold, we'll be okay. My teeth are chattering. It is the cold where the weather doesn't even suggest cold now. Cold as the metal I'm gripping in my pocket.

"You all leaving town already?"

"For a while," Lazarus answers.

"Headed in the wrong direction, aren't you?"

Flashlight in our faces.

"It's the direction we're going in."

"Let's see some licenses."

"Certainly, Officer." Lazarus starts to take his wallet out. Then he stops and does everything slow motion with commentary. "I'm reaching for my wallet. I'm going into my back pocket."

"I can see, boy."

"Just wanted to be sure you understood."

The sheriff goes over to his car and leans into his flashlight's beam, scrutinizing the license.

I am thinking of the warmth of the Gulf. There be hurricanes down there. But a way to circumvent the freeze. The islands are balmy with problems of their own. But it's not this cold. And the coves and little houses and the smiles of the dark people offer places to hide inside. If I think about the island, I won't break my teeth chattering, or grind them down holding what rages in. I won't panic and ease the piece out and pull the trigger, aiming for the ear.

Sheriff Columbine's careful reading the document and looking at us to be sure we are nervous. So careful is he he doesn't pay much attention to the old Buick that slides on past at an easy speed. The driver, Miss

Ruby Collins, doesn't even look our way. We don't look hers. The sheriff looks up. Almost absentmindedly. The sheriff says, "I got word that Stone fella might not be dead."

We don't leave room for a silence in which he might ruminate. We act surprised, amazed, and scared. Essie acts mad. My hand is cramping.

"Of course he's dead." Essie sounds outraged. Looking at me real fast. Knowing what I am doing.

"How would you know that, young lady?"

"The dirt he had hanging around him was enough to bury him."

Out of the corner of my eye I can still see Ruby Collins's car. Essie keeps on. Talking loud as an ambulance siren. Afraid I will do it.

"He had ex-convicts and thugs for something called ASANTE. I knew he'd wind up blown apart. One of his lieutenants I know wasn't nothing but a child molester. And I know birds of a feather flock together. He just had a lot of people fooled. But he didn't fool everybody, because you can't fool all of the people all the time. That's why the gangs got rid of him. I'm—"

"Essie," Leona says.

"If you hated this fellow so, what are you doing with his friends?" The sheriff has done his homework or someone has done it for him. Just as Aunt Silence said it would be when she gave me her derringer instead of Lazarus.

"He came between me and my best friends. He's dead now. So it doesn't matter. Now that his friends have killed him. Now they'll appreciate me and what I tell them." She waves her arms to take us in. Her grin is sloppy and wide like Charlotte's when she was crazy before Bertram was born.

He looks at her a long time.

"I've never been south before. I grew up in the Homes, a housing project."

"Know 'bout that."

"I just wanted to see the South. And maybe meet Maggie's grandmother. The one she swear ain't got no head." She giggles a little.

He snaps off his flashlight. Sending our faces and his own into the governance of darkness. "So you on this road looking for a ghost?"

"Hate to be so superstitious."

352

"Go on home," he says harshly. "You don't want to see what ain't human no more. Git! Git now. All of you all." He's waving the flashlight. Shooing us like chickens. But the waving doesn't stop his arms and hands from trembling. "Ain't no such thing as a ghost."

"But we saw something in the trees!" Bertram protests.

"I said git now."

He watches us get back into the car. Then he goes to his. I can see him, his eyes searching the road and the sides of the road for stirrings, a brief glimpse, a wavering light, a movement.

When something jiggles the leaves like the coins in his pocket, he reaches for his holster, drawing the gun, and sighting the wild pigeon when it pulls up out of the bushes. He follows the jagged ascent and aims, his arm wavering, then fires. We jump, hit by the sound. He's missed. My hand is like a block of ice.

"Look like one of Ike's pigeons. He better keep 'em cooped or he'll lose 'em." All this talk to himself, and to us, to restore his pride at the failed attempt. "I oughta take you all in. But I'm gonna tell you to get out of town fast. We don't want no angry young militants down here disturbing the peace. The South is building up. I'm a businessman. I aim to keep Mimosa and Letha conducive to investment. The Nigras can vote. We got a reputation as a fair city. We don't want no black marks against us."

"All the Blackpeople in Mimosa-Letha are happy?" That's me. Talking in a voice I've never heard before.

"I haven't heard no complaints. And I don't intend to."

Have you ever had someone look at you and try to will you to stop breathing? He makes himself look hard at me. I can see that. The way his jaw juts out and his chest tries to swell to make him bigger. His mouth meaner.

The wind dances now under the full moon where if you look close enough you can see the footprints of astronauts and an American flag standing still because there is no wind there. Is there? The wind here slaps leaves and carries water. Way down the road there is a light flickering and smoky. The sheriff peers into it, then, looking nervously at us, he climbs into his car. "Git!" he throws out the window. "Git!"

The light down the road grows. I can make out the woman figure. The light at her side. Then she opens, the woman does, and winging things

353

come out, rising and falling like notes in a song by Mockingbird July. Pretty. They shadow-fly and rise away from her. And soar and soar. Big wings angling out and sliding away into trees and beyond trees. Away and over and beyond the fields of Letha.

The woman figure keeps walking. The light at her side.

"Git!" the sheriff yells hysterically as he takes off. His eyes like plates. So big and blank and childlike with terror, I ease my hand.

We git. Taking our own sweet time. I keep looking at the hand that held the gun. The same hand that holds the paintbrush. Something has changed. Lazarus is driving slow, stopping after Sheriff Columbine's taillights are extinguished by the darkness, so that Silence, walking, carrying the lantern, can turn and wait for us.

On the road where he will meet Uncle Ike and Uncle Ike will take him down to the unprotected strip of beach on the Gulf, we meet at Miss Ruby Collins's car. We stop in the veil of darkness. I only see Tree. He reaches out for me and kisses me a long time. He breathes, "I don't want to leave you, Maggie. But I can't stay now." He lets me go. He takes the gun from my pocket where he felt the hardness. "You don't need this. That's not your way. And you know it. You've always known it."

I start to mouth his name as he gathers his belongings and runs into the deep darkness to meet Uncle Ike.

In the car, driving away from the Gulf, I see him in my mind's eye: He is on a boat, lost among American goods, toothbrushes, Afro combs, go-go boots (out of style and season), hot pants, reams of denim, raw silk waylaid from the East, bicycles, hooks and eyes, leather and suede, chicken feed, umbrellas, and compasses, radios, and TVs that catch broadcasts from the tip of the United States. His bag under his head, he lies down between the hooks, between the eyes, covered on all sides by boxes of umbrellas, wedged against the stationary wheels of bicycles. He dreams and I dream he dreams of me.

The boat docks in darkness, and he rides down the ramp on a bicycle. One bag on his back, the other tied to the back of his bike. He speeds. In the dark his wheels spin a soft light. Whoever he will be for a time. He is Steve Rainey. Sometimes a hundred others. The names spin around him. He could cry. A long way from home.

His bike propped against a tree. He closes his mother's eyes. He dreams. I dream he dreams of me.

I know he will be back. And I have to live without him. There are things I have to do. Works for me to do that only I can do. Changes to make. I have to.

"Only you," my grandmother whispers in my ear. "Only you," she and he whisper as I ride into the life that is waiting for me to make.